This special signed edition is limited
to **1000** numbered copies and **26** lettered copies.

This is copy 336

In the Beginning:

TALES FROM THE PULP ERA

In the Beginning:

TALES FROM THE PULP ERA

ROBERT SILVERBERG

SUBTERRANEAN PRESS 2006

ISBN
1-59606-043-3

Subterranean Press
PO Box 190106
Burton, MI 48519

TABLE OF CONTENTS

For Howard Browne, William L. Hamling,
Paul W. Fairman, and W. W. Scott.
And for Randall Garrett, who opened the doors.

INTRODUCTION

I have to confess, right up front here, that you will not find a great deal in the way of poetic vision in these stories, or singing prose, or deep insight into character. Nor are these stories that will tell you much that is new to you about the human condition. These are stories in what is now pretty much a lost tradition in science fiction, the simple and unselfconsciously fast-paced adventure story of the pulp-magazine era. They are stories from the dawn of my career, which began in the closing years of that era, and are straightforward tales of action, in the main, that were written partly for fun and partly for money.

The money part first: I needed the income that these stories brought in, because I wrote the first of them in 1954, when I was nineteen years old and still in college, and the rest followed over the next four years, when I was newly married and just starting out in the world. Writing was my job. By choice, I had no other. Nor was I being supported by my indulgent parents or by a trust fund that some thoughtful ancestor had established for me. My wife had a decently paying job, yes, so I can't say I was completely on my own, but we could hardly have lived on her earnings alone. Rent had to be paid; furniture for our new apartment had to be bought; the pantry had to be stocked with food; whatever medical expenses we might have came out of our own checkbooks, not out of any medical insurance plan, since such things were rarities then, especially for self-employed writers. Telephone bills, electricity, the cost of typewriter ribbons and typing paper, a haircut now and then, movie tickets, restaurants, subway fares (we lived in

Manhattan, where even back then it was madness to own a car), the occasional new pair of shoes—well, writers have expenses just like everyone else. What they don't have is regular paychecks. I had not chosen an ivory-tower sort of life for myself.

Since what I had chosen for myself was the next-to-impossible task of earning my living as a full-time science-fiction writer in an era when only two publishers were regularly issuing science-fiction novels in the United States and their total output was something like three or four titles a month, and the handful of science-fiction magazines that existed then paid between $50 and $200 for most of the stories they published, I knew I had to write quickly and to tailor most of my stories to the needs of the marketplace. Coming straight out of college as I was, without any day job to see me through times of thin inspiration or editorial rejection and having no significant savings to draw on, there was no other option. I didn't want to dilute my energies by putting in eight hours at some mundane job and trying to write science fiction in the evenings, as so many of my well-known colleagues did. I wanted to be a writer, not a public-relations man or a bookkeeper or a shoe salesman. But I wasn't of the sort of temperament that encouraged me to starve for the sake of my art, either. I have never been much into asceticism. I loved science fiction and yearned to write it as well as those of my predecessors whose work had given me such delight as a reader, but there was time to be an artist later, I reasoned: right now, if I wanted to make a go of it as a writer, I had to write things that editors would be willing to pay me for.

Not that I didn't *want* to tell you all sorts of profound things about the human condition, or to win your admiration with unique and unforgettable visions of the worlds to come. I would, of course, have been happy to be earning my living writing nothing but searching, weighty stories of unparalleled artistry and power that would rank me with the greats of the field. Certainly that was my ultimate ambition, and in such early stories as "Road to Nightfall" (1954) and "Warm Man" (1957) I took my best shot at it.

The trouble was that the greats of the field were already in place, and I wasn't remotely their equal. In the early 1950s when I set out to become a writer the science fiction field already had such people as Theodore Sturgeon, Ray Bradbury, James Blish, Cyril Kornbluth, Alfred Bester, and Fritz Leiber in it, all of whom were fifteen or twenty years older than I was, and who had had first-hand experience of a great many aspects of real life (military service, parenthood, financial or marital crisis, the deaths of parents and friends) that I knew about mainly from having read about such things.

Precocious though I was, I couldn't begin to match those writers in worldly wisdom and I had nowhere near their level of craftsmanship, either. Now and then one of my "serious" stories would find its way onto a magazine's contents page, tucked away between the newest work of Sturgeon or Bester or Blish or Leiber, but I had no illusions about which writer would get more attention from an editor if manuscripts by Sturgeon and Silverberg were to show up in the same batch of morning mail. So if I wanted to write science fiction for a living, I was going to have to earn the bulk of that living writing unpretentious stories to order for the unpretentious pulp-style magazines that catered to youthful and/or relatively undemanding readers simply looking for a lively read.

But there was also the fun aspect of writing that kind of action-adventure fiction. I had been reading science fiction since I was about ten years old, and, although I had been an earnest and scholarly little boy who inclined naturally toward the more literary side of science fiction (represented then by the books of H. G. Wells, S. Fowler Wright, Aldous Huxley, John Taine, and Olaf Stapledon and such high-level magazine writers as Sturgeon, Leiber, and Bradbury), my teenage self also had an unabashed fondness for the rip-roaring adventure stories to be found in such gaudily named pulp magazines as *Amazing Stories*, *Planet Stories*, *Startling Stories*, and *Thrilling Wonder Stories*. In their pages I found stories by writers like Leigh Brackett, Poul Anderson, Henry Kuttner, and Jack Vance that were every bit as pleasing to me as the statelier kind of s-f (often by the very same writers) that I could read in the three "adult" magazines, *Astounding, Galaxy*, and *Fantasy & Science Fiction*. I loved the colorful, lively work of the best of the pulp writers, and emulated it in many of my own early stories. So my career got off to a schizoid start, back there in the 1950s: one part of me labored over carefully worked tales intended for such demanding editors as John W. Campbell of *Astounding*, Horace Gold of *Galaxy*, and Anthony Boucher of *Fantasy and Science Fiction*, while another reveled in the opportunity to write slam-bang adventure stories in the Brackett-Anderson-Kuttner-Vance mode for the editors of the lesser magazines that were intended for less demanding readers of the kind that I myself had been only five or six years before.

There was nothing very unusual about operating on both these levels of science fiction at once. Such cerebral writers as Blish and Isaac

Asimov and Damon Knight, and such poetic ones as Sturgeon and Bradbury, were unabashed contributors to *Planet Stories,* the wildest and pulpiest of all the slam-bang s-f magazines. (I came along just a little too late to join them there: to my great regret, *Planet* went out of business just as I was getting started.) For them, as it would be for me a few years later, the motives were mixed ones—the need to earn some quick dollars, sure, but also the jolly pleasure of turning out an uninhibited action story at high speed. None of them saw any kind of rigid compartmentalizing in what they were doing: a story was a story, science fiction was science fiction, and not everything they wrote had to be something intended for the ages. My own particular hero, Henry Kuttner, who under an assortment of pseudonyms had written dozens of the greatest science-fiction short stories ever conceived, had also, quite cheerfully, given the world reams and reams of pulpy non-masterpieces with titles like "War-Gods of the Void," "Crypt-City of the Deathless One," and "Avengers of Space." If the great Kuttner could do it, I told myself, so could I. Maybe not as well as he could, not then, but in the same mode, at least.

When I was twenty years old, the doors to that pulp-magazine world opened for me (or, more precisely, were opened for me by my friend and collaborator of those days, Randall Garrett) and I was given my own chance to produce reams and reams of stories, all of them accepted and sometimes paid for in advance, for the action titles. Sure, I went into it for the money. As I've said, I had the rent to pay, just like everyone else. But also I found real joy in writing at such great velocity, creating cardboard worlds with flying fingers and sweaty forehead— a 20-page story in a morning, a 40-page novelette in one six-hour working day. I had the youthful energy to do that, day in and day out, throughout the year. I was, somewhat to the consternation of my older colleagues, a juggernaut, unstoppable, who was destined to break all records for prolificity in science fiction. And I loved the cognate fun of knowing that I had made myself part of a pulp-writer tradition that went back through those early favorites of mine, Henry Kuttner and Leigh Brackett and Poul Anderson and the rest, to Edgar Rice Burroughs, Max Brand, Robert E. Howard, and the other famous high-volume writers of a pulp generation that had thrived before I was born.

Even as I wrote these stories, I knew them for what they were: work meant primarily to entertain, not to blaze new literary paths or to help establish a place for myself among the great writers of science fiction. I never abandoned my hope of achieving that, of course, and as time went along I concentrated less on the problem of merely paying the rent and more on the challenge of adding something new and memorable of my own to the literature of science fiction. And, by and by, the emphasis on quality overtook the emphasis on quantity for me, and these early stories of mine receded into oblivion, although those readers with a sense of the history of the field remained aware that I had written such things once.

As I reread them for the present book, I felt the temptation to touch up these early works here and there, of course, to add a bit of extra color, to replace this or that semi-colon with a dash, to remove some bit of sensationalizing plot machinery, or otherwise to modify the text in the light of all that I've learned about storytelling in the past forty-odd years. But I resisted it. Doing that sort of ex post facto rewrite job would have been unfair to the young man who turned these stories out. I have no business imposing on them the accumulated wisdom, such as it may be, of the veteran writer I now am, and also it would have defeated the main purpose of this book, which is to bring back into view, as an archaeologist might, certain artifacts of the dawn of my long writing career as examples of a certain kind of science fiction, typical of its time, that virtually every one of us chose to write, back then, at some phase of his career.

Here, then, is a group of stories I wrote for long-forgotten magazines, stories written extremely quickly, stories in which, for the most part, I stayed rigorously within the boundaries of the pulp-magazine tradition. By way of deviating from the tried and true narrative formulas I allowed myself only the luxury of killing off my protagonist now and then, something that would have been unthinkable in the pulps of the 1940s but which was sometimes permissible in the decade that followed; but in general, good struggles with evil in them and evil usually (not always) loses.

I will not try to deceive you into thinking that there are any unjustly neglected masterpieces here. I think I've made it sufficiently clear that even at the time I wrote them these stories weren't meant as high art—the magazines that bought them had no interest in publishing high art, only good solid basic pulp fiction—and I offer them here in that archaeological spirit I mentioned a few lines back, delvings into long-buried strata that provide demonstrations of who I was and what I was doing as a writer fifty years ago.

I did, it must be said, learn a great deal about writing fiction from writing these stories: how to open a story in an interesting way and keep it moving, how to set a scene and sketch in a character (however roughly) without a lot of ponderous exposition, how to provide with a few quick touches the sort of color and inventiveness that make people want to read science fiction in the first place. So these stories have some technical interest and some historical interest, too, for they are, after all, the work of the same man who would write *Dying Inside*, "Sailing to Byzantium," "Born with the Dead," and all the other books and stories for which the Science Fiction Writers of America would reward me, in 2004, with the highest honor of the science-fiction world, its Grand Master award. Is it possible to detect the touch of a future Grand Master in these early stories? Maybe not, because even when they were written they represented the side of him that was producing, at improbably high volume, stories intended mainly to pay the rent, stories meant to be fun to read and nothing more. I never pretended that stories like "Guardian of the Crystal Gate" or "Citadel of Darkness" were the best science-fiction I had in me. But, for better or for worse, they were part of my evolutionary curve. I have never repudiated them, or anything else that I wrote along the way. And here they are again, these artifacts of a vanished age, sixteen of my earliest stories reprinted in book form for the first time, brought forth now into the bright eerie light of a new century that was far in the future when I wrote them.

YOKEL WITH PORTFOLIO
(1955)

*All through my adolescence I dreamed of becoming a science fiction writer.
Feverishly I wrote stories, typed them up, sent them off to the magazines of
the day* (Astounding Science Fiction, Amazing Stories, Startling Stories,
and so forth.) *They all came back.*

*But then, in 1953, when I was 18 and a sophomore at Columbia, I
began to make my first sales—an article about science-fiction fandom, then
a novel for teenage readers only a few years younger than myself, and then
a short story. On the strength of these credentials I was able to get myself a
literary agent—Scott Meredith, one of the pre-eminent science-fiction spe-
cialists of that era, who represented such notable clients as Arthur C.
Clarke, Poul Anderson, Philip K. Dick, and Jack Vance.*

*My hope was that under the aegis of so powerful an agent my stories
would get faster and more sympathetic attention from the editors than they
had been getting when I sent them in myself. It didn't quite work that way—
maybe I got faster readings, sure, but my stuff was still competing with the
stories of Messrs. Clarke, Anderson, Dick, and Vance for space in those editors' magazines. Still, during the course of the next year or so Scott did
manage to make a few tiny sales for me to a couple of minor s-f magazines.
The first, in June, 1954, was a 1500-worder called "The Silent Colony."
Eight tense months later, in February of 1955, he produced a second one:
"The Martian," 3000 words, which Scott sold to William L. Hamling's*
Imagination, *an unpretentious little penny-a-word market that filled its
pages with stories that various top-level writers (Gordon R. Dickson,
Robert Sheckley, Philip K. Dick, Damon Knight) had been unable to sell to*

better-paying magazines. I was pleased to be joining their company. Even though these two sales had netted me a grand total of $40.50, I felt I was on my way toward the start of a career. And I was still only a junior in college, twenty years old, after all. There would be time later on to consider whether I could actually earn a living this way.

Three more months went by before my next sale: a second one to Hamling, "Yokel with Portfolio." Looking at it now, I suppose that I wrote it with Horace Gold's Galaxy Science Fiction *in mind, or Anthony Boucher's* Fantasy & Science Fiction, *since those two top-of-the-field editors were particularly fond of the sort of light, slick science fiction that I imagined "Yokel with Portfolio" to be. But the Meredith agency obviously didn't think I was quite ready for prime time yet, for I see from the agency records that they sent it straight to* Imagination *in March of 1955 and that on May 8 Hamling bought it for $55. It was published in the November, 1955 issue of* Imagination's *new companion magazine,* Imaginative Tales, *and here it is again for the first time in half a century—my third published short story, no classic but, I think, a decent enough job for the lad of twenty that I was at the time I wrote it.*

I t was just one of those coincidences that brought Kalainnen to Terra the very week that the bruug escaped from the New York Zoo. Since Kalainnen was the first Traskan to come to Terra in over a century, and since the bruug had lived peacefully in the zoo for all of the three or four hundred years or more since it had been brought there from outer space, the odds were greatly against the two events coinciding. But they did.

Kalainnen, never having been on a world more complex than the agrarian backwater of civilization that was his native Trask, was considerably astonished at his first sight of gleaming towers of New York, and stood open-mouthed at the landing depot, battered suitcase in hand, while the other passengers from his ship (*Runfoot*, Procyon-Rigel-Alpha-Centauri-Sol third-rate runner) flocked past him to waiting friends and relatives. In a very short time the depot was cleared, except for Kalainnen and a tall young Terran who had been waiting for someone, and who seemed evidently troubled.

He walked up to Kalainnen. "I'm from the *Globe*," the young man said, looking down at him. "I was told there was an alien from Trask coming in on this ship, and I'm here to interview him. Sort of a feature angle—weird monster from a planet no one knows very much about. Know where I can find him?"

The young Terran's hair was long and green. Kalainnen felt acutely aware of his own close-cropped, undyed hair. No one had warned him about Terran fashions, and he was beginning to realize that he was going to be terribly out of style here.

"I am from Trask," Kalainnen said. "Can I help you?"

"Are you the one who came in just now? Impossible!"

Kalainnen frowned. "I assure you, sir, I am. I just arrived this very minute, from Trask."

"But you look perfectly ordinary," said the reporter, consulting some scribbled notes. "I was told that Traskans were reptiles, sort of like dinosaurs but smaller. Are you *sure* you're from Trask? Procyon IV, that is."

"So that's it," Kalainnen said. "You're mistaken, young man. The inhabitants of Procyon IV are reptiles, all right, in more ways than one. But that's Quange. Trask is Procyon of Terran descent; the Traskans are not aliens but from Terra. We were settled in—"

"That doesn't matter," said the reporter, closing his notebook. "No news in you. Reptiles would be different. Hope you enjoy your stay."

He walked away, leaving Kalainnen alone in the depot. It had not been exactly a promising introduction to Terra, so far. And he hadn't even had a chance to ask for anything yet.

He checked out of the depot, passed through customs without much difficulty (the only problem was explaining where and what Trask was; the planet wasn't listed in the Registry any more) and headed out into the busy street.

It made him sick.

There were shining autos buzzing by, and slick little copters, and hordes of tall people in plastiline tunics, their hair dyed in fanciful colors, heading for unknown destinations at awesome speed. The pavement was a deep golden-red, while the buildings radiated soft bluish tones. It was not at all like Trask, quiet, peaceful Trask. For an unhappy moment Kalainnen wondered whether the best thing for Trask would not be for him to turn around and take the next liner back; did he really want to turn it into another Terra? But no: the technology of Trask had fallen centuries behind that of the rest of the galaxy's, and he had come for aid. Trask had been virtually forgotten by Terra and was stagnating, off in its corner of the sky. Kalainnen's mission was vital to Trask's continued existence.

Before he left they had dressed him in what they thought were the latest Terran styles and cropped his hair in approved fashion. But, as he walked through the crowded streets of the metropolis, it became more and more apparent that they were centuries behind in dress, as well. He was hopelessly out of date.

"Yokel!" called a high, childish voice. "Look at the yokel!" Kalainnen glanced up and saw a small boy pointing at him and giggling. A woman with him—his mother, probably—seized him roughly by the wrist and pulled him along, telling him to hush. But Kalainnen could see on her face a surreptitious smile, as if she agreed with the boy's derision.

The rest of the walk was a nightmare of snickers and open laughs. Even the occasional alien he saw seemed to be sneering at him, Kalainnen trudged along, feeling horridly short and dumpy-looking, regretting his old-fashioned clothes and close-cut hair and battered suitcase, and regretting the whole foolish journey. Finally he found the address he was heading for—a hotel for transient aliens—and checked in.

The hotel had facilities for all sorts of monstrosities, but, since Trask was an Earth-type planet, he accepted one of the ordinary rooms, and sank gratefully down on a pneumochair.

"Hello," said the chair. "Welcome to Terra."

Kalainnen leaped up in fright and looked around the room. There was no one else present. Probably some sort of advertising stunt, he concluded. Piped in from above. He sat down again in relief.

"Hello," said the chair. "Welcome to Terra."

He frowned. How often were they going to welcome him? He looked around the room for the loudspeaker, hoping to find it and rip it out. There was no sign of one. He sat down again.

"Hello," the chair said a third time. "Welcome to Terra."

"So that's it!" Kalainnen said, looking at the chair. He wondered if every chair in the hotel spoke to its extraterrestrial occupant, and, if so, how long the occupants could stand it.

Pressing gingerly on the seat of the pneumochair revealed that the voice was activated by weight. He dropped his suitcase heavily on the chair, ignoring the fourth welcome, and sat carefully on the edge of the bed, waiting for chimes or some other sign of welcome. Nothing was forthcoming. He leaned back, and rested.

Tomorrow he would have to try to get an audience with the Colonial Minister, in hopes of arranging some sort of technical-assistance program for Trask. But now, he thought, as he swung his legs up and got under the covers, the first thing was to get some sleep. Terra was a cold and unfriendly world, and his appearance was not calculated to win him any friends. He would rest. The bed was much too soft, and he longed for the simple life on Trask.

Just as he began to drop off into sleep, a sudden and powerful buzzing noise jolted him out of bed.

Astonished, he looked around, wondering what the buzzing meant. It was repeated, and this time he realized it was a signal that someone was at the door. A visitor, so soon? There were no other Traskans on Terra; of that, he was fairly certain.

After a moment's confusion with the photo-electric device that controlled the door, he got it open. The green, reptilian face of a Quangen stared blandly up at him.

✳

"Oh," the Quangen said. "They told me someone was here from the Procyon system, and I was sort of hoping—"

"Yes," said Kalainnen. "I know. You were hoping I was from your planet, not mine. Sorry to disappoint you. Anything else I can do for you?" He stared at the Quangen coldly. Little love was lost between the neighboring planets.

"You needn't be so inhospitable, friend," said the Quangen. "Our peoples are not the best of friends at home, but we're almost brothers this far from Procyon."

The Quangen was right, Kalainnen conceded to himself. Poor company was better than none at all, anyway.

"You're right. Come on in," he said. The Quangen nodded his head—the equivalent of a smile—and stomped in, flicking his tail agilely over his shoulder to prevent it from being caught in the door.

"What brings you to Terra?" said the Quangen.

"I might ask the same of you," Kalainnen said.

"You can, if you want too," said the reptile. "Look, fellow: I told you before, maybe our planets don't get along too well, but that's no reason why we shouldn't. I see no harm in telling you that I'm here on a technical-aid mission. It's about time Quange caught up with the rest of the galaxy. I'll bet that's why you're here, too."

Kalainnen debated for a moment and then decided there was no reason why he shouldn't admit it.

"You're right," he said. "I have an appointment with the Colonial Minister for tomorrow." It wasn't quite the truth—he was only going to *try* to get an appointment the next day—but an old Traskan proverb warns against being too honest with Quangens.

"Oh, you do, eh?" said the Quangen, twirling the prehensile tip of his tail around his throat in an expression of, Kalainnen knew, amusement. "That's very interesting. I've been waiting two years and I haven't even come close to him. How do you rate such quick service?" He looked meaningfully at Kalainnen, flicking his tail from side to side.

"Well," said Kalainnen, nearly sitting down in the chair and avoiding it at the last moment, "well—"

"I know," said the Quangen. "You can't help being a Traskan, even on Terra. I'll forgive you. But you don't really have an appointment tomorrow, do you?"

"No," Kalainnen said. "As a matter of fact, I haven't even applied yet. I just got here."

"I thought so," the reptile said. "In two years I've gotten as far as the First Assistant Undersecretary. The Colonial Minister is a very busy man, and there are more outworld planets than you can imagine. I've been living here. The hotel's full of outworlders like us who are stuck here waiting to see some bureaucrat or other. I'll introduce you around tomorrow. After two years it's good to see someone from the same system."

Kalainnen frowned. They hadn't told him the mission might go on and on for a matter of years. As it was, a single afternoon on Terra had been a profoundly distressing experience. And two years?

"By the way," the Quangen said. "There's one little feature of the furniture here that must be bothering you. We more experienced hands know how to circumvent it." He extended his tail under the seat of the pneumochair, explored the insides of the chair for a moment, and then pulled his tail out quickly. An abortive "Hello, welcome to—" started out of the chair and died.

"Sit down," the Quangen said. Kalainnen did. The chair was silent.

"Thank you," Kalainnen said. "The chair was bothering me."

"It won't any longer," said the Quangen. "I'm Hork Frandel, by the way."

"My name's Kalainnen," Kalainnen said. He stared glumly out the window. "What's that box over there?" he said.

"The video," Frandel explained. "Put a quarter in the slot and it plays. It's entertaining, but it's one aspect of Terran technology I'd just as soon not bring back to Quange. You may like it, of course."

"I don't have any coins," Kalainnen said. "All I have is Galactic Traveler's Checks."

"Allow me," said the Quangen. He reached into his upper hip pocket with his tail and withdrew a small coin, which he inserted in the appropriate slot. The video flickered and came to life.

"The big news of the day!" said a deep, robust voice, and the screen showed a fleeing multitude, "All New York is in terror today. For the first time in over a century, a dangerous alien beast has escaped from New York's famed Zoological Gardens and is roaming the city." The camera showed a deserted cage.

The scene cut to a very scientific-looking office and the camera focused on a dapper man with extravagant mustaches. "I'm Carlson," he said, "head of the zoo. We're unable to account for the escape. The animal lived here peacefully for centuries. It's something like an ape, something like a tiger. Eats anything. Completely indestructible, perhaps immortal, hitherto quite docile though frightening-looking. Skin like stone, but flexible. Origin is somewhere on one of the smaller outworlds; unfortunately our records have been misfiled and we're not sure exactly where the animal comes from. My guess is Rigel II, possibly Alpheraz VI." He smiled, doing impossible things with his mustaches, and radiating an aura of complete confidence.

"We're taking all possible steps for the beast's recapture; meantime DO NOT PANIC, but avoid unnecessary going out."

Kalainnen looked at the Quangen, who looked back balefully.

"Things like this happen all the time?" Kalainnen asked.

"Not too often," Frandel said. He looked boredly at the screen, which was showing shots of some incomprehensible sporting event, apparently having lost interest in the escaped animal. He glanced at his watch—Kalainnen noted how incongrous the Terran-type watch seemed against the Quangen's scaly skin—and got up.

"I've got to be moving on," he said. "But maybe I'll see you at the Colonial Ministry tomorrow, if it's safe to go out. I've got an appointment to ask for an appointment." The Quangen grinned, waved his tail in salute, and left.

❋

Kalainnen watched the video until the time Frandel had bought for him expired. The camera had gone to another office, the mayor's, and he was discussing the situation. The plans being concocted for capture of the beast were growing more and more elaborate as the minutes went on; the animal had taken up headquarters in an office building (hastily evacuated) and Terran police had established a cordon around the building, with heavy artillery trained on the entrance waiting for the animal to appear. Kalainnen wondered what the point of using artillery on an indestructible beast was, but the mayor did not dwell on the point.

Suggestions offered by various authorities over the video included flooding the building with radiation, building a steel wall around the edifice, and bombing the whole area. Erecting the wall seemed the only solution of any value, but there was always the consideration that the hungry animal might appear before the wall was finished, causing all sorts of difficulties. Kalainnen had no coins, and so he climbed into the too-soft bed and, after a while, fell asleep, pondering the state of affairs.

The next morning he went down to the Colonial Ministry. Since the animal was, at least in theory, under control, people were going about business as usual, but they were moving quickly and cautiously through the streets as if they expected to be devoured at any instant.

It was not difficult to find the Ministry—it was one of the biggest of a great many immense buildings. But it was crowded. There were colonists of all shapes and sizes pleading their various cases. Lines of outworlders extended in all directions—humans, humanoids, and grotesque total-aliens wearing protective devices of great complexity. Besides those on line, many more milled around aimlessly, apparently too confused and too deafened by the enormous hubbub to do anything else. Kalainnen could see now why the Quangen had got no farther than a First Assistant Undersecretary in two years.

"Where is this line heading?" he asked a tall purple beanpole, probably hailing from an inner world of Arcturus.

"I don't know," the beanpole said. "But it seems to be a short one."

A cucumber-like alien from a planet Kalainnen didn't know turned around and said, "Just got here? Try that line over there." Kalainnen followed where the stubby tentacle pointed, and joined the other line, which seemed to stretch off endlessly. The new line seemed to be composed almost exclusively of humans and humanoids; occasionally a small dog-like being ran up and down the line, laughing wildly. In two hours the line moved seven feet. By late afternoon the line had unaccountably moved back until it was almost four feet behind where Kalainnen had joined it. Sensing there was no point in waiting any longer, since he still had not been able to find out what line he was on (not that it seemed to matter) and he had not been able to get anywhere in particular, he left, completely discouraged.

The Quangen, he knew, was a slick, shrewd operator—it was a characteristic of the race—and yet even he had failed to reach any appreciable proximity to the Colonial Minister. What chance, then, did he, Kalainnen, a visiting yokel from a backwater planet, have?

It didn't look as if Trask were going to get the technological assistance it needed, he thought—not if every day were like this one. In a way it wasn't so bad—Trask seemed to get along all right on tools five centuries out of date—but he would feel terribly unhappy about returning empty-handed. The whole planet had contributed to pay his passage, and he had been hailed as the savior of Trask. He had been a hero there; here he was just a stubby little man of no particular importance.

He walked all the way back to the hotel, feeling dismal. Everyone he passed seemed to be discussing the monster loose in the city, and he found himself wishing devoutly that the animal would eat them all, slowly.

✵

"Get anywhere?" asked Frandel that evening.

Kalainnen shook his head.

"That's too bad," the Quangen said, soothingly. "It took me a month to get my petition received, though, so don't worry too much. It's just a matter of going there regularly, and getting there before everyone else."

"What time does it open?" Kalainnen asked, too weary to look up.

"About 0800, I think. But you'll have to get there about midnight the night before to make any headway. In fact, you'd be wise to start out right now and wait on line till it opens. You might be one of the first."

"Leave now? Stand on line all night?"

"You don't like the idea?" The Quangen grinned toothily. "Unfortunate. But you're likely to disappoint all the folks back on Trask unless you do it. I didn't enjoy it, either. Oh, by the way—I moved up a notch today. My application is now up to the Second Assistant Under-Secretary, and I might get to the First Associate in a couple of weeks. I should be bringing quite a load of valuable data back to Quange before long. In fact, there's a very good chance that we'll be leaving Trask far, far behind." He curled his tail derisively.

That's all we need, Kalainnen thought. He waved his hand feebly. "Congratulations. Fine. Leave me alone, will you?"

The Quangen bowed, grinned, and left.

Kalainnen stared at the video set for a long time after the reptile's departure. The Quangen certainly was a slick operator. It might be ten years before Kalainnen got close to the Colonial Minister. Even for as slow-moving a planet as Trask, ten years was a long tine. They might think he was dead.

He played with the handful of coins he had accumulated during the day, and finally dropped one in the video. He stared glumly as the set came to life.

"New York remains paralyzed by the unknown alien monster in its midst," a staccato voice said. "The animal is still somewhere in the building in the heart of the business district that it took over late yesterday, and a fearsome range of artillery is waiting for it to emerge. *Do not panic.* The situation is under study by our foremost experts on extraterrestrial life.

"And now, for the first time, we can show you what this monster looks like. Zoo officials have supplied a photograph of the animal." The photograph appeared on the screen. Kalainnen reached to turn off the set, then stopped as the features of the beast behind the bars registered.

It was a bruug.

He sat back in his chair, startled. His first thought was one of incredulity. The whole city terrorized by a bruug? They were the most peaceful, the most—

Then he thought of calling the video station. They would be interested in learning the identity of the monster, the planet it came from, all the data that the zoo officials had misplaced or (more likely) forgotten.

Then he realized he was the ace in the hole.

At the rate he was going, he would never come to the Terrans' notice, and, just as Trask was a forgotten backwater of the Galaxy, he would remain in this hotel, forgotten by Terra and, eventually, by Trask.

But there was one thing he could do. He was of vital importance to Terra, though they didn't realize it. The bruug, the familiar red beast, was virtually a domestic animal on Trask; every Traskan could handle one like a pet. It was all a matter of understanding animals, and this the Traskans did superbly. No bomb would do any good—not on an animal with a hide like that. No; it was understanding. A few gentle words from a Traskan and the animal would lie down placidly. Understanding.

And who understood the bruug? Kalainnen. His way seemed perfectly clear to him.

Of course, the bruug might not be red. It might be blue. The only way he could tell was by close examination. And if the bruug were blue—but he preferred not to think about that.

Anyway, it would be good to see something from home again.

※

The streets were deserted. No Terran cared to venture out into the night while the bruug was loose in the city, no matter how many guns were trained on it. The spectacle of an immense city completely terrorized by an animal of which he himself had no more fear than of a butterfly amused Kalainnen as he walked down to the building where they bruug was.

It was a long walk, but the city was intelligently planned and he had no trouble finding his way. He enjoyed the walk; the air was clean and fresh at night, almost like Trask, and there were no people in the streets to snicker at him.

Finally, in the distance, he glimpsed some big guns and a group of soldiers. He began to trot a little. When he reached the guns, the soldiers stopped him.

"What do you want?" said a very tall man in a very resplendent uniform. In the dim light Kalainnen saw that his hair was dyed a flaming bronze-red. "Are you crazy, walking right in here?"

"I'm from Trask," Kalainnen said. "We know how to handle these animals. Let me through, please." He started to walk on.

"Just a minute!" The big soldier grabbed him; Kalainnen twisted loose. Two other soldiers dove for him and caught him, and he found himself looking up at an even taller and more resplendent one.

"This guy says he's from Flask, sir," the first soldier said. "Says he knows how to handle the animal."

"That's right," Kalainnen said. "They're domestic animals on Trask."

The officer looked at him—he was more than a foot taller than Kalainnen—and laughed. "Domestic animal, eh? Pet for the kiddies? Take him away—anywhere, just out of my sight."

As the first soldier reached for Kalainnen, a mighty roar erupted from the office building. Kalainnen felt a thrill of familiarity; knowing there was a bruug in the vicinity—even a blue one—was a comforting feeling.

"All hands to battle stations!" the officer roared. "Prepare to fire!"

The bruug roared again from somewhere inside the building. The soldiers dashed to the gun installations, and suddenly Kalainnen found himself standing alone and ignored. He looked briefly around and began to run as fast as he could for the entrance to the building, ignoring the outraged and amazed yells of the soldiers who watched him.

●

The building was unlighted and very big. Kalainnen wandered around in the dark for a moment or two, hoping the bruug would not appear before he had acclimated his vision to the darkness. From somewhere on an upper floor, he heard the deep-throated roar he knew so well. The poor beast was hungry.

Bruugs were docile animals. But the blue bruugs of Kandarth, the deserted island in South Trask, were hardly so. And they refused to be understood.

As he wandered through the darkened building, he began to wonder whether or not he was biting off more than he was going to get down his throat. If the bruug were blue, well, that was it. But even if it were the domesticated kind, it had, after all, been captured (or, more likely, given away by the Traskans) centuries before. Perhaps it had forgotten.

The roaring grew louder. Kalainnen mounted the stairs.

It was dark, but he was growing accustomed to the darkness and could see fairly well. Not well enough to discern the color of the bruug's skin at a distance, though; he would have to look under the thick fur, and by the time he got that close it no longer mattered much.

On the fourth floor he came across the bruug, sprawled out in the corridor and munching angrily on a splintered door. The bruug was a big one; he had prospered in captivity. He scented Kalainnen and looked up slowly at him and emitted a great roar.

"Hello," Kalainnen said, looking at the beast's eyes. As it began to lumber to its feet, Kalainnen walked toward it, smiling, trying desperately not to let his fear show through and destroy his chances of mastering the animal. The roars of the bruug filled the hall. Kalainnen began to talk to it, calmly, in Traskan.

It rose to its full height and began to charge.

"No. You don't want to do that at all," Kalainnen said, listening to the echoes of his voice rattling down the corridor. "You don't want to do that."

Ten minutes later he emerged from the building, with the bruug following docilely behind.

It had been a red one.

✸

The Colonial Minister was a jovial-looking rotund man, one of the few unimpressive-looking Terrans Kalainnen had ever seen. Kalainnen studied his features for a moment or two, and looked down again at the text of the agreement whereby Terra would supply the planet Trask with a team of technologists and whatever aid would be necessary, in return for valuable services rendered by an inhabitant of the aforementioned planet Trask, etc., etc.

"It sounds reasonable enough," Kalainnen said. "I think it'll meet our needs admirably."

"I'm pleased to hear that, Mr. Kalainnen," the Colonial Minister said. "But I still don't understand how a planet whose people have such skills as you showed can need any help from us."

"It's a matter of different kinds of skills, Mr. Minister," Kalainnen said. "Every planet understands certain things that no other one does. Once in a book of Terran folklore—we have a few old Terran books on Trask—I read a story that reminds me of this. It seems a backwoodsman came to a big city, and, amid the roaring of traffic, said he heard a cricket chirping. They laughed at him, but he walked down a street and pointed out a nearby sewer opening and sure enough, they found a little cricket in the opening. Everyone congratulated him for his miraculous powers of hearing. But he proved that he didn't hear any better than anyone else, just that he heard different things."

"How did he do that?" the Minister murmured.

"It was easy. He took a small coin out of his pocket and dropped it on the sidewalk. Two hundred people stopped and looked around at the sound."

The Minister smiled. Kalainnen knew from experience that he was a busy man, but at the moment he had the upper hand and he wanted to make the most of it.

"The moral of the story is, sir, that some planets are good for one thing and some for another. And so if you'll give us the tools we need, we'll show you why ferocious monsters on Terra are pleasant pets on Trask. Fair enough?"

"Fair enough," said the Minister. He extended his pen to Kalainnen, who signed the agreement with a flourish.

On his way out of the Ministry he passed Frandel, who was standing gloomily in the midst of a seemingly endless line.

"Let's get together again some time," Kalainnen said, pausing for a moment. The Quangen just glared at him angrily. "Let me know when you get back to our system, old man. Perhaps you'd like to come over to Trask and study our technology." Kalainnen smiled. "Best of luck, friend. The Minister is a fine man; you'll see that as soon as you get to see him. *If* you get to see him, that is."

And Kalainnen walked on, feeling very pleased, and—unintentionally, of course—treading on the tip of this Quangen's prehensile tail, which he had wanted to do all his life.

LONG LIVE THE KEJWA
(1956)

A great deal happened to me, professionally, between the publication of "Yokel With Portfolio" in the autumn of 1955 and the appearance of this one seven months later. The most important development was the arrival in New York City, where I was living then, of one Randall Garrett.

Garrett, a charming, roguish fellow seven or eight years older than I was, came from Texas but had been living in the Midwest, working as a chemist and writing science fiction on the side, in the early 1950s. He was a natural storyteller and had a good grasp both of science and of the traditions of science fiction, and very quickly he sold a dozen stories or so to most of the major markets, including two excellent novelets ("The Waiting Game," 1951, and "The Hunting Lodge," 1954) to John W. Campbell's Astounding, *one of the leading magazines of the field. But like too many science-fiction writers Garrett had an unfortunate weakness for the bottle, which led early in 1955 to the end of his marriage and the loss of his job; and then the friends in Illinois with whom he had taken refuge wearied of his wayward ways and suggested he move along. That spring he packed up his few possessions and a box of unfinished manuscripts and headed for New York to establish himself as a full-time science-fiction writer.*

One of the few people he knew in New York was Harlan Ellison, who had come from the Midwest a year before Garrett with the same goal in mind. Harlan and I were close friends, and at my suggestion he had taken a room next door to me in the seedy Manhattan residence hotel where I was living during my college years, on West 114th Street, a couple of blocks from the Columbia campus. It was a place inhabited by a sprinkling of undergraduates, an assortment of aging graduate students, a few aspiring writers like Harlan and me, some very aged ladies living on pensions, and an odd collection of down-on-their-luck characters of no apparent profession. When he reached New York, Garrett phoned Ellison, who was still meeting only frustration in his attempts to break into print. Harlan told him about our hotel, and very suddenly we had him living down the hall from us. Almost immediately thereafter Garrett and I went into partnership as a sort of fiction factory.

He and I could scarcely have been more different in temperament. Randall was lazy, undisciplined, untidy, untrustworthy, and alcoholic. I was a ferociously hard worker, ambitious, orderly, boringly respectable and dignified, and, though I did (and do) have a fondness for the occasional alcoholic beverage, I was (and am) constitutionally unable to drink very much without getting sick. But we did have one big thing in common: we both were deeply versed in the tropes of science fiction and intended to earn our livings entirely by writing science fiction. We had the same agent, too. Furthermore, we had complementary sets of skills: Garrett's education had been scientific, mine literary. He was good at the technological side of s-f, and also was a skillful constructor of story plots. I, though still a beginning writer, was already showing superior stylistic abilities and the knack of creating interesting characters. I was tremendously productive, too, able to turn out a short story in a single sitting, several times a week. Garrett was a swift writer too, but only when he could stay sober long enough to get anything done. It occurred to him that if we became collaborators, my discipline and ambition would be strong enough to drive both of us to get a great deal of work done, and his more experienced hand as a writer would help me overcome the neophyte's flaws in my storytelling technique that had kept me from selling stories to any but the minor magazines. And so we set up in business together. (Harlan, having not yet reached a professional level of writing ability, remained on the outside, somewhat to his displeasure.)

Garrett was a man of grandiose ideas, and so he and I aimed for the top right away: we meant to sell a novel to Campbell's Astounding. As soon as my third year of college was over that June, he and I began plotting a three-part serial built around one of Campbell's favorite formulas, the superior Earthman who helps benighted alien beings improve their lot in life. Since Campbell was of Scottish ancestry, Garrett suggested that we make our hero a Scot, one Duncan MacLeod. I cheerfully agreed. We worked it all out in great detail, and then, to my surprise, Garrett told me that we were going downtown to Campbell's office to pitch the idea in person.

I had never expected anything like that. I thought we would let our agent handle the marketing of the project. But Garrett, a supremely gregarious man, believed in personal contact with his editors; and so one summer morning he swept me off to Campbell's office, where I was introduced as a brilliant new talent with whom he would be collaborating thenceforth. We pitched our story; Randall did most of the talking, but I added a thoughtful bit of Ivy League eloquence every now and then. Campbell loved the idea. He had a few improvements to suggest, though—in fact, by lunchtime he had transformed our story beyond all recognition. Then he told us to go home and write, not a novel, but a series of novelets, first, and then a novel. I went back to West 114th Street in a daze.

Of course, I never thought anything was going to come out of this. Me, not even old enough to vote yet, selling a series of novelets to John W. Campbell? But we sat down and wrote the first in our series almost instantly, sticking the joint pseudonym "Robert Randall" on it, and Campbell bought it on the spot, reading it in his office before our eyes, in August, 1955. I was so stunned at the idea that I had sold something to Astounding that I couldn't sleep that night.

Garrett didn't want us to stop there. It was the personal touch that did it, he was convinced. Editors wanted to put faces behind the manuscripts. So we needed to visit all the other editors, too—Howard Browne of Amazing, Bob Lowndes of Future, Larry Shaw of the new magazine Infinity, etc. Later in August, Garrett and I attended the World Science Fiction Convention in Cleveland, where I met William L. Hamling, who had bought two stories from me that year and let me know now that he'd like me to send him some others. Garrett was right: in the small world that was science fiction in 1955, the personal touch did do it. On the strength of my collaborative sale to Campbell's Astounding, coming on top of my scattering of sales to a few lesser magazines, I had acquired enough professional plausibility to find the doors of the editorial offices opening for me, and Garrett's prodding had brought me inside.

Bob Lowndes, who had already bought a story from me the year before, seemed glad to meet me, and by way of our shared love of classical music struck up a friendship right away. He had high tastes in science fiction, and would buy many more stories from me, usually the ones I had tried and failed to sell to the better-paying magazines. Browne, about whom I will have more to say a little further on, also gave me a ready welcome. He ran a different sort of magazine, featuring simple action tales staff-written by a little stable of insiders—Milton Lesser, Paul W. Fairman, and a couple of others. It happened *that in the summer of 1955 Browne had two vacancies in his stable, and he offered the jobs to Garrett and me the day we showed up in his office. So long as we brought him stories every month and maintained a reasonable level of competence he would buy everything we wrote, sight unseen.*

That struck me as almost as improbable as my selling novelets to John Campbell. Here I was, a kid still in college who had sold less than a dozen stories, and a cagy old pro like Howard Browne was offering me what amounted to a job, with a guaranteed rate of pay, to keep his science-fiction magazine supplied with copy!

I didn't hesitate. I had a story called "Hole in the Air" that Scott Meredith had returned to me because he didn't think he could sell it to anyone. I handed the manuscript to Howard Browne on an August day and he bought it. The following week Garrett and I batted out a novelet, "Gambler's Planet," and he bought that too. We did another for him in September, "Catch a Thief," and I sold two stories to Bob Lowndes, too, and another novelet to Campbell, and then more to Browne, and so on. In the first five months of the Garrett partnership I made a phenomenal 26 story sales— some of them collaborations, but many of them solo stories, for with Randall's help I had acquired the momentum for a career of my own.

One thing I did, as I grew more confident of my relationship with Howard Browne, was to feed him some of the unsold stories that I had written in the pre-Garrett days, when I was simply sending them off to Scott Meredith and hoping that he would find a market for them somewhere. In June of 1955 I had written "Long Live the Kejwa," built around a classic theme that I had encountered in my anthropology class. Toward the end of the year, since it was still unsold, I asked Scott to send it over to Browne as part of my quota of stories for the month. It was published in the July, 1956 issue of Amazing Stories *under Howard's title, "Run of Luck," which was, perhaps, a better title than mine. But as I restore it to print here after five decades in limbo I prefer to use the original title for it.*

That July 1956 Amazing *provided another milestone for me in that dizzying year, because "Run of Luck" was one of three stories that I had in the issue. Its companions were "Stay Out of My Grave," another early unsold story that I had salvaged by selling to Browne, and "Catch a Thief," a Garrett collaboration published under the byline of "Gordon Aghill." Fifteen months earlier it was an awesome thing for me to get any story published, and now here they were showing up in threes in a single issue!*

Steve Crayden growled in anger as the dials on the control panel spun crazily around, telling him that the little cruiser was out of control.

He frowned and glanced at the screen. There was only one thing to do—crash-land the ship on the tiny planet looming up just ahead. It was the lousiest twist possible—after he had lied and cheated and killed to get off the prison planet of Kandoris, here he was being thrown right back into cold storage again. Maybe not behind bars, this time, but being marooned on a little bit of rock was just as much an imprisonment as anything.

He brought the stolen ship down as delicately as he could. It maintained a semblance of a landing orbit until a hundred meters above planetfall, and then swung into a dizzying tailspin and burrowed into the soft ground.

Crayden, jarred but unhurt, crawled out of the confused tangle of the control cabin and checked the dials. *Air 68, Nitro, 21, Oxy. Water normal.*

At that, he smiled for the first time since the ship had conked out; things looked different all of a sudden. This new place had *possibilities,* he saw now. And any place with possibilities beckoned to a born opportunist like Crayden.

He climbed out of the ship and smelled the warm air, and shook his head happily. *I'll make the most of it,* he told himself. If Fate wanted to kick him in the teeth again, that was O.K. He'd bull his way through it. If he was stuck here—and the way the ship looked, he was—then he'd have a good time of it.

He looked around. It was almost a perfect Earth-type planet, probably uninhabited, not listed on any of the charts in his stolen ship, and it was a nice cozy place for him to stay. Things could have been worse, Crayden thought. There'd be hunting and fishing, he hoped, and he'd build a small cabin near a waterfall. *I'll make out,* he said, as if in defiance of whatever Power had let him escape from one prison and then had thrown him immediately into another.

He had left so quickly that he hadn't taken anything from his prison-barracks on Kandoris. He returned to the ship, and a quick check revealed a thought-converter, somewhat jarred by the crash, and a rescue-beam radiator. No weapons were to be found.

That didn't stop him. *I'll make a bow and arrow,* he decided. *I'll go real primitive.* He tucked the damaged thought-converter under one arm, the rescue-beam radiator under another, and climbed out.

The patrol won't ever use that one again, he thought as he looked at the wrecked cruiser. Its nose was buried in ten feet of mud at the side of a lake, and the ship was bent almost in half. The tail jets were all but ruined.

I'm here for good, he decided. *But it's going to be a picnic. It better be.*
He turned to survey the little world.

The gravity was about the same as that of Kandoris, which meant Earth-normal. He found that out as soon as he took his first step. He had expected to go sailing twenty feet, but he moved only the Earth-type two or three feet at a stride. That meant unusual density, heavy mass, since the little planet's diameter couldn't have been much over 700 miles. He had landed on a freak world. He scanned it some more.

But it didn't look like a freak. It might have been a lost corner of Earth. The sky was just a shade off-blue, and the sun was a trifle reddish, but the soil was brown, the grass was green, and the air was fresh, clean, and good to breathe. He was standing in a valley, by the side of a long, deep-looking blue lake. Small mountains, almost hills, hemmed in the valley, and heavy clusters of trees sprouted on the hills. A little stream wound down out of the nearest hill and trickled into the lake.

Crayden felt a warm glow. In a way, this was the best thing that could have happened. Instead of going back to the old con games, the shabby routines he'd lived on, he'd have a new, fresh life beginning. He grinned. It was a talent he had, making the most of what seemed like a rough break. It was the way to stay alive.

He started off to follow the stream. After walking a few steps, he stopped.

"I name this planet Crayden," he shouted. "I take possession of it in the name of Steve Crayden."

"Crayden," came back the faint echo from the hill.

The effect pleased him. "I hereby proclaim myself King Stephen of Crayden!"

The echo replied, "Of Crayden."

Thoroughly satisfied, the new king began to trudge along the side of the stream, carrying the damaged thought-converter under one arm, the rescue-beam radiator under the other.

He followed the stream several hundred meters up into the hills. Looking ahead, he noted what seemed to be a thin trail of smoke curling into the sky. Natives?

He stopped and watched the smoke. The first thought that came to him was to hang back cautiously, but then he shook his head and kept moving. This was his world, and he was going to keep the upper hand.

They saw him first, though, and before he was aware of anything, ten blue-skinned men had stepped out of the woods and were kneeling at his feet.

"Kejwa!" they shouted. "Kejwa, Kejwa!"

Crayden was too startled to react. He stood there frozen, staring down. They were all burly humanoids, perfectly manlike as far as he could tell, except for the bright blue skin. They were clad in loincloths and beads, and were obviously friendly. Crayden relaxed; King Stephen had found his subjects.

Gingerly he touched the nearest native with the tip of his toe. The alien sprang up instantly and faced him. The man was well over six feet tall, and powerfully built.

"Kejwa endrak jennisij Kejwa," the native jabbered, pointing to the smoke that indicated the village.

"Kejwa! Kejwa!" came the chorus from the ground.

"I wish I could understand you chaps," Crayden said. "Kejwa, eh? That's the best compliment I had since the warden said I looked like an honest man."

They were dancing around him, stamping on the ground and slapping their hands, and emitting cries of "Kejwa! Kejwa!" until the trees began to tremble from the noise. Other blue-skins began to appear from further upstream, naked children and women in loincloths. They gathered around Crayden, chanting that one word over and over, now softly, now at the top of their lungs.

Crayden grinned at them. This was working out better than he'd dare dream. Slowly, with all the dignity his new rank afforded, Crayden began to move upstream toward the village, clutching the useless thought-converter like a scepter in his outstretched right hand.

When they reached the village, a tall, wrinkled native wearing a great many beads and a flowing white beard stood in front of the community fire, watching Crayden's approach. The beard looked strange against the blueness of the old man's chest.

As Crayden drew near, the old one sank down on both knees. "Kejwa," he said slowly, in a very deep, solemn voice.

Crayden took the cue. He stepped forward and touched the old man on the left shoulder with the tip of his thought-converter. The oldster rose as if transfigured.

The villagers clustered around, keeping a respectful distance, and chattered away. He pointed to the thought-converter. "I'll have this fixed soon," he promised. "Then I'll be able to talk to you."

They continued to chatter. Every third word seemed to be "Kejwa." Crayden happily wondered whether it meant "king" or "god."

* * *

They installed him in a large hut, the best in the village. The old man took him there personally—Crayden decided he was either the chief or the high priest, or, most likely, both—and indicated a bed of thick grass in one corner. It was the only furniture.

"Thanks, pop," he said lightly. "Usually I expect better accommodations in my hotels, but I won't kick. See that the bellhop comes when I ring, will you? I hate having to wait."

The old man looked at him without a trace of comprehension or anything else but worship in his eyes.

"Kejwa emeredis calowa Kejwa," he said.

Crayden watched him depart, and sat for a while on the big stone at the entrance to his hut. From time to time little groups of children would approach timidly and stare at him and back away, and occasionally one of the blue-skinned women would come by. There hadn't been any women on Kandoris. Crayden rubbed his chin. Even a blue-skinned one would do right now, he thought. Yes, even she would be welcome.

He stared at the bare hut, with its low bed. The only other things in it were the thought-converter and the rescue-beam radiator. He hefted the compact rescue-beam radiator in his hand.

I'd better get rid of this, he thought. One of the natives might accidentally turn it on and call down the patrol.

He walked to the stream, held the radiator reflectively for a moment, and then pitched it into the water.

"Good riddance," he said. His last link with Kandoris and the worlds of the galaxy was gone. They couldn't find him unless he tipped them off by using the rescue-beam radiator, which would attract any patrol ship within a dozen light-years. And the radiator was under the flowing waters of the stream.

When he returned to his hut he looked at the remaining piece of equipment, the thought-converter. "I'll really be able to make this town jump once I can talk to them," he said. "Women, food, fancy furniture—

I'll just have to ask for them, and they'll jump. They wouldn't want their Kejwa to be displeased."

The thought-converter didn't seem to be too badly damaged. A few delicate wires had come out of their sockets, that was all. He tried to put them back, but his fingers were too thick and clumsy, and he had to give up.

He realized he hadn't slept in almost three days. He put the converter in his prison shirt, wrapping it carefully to protect it from the moisture of the ground, and curled up on the bed of grass. It wasn't much better than lying on the ground, but he was too tired to notice.

✺

For the next three days he did nothing but sit on the stone outside the hut and toy with the thought-converter while the natives brought him food three times a day. He didn't recognize any of the delicacies they brought—something which looked like a black apple and tasted like a red one, another something which looked like nothing he'd ever seen on Earth and tasted like a shot of bourbon filtered through a banana, and plenty of fresh, red meat, almost raw despite the perfunctory roasting they gave it.

Crayden felt his frame expanding, and, though he had no mirror, he knew the prison-planet pallor had left his face. This planet was agreeing with him, all right. Being Kejwa was a grand life. He'd never had it so good.

When he got tired of sitting around being worshipped, he decided to survey the area. He was curious about this world—his world—and he wanted to know all about it.

All the huts were something like his, only smaller, and the ones near the stream seemed to belong to the more important people of the tribe. The huts were arranged in a roughly semi-circular fashion, with the community fire at the entrance to the semicircle. All around was the thick forest—Nature's fortress.

Crayden wandered off toward the forest, hoping to see some of the native wild-life in action, but was surprised to find himself confronted by a little ring of blue-skins.

"Kejwa," they murmured, pointing to the forest. "Nek nek konna je Kejwa."

"'My country, 'tis of thee,'" he replied gravely, and continued to move toward the forest.

They became more insistent. Two of the biggest stood in front of him and barred his way. "Nek nek konna je Kejwa," they repeated more loudly.

Obviously they didn't want him straying. So his powers were limited after all. He frowned. "If that's the way you want it, I'll give in. Never argue with the boys in blue, the saying goes." But he was angry all the same.

✵

Every night they danced in front of his hut, and every day they let him sit there while they came by and bowed and mumbled "Kejwa." But Crayden was getting restless.

They treated him as a king, or as a god, and he took full advantage of the privilege the way he did everything else—but he was required to stay in the vicinity. The constant worship was starting to bore him, and the steady diet of rich food combined with lack of exercise had put a definite bulge around his stomach. He felt like a prize bull being groomed for the cattle show, and he didn't like it. He decided the quickest way to fix things was to repair the thought-converter and talk to them.

But he couldn't do it himself. The repairs involved nothing more complex than putting three wires back in place, but he couldn't fit his fingers through the opening to do it. He tried improvising tweezers out of two twigs, but that didn't do it. He needed someone with small fingers—a child, perhaps. Or a woman.

A woman. Here was where his Kejwahood was going to come in handy.

One night as the tribe was gathered outside his hut he raised the thought-converter high over his head as a sign for silence. "Hold everything!" he thundered. "As your Kejwa, I declare this morsel strikes my fancy."

He pointed at a girl whom he'd noticed before—she seemed to be about seventeen or eighteen by Earthly standards and she wore her loincloth with the dignity of a matron displaying a mink. Some large precious-looking stone was strung on a necklace that dangled down between her breasts.

She was the best of the lot. Crayden pointed to her, then to his hut—an unmistakable gesture.

The girl flashed a glance at the old man. He nodded benignly, stroked his great beard, and smiled as she stepped forward shyly and stood before Crayden.

"You'll do," he said approvingly. "A dish fit for a Kejwa." He waved dismissal to the tribespeople and took her inside the hut.

During the night he looked out the open entrance and saw a knot of tribespeople staring in with evident curiosity, but he didn't let that disturb him.

*

She seemed happy with the arrangement, and so did he. The blue skin didn't trouble him at all. He had come to think of himself as the white-skinned freak among the normal people. It had been three long years on Kandoris since Crayden had had a woman, but he hadn't forgotten anything. And this one knew all the tricks.

The people began to bring him dead animals—strange-looking beasts, resembling Earthly ones but with differences—and left them at his door, as sacrifices. One morning there was a squirrel with horns, the next a fox with a prehensile tail.

Whenever he walked through the village, they followed him, always at a respectful distance, and soft cries of "Kejwa" drifted through the air. His woman—he named her Winnie, after a girl he'd known on Venus—was getting the same treatment. She had become someone important now that she belonged to the Kejwa.

He spent a full day trying to get her to fix the thought-converter. Her fingers were slim and tapering, and would fit into the opening easily. But it wasn't simple to convey what he wanted her to do. After hours of gesturing and indicating what he wanted, she still couldn't grasp it. Laboriously he went through it again. She looked up at him imploringly, and seemed ready to burst into tears.

"Look, Winnie. For the last time. Just pick up these little wires and put them in here." He showed her. "If you only understood English—"

He showed her again. She still did nothing. He slapped her left hand, and left her in a little whimpering heap in a corner of the hut. He strode angrily out and stalked around the village. He wasn't going to be stymied here, not when he got past every other hurdle so well.

When he returned, night had fallen, and she was waiting for him, holding the thought-converter. She had a bright little smile, and seemed to have forgotten all about the slap. He looked at the thought-converter. The wires were in place. The Crayden luck was holding true to form.

He kissed her, and she responded as he had taught her. After a while, he picked up the thought-converter and held it fondly.

"Kejwa," she said.

This was his chance to find out, he thought. He reached underneath and snapped on the converter.

Her lips formed the word "Kejwa" again.

But through the converter came a stream of unexpected concepts. "Placator of the gods...noble intervener...royal sacrifice."

"Sacrifice? What? When?"

She launched into a string of words, and the converter brought them over all too clearly. "Tomorrow is the day you go to the gods, and I should be happy. But I'm sad. I'll miss you."

"You mean the Kejwa gets killed?" he asked desperately.

"Oh, no," the converter translated. "Not killed. You go to meet the gods, to intervene in our favor. One of us is chosen every year. This year you came to us from above and it was good."

"Where do the gods live?"

She pointed. "Down there. At the bottom of the lake. It is deep. We have never been able to reach the bottom."

Crayden's insides jangled. Royal sacrifice? Bottomless lake? So *that* was the catch?

The Crayden luck was just about being stretched to the breaking-point. For a second his old optimism asserted itself, and he told himself confidently that now that the converter worked he'd be able to talk the natives out of sacrificing him.

But the bleak truth was apparent, and for the first time in his life Crayden saw there was no opportunity he could cling to. Except—except—

❋

He looked out the door of the hut. The night was black. He tiptoed out softly. "Keep quiet," he told her.

He crept through the sleeping village to the stream where he had so boldly disposed of the rescue-beam radiator the other day. He hadn't needed it, then, but he did now. If he could find it, he could call the Patrol and get taken back to the prison planet, where he could start all over. He'd break out again, he was sure. For Steve Crayden, optimism was an incurable disease.

Grimly calling on whoever had been taking care of him up till then, he got down on his knees in the water and began to grope frantically for the rescue-beam radiator he'd thrown—who knew where?—somewhere in the stream.

He moved inch-by-inch over the stream's shallow bed, searching fruitlessly. He refused to give up. The cool waters of the stream washed the feverish sweat from him and left him chilled and shivering.

When the aliens came for him the next morning, he was a hundred yards upstream, blindly rooting up handfuls of mud, still confident he was going to find the rescue beam. It wasn't till the priest held him poised above the sparkling blue waters of the bottomless lake and started to release him, as a glad cry went up from the watchers—it wasn't until then that he came to the final realization that there were no angles left for him to play.

But he was still expecting a last-minute miracle as he hit the water. This time there wasn't any.

GUARDIAN
OF THE CRYSTAL GATE
(1956)

Amazing Stories and its companion magazine, Fantastic Adventures, *were big, shaggy pulps published by Ziff-Davis of Chicago. They featured fast-paced adventure stories aimed at adolescent boys, a group to which I belonged when I started reading them in 1948. I loved nearly everything I read, had fantasies of writing for them some day, and had no idea that the two books were staff-written by a dozen or so regular contributors whose work was bought without prior editorial reading and who worked mainly under pseudonyms that the editor, Ray Palmer, would stick on their material at random. (About fifteen different writers were responsible over the years for the stories bylined "Alexander Blade," who was one of my special favorites when I was about 14.)*

While I was still an Alexander Blade fan Ziff-Davis moved its operations to New York. Editor Palmer preferred to stay behind in Chicago. The new editor was a big, burly, good-natured man named Howard Browne, who had been one of Palmer's stable of regulars, producing undistinguished stories for him in the mode of Robert E. Howard and Edgar Rice Burroughs under an assortment of names. Indeed, Browne thought that science fiction and fantasy was pretty silly stuff. What he preferred was detective stories. His own favorite writer was Raymond Chandler and he had written a number of creditable mysteries in the Chandler vein. Gossip had it that he had taken over Palmer's job mainly in the hope, never realized, of talking Ziff-Davis into letting him edit a mystery magazine as well.

By the time Browne had been on the job a couple of years my own tastes in reading had grown more mature, and I was no longer very enamored of the work of Alexander Blade and his pseudonymous colleagues. Truth to tell, I had come to think of Amazing and Fantastic Adventures as pretty awful magazines, and, with the high-minded fastidiousness common to young men in their mid-teens, said so very bluntly in a 1952 article that I wrote for an amateur magazine of s-f commentary named Fantastic Worlds. They were, I said, "the two poorest professional magazines of the field," magazines of "drab degeneracy" that were devoted to "a formula of adventure and 'cops and robbers on the moon.'" I said a lot of other things too, some of them fairly foolish. Fantastic Worlds allowed Browne to reply to my diatribe, and he did so quite graciously, under the circumstances, defending himself by pointing out that "magazines, like bean soup and bicycles, are put out to make money." He offered reasoned and reasonable arguments for his editorial policies and in general resisted matching my intemperate tone. He did call my piece "unrealistic and irresponsible" but added that "it is axiomatic that only the very young and very old know everything," and obviously I belonged to one of those two categories.

We now jump three years. It is the summer of 1955, and, thanks to Randall Garrett, I have unexpectedly become part of Howard Browne's stable of writers myself, turning in a monthly quota of formula fiction. I would deliver a story on Tuesday or Wednesday, Howard would let the accounting department know, and the following Monday my payment would go out. He rarely bothered to read them. Now and then he would check to see that I was maintaining the minimal level of competence that the magazines required, but he understood that I was, by and large, capable of consistently giving him the right stuff. In fact, after I had been part of his staff for six months or so, he paid me the considerable compliment of asking me to write a story around a cover painting that Ed Valigursky, one of his best artists, had just brought in.

The painting showed two attractive young ladies in short tunics fiercely wrestling atop a huge diamond. I produced a 10,000-word story called "Guardian of the Crystal Gate," which Howard published in the August, 1956 issue of Fantastic, the successor to the old Fantastic Adventures. My name was prominently featured on the front cover and an autobiographical sketch of me, along with a lovely drawing of me as the beardless young man I still was, went on the second page of the issue.

During one of my visits to the Ziff-Davis office about this time, Howard Browne greeted me with a sly grin and pulled a small white magazine from his *desk drawer. "Does this look familiar?" he said, or words to that effect. It was that 1952 issue of* Fantastic Worlds, *with my blistering attack on the magazines he edited. He had known all along that the bright young man he had hired for his staff in 1955 was the author of that overheated polemic of three years before, and finally he could no longer resist letting me in on that. He had, of course, calculated how old I must have been when I wrote that piece, and had gallantly chosen not to hold my youthful indiscretion against me.*

That August 1956 Fantastic *was pretty much an all-Silverberg issue, by the way. I had broken my personal record of the month before, because I was the author or co-author of four of the six stories it contained. Besides "Guardian of the Crystal Gate," there was a collaborative novelet called "The Slow and the Dead," under the "Robert Randall" byline, and I appeared as "Ralph Burke" with a short entitled "Revolt of the Synthetics." The fourth story, "O Captain My Captain," was one that I had written while still an unknown freelancer back in 1954; unable to sell it the normal way, I had eventually fobbed it off on Browne as part of my regular quota. The interesting thing here is that Browne published it under the byline of "Ivar Jorgensen"—a writer who had been one of my early favorites in the days before I knew that the Ziff-Davis magazines were entirely written by staff insiders using pseudonyms. "Jorgensen" had originally been the pen name of Paul W. Fairman, Browne's associate editor, but now the name was being spread around to the other contributors. So after having been an Ivar Jorgensen fan in my mid-teens, I had, four or five years later, been transformed into Jorgensen myself! It would not be long before I could lay claim to "Alexander Blade" as well.*

I t started very simply, with the routine note on my desk, saying that the Chief had a job for me. Since there's generally some trouble for me to shoot ten or a dozen times a year, I wasn't surprised. The surprises came later, when I found that this particular job was going to draw me a hundred trillion miles across space, on a fantastic quest on a distant planet. But that came later.

It began quietly. I walked in, sat down, and the Chief, in a quick motion, dropped a diamond in front of me on his desk.

I stared blankly at the jewel. It was healthy-sized, emerald-cut, blue-white. I looked up at him.

"So?"

"Take a close look at it, Les." He shoved it across the desk at me with his stubby fingers. I reached out, picked up the diamond—it felt terribly cool to touch—and examined it.

Right in the heart of the gem was a thin brown area of clouding, marring the otherwise flawless diamond. I nodded. "It looks—like a burnt-out fuse," I said, puzzled.

The Chief nodded solemnly. "Exactly." He opened a desk drawer and reached in, and grasped what looked like a whole handful of other diamonds, "Here," he said, "Enjoy yourself." He sent them sprawling out on the desk; they rolled across the shiny marbled desktop. Some went skittering to the floor, others dropped into my lap, others spread out in a gleaming array in front of me. There must have been forty of them.

The Chief's eye met mine. "Each one of those diamonds," he said, "represents one dead man."

I coughed. I've had some funny cases since joining the Bureau, but this was the fanciest hook the Chief had used yet. I started scooping up the diamonds that had fallen to the floor. They were of all sizes, all cuts—a million dollars' worth, maybe. More, maybe.

"Don't bother," the Chief said. "I'll have the charwoman pick them up when I leave. They're not worth anything, you know."

"Not worth anything?" I looked at the ones I had in my hand. Each was marred by the same strange brown imperfection, that fuse blowout. I closed my hand, feeling them grind together.

"Not a cent. For one thing, they're all flawed, as you can easily see. For another, they're all synthetics. Paste, every one of them. Remarkably convincing paste, but paste all the same."

I leaned back in my chair, put my hands together, and said, "Okay. I'm hooked. Put the job on the line for me, will you?" I was thinking, *This is the screwiest one yet. And I've had some corkers.*

"Here's the pitch, Les." He drew out a long sheet of crisp onionskin paper, and handed it to me. Neatly typed on it was a list of names and addresses. I ran down the list quickly without hitting any familiar ones.

"Well? Who are they?"

"They're missing persons, Les. They've all disappeared in this city between—ah—" He took the list back—"27 November, 2261, and 11 February of this year. The list totals sixty-six names. And those are just the ones we know about."

"And the diamonds?"

"That's where this Bureau comes in," he said. "They only send us the screwy ones, as you've no doubt discovered by now. In each disappearance case listed on this sheet, one of those burnt-out diamonds was found in the room the missing man was last seen in. In every case."

I frowned and scratched an ear reflectively. "You say there's a tie-in with the diamonds, Chief?"

He nodded. "One burnt-out diamond in exchange for one man. It's a recurrent pattern of correlation. Those men are going somewhere, and those diamonds have something to do with it. We don't know what."

"And you want me to find out, eh?" I asked.

"That's only part of it." He moistened his lips. "Suppose I tell you where you fit into the picture, and let you decide what you want to do yourself. I can't force you, you know."

"I haven't turned down a case since I've been with the Bureau," I reminded him.

"Good." He stood up. "Let's see you keep that record intact, then. Because we've just found one of these diamonds that *isn't* burnt out!"

※

The vault swung open, and the Chief led the way in. He was a short, blocky little man, hardly impressive-looking at all. But he knew his job perfectly—and his job was to maneuver muscleheaded underlings like myself into positions where they were just about committed to risk life and limb for the good old Bureau without knowing quite what they were going into.

I was in that uncomfortable position now. It wasn't going to be easy explaining this gambit to Peg, either, I thought.

He crossed the shadowy floor to an inner safe, deftly dialed the combination, and let the door come creaking open. He drew out a little lead box.

"Here it is," he said.

I reached for it, in my usual melon-headed manner, but he drew it back quickly out of my grasp. "Easy," he said. "This thing is dangerous." Slowly, terribly slowly; he lifted the top of the box just a crack.

A pure, silvery beam of brightness shot out and lit up the whole room.

"It must be a beauty," I said.

"It is. Diamonds like these have lured sixty-six men to what we assume is their death, in the last three months. This particular one hasn't had a chance to go into action yet."

I took the box from him. It was hard to resist the temptation of lifting the top and staring at that wonderful diamond again, but I managed. I wanted to find out all the angles of the job before I got involved.

"One of our cleaning-women found the stone yesterday, right after I left. She called me at home. At first I thought it was one of the ones I was working with—one of the burnt-out ones. But from the way she described it, I knew it was something special. I had her box it up this way at once. No one's seen it yet, except in little peeks like the one I just gave you."

He tapped the box. "I'll tell you my theory," he said, "and you can take it from there." His voice ricocheted around unpleasantly in the silent vault. "This diamond is *bait,* in some way. The things have been appearing, and men have been doing something with them; I don't know what. But the diamonds are directly connected with this wave of disappearance."

I started to object, but he checked me.

"Okay, Les. I know it sounds crazy. How would you like to prove otherwise?"

"You're a sneaky one," I told him, grinning. Then the grin vanished as I stared at the little lead box. "I'll do it," I said. "But make sure that Peg gets the pension, will you?"

"Don't worry," he said, matching my grin. "She'll get every penny she deserves—after *I* get through grabbing, of course." He started to lead the way out of the vault. I followed, and he closed the door behind me.

"You take that diamond along with you," he said, indicating the box. "Play with it. Do anything you like. But come back with a solution to this vanishing business. Here," he said. "Take a few of these burnt-out ones too."

"Yeah. Peg might like them," I said. " They'll look swell with black."

I turned to go. As I reached the door, something occurred to me, and I paused.

"Say—I think I've found a hole in your theory. How come that charwoman didn't disappear when she found the diamond?"

He smiled. "Take another look at the list I gave you, Les. All the names on it are *men's* names. Whatever this is, it doesn't affect women at all."

"Hmm. Thought I had you there, for a minute."

"You ought to know better than that, Les."

✺

Peg didn't like the idea one little bit.

I called her right after I left the Bureau office, and told her the chief had a new project for me. I didn't tell her what it was, but from the tone of my voice she must have guessed it was something risky.

I saw her face in the screen go tight, with the mouth pulled up in the little frown she's so fond of making every time I get stuck into another of the Bureau's weirdies.

"Les, what is it this time?"

"Can't tell you over the phone," I said, in mock accents of melodrama. "But it's a doozie, that's for sure." I fingered the leaden box in my pocket nervously.

"I'll come over after work," she said. "Les, don't let that man get you doing impossible things again."

"Don't worry, baby. This new business won't take any time at all," I lied. "And the Bureau pays its help well. See you later, doll."

"Right," I broke the connection and watched her anxious face dissolve into a swirl of rainbow colors and trickle off the viewer, leaving the screen looking a dirty grey. I stared at the dead screen for a couple of minutes, and then got up.

I was worried too. The Bureau—that's its only name, just plain The Bureau—was formed a while back, specifically to handle screwball things like this one. In a world as overpopulated and complex as ours is, you need a force like the Bureau—silent, anonymous, out of the limelight. We take care of the oddball things, the things we'd prefer the populace didn't get to hear shout.

Like this one. Like this business of people fooshing off into thin air, leaving burnt-out diamonds behind. The only people on Earth who could have even a remote chance of worming some sanity out of that one were—us. More precisely, me.

I stopped at a corner tavern and had a little fortification before going home. The barkeep was an inquisitive type, and I rambled on and on about some fictitious business problems of mine, inventing a whole sad story about a lumber warehouse and my shady partner. I didn't dare talk about my real business, of course, but it felt good to be able to unload some kind of trouble, even phony trouble.

Then I caught a quick copter and headed for home. I got out at the depot and walked, feeling the leaden box tapping ominously against my thigh every step of the way. Peg was there when I came in.

"You made it pretty quick," I said, surprised. "Seems to me you don't get out of work till four, and it's only three-thirty now."

"We got let off early today, Les. Holiday." She looked up at me, with strain and worry evident on her face, and ran thin, nervous fingers through her close-cut red hair. "I came right over."

I went to the cabinet and poured two stiff ones, one for each of us.

"Here's to the Chief," I said. "And to the Bureau."

She shook her head. "Don't make jokes, Les. Drink to anyone else, but not to the Bureau. Why don't you drink to *us?*"

"What's wrong, Peg? The Bureau is what's going to keep *us* going, doll. The salary I get from them—"

"—will be just adequate to get you the finest tombstone available, as soon as he gives you a ,job you can't handle." She stared up at me. Her eyes were cold and sharp from anger, but I could also see the beginnings of two tears in them. I kissed them away, and felt her relax. I sat down and pulled out the handful of burnt-out diamonds.

"Here," I said. "You can make earrings out of them."

"Les! Where did these—"

I told her the whole story, starting at the beginning and finishing at the end. I always tell Peg exactly what each mission of mine is about. Doing that violates security regulations, I know, but I'm sure of Peg. Absolutely sure. When I tell her something, it's like telling myself; it doesn't get any further. Which is why I was able to keep company with her, with the eventual idea of marrying her. In the Bureau, you don't think of getting married unless you can find a woman who could keep her mouth shut. Peg could.

"You mean these diamonds are instrumental in the disappearances?" she asked wonderingly.

I nodded. "That's what we think, baby. And I have one other little exhibit for you." Slowly I drew out the lead box and opened it, only a crack, and let a single beam of radiance escape before slamming it shut again.

She gasped in awe. "That's *beautiful!* But how—"

"That's where my job begins," I said. "That diamond is an unused specimen, one that hasn't functioned yet."

"Just how do *you* fit into this?" she asked suspiciously.

I stood up. "I'll find out soon enough. I'm going to go into the next room," I said, "and see how this diamond works. And then I'm going to go wherever it takes me, and worry about getting back after I get there."

The words fell so easily from my mouth that it seemed as if that had actually been my plan along. Really, it hadn't; I didn't have any idea where I was going to begin this case, but certainly that wasn't any way to go about it.

But as I spoke the words, I saw that that was what I had to do. That was the way the Bureau worked. Go straight to the heart of the matter, and worry about the consequences to yourself later.

"Les—" Peg began, and then knocked it off. She knew it wouldn't do her any good to complain, and she didn't try. I loved her for it. I knew she didn't like my job, and I knew she'd give anything to have me go into some sane, safe industry—like jetcar racing, or something, I suppose— but at least she kept her mouth shut once I got going on a project.

"You wait here," I told her. "Fix a couple of drinks for us. I'm going to adjourn to the next room and play around with this piece of glitter for a while."

"Be careful," she urged.

"I always am," I said. I gave her a kiss, and as I felt her soft, responsive lips against mine I wondered just where in hell that diamond was going to lead me. I didn't want to get too far from Peg, I thought suddenly.

Then I broke away, scooped up the lead box, and went into my tiny den, closing the door behind me.

❂

I sat down at the desk and spread the burnt-out diamonds in a little semi-circle around the box. The room was cold, and I was shivering a little—not only from the draft, either.

I turned on my desk light and sat there for a while, staring at the glistening row of gems, staring at the odd little brown cloud disfiguring each one.

Then, slowly, I reached for the box.

Sixty-six men—only men, for a reason I didn't understand—had disappeared. The diamonds had something to do with it. I didn't know what. But I had an overriding feeling that *I* was slated to be Number Sixty-seven.

It's a job, I thought. *It's my job.* And there was only one way to do it. My fingers quivered a little, just a little, as I started to open the box.

Brightness began to stream from it as soon as the upper half had parted from the lower, and I felt a bead of sweat break out on my forehead and go trickling down back of my ear. With perhaps too much caution, I lifted back the lid and lay bare the diamond nestling within, like a pearl inside an oyster.

I had never seen anything so lovely in my life. It was emerald-cut, neat and streamlined, with uncanny brilliance lurking in its smooth facets. It was small, but perfect, symmetrical and clear. It looked like a tiny spark of cold, blue-white fire.

Then I looked closer.

There was something in the heart of the diamond—not the familiar brown flaw of the others, but something of a different color, something moving and flickering. Before my eyes, it changed and grew.

And I saw what it was. It was the form of a girl—a woman, rather, a voluptuous, writhing nude form in the center of the gem. Her hair was a lustrous blue-black, her eyes a piercing ebony. She was gesturing to me, holding out her hands, incredibly beckoning from within the heart of the diamond.

I felt my legs go limp. She was growing larger, coming closer, holding out her arms, beckoning, calling—

She seemed to fill the room. The diamond grew to gigantic size, and my brain whirled and bobbed in dizzy circles. I sensed the overpowering, wordless call.

Then I heard the door open and close behind me, and I heard Peg's anguished scream: *"Les!"*

There was the sound of footsteps running toward me, but I didn't turn. I felt Peg's arms around my shoulder. She seemed to be holding me back.

I tore loose. The girl from the diamond was calling to me, and I felt inexorably drawn. *"Les!"* I heard Peg call again, and then again, more faintly. Her voice seemed to fade away, and the diamond grew, and grew, and seemed to take up the entire universe. And within it, now life size, was that girl, calling to me.

I went to her.

❉

There was greyness, and void.

I found myself alone. Somewhere.

I was flat on my face, breathing in a strange, warm, alien air, lying stretched out with my nose buried in a thick carpet of blue-green moss. I stumbled to my feet and looked around, still hearing the echoes of Peg's fading cries resounding in my head.

Strange twittering noises sounded from above. Still too stunned to do much besides react to direct stimuli, I glanced up and saw a vicious-looking black-feathered bird with gleaming red talons leap from one tree to another.

Once I recovered my mental equilibrium, my first feeling was one of bitter, irrational anger—anger at the Chief for having let me fall into this job, anger at Peg for not forcing me to turn down the assignment, anger at myself for letting that diamond suck me into its field.

I was Number Sixty-seven, all right. Lee Hayden, Vanished Man. I could imagine Peg's terror-stricken face as she saw me disappear before her eyes and then picked up—

A burnt-out diamond.

Wherever those sixty-six guys had gone, I had followed. I looked around again. I had landed on some alien world, evidently, and I took the realization a lot more calmly than I should have. I was pretty blase, as a matter of fact.

It *could* have been the Congo, of course, or the Amazon basin—but that wasn't too probable. For one thing, most of the places like that on Earth are pretty well civilized-looking by now. For another, no place, not even the Amazon, had birds like the ones that were flitting through the trees here. No place.

After the anger had washed through me, I calmed down a little. I leaned against one of the gigantic trees and groped for a clue, something to pick on as a starting point for the investigation I was about to conduct, the investigation that would clear things up. I was here on *business*.

I was in the middle of a vast jungle. The air was warm and moist, and clinging vines dangled down from the great trees. There didn't seem to be any other animal life, except for the myriad infernal birds.

Overhead, behind the curtain of vines, I could see the sun streaming down. It wasn't the familiar yellow light of Sol, either; the sun here was small, blue-white, and hot. I was sweating—me, in my business suit.

I stripped the jacket off and dangled it on the limb of a tree nearby, as a landmark, and started to walk. Meantime, pounding away in my head, was the vision of that impossible girl inside that impossibly lovely diamond. She was the bait that had trapped me.

I saw how the process worked. These diamonds appeared, and the lucky recipient would stare at them, as I did, hypnotized by the unearthly beauty of the stone into thinking there was a beckoning girl inside.

Then, through some magic, the trap snapped, and the unsuspecting victim—me—got drawn in and carried across space to an uninhabited jungle planet—here.

Why? That was what I was going to find out—I hoped.

❋

I started to walk, moving slowly through the thick haze of the steaming jungle. I kept hearing the twitter of the birds, as a sort of chirping mockery from above, and now and then a little animal jumped out from behind the trees and scurried across my path, but otherwise there wasn't a sign of another living being. I wondered if each victim of this thing got sent to a planet of his own; I hoped not. I was starting to feel terribly alone here.

The jungle seemed endless, and that blue-white sun was getting hotter and hotter with each passing minute. I began to think that I was moving in circles. One tree looked just like the next.

I walked for perhaps an hour, with the sweat pouring down my arms and shoulders and my legs getting wobbly from the strain and the heat, and floating in front of me all the time was the vision of Peg's face as she must have looked the moment I vanished.

I tried to picture the scene. Probably the first thing she'd do, when she got her balance back, would be to call the Bureau, get the Chief on the wire, and curse him black and blue. She wasn't a weak woman. She'd let him know in no uncertain terms what she thought of him for giving me this job, for sending me out to do and die for the Bureau.

But what would she do then? Where would she go? Would she forget me and find someone else? The thought chilled me. I kept slogging on through that infernal mudhole of a planet, and there was nothing in sight but trees and more of them. After a while longer, I peeled off my shirt and wrapped it around the bole of a lanky sapling. Another landmark, I thought.

I was starting to get dreadfully depressed by the loneliness, by the dead, paradoxical emptiness of this fantastically fertile world. There didn't seem to be any way out, any hope at all, and I was beginning to give in to my fears in a way I usually didn't do.

But just then a brown something came bounding out of the tangled nest of vines above me and struck me hard, knocking me to the ground. I hit the springy moss with a terrific impact, recoiled, and rolled over, feeling my lip starting to swell where I'd split it.

I found myself facing what looked like an ape, about the size of a small, wiry man. The beast had two pairs of arms, two glowing, malicious eyes, and as nice a pair of saber teeth as you could find outside the Museum of Natural History. I scrambled a foot or two back, and lashed out with my feet.

I wasn't alone here any more, for sure.

The animal fought back furiously, wrapping its four arms around me, bringing its two razor-sharp teeth much too close to my throat to make me happy.

But I had just been waiting for something like this. I needed something concrete on which I could take out all my fear and rage and resentment, and I met the animal's attack firmly and came back on the creature's own grounds, fighting with arms and legs and knees and anything else handy. Overhead, I heard the chattering of the birds grow to a tumultuous frenzy.

I pounded away, smashed a fist into those two gleaming yellow sabers and felt them crack beneath my driving knuckles, felt the teeth give and break beneath the impact. A hot lancet of pain shot down my hand, but the animal gave a searing cry and jumped back.

I was on him immediately. All its attention was being given to the two broken teeth; its upper pair of hands was busy trying to stanch the flow of bright blood from its mouth, and the other two were waving in feeble circles. I came down hard with my feet, once, twice, a third time, and then the arms stopped waving.

I walked away, looking cautiously around to see if the animal had any relatives in the neighborhood. Suddenly, the empty, lonely jungle seemed overcrowded; behind every spreading leaf, there might be another of these saber-toothed horrors. Breathing hard, feeling the blood dripping from my cut knuckles, I started to edge on through the jungle.

My face was set in a grim mask. It looked like life on this planet was going to be a permanent struggle for survival, judging from my first taste of its wildlife—with no way out. I thought of Peg, back on Earth, and wondered what she was doing, what she was thinking of.

●

I kept going, determined now to keep moving at all costs, determined to beat this world and find my way back to Earth. The fight had set my hormones rolling, apparently; the outpour of adrenalin was just what I needed to galvanize me out of the fit of depression I had been sinking into. Now I was fully alive, wide awake, and wanting out desperately.

Then I glanced up. There seemed to be a fire up ahead; white, brilliant light was streaming through the jungle, illuminating the dark recesses around me. I drew in my breath. If it really was fire, that meant people—savages, perhaps? I advanced cautiously, dying a dozen times whenever I scrunched dawn on a twig.

After about fifty yards, the path swivelled abruptly at a right-angle bend, and I found myself suddenly out of the jungle. I emerged from the thickly-packed trees and saw what was causing all the light. I whistled slowly.

It wasn't a fire. It was a *diamond,* planted smack in the middle of a wide treeless clearing—the biggest diamond anyone ever dreamed of, looming ten feet off the ground, lying there like a gigantic chunk of frozen flame. It was cut with a million facets from which the bright sunlight glinted fiercely. All around it, the trees had been levelled to the ground. The great gem stood all alone, in solitary majesty.

Not quite alone, though. For as I stood there, at the edge of the jungle, staring in openmouthed astonishment, I saw a figure come up over the top of the diamond, poise for a moment on the narrow facet at the very peak, and then leap lightly to the ground.

It was the girl—the girl whose beckoning arms had enticed me into this nightmare in the first place. She was coming toward me.

The girl in the diamond had been nude, but I guess that was only part of the bait. This girl was clad, though what she was wearing took care of the legal minimum and not much more. Otherwise, it was the same girl, radiant with an incredible sort of magnetism. In person, she had the same kind of effect that the image in the diamond had had.

I stood there, dazzled.

❖

"I've been waiting for you," she said. Her voice was low and throbbing, with just the merest echo of something alien and strange about it. "It has been so long since I called, and you did not come."

I just stared at her. Up till this moment I had thought Peg was about as sexy as a girl could be, as far as I was concerned. But I was wrong. This item made Peg look almost like an old washboard by comparison.

She was all curves, but with a rippling strength underneath that was a joy to see. Her hair was deep blue-black, with glossy undertones, and her eyes were deep and compelling.

"My name is Sharane," she said softly. "I have been waiting for you."

The sunlight kept bouncing down off that colossal diamond, and Sharane stood there, brilliant in its reflected light. Her skin seemed to glow, it was so radiant. She took another step toward me, arms outstretched.

I moved back a step. So much glamor in one body frightened me. The last time I had listened to this girl's call, it had drawn me across space and brought me to this planet. Devil only knew what might happen this time.

Besides, there was Peg. So I backed off.

"What do you want?" I demanded. "Why have I been brought here? Where is this place?"

"What does it matter?" Sharane asked lightly, and from the tone of her voice I started to wonder myself. "Come here," she urged.

I started to laugh, I'm afraid. It was all so preposterous, this whole business of diamonds that make people shoot off to some world in space, and this lynx-eyed temptress coming toward me—I dissolved in near-hysterical laughter.

But I was laughing out of the other side of my face a moment later, when Sharane stepped close to me and I felt her warmth near me. She looked up at me, with the same expression on her face that the image in the diamond had had. I was defenseless.

Peg, I thought. *Peg, help me!*

She put her arms around me, and I started to pull back and then stopped. I couldn't. She came close, enfolded herself around me.

Somehow at that moment the distant Peg seemed pretty pale and tawdry next to Sharane. I forgot her. I forgot Peg, I forgot the Chief, the Bureau, Earth—I forgot everything, except Sharane and the blindingly brilliant diamond in front of me.

She drew my head down, and our lips met. The contact was warm, tingling—

And I felt myself grow rigid, as if I were rooted to the ground.

※

Sharane pulled her lips away, and took a step back, She looked at me, strangely, half triumphantly and half sadly. I saw her sigh, saw her breasts rise and fall.

I strained to move, and couldn't. I was frozen!

"Sharane!"

"I am sorry," she said. Her musical voice seemed to be modulated into a minor key, as if she *were* really sorry. "This is the way things must be."

And then she lifted me up, slung my stiffened form over her shoulder as easily as if I were an empty sack, and started walking away!

I struggled impotently against the strange paralysis that had overcome me, and cursed bitterly. A second time, Sharane had trapped me! Once, when she called from the depths of the crystal; now, when she betrayed me with a kiss.

I rolled my eyes in anguish, but that was as close as I could come to motion. Sharane carried me lightly, easily, around to the other side of the gigantic diamond. "You will have friends here," she said softly.

I looked around, and blinked in surprise. For half a dozen other Earthmen lay, similarly frozen, behind the great diamond.

Sharane very carefully laid me down in their midst, and left me.

She had put me between two other frozen prisoners. Further away, I saw four more. All six were gripped by the same strange force that held me.

"Greetings, friend," I heard the man on my left say. "The name is Caldwell—Frederic Caldwell. What's yours?" It was almost as if we were meeting in a cafeteria, he was so casual.

"Les Hayden," I said.

"My name is Strauss," said the one on my right. "Ed Strauss. Glad to meet you, Hayden. Join our merry band."

Strauss—Caldwell—those were two of the names on that list of sixty-six vanishers. And I'm *Sixty-Seven. Welcome to the fold,* I thought.

"How long have you been here?" I asked.

"Ten days," said Strauss.

"A week," Caldwell said. "But you'd never know it. When you're frozen like this, you don't need food or anything. You're out of circulation, period. You just lie here, waiting for the next sucker to be deposited in the vault."

"Yeah," said Strauss. "There were about forty guys here when I came, but one day a ship came down and some huge *things* packed most of them up. That made things pretty quiet for a while. We've just been lying here, those of us that are left. Every once in a while Sharane catches someone new."

"Did both of you get snagged the same way?"

"I found a diamond on my desk one day," said Caldwell. "Came out of nowhere. I started staring at it—and I guess you know the rest of the story."

"It's Sharane's kiss that does it," Strauss said. "I think it sets up some kind of force field that freezes us. And we stay here, and wait for the alien ship to come pick us up and take us away."

"To the slaughterhouse," said Caldwell dully.

I pushed and struggled, but it was to no avail. I was efficiently straitjacketed. Above me, the big diamond stared coldly out, its radiant brilliance seeming to mock us.

Caldwell and Strauss had been trapped the same way I had—by the beckoning diamond. I wondered how many more Sharane would catch, would draw across space to this strange planet. And I wondered *why?* Who was this strange woman, what power did she have, why was she doing what she did? What motivated her?

I didn't know. And it didn't look like I was ever going to find out.

All I knew was I was caught, and there didn't seem to be any way out. But I wasn't going to give up. I could still keep on hoping.

We lay there for hours, talking occasionally, more often remaining silent, staring up at the cloudless sky. I could see how the days would roll by, in empty, mindless waiting, until the mysterious ship returned for its next load of Earthmen.

By dint of much eyeball-rolling, I was able to make out what my two companions looked like. Strauss was balding, sandy-haired, middle aged, Caldwell much younger, dynamic-looking.

There wasn't much we could say, and after a while conversation ceased entirely. We were so placed that I could see the giant diamond clearly, and I started to pass the time by staring at its peak, wondering how many carats the thing could weigh. Millions, no doubt.

Then I began searching the sky, waiting for the ship to come, the ship that would carry us off to our unknown next destination. After a while longer I grew tired, and closed my eyes. I slept, uneasily, and no doubt I would have been tossing and turning if only I could move at all.

I was awakened by the sound of Caldwell's deep, sharp voice exclaiming, "Look! Here comes a new one!"

Then Strauss commented, "And it's a girl!"

I struggled to get my eyes open and keep them that way, and swiveled them around, searching for the newcomer. And then I saw her.

She was just emerging from the edge of the jungle. I saw her plainly, clad in sweater and tight-clinging khaki trousers; she had evidently had a rough time of it in the jungle, because her sweater was torn and shredded and her hair was wildly disheveled. But she kept moving onward, her eyes wide in amazement at the sight of the diamond.

She was Peg.

※

I watched her almost dazedly as she made her way across the clearing. I knew she couldn't see me yet, but I could see her. It was Peg, all right. How, why she had come, I could only conjecture, But she was here, madly, unbelievably, and I was glad to see her.

"Where'd *she* come from?" Caldwell asked.

"I thought only men came through," said Strauss. "Maybe she's an accomplice of Sharane."

"No," I said. "I know her."

I tried to call to her, to attract her attention in some way. I didn't know where Sharane was.

"*Peg!*" I called. My voice was a hoarse croak, barely more than a whisper. I tried again. "Peg! Peg!"

The third time she heard me. I saw her mouth drop open as she turned slowly and saw us spread out on the ground, and then she started running joyfully toward us.

"Les! Oh, Les!" she called, from a hundred yards away. Her voice came across clearly, and at the moment it seemed like the most wonderful sound I had ever heard.

I watched her as she ran, drinking in the sight of her—the smooth stride, the long, powerful legs, the bobbing red hair that fluttered up and down as she ran. And a hot burst of shame flooded my face as I remembered the kiss—Sharane's kiss.

Peg would forgive me, though. I knew she would.

She kept running, running toward us—and then, she stopped and recoiled back, as if she had struck a glass wall.

I saw her move back a few paces and rub her nose as if she had bruised it. Then she stepped forward again, and, in perplexity, extended a hand in front of her. It stopped short at the same barrier.

She began to edge around in a wary semicircle, feeling in front of her, and everywhere it was the same. An invisible barrier, blocking us off from her. She wouldn't be able to reach us. Whoever had snared us really knew his business.

Tears of frustration came to her eyes, but she wiped them away and continued to search for some break in the barrier, while I shouted words of encouragement to her. It was a miracle that Peg was here at all, Peg whom I thought I'd never see again, and I wanted desperately to be holding her tight.

She completed the circle around us, without finding any way in. I saw her kick the barrier viciously, saw her foot stop in mid-air as the invisible field rebuffed the blow.

And then I saw Sharane come up behind her.

"Watch it!" I yelled, but there was no need of the warning. Peg turned, and the two women faced each other uneasily.

I felt torn apart when I saw the two of them together. Peg was a wonderful girl, wonderful to look at, wonderful to be with—but Sharane! Sharane was something different, something unearthly, something irresistible. No wonder she had trapped sixty-seven men so far. Sixty-seven, plus Peg—if Peg had been trapped.

The two women moved closer to each other, and then, incredibly, I heard Sharane say, in the same throaty, erotic voice she had used on me and on everyone else who had come through the crystal gateway, "I've been waiting for you."

Peg's sarcastic answer rang out sharp and clear. "I'll bet you have," she snapped.

"It has been so long since I called, and you did not come," Sharane said caressingly.

My eyes popped. Was Sharane trying to make love to Peg? What kind of thing *was* Sharane, anyway?

"Let me through that barrier," Peg demanded.

Sharane made no answer, but merely moved closer. "My name is Sharane," she said. "I have been waiting for you."

Word for word, the same routine she'd given me! Only how did she expect it to work on Peg?

It didn't. Sharane moved even closer, reached out her arms, started to embrace Peg—

And Peg knocked her sprawling with an open-fisted blow.

Sharane went reeling back on the ground, but picked herself up with no apparent bruises, and returned to her strange task. She moved back to Peg, turning on all her siren charms.

It was incredible, unbelievable. But Peg wasn't to be tempted as easily as a mere man would be. As Sharane approached, Peg whipped out at her with another blow, and followed with a neat fist to the dark-haired woman's stomach.

Sharane backed up, and apparently caught on that she wasn't getting the usual reaction from Peg. She charged in a mad flurry, failed to get much of a handhold on Peg's short-cut hair, and launched out in an attack of wild violence.

Peg parried most of the punches, but a stray fingernail got through the defense and raked down her cheek, leaving a long, bloody line, and one of Sharane's frantic blows landed in her mid-section, throwing her back gasping for breath.

I heard my own voice shouting encouragement, roaring as if I were at a prizefight. And, from around me, I heard the other men cheering Peg on too.

I had never seen two women fight before. It was quite a sight.

Sharane kept the upper hand for a few moments, forcing Peg back, and on the areas of flesh exposed where Peg's sweater had been torn in the jungle, I saw livid bruises starting to appear.

Then Peg regained the initiative, and with an outburst of kicks, punches, and slaps she drove Sharane back. Peg used every tactic in the book, and some that weren't—such as reaching out, seizing Sharane's lovely blue-black hair, and yanking.

Suddenly I saw Sharane break away out of a clinch and dash back, toward us, through the barrier. Peg followed on her heels, just a step behind.

Sharane must have dissolved the barrier she'd set up in order to let herself get through, but the maneuver turned out a flop, because Peg came right through with her. Sharane turned, glared angrily at her when she saw the strategy had been negated, and set out in a run—straight for the giant diamond!

"Go get her, Peg!" I shouted, almost breathless myself from the strain of watching the women fight while I myself was unable to move a muscle.

Sharane was climbing the diamond, pulling herself up by grasping the sharp corners of the facets, hauling herself up over that great shining eye. And Peg was right behind her.

I watched as Peg started the ascent, slipping and sliding, cutting her hands on the keen edges. Sharane was at the top, balanced precariously on the uppermost facet. The sun was beating down hard, shooting blinding flashes of light slashing off the diamond into our eyes.

As Peg approached the top, Sharane stooped and pushed her off. She went sliding back down, catching hold half way to the ground. I saw that she had ripped the leg of her slacks open, but she didn't appear to be cut herself. She dangled for a moment and then with dogged determination she climbed her way back to the top. My heart pounded as frantically as if I were taking part in the struggle myself.

Sharane kicked out viciously. I saw Peg start to lose her grip, begin to fall back—and then seize Sharane's flailing foot, and, holding on with an unbreakable grip, begin to haul herself to the top of the diamond!

She reached it at last, and the two of them stood here, rocking shakily back and forth in the narrow area, while the blazing sun burnt down fiercely on them, sending rivers of perspiration coursing down their bare flesh. They were locked in a double grip, shivering from exhaustion, neither one able to gain advantage over the other.

Then I saw Peg's muscles flex, and she began to bend Sharane back, back, until the other woman was almost doubled over. Suddenly Sharane's leg gave way, and she toppled; through some miracle, she landed on her back, still atop the diamond, and Peg pounced down on her. Peg clamped her hands on Sharane's lovely throat, and started to squeeze.

Sharane's arms began to thrash wildly—and then, then, as we watched dumfounded, Sharane began to *change!* As Peg kept up the relentless pressure, Sharane's shape began to alter; arms became tentacles, skin thickened and became something else, changed color from radiant white to loathsome purple. Where there had been a lovely seductress a moment before lay a ghastly *thing.*

Peg jumped back, startled at the transformation; Sharane, or the thing that had been Sharane, lashed out with a tentacle, and Peg, still clinging to the other, toppled back and off the diamond, pinwheeling to the ground.

The Sharane-thing lost its balance and dropped off the other side. I saw Peg lying unconscious on the ground, watched in impotent horror as the alien being started to rise—

And suddenly I discovered I was free! My arm moved, my leg! Apparently the alien had needed all its power to fight Peg, and had been unable to spare the concentration needed to maintain our imprisonment.

I was up and running in an instant, feeling strength ebb back into my stiff, cramped muscles. I leaped on the monster before it could rise, felt its strange, dry, alien odor, and then my hands were around its scaly throat. I looked down, searched for some trace of the loveliness that had once tempted me, and could find none. I saw a weird, terrifying face with glinting many-faceted eyes and a twisted, agonized mouth. I kept up the pressure.

I heard the creature's breath gasping out, and then I felt hands on my shoulders—Peg's, on one shoulder, and a man's hand, on the other.

I looked up and saw Strauss' pudgy face. "Don't kill the thing," he said. "Get up, and let's find out what's been going on."

"No," I said. But they pulled me off.

I stood up, and watched the alien writhing on the ground, struggling to recover its breath. A surge of hatred ran through me as I saw the strange thing down there.

"What are you?" I demanded. "Where are we?"

"Give me some time," it said, barely able to speak—but I could still detect in its voice the same underlying hypnotic tone that Sharane's voice had had. It was the only point the thing had in common with the girl. "Let me recover. I mean no further harm."

"I don't trust it," I said uneasily.

"Why not wait?" asked Strauss. "It can't make any trouble for us now—obviously there has to be some kind of emotional surrender or it can't take control of us. That must be how the girl was able to defeat it."

I nodded. "That sounds reasonable." I stared coldly down at the battered, suffering alien. "All right. Let's let it catch its breath, and we'll find out what's what."

I was glad, now, that they had pulled me off. Carried away the way I was, I would undoubtedly have throttled the creature—and the Chief would undoubtedly have throttled me for it when I got back—*if* I got back. For one thing, with the creature alive there was a chance we might find out what this was all about. For another, with the creature dead we might have no way of getting back to Earth.

So I stood back, letting the anger seep out of me, and turned to Peg.

She had come off on top in the fight, but she was pretty well battered. One of her lovely blue eyes had an even lovelier shiner, and she was thoroughly scratched and bruised. Her sweater was just about ripped clean off her, and she was holding the tatters together self-consciously.

"How did *you* get here?" I asked.

She smiled, and through all the blood and bruises it still looked wonderful.

"I went to the Chief, after you—disappeared."

"I wish you hadn't," I said. "I didn't want him to know I was letting you in on anything."

"He doesn't know. All I did was ask him to tell me what kind of job you had been sent out on. After I told him what had happened to you, he explained."

"And then?"

"Then I requested that the next unused diamond that was found be turned over to me. He didn't want to, but finally he agreed to it."

I looked at the slowly twisting creature lying on the ground, and back to Peg. "So?"

"So another diamond materialized that night, and the Chief called me. I came and picked it up, and when I was alone I looked at it. There was that girl in it, calling to me." She made a face. "It was disgusting."

"And then you were drawn in?" I asked, remembering the way Sharane had trapped me.

"Of course not, silly. I didn't respond to that posturing girl at all, and so I couldn't be caught. But I *voluntarily* came through. I willed myself to be drawn in, and I was. I landed up in that jungle, and wandered out here when I saw the light of the diamond."

I nodded. "And then Sharane came after you with her song and dance. Since Sharane was actually an alien with no real idea of the difference between the human sexes, she—it—thought her act would work on you too. But it didn't."

I walked over to where the alien was, and Peg and the six freed captives followed me. Sharane—the Sharane-thing—was sitting up.

"Hurry," it said. "We must talk before the Llanar ship arrives, or there is great danger."

"Who are the Llanar?" I asked, surprised.

"My captors," said the alien. Its weird face was twisted into an expression of cosmic sadness.

"What do you mean, your captors?"

"The Llanar," Sharane said, "are a great race from out there." She gestured at the sky. "They conquered my people, and they wish to enslave yours through us. They have placed me here, against my will, and shown me how to disguise myself as a human. All who were drawn by the diamond were powerless against me—except—"

She pointed to Peg.

I smiled. "The only thing as hard as a diamond is another diamond. The only thing that could resist Sharane's womanly wiles would be another woman. Those diamonds were set up to trap *men*—and when a woman came through, Sharane here didn't know what to do with her. She had never experienced a human woman."

"I have now," the alien said weakly. "I hope to never again."

"How does this trap work?" Caldwell asked.

"The great diamond here is the focus," Sharane said. "The smaller ones serve as transmitting poles, at the other end of the channel. We send them to Earth, and when men find them they are drawn in. I then tempt them to surrender themselves—and as soon as they do, I freeze them." The alien broke into the alien equivalent of a sob. "Then the Llanar come, and take them away. They make them slaves, on their home worlds."

The alien sat up, and rubbed itself. "But you have won your freedom from me," it said. "You may return to your planet."

"And you?"

"I must sit here," the alien said. "I must continue to prey on Earth, or the Llanar will kill me."

"We'll close that damnable gateway, don't worry," muttered Caldwell, but I ignored him.

Suddenly all my hatred for Sharane had vanished. I saw the strange thing before us as a *person,* not a thing—a suffering, sensitive person. An alien, true, but very human under the to-me-grotesque exterior. In just those few minutes I learned a lesson: you don't have to have arms and legs and two blue eyes to be a human being.

I saw the whole picture now. Sharane's people were under the domination of still another alien race from deep in the galaxy—the dread Llanar. And the Llanar were forcing Sharane to operate this lonely trap on the edge of the universe, waiting like a spider to net the unfortunates who happened to find one of the treacherous diamonds she scattered.

"You can send us back to Earth?" I asked.

"Yes," Sharane said. "But—"

Then she looked upward, and I saw the sky darken. Coming down, straight above us, was a gleaming golden-hulled spaceship!

✺

Suddenly Sharane came to life. "The Llanar!" she cried. "Run into the jungle—hide, or they'll carry you off! I'll stay out here and get rid of them."

Her form melted and coalesced weirdly, and once again I saw before me the woman-shape. She pointed toward the jungle, and I didn't waste any time arguing. I seized Peg's hand and we broke into a frantic trot, heading for the woods.

We got there breathless, and all six of the freed men came racing in right behind us. We squatted there, silently, watching the Llanar ship descend.

It came down in slow, graceful spirals, hovered overhead, finally settled to the ground—and the Llanar came out.

I won't try to describe them. They were huge, thick-bodied, and I still shudder when I think of what they looked like. They were hideous, hateful, fearsome creatures. I imagined what a whole world of them would be like.

Three of them emerged from the ship, came out, walked up to Sharane. They stood around her, dwarfing her lovely body among them.

They talked for a long while; I heard the low, booming rumble of their voices come crackling over the ground to us. After an extensive discussion, they turned and left. Sharane stood alone.

I watched, quivering with revulsion, as they marched slowly back to their ship, got in, and a moment later a fiery jet-blast carried them aloft. We remained in the forest for a moment or two longer, waiting until the Llanar ship was completely out of sight. Then we dashed out.

Sharane was waiting for us at the base of the great diamond.

"They wanted to know where the new batch of captives was," she said. Her breasts were heaving in obvious terror, and it was hard for me to remember, as I looked at her, that minutes before she had been a hideous alien being writhing on the ground. "I told them none had come through since their last pickup."

"What did they say?"

"They were very angry that no new slaves were on hand. But I promised to have some soon, and they left."

I looked at Peg in gratitude. "If it weren't for you, I'd be on my way in that ship," I said. "And all these other people too."

"It's lucky I came through when I did, darling."

"It certainly is, Miss," said one of the men. "We owe our lives to you."
I turned to Sharane. "Can you send us back?"

"It is simple." She reached up, pulled eight diamonds—small ones—from nowhere, and handed one to each of us. "Concentrate," she said.

One by one, the men blinked out and vanished, until only Caldwell and Peg and myself were left. Caldwell looked at me.

"You know," he said, "if you destroy that big diamond, I think it'll close this hellish gateway forever. No one else on Earth will be trapped the way we were."

"I know," I said. "But I don't intend to do it."

His eyes blazed angrily. "Why not? Do you want the Llanar to carry off everyone? For all you know, you'd be a slave on some stinking planet now if your girl hadn't shown up."

"I know," I said again. I turned to Sharane. "But I'm not going to close the gateway."

"They would kill me if you did," Sharane said.

"That's not the reason."

"What is, dear?" Peg asked.

"I'm leaving the gateway open so we can come back through. Someday we'll return, when we're ready—more of us, Sharane. And our people and your people together will end the Llanar tyranny." I thought of those gigantic creatures again, and shivered.

"Do you mean that?" Sharane asked.

"I mean it," I said firmly. "As soon as I get back to my world, to the Bureau, I'll start getting things rolling for the counterattack."

I smiled. This job was over; I had solved the mystery of where the sixty-six had gone. But a new job was beginning.

"I will be waiting for you," Sharane said. "But in the meantime—I must stay here, preying on all who come through. The Llanar will only kill me and replace me with another I don't." There was a note of genuine regret in the alien's voice.

"Go through," I said bluntly to Caldwell. He frowned in concentration and vanished, leaving just Peg and myself facing Sharane. The great diamond formed a backdrop for the scene.

"I am glad you defeated me," Sharane told Peg. "It may mean the beginning of a long friendship between our peoples."

"Many friendships begin after a deadly battle," I said. I turned to Peg. "Let's go through," I said.

"All right. Goodbye, Sharane."

"Farewell." The alien turned and walked away, slowly, toward the jungle.

We watched her go, standing there, watching that lovely false woman-form glide smoothly away. I was thinking, *you never can tell*. The normal thing would be to hate, to destroy the horrid alien thing that lurks in wait for unsuspecting Earthmen—but we couldn't hate Sharane. She was a tool, serving powerful masters. She was not evil in herself.

The Llanar were powerful, all right—but not so powerful that they couldn't be beaten. I took a last look at the gleaming diamond, and at Sharane's retreating form—the lonely, pitiful guardian of the crystal gate.

Then she was at the very edge of the jungle, and waving to us. We waved back. Grasping our diamonds firmly and holding hands, Peg and I concentrated on returning to Earth.

The giant diamond slowly faded into the greyness that swept over us, as did Sharane. We were on our way back to Earth at last.

But I knew I'd be seeing her again, someday. We'd be coming back through the gateway. We'll come back, all right.

And when we do, the Llanar will tremble.

CHOKE CHAIN
(1956)

It was the busy month of February, 1956. I was four months away from graduation at Columbia, but by now I was selling stories all over the place, and I was going to classes only when absolutely necessary, spending most of my time holed up in my little room on West 114th St. turning out new material, singly or in collaboration with Randall Garrett. We had sold a second and then a third "Robert Randall" novelet in our series to John Campbell, I had placed stories of my own with Campbell, Bob Lowndes, Larry Shaw, and several other editors, and there was the monthly task of meeting my quota for Howard Browne's two magazines.

Hardly had I finished "Guardian of the Crystal Gate" for Howard and sold him the "Ralph Burke" story "Stay Out of My Grave," but I was at work on an 8000-worder that I called "The Price of Air" for him. It saw print in the December, 1956 issue of Fantastic. *By then Howard Browne had resigned from Ziff-Davis so he could return to writing mystery novels, and the new editor was Howard's former associate, Paul Fairman, a much less jovial man with whom I never attained much of a rapport. Fairman kept me on as a staff writer, but it was strictly a business matter, whereas I think the amiable Howard Browne had regarded me as something of an office mascot.*

When he published "The Price of Air," Fairman changed the title to "Choke Chain," which puzzled me, because I didn't know what the term meant. Later I discovered that it's a dog-owner thing. I am a cat-owning sort of person. It is, I suppose, an appropriate enough title for this story, and I have left it in place this time around.

Callisto was supposed to have been just a lark for me, a pleasant stopoff where I could kill time and work up the courage to tackle the big task—Jupiter. I felt that exploring the big, heavy planet was, well, maybe not so grand a thing as my destiny, but yet something I had to do.

There was only one trouble: the immenseness of Jupiter's unknown wastes scared me. Fear was a new sensation for me. I got as far as Jupiter's moon Ganymede, a thriving world bigger than Mercury, and suddenly, with great Jupiter looming overhead in the sky like a bloated overripe tomato, I knew I wasn't ready for it. I've been to a lot of places and done a lot of things, and this was the first time I'd ever drawn back from an adventure.

I dallied on Ganymede for a couple of days, not knowing quite where to turn. Then one night in a bar someone hinted to me that something funny might be going on on Jupiter's largest moon, Callisto, and I set my sights there.

It seemed Callisto had recently clamped down on tourists, had booted out a couple of newspapermen, and had done some other mighty peculiar things, and rumors were spreading wildly about what might be taking place there.

It looked like a fine idea, at the time: go to Callisto, find out what the trouble was, spend a few days putting things in order. It was the kind of jaunt I thrive on, the sort of thing that's been my specialty since I began roaming the spaceways. By the time I was through on Callisto, I thought I'd have the blood flowing smoothly in my veins again, and I'd feel more like tackling the Big Project: Jupiter.

Only Callisto wasn't the picnic I thought it would be. It turned out to be something more than a refresher for weary adventurers. I found that out as soon as I got there.

❁

It had been rough to get a passport, but I finally signed on a slow tug as a mechanic, and that was good enough to get me a landing permit for Callisto.

I helped pilot a tugload of heavy crates from Ganymede to its nearby twin moon, Callisto. I didn't know what was in the crates, I didn't ask, and I didn't care. The job was getting me to the place I wanted to get to, and that was what counted.

We reached the satellite in a couple of days, and the skipper put the ship down in a vast, windswept desert of blue-white ammonia snow. As soon as we were down, the captain radioed Callisto City to let them know we were here.

Callisto City is a giant dome, a plastine bubble that covers a fair-sized chunk of Callisto and houses several tens of thousands of colonists. We were outside it, in the snow.

I waited impatiently, staring out the port of the ship at the empty swirls of snow, watching a little convoy of trucks come crawling out of Callisto City like so many black bugs and go rolling through the snow to meet us.

Then they arrived. A gong sounded, and I heard the captain yell, "Into your spacesuits, on the double! Let's get the cargo loaded extra quick."

We suited up, and by that time the trucks had arrived. We loaded our cargo aboard them, and one by one they started back to the dome. That was all there was to it. No contact between Callistans and outsiders at all.

When the last crate was swung aboard the last truck, the captain said, "Get back in and let's blast off!"

I turned to him. "I'm not going. I'm resigning, sir."

He looked at me blankly, as if I'd just said, "I'm dead, sir." Finally he said, "You're *what?*"

I nodded. "I'm quitting? Right here and now. I'm going to grab one of these cargo trucks back to Callisto City."

"You can't leave in the middle of the trip!" he protested. He went on objecting, violently, until I quietly told him he could pocket the rest of my uncollected wages. At that he shut up in a hurry, and gestured for me to get going. These guys are all alike.

❋

I climbed into the rear truck of the convoy, and the startled driver looked at me wide-eyed.

"What the hell are you, buddy? There's nothing about you on my cargo invoice."

"I'm just going along for the ride, friend," I told him softly. "I'm a sightseer. I want to get a look at your fair city."

"But you can't—" he objected. I jabbed him in the ribs, once, in exactly the right place, and he subsided immediately.

"Okay, buddy," he grunted. "Lay off. I'll take you—but remember, it's only because you forced me." He wrinkled his brow in puzzlement. "But it's beyond me why in blazes anyone would *want* to get to Callisto that bad—when we'd all give our left ears to get away."

"It's my business," I said.

"Sure, sure," he said placatingly, afraid of another poke. "Do whatever you damned please. But it's your funeral—remember that."

I smiled to myself, and watched the shining dome of Callisto City grow nearer. I was wondering what was going on beneath that peaceful-looking arc of plastine. It didn't sound very good.

* * *

Finally we reached the city, and the truck edged carefully into the airlock. My helmet-window went foggy as the icy air of outside was replaced by the warm atmosphere of Callisto City, and then I saw my fellow truck-drivers climbing down and getting out of their spacesuits, in obvious relief at being able to shuck the bulky, uncomfortable things.

As I slid out of mine, I noticed one very strange thing. All the truck-drivers—every last one—wore curious golden collars around their necks. The collars were almost like dog-collars, thick, made of what looked like burnished bronze. They seemed oddly flexible and solid at the same time, and set in the middle of each was a little meter that kept clicking away, recording some kind of data.

I looked around. There were twenty or thirty Callistans near me, and they all wore the collar. And they all wore the same facial expression, too. The best way to describe it is to call it a *beaten* look. They were all beaten men, spiritless, frightened—of what?

The intense fluorescent lights from above glinted brightly off the collars. Was wearing them some kind of local custom, I wondered? Or a protection against something?

I heard low whispering coming from them as they stowed their spacesuits in dull-green lockers ranged along the side of the airlock, and headed back toward their trucks. They were all looking at me, and obviously they were commenting on the fact that I didn't have any collar. They seemed shocked at that, and very worried.

"What's this collar business?" I asked the driver of my truck, as we moved through the inner lock and into the city proper.

"You'll find out, chum. Just make sure you can run fast when they spot you, though."

"When who spots me?"

"The guards, dope. The Tax Agents. You don't think you can breathe for free on Callisto, do you?"

"You mean they *tax your breathing?*" I asked, incredulously, and before I could get an answer I saw a cordon of guards forming around our truck.

※

There were half a dozen of them, burly men in blue uniforms, all of them wearing the ubiquitous metal collar. They had halted our truck, which had been last in the procession. I saw the other trucks in the convoy rolling on toward their destination somewhere in the city.

"Don't make trouble for me," my driver said pleadingly. "I'll be docked if I don't get my cargo back on time."

One of the men in uniform reached up and opened the cab of the truck. "Come on out of there, you."

"Who, me?" I asked innocently. "What for?"

"Don't play games," he snapped. "Get out of that truck." He waved a lethal-looking blaster at me, and I decided not to argue with it. I leaped lightly to the ground, and as I did so the uniformed man signalled to my driver that he could go ahead.

The six men ringed threateningly around me. "Who are you?" the leader demanded. "Where'd you come from?"

"That doesn't matter," I said belligerently. He put his hand on my arm, and I jerked away. "I'm a tourist. Want to see my landing permit?"

"Landing permits don't mean a thing here," he said. "Where's your respirometer?"

"My *what?*"

"According to statute 1106A, Book Eleven, Civil Code of the Principality of Callisto City," he reeled off, "all inhabitants of the Principality of Callisto City are required by law to wear respirometers at all times, whether they are transients or permanent inhabitants." He finished his spiel and gestured boredly to one of his assistants. "Give him the collar, Mack."

The man named Mack opened a wooden box and revealed one of those metal collars, the kind that seemed to be all the rage in Callisto just then. He held it out invitingly.

"Here you are, dear. The finest model in the house."

I drew back. "I don't want your goddam collar," I snapped hotly.

"You've heard the regulation," the head man said. "Either you put the collar on or you turn around and walk out the way you came."

I turned and looked through the translucent airlock out at the barren wastes of frozen ammonia. "I'm staying here, for the time being. And I don't plan on wearing any collars."

He frowned. I was being particularly troublesome, and he didn't like it. He waved his blaster in an offhand gesture. "Put the collar on him, boys."

Mack and one of the others advanced toward me, holding the gleaming metal circlet. I took one look at it, smiled, and said, "Okay. I know when I'm licked. I can't fight all of you."

They relaxed visibly. "Good to see you cooperate. Put it on him."

I let them come close, and Mack was starting to lower the thing over my head when I went into action. I batted the collar out of his hands and heard it go clanging across the floor, and at the same time I lashed out with my foot and nipped the boss' blaster right out of his amazed hand. The gun went flying thirty feet or more.

Then they were all on me at once. I pounded back savagely, feeling solid flesh beneath my knuckles and occasionally the unyielding coldness of someone's collar as I drove a fist past it into his jaw.

Some picnic, I thought, as I waded gleefully in, flattening Mack with a poke in the stomach and sending another one reeling to the ground with a swift kick. Luckily for me, the head man had been the only one wearing sidearms—and apparently some street urchin had made off with the blaster before he could find it again, because I wasn't getting cooked.

I crashed two of them together, pushed the remaining two aside, and dashed away toward the entrance to the city. I heard them pounding after me in hot pursuit.

It was about a hundred yards to the edge of the city. I made the dash in a dozen seconds and found myself in a crowded thoroughfare, with a number of people watching my fight with evident interest.

I broke into the crowd and kept on running, pushing people aside as I went. Behind me, I could see the six policemen jostling their way along. One of them had found another blaster somewhere, but he didn't dare use it in such a crowd.

I rounded a corner, nearly slipped, and then doubled back and headed for the main thoroughfare again. The cops weren't taken in by my maneuver, though, and as I looked back I saw them following grimly, shouting something at me. There were more of them now.

Suddenly I felt a hand slide into mine, soft and warm, and a gentle voice at my side said, "Come with me."

I didn't argue. I saw the crowd close up into a solid mass behind us, and heard the roaring of my frustrated pursuers, as my unknown rescuer led me away to safety.

❋

As we ran, I glanced down and saw a girl at my side, with her hand grasping mine. She was about twenty-two, wearing a clinging blue tunic that cut off above her knees. She had copper-red hair, and around her neck was that curious collar.

After running a block and a half, we came to a small tenement-house of the kind common in Callisto City. "In here," she whispered, and we ducked inside.

Then up a flight of stairs, around a corridor, down a dimly-lit hallway. We stood for an anxious moment outside her door, while she fumbled nervously in an attempt to touch her thumb to the doorplate, and then finally she managed to impress her print on the sensitive photo-electronic plate and the door slid noiselessly open.

We stepped inside, and with a feeling of relief I watched the heavy door roll back. I was safe—for now.

I turned to the girl. "Who are you? Why'd you bring me here?"

The run had tired her. Her breasts rose and fell as she gasped for breath, and she smiled and held up a hand for time as she struggled to talk. Finally, panting, she managed to say, "I'm June Knight. I saw the whole scene with the guards. You're safe here, for a while. But tell me—why have you come to Callisto?"

"Why does everyone wear these collars?" I countered, ignoring her question.

Her pretty face grew sad. "They make us—the Three, that is. Come on inside, and I'll get together something for you to eat. You must be starved, and we can talk later."

"No," I said quickly. "I'm not hungry. I'm more anxious to find out what's been happening here."

"Well, even if you're not hungry, I am," she said. "Come into the kitchen and I'll tell you the whole story—the story of how this whole city's been enslaved."

She went into the adjoining room of the little flat, and I followed her. She punched keys on the robocook, dialing a small but nutritious meal, and when the food was placed before her on the table she turned to me.

"First," she said, "when's the last time any news came from Callisto to the outside world?"

I shrugged. "I haven't been keeping up with the news. I've been on Mars the last two years, hunting *rhuud* in the lowlands. The papers don't get there often."

"Oh. You've been out of touch. Well, you haven't missed any news from Callisto, because we've had an efficient news blanket in operation for almost a year and a half. And for a while it was a voluntary one— just about two years ago, when the air started going bad. We didn't want outsiders to know."

I blinked. "The *air?*" In a dome-city like this, the air supply was, of course, wholly artificial, and its proper maintenance was of vital importance to the entire community. "What happened to the air?" I asked.

"I'm not sure," she said. "None of us are. Suddenly it became impure. People began sickening by the hundreds; some died, and almost everyone else was ill in one way or another. A tremendous investigation was held by the people who were our government then—Cleve Coldridge was our mayor, a fine man—and nothing could be determined about the source of the impurities. And then my father—he's dead now—invented this." She tapped the metal collar she wore around her throat.

"And what, may I ask, is that collar?"

"It's a filter," she said. "When the collar is worn, it counteracts the impurities in the air, through some process I don't understand. My father died shortly after he developed it, and so he didn't get a chance to offer it to the public. He willed the design and the process to three— friends—of his." Her mouth clamped together bitterly, and I saw her struggling to fight back tears. Almost automatically, I put my arm around her.

"I'll be all right," she said. "Every time I think of those three, and what they've done to Dad's invention—"

"Tell me about it later, if you want."

"No. You might as well know the whole story. The three of them—Martin Hawkins, an Earthman, Ku Sui, a Martian, and Kolgar Novin, a Venusian—announced my father's device to the public as if they had discovered it themselves. It was the solution to our air-impurity problem. They started turning out the collars in mass production, and within a month everyone in Callisto City was wearing one."

"Did that stop the sickness?"

She nodded. "Immediately. The hospitals emptied out in no time at all, and there hasn't been a case of that disease since then."

"Is that all?" I asked.

"Hardly. The trouble didn't start until after we were all wearing the collars." She took my hand and guided it along her collar to the back of her neck, where I felt a tiny joint in the metal.

"What's that?" I asked.

"That joint is the weapon those three hold over us at all times. These collars, you see, can be tightened at will by remote control—and my father's three friends operate the controls!"

I whistled. "What a hideous kind of dictatorship! You mean—anyone who makes too much of the wrong kind of noise gets his collar tightened."

"Exactly. As soon as the whole city was wearing the protective collars—the collars that we thought were our salvation—the Three called a public meeting, and announced that they were taking over the government. Mayor Coldridge stood up to protest such a high-handed move—"

"And suddenly felt his collar tightening around his neck!" I concluded. I could picture the scene vividly.

"It was terrible," she said. "Right in the middle of his speech, he clutched at his throat, went red in the face, and sank to his knees. They let him up after a minute or so, and explained what they had done. Then they announced that anyone who protested against what they were doing would get similar treatment. We've been against them ever since."

I stood up, almost overwhelmed with anger. I had come to the right place this time! Maybe giant Jupiter was something I needed to explore someday for my own peace of mind, but this mess on Callisto required immediate attention. I didn't see how I was going to fight it, either, but I swore to myself that I wasn't going to leave here until the last collar had been removed from a Callistan throat.

"What about this breathing-tax?" I asked.

She nodded. "That's the latest thing. They've decided the regular taxes aren't enough for them, and so they're bleeding us white with this new one. They installed meters in all the collars, to measure the amount of air we consume, and—" her voice was choked with hatred—"they tax us. There's even a price of air here. Every Friday, we have to pay a certain amount."

"And if you don't?"

She put her hand to her throat, and made a swift squeezing motion. I shuddered. I'd never come across anything so vicious as this. When I was hunting *rhuud* on Mars, I thought I was against an ugly beast—but those Martian land-serpents weren't half so cold-blooded as the Three who held Callisto in their iron grip.

I was going to break their hold. I vowed it, as I looked at the red-eyed girl staring solemnly at me.

* * *

Suddenly there was a knock on the hall door. I sprang up at once, and June looked at me with alarm.

"Hide in there," she said, pointing to the bedroom. I dashed inside and crouched behind the bed, wondering who was at the door.

I head a male voice say, "It's me, June. You decent?"

"Come on in," she said, and I heard the door slide open. I peeped out and saw a tall, good-looking young man enter. Around his throat was the inevitable collar. He ran to her, put his arms around her, embraced her. I felt a sour twinge of jealousy, though I had no conceivable right to.

"Hello, Jim," she said warmly.

The newcomer was frowning worriedly. "Have you heard about this new trouble?" he asked without preamble. "They've just announced it from the capitol building."

"What is it?"

"There's a fugitive loose in the city somewhere," the man named Jim said rapidly. "Apparently he broke in by stowing away in a cargo shipment from Ganymede, and he escaped when Hawkins' guards tried to put a collar on him. He's been at large for the past half hour—and Ku Sui and Hawkins have just announced that they're going to start tightening the collars gradually until he turns himself in!"

June gasped. "Everyone's collar?"

"Everyone. There's a gigantic manhunt going on now, with the whole city out trying to find this guy. If we don't get him and turn him in, those three madmen are liable to choke us all as a punitive measure."

As he spoke, he winced and put his hand to his throat. "They're starting now!"

A moment later, June uttered a little cry as the remote-control torturers went to work on her collar as well. I went almost insane with rage at that.

I got off the floor and went inside.

"I'm the man they're looking for," I announced loudly. Jim turned, startled, and flicked a glance from me to June and back to me again.

"Where'd *he* come from, June?" Jim asked coldly.

"He's the fugitive," she said hesitantly. "He was running from the Tax Guards and practically ran into me. I brought him here."

"Great Scot!" he shouted. "Of all the crazy stunts! Come on—let's turn him in before they choke us all."

He started toward me, but I held up a hand. I'm a big man, and he stopped, giving me the respect my size deserves. "Just one moment, friend. Don't be so quick to turn people in. Suppose you tell me who you are?"

"What does that matter to you?" he snapped.

"Jim's my brother," June said. "Have you heard what they're going to do unless they find you?"

I nodded grimly. "I heard you talking from inside."

"I'm going to call the Guards," Jim said. "We can't let you roam around free while our lives are in danger. It's for the good of the whole city."

He moved toward the phone, but I tripped him and shoved him into a chair. "Hold on a second, buddy."

He popped up almost immediately and came at me with a savage right. I heard June utter a little scream as his fist caught me off-guard and cracked into my jaw; I backed up a step or two, shaking off the grogginess, and hit him carefully just below the heart. He folded up and dropped back into the chair.

"Sorry, June," I said apologetically. "But I have to have this thing done my way."

Jim opened one eye, than another, and sat there without making any further disturbance. "June, get your video on. Find out if what your brother says is true."

"Can't you believe me?" he asked.

"No," I told him bluntly. I wasn't taking any chances.

June was fumbling with the dials of her video, and a moment later a newscaster's face came on the screen. I listened stonily as he proceeded to give my description, or a rough approximation thereof, and repeated "President" Hawkins' bone-chilling threat that the collars would be gradually tightened unless I was turned in.

"Okay," I said. "I've heard enough. Shut that thing off." I whirled and faced them. Both June and her brother were pale-faced and frightened; they wore the same beaten, cowed look I'd noticed on the truck-drivers. This was a city of perpetual terror.

"Look," I told them. "I'm going to turn myself in, as soon as possible."

"But—" June started weakly to say.

"No. There's nothing else I can do. I'm going to turn myself in and let them put a collar around my neck." The words came tumbling out easily, and I was forming my plan even as I spoke.

"Why don't you just escape through the airlock?" June asked. "Go back where you came from. You can still get away, and you won't have to wear the collar."

I shook my head firmly. "No. Two reasons. The first is that your benevolent administrators may take punitive measures against you anyway; the second is that you're suggesting I run away—and I just don't believe in running away. I'm going to stay here till the job is done."

Jim Knight stood up and took my hand. "I'm sorry I got so hotheaded before, fellow. But why'd you knock me down when I went to the phone?"

"I wanted to tell you some things first, Jim. I'm sorry I had to rough you up, but it was necessary. There was one plan I had to let you know."

"Which is?"

"I'm going to go to the capitol building now to get collared. I want you two to go gather up all your friends and see to it that there's a considerable mob outside the building after I go in. Get the whole populace down, if possible. I don't know if I can carry off what I'm planning, but I'll need help on the follow-through if I do."

"Right. Anything else?"

I rubbed my throat speculatively. "No. Nothing else. How does it feel to wear one of those things?"

I stepped hesitantly into the street, expecting to be grabbed at any moment. The artificial air of Callisto City was warm and mild, and the atomic furnace that heated the domed city was doing a good job. But I detected a curious odor in the air, and my sensitive nostrils told me that whatever had been polluting the air was still present. June had said it wasn't fatal, and with my strength I knew I wouldn't have much to fear for a while, so I didn't worry about it.

I got about four steps down the street, walking by myself. I had insisted that June and her brother keep away from me, for fear they get involved as accomplices. I reached the corner and started up the thoroughfare, and at once a dozen hands grabbed me.

"There he is!" someone said.

"Thank God we've caught him before these collars get any tighter!"

I looked at them. They weren't wearing uniforms; they were just townsfolk, honest, worried men who turned into vigilantes only to save their own necks. I pitied them.

"I'm the man you're looking for," I said. "You can let go of me. I won't run away."

The mob was getting bigger by the moment, and I was anxious to calm them down before they started transferring some of their hatred for their three tyrants to me, and ripped me apart in a mob's wild, illogical way.

"I'm going to turn myself in," I assured them hastily. "Where do I go?"

"To the capitol building," someone said. "And you'd better get there in a hurry. You know what they're going to do to us if you're not found?"

"I've heard," I said. "That's why I'm turning myself in. Take me to wherever I'm supposed to go."

A couple of them led me through the streets, with the rest tagging along behind. The poor, timid, frightened people! I was almost ready to explode with indignation; I felt I wanted to tear their unspeakable overlords apart with my bare hands.

And I could do it, too.

Finally we reached the capitol—a lofty affair that towered right up to the highest point of the great dome. I looked up. The dome formed a shining arc that covered the entire city; outside, beyond the dome, all was black, except for the swollen red orb of Jupiter hanging monstrously in the sky.

Jupiter. I wondered if I was ever going to get out of Callisto City to cross the gulf of space to the planet that seemed to beckon to me, the unexplored giant that called to me from afar.

"Here he is," one of my captors said, to a guard at the capitol door.

*

I recognized him. He was the leader of the group of six who had originally tried to stop me back at the airlock. He gestured with his arm, and a whole host of blue-clad guards came forth and seized me roughly.

"Bring him inside," he said. "Hawkins is waiting to see him."

I was waiting to see Hawkins, too. I wanted to see just what sort of monster was capable of enslaving a whole city this way.

They led me through the richly-appointed lobby, hung with luxurious furnishings from every planet, no doubt imported at fantastic cost with money wrung from the Callistans by the infamous breathing-tax, and bustled me into an elevator. We shot up rapidly to the twelfth floor, where I was shoved out. I submitted as patiently as I could to this sort of treatment; if I wanted to, I could have smashed their faces and escaped with ease, but that kind of answer didn't suit me.

I was taken down a long, well-lit corridor, and pushed into a large room that seemed to be completely lined with machinery. A row of dials and clicking computers ran down one wall, and a giant electronic brain sprawled ominously over the entire back half of the room. Up at the left side were two men, seated in lofty chairs surrounded by metal railings.

One was a Martian, spindly, elongated, with a weirdly-inflated chest and thick, leathery reddish skin. The other was an Earthman, small of stature, balding, totally ordinary-looking. There was something familiar-looking about both of them.

The Earthman, who must have been Hawkins, turned to the other—evidently Ku Sui, the Martian, the second of the triumvirate that ruled Callisto.

"Here's our troublemaker," Hawkins said. "Let's collar him before he can do any damage."

The Martian got off his throne-like chair and came rustling down to examine me at close range. They have notoriously poor eyesight. As he drew near, I recognized him, and a moment later he spotted me.

He turned in surprise to Hawkins. "You know who this is?" he asked sibilantly. "This is our old friend Slade."

Hawkins was up from his chair in a second. *"Slade?"* I saw him go pale. "Get that collar on him as fast as you can!"

It came back to me now. Hawkins, and Ku Sui, and yes, the Venusian Kolgar Novin. I should have remembered as soon as June told me their names. Yes, we were old friends. Someone who leads the kind of life I do tends to forget some of his earlier adventures; they get blurred under the successive impressions of later encounters. But I recalled these three, now, and how I had foiled them, some ten years ago.

"Now I remember you," I said, as Ku Sui came toward me holding an ominous-looking collar. "Remember the Pluto Mines, and the neat slave-trade you three were running out there? I chased you out of there fast enough!"

"You were a considerable nuisance," Hawkins said. "But I think we have you in a better position now."

I nodded. "This dog-collar racket is the best thing you've come up with yet. And you're just vile enough to be operating something like this. I notice you three don't wear collars."

"The air-pollution does not affect us," Hawkins said. "But I don't intend to stand around discussing things with you." He seemed quite distressed that the two guards who pinioned my arms were overhearing my recollections of the Pluto Mines incident. "Collar him, Ku Sui."

"Here you are," the Martian said, rustling dryly like the remnant of a past age he was. "Extra large, to fit your bull neck." He lifted the collar and brought it down around my throat. At last, I had forfeited my liberty, at least for the time being

❋

The collar was cold and somehow slimy. I made up my mind not to wear it for long.

"How does it feel, Slade?" Hawkins asked tauntingly.

"It's a good fit," I said.

"You can go now," Hawkins said to the guards. "He's amply under control." They nodded and backed out, and I was free. Just the two of them, and me, in the room with the machines. As they left, the door in the back opened and Kolgar Novin, the Venusian, entered. Now they were all three together.

Hawkins left his throne and crossed the room to a control panel. "Now you're a taxpayer, just like the rest, Slade."

"I hear the price of air's pretty high in these parts," I said wryly, rubbing my finger around the collar.

Hawkins nodded. "We get a good rate for it."

"And what if I don't care to pay?"

Hawkins smiled. "We have methods of persuasion," he said. "I was just about to demonstrate one of our best."

He reached for a switch and nudged it down. Immediately that damnable collar tightened like a deadly hand around my neck. I felt the pressure increase.

"How do you like that, Slade?"

I didn't. But I didn't tell him that. I had decided the time had come for action. I flicked out my hands and drew the startled Martian, Ku Sui, toward me. Apparently the collar was such a foolproof protective device that they had gotten careless, for Ku Sui had been standing within my reach all the time Hawkins was talking.

I sensed the dry alien smell of the Martian, who was gesturing wildly to Hawkins. I got my hands around the Martian's scrawny throat.

"Now *I've* got a collar on you!" I said, "And it doesn't operate by remote control! How does it feel?"

"Hawkins—increase the pressure," Ku Sui grated brokenly. *"Kill him,* Hawkins. He's...choking...me!"

I looked up from the Martian and shouted at Hawkins, "Shut your machine off! Get the pressure down or I'll kill Ku Sui!"

The grip of the collar around my throat was almost unbearable. I flexed my neck muscles and tried to fight the slowly intensifying grip of the collar, but my face was fiery red and I was having trouble breathing. I could hear the sound of my blood pounding through my veins.

"Shut it off, Hawkins! I'll strangle the Martian!"

It was a mistake on my part to assume that Hawkins gave the faintest damn about what happened to his partner in crime. I kept increasing my grip on Ku Sui's throat, and Hawkins up there at his control board kept tightening his grip on mine. Everything was starting to swim around my head, and I didn't know how much longer I could hold out.

"Don't...call...my...bluff," I gasped. I wrung Ku Sui's leathery neck and hurled the corpse across the room at the motionless Venusian standing bewildered in the back. Venusians have a way of freezing up when there's trouble, and I was thankful Kolgar Novin wasn't taking a hand in the action.

I saw Hawkins through a red haze. He was obviously surprised that I still hadn't succumbed to the choking, but he didn't seem very disturbed about Ku Sui. I gasped in as much air as I could and began the slow, leaden-footed climb up the steps to the control panel.

I saw Hawkins go white with fear as I approached. I was moving slowly, deliberately, my head swimming and my eyes popping from my head.

"Why don't you drop?" he asked in terror. "Why don't you choke?"

"I'm too tough for you!" I said. He started to scream for the guards, but I reached up, plucked him away from his control panel, and hurled him over the railing into the middle of the floor. He went flying heels over head like a chubby little basketball, and bounced on the concrete.

He continued to moan loudly for his guards, and Kolgar Novin was still a statue at the far end of the room.

Desperately, I reached for the lever he had been pushing down and I hurled it as far up as it would go. The collar opened immediately, and the air went rushing into my lungs. I reeled against the railing, trying to recover, as the blood left my head and the room tilted crazily around me.

Then I heard footsteps outside, and the door broke open. The Guards! I made up my mind what I was going to do in an instant.

I started smashing my fists into the delicate machinery, raging up and down the room destroying whatever I could. I ripped up the intricate wiring and watched blue sparks lick through the bowels of the giant electronic brain and the smaller computers, watched the whole edifice of terror come crashing down. I pulled out levers and used them as clubs to bash in the dials and vernier gauges, and when I was through I turned to see what the guards were doing.

To my surprise, I saw they were struggling among themselves. They were divided—half of them, the most evil half, were still loyal to Hawkins, while the others, the native Callistans impressed into the guards, were rebelling now that they saw the overlords were destroyed, their machines of coercion in rubble. I saw one guard rip off his collar and hurl it into the ruined machines with a shout of savage glee.

There still was a nucleus of guards clustered around Hawkins and Ku Sui, but their numbers were growing smaller as more and more of them realized the game was up for the three tyrants.

Then the room was suddenly crowded, and I smiled happily. June and her brother had roused the people! They were coming! I leaned against the railing, weak with strain, and watched as the angry, newly-free Callistans swept the remaining guards out of the way and exacted a terrible revenge on Hawkins and Kolgar Novin and even the dead body of Ku Sui.

The lynching was over eventually, and the guards, taking charge in the name of the people, managed to restore some semblance of order. Blankets were thrown over the mutilated bodies on the floor.

Then, with grim methodicality, the Callistans completed the job of wrecking Hawkins' machines. The room was a shambles by the time they were through.

June finally made her way through the confusion to my side. She looked up in concern, and ran her fingers gently over the angry red lines the collar had left on my throat.

"You were wonderful," she said. She was crying from relief and gratitude, and I took her in my arms and held her.

Then I released her. "Let's go downstairs," I said. "I need some fresh air after that battle."

We left the building and I stood in the warm artificial sunlight of Callisto City, recovering my strength.

"I've heard how you overthrew them," June said. "But I don't understand how you survived the choking."

"I'm stubborn," I said simply. I was hiding the truth from her—the bitter truth that I wanted no one to know. "I just wouldn't let them strangle me, that's all." I grinned.

She took a deep breath. "You know, I just thought of something—we're not wearing collars, and yet we don't mind the air! It's not polluted any more!"

I stopped to consider that, and then shook my head in disgust as the obvious answer came to me. "Those worms! You know what was causing the pollution?"

"No," she said.

"It must have been maintained artificially by one of those machines up there! I remember, now—Hawkins was quite a chemist. He must have synthesized some chemical that polluted this air, and then gave your father enough leads so he could develop a filter to counteract it. It was a devilishly well-planned scheme, neatly calculated to reduce Callisto City to a state of servitude!"

We took a few steps away. It was bright midday, but I could see the bulk of Jupiter high in the sky above the dome. In the great square in front of the capitol building, a huge golden mountain was growing—a heap of discarded collars, getting bigger and bigger by the moment as the Callistans hurled the impotent symbols of their slavery into the junkheap. For the first time, I saw smiling, happy faces on Callisto. The air was pure again, and the time of troubles was over. It didn't cost anything to breathe on Callisto any more.

The happiest face of all was June's. She was beaming radiantly, glowing with pride and happiness. "I'm glad I decided to rescue you," she said. "You looked so brave, and strong, and—lonely. So I took a chance and pulled you away."

I looked at her sadly, not saying anything.

"Where will you stay?" she asked. "There's a flat available next door to mine—"

I shook my head. "No. I'm leaving. I must leave immediately."

The sunshine left her face at once, and she looked at me in surprise and shock. *"Leaving?"*

I nodded. "I can't stay here, June. I've done my job, and I'm going."

I didn't wait for another word. I strode away, and she took a couple of steps after me and then stopped. I heard her sobbing, but I didn't turn back. How could tell her that I loved her? How could I dare to love her? Me—an android. A laboratory creation? Sure, I was stronger than a human being—the factor Hawkins didn't figure on. Only an android could have withstood that choking.

I have human drives, human ambitions. When you cut me, I bleed red. You can only tell by microscopic analysis that I'm not human. But resemblance isn't enough. I couldn't fool myself, and I wouldn't fool June. I couldn't allow her to waste herself on something like me. She'd make a good mother, someday.

I turned away, feeling bitter and empty, and made my way through the streets crowded with jubilant Callistans. In my mind's eye I could see June's pale, bewildered face, and my synthetic heart wept for her. She'd never understand why I was leaving.

I looked up through the dome at the black curtain of the skies, at mighty, lonely, unapproachable Jupiter. It was a fitting challenge for me. We had a lot in common, big Jupiter and I. I knew where I was going, now, and I couldn't wait to get there.

CITADEL OF DARKNESS
(1957)

As 1956 moved along, my new career as a science-fiction writer, and all the rest of my life as well, began to expand in ways that I would scarcely have dared to fantasize only a couple of years previously. I continued selling stories at the same torrid pace, and in May succeeded in placing one with the prestigious magazine Galaxy, *edited by the exceedingly difficult, tough-minded Horace Gold. Selling one to him was a big step forward for me. In June I got my Columbia degree and set up shop as a full-time writer. Randall Garrett and I spent two weeks that summer writing the novel for John W. Campbell that we had so grandly imagined selling him the year before—*The Dawning Light, *it was called—and he bought it in August. Later that month I married my college girlfriend, Barbara Brown, and we found a splendid five-room apartment on Manhattan's elegant West End Avenue, a short walk from the Columbia campus but light-years distant from the squalid hotel room where I had been living for the past three years. About ten days later I attended the World Science Fiction Convention, where I was greeted as a colleague by science-fiction writers like Edmond Hamilton and Jack Williamson who were old enough to be my father, and where to my amazement I was given the Hugo award as that year's most promising new author.*

It was all pretty startling. I was getting published all up and down the spectrum of science-fiction magazines, from Astounding *and* Galaxy *at one end to* Amazing *and* Fantastic *at the other, and soon after the convention I had deals with two book publishers, Ace (for an original novel) and Gnome*

(for a two-volume reprint of the "Robert Randall" series from Astounding.*)
Everything was happening at once.*

*In the midst of it all I plugged away at my Ziff-Davis obligations,
visiting Paul Fairman's midtown office two or three times a month to
bring him new stories. He used "Citadel of Darkness," which I wrote in June,
1956 a couple of days after my Columbia graduation ceremony, in* Fantastic
*for March, 1957. Once more I turned the four-stories-in-an-issue trick, for
"Citadel," a "Ralph Burke" story, was accompanied by a story under my own
name, one as "Calvin Knox," and one as "Hall Thornton." I wasn't taking
anything for granted, but it was pretty clear to me by this time that what was
going on wasn't likely to stop, and that, improbable as it had once seemed, I
really was going to be able to earn my living as a writer.*

T he wavering green lines of the mass detector told me that there was
a planet ahead where no planet ought to be, and my skin started to
crawl. I checked the star-guide a second time, running down the tight-
packed printed columns with deliberate care.

Karen's soft hand brushed lightly across my shoulder, and I glanced
up. "The guide doesn't say anything about planets in this sector of
space," I told her.

"Have you checked the coordinates?"

I nodded grimly. "I've checked everything. There's a planet out ahead,
approximately two light-months from us. And you know what it has to be."

Her fingers dug tightly into my neckmuscles.

"It can't be anything else. There's no star within sight, none
supposed to be here, and yet the mass detector's popping like
sixty. The only answer is a wandering sunless world—and there's only
one of those."

"It's Lanargon," she said simply. "Lanargon. The marauder world."

I turned away and busied myself over the control panel. My fingers
flew lightly over the computer levers, and microrelays clicked and
buzzed behind the green plexilite screen.

After a moment, Karen said, "What are you doing?"

"Setting up a landing orbit," I told her without looking up. "As long
as we're here, we might as well investigate. We can't pass up a chance
like this."

I expected opposition, but I was surprised. All she said was, "How soon before we land?" No nervousness, no hesitation. She looked a lot cooler than I felt as I went about the job of preparing for our landing on Lanargon, the galaxy's most dreaded—and most mysterious—planet.

❉

It was in the year 3159 that the Terran colony on Faubia III was wiped out by armed attack, and word came to the universe that war was with us again. The worlds of mankind looked at each other in suspicion and fear. Five centuries of galactic amity had brought about the feeling that armed strife was a buried relic of antiquity—and then, without warning, came the attack on Faubia III.

There were universal denials. A year later, Metagol II was sacked by unknown invaders, and later the same year Vescalor IX, the universe's greatest source of antivirotic drugs, was conquered.

The circumstances were the same each time. An army of tall men in black spacesuits would descend suddenly upon the unsuspecting planet, destroying its capital, seize control of the planet's leaders, and carry off plunder. Then, mysteriously as they came, they would depart, always taking many prisoners with them.

The attacks continued. The marauders struck seemingly at random here and there across the face of the galaxy. Trantor was hit in 3163, Vornak IV three years after that. In 3175, Earth itself was subjected to a raid.

The universe recoiled in terror. The Multiworld Federation searched desperately for the answer—and found it. It made us no more comfortable to learn that the marauders were aliens from some far island universe who rode their sunless planet like a giant spaceship, who had crossed the great gulf of space that separated their galaxy from ours and now, under cloak of their virtual invisibility, travelled through our group of worlds, burning, pillaging, and looting as they went.

We were helpless against an invader we could not see. And now, possibly for the first time, someone had taken Lanargon by surprise. The marauder world had crossed our orbit as we returned to Earth from Rigel VI, and it lay squarely in our path, wrapped in its cloak of darkness out there in the eternal black of space.

I watched its bulk grow on the mass detector, and wiped away a trickle of perspiration that had started to crawl down my forehead. Two people—a man and a woman—against a world of the deadliest killers ever known.

As an Earthman, as a member of the Multiworld Federation, it was my duty to aid in Lanargon's destruction. And I had an idea for doing it.

I locked the ship into automatic, watched the computer buzz twice to confirm that it had taken control, and got up. Karen was still standing behind me. Her face was pale and drawn; all the color seemed to have left it, though her eyes glowed with courage.

She reached out and took my hand as I stepped away from the controls. I folded her hand in both of mine, and squeezed.

"It has to be done, doesn't it" she asked softly.

I nodded, thinking of the home that awaited us on Earth, the friends, the children. Heroes don't have to be born; sometimes they're made by a trajectory-line charted between two worlds.

"It has to be done," I said. I drew her close. For all I knew, it was going to be the last time.

◉

Our ship taxied in slowly, spiralling around Lanargon in ever-narrowing circles. I could see it plainly now from the viewport, a rough, ugly-looking, barren world, boasting not even the drifts of snow that would be a frozen atmosphere. Lanargon was just a ball of rock, seen dimly in the starlight. Great leaping mountains sprang up like dragon's teeth from the rocky plains beneath. There was no sign of life. None.

I glanced over at Karen, who was strapped securely in her acceleration cradle at my side. She was smiling.

"We'll be there soon," I said.

"Good. This suspense is starting to get me. I'd like to get down there and get it over with—whatever it is we're going to do."

"I've got bad news for you, if you're in a hurry," I said. "We may need months before we get through."

"Why? What will happen?"

"We're going to tell the universe about Lanargon," I said. "Where it is, where it may be going, how to come get it. We're in a pretty empty part of space, though. Even by subradio, it may take weeks before we get within range of some other world."

"You mean we're going to stay on Lanargon until you make radio contact with some other planet?"

I nodded. "We're going to turn ourselves into living signal buoys. We're going to ride on Lanargon like fleas on a gorilla's back for a while. I hope they don't notice us, and just keep on moving until they come close enough to some inhabited planet for us to get out an SOS."

"And then?"

"Then we get out of here as fast as we can, and wait for the Multiworld Fleet to home in on the coordinates we've given and blast Lanargon to the fate it so thoroughly deserves," I said. "The only problem is staying unfound long enough to give the message. At the moment, we're well out of range of anyone who could pick it up."

I leaned back and moistened my dry lips. "Hold tight, kid. We're almost there."

❋

Within the hour, we had approached Lanargon's surface and were hovering no more than a hundred miles above, moving into the final stage of our landing. Minutes later, our ship dropped gently down and touched ground.

I was the first one up, and was half into my spacesuit before Karen had climbed out of her acceleration cradle. She followed me into the airlock when she was ready, and together we stepped outside.

It was a dead world. Perhaps it once had had a sun and an atmosphere and the warmth of life, but now it was but the corpse of a planet—inhabited, who know where, by the merciless aliens who had terrorized the universe.

"It's—its the most horrible place I've ever seen," Karen said, as we stood together at the base of the ship, looking around at the planet that would be our hone until we made contact with some inhabited world.

"That's the only word for it," I agreed. I almost shivered, though I was fully protected from the cold by my spacesuit. We could see— dimly, by the faint glow of the sprinkling of stars above—a few miles of the planet's surface, and it was hardly a cheering sight. Lanargon was a slagheap, a vast desert of twisted lava forced into tortured convolutions, of ageless rocks and jutting mountains, stony and bleak.

"I hope it's over quickly," Karen said.

"I hope so too. Let's go back in and send out the SOS—suppose we beam it five times a day until we get response—and then start exploring a little. I'd like to know just where the aliens are."

"Underground, maybe," Karen suggested. "Or in a domed city hidden somewhere in those awful mountains."

"That's probably it," I said, nodding.

We returned to the ship and started the message on its way, announcing that we had discovered Lanargon accidentally, had landed, and would remain here acting as a signal-beacon until contacted by a member of the Multiworld Federation.

I snapped off the transmitter when we were through. "That should do it," I said. "Now we'll just have to wait, and keep sending it, and wait some more. One of these days we'll get a reply, and we'll tell them exactly how to go about getting to Lanargon and blasting it out of the skies. Then our job's done."

Karen frowned. "What if the aliens discover what we're doing, and set out to find us?"

"No use thinking about it, honey. We'll just have to sit here quietly and hope we're not noticed by the wrong people. It won't be fun, but what else can we do?"

"It's like sitting on the rim of a live volcano," Karen said. "And taking bets on when the top will blow off."

"Come on," I said. "Let's go outside and do some exploring. For all we know, we've landed right next door to an alien city."

I stood up and led the way. I knew some exercise would loosen her tight-stretched nerves a little.

❉

I stared for a moment at the dreary stretch of slag and needle-edged rocks. "You go to the left," I said. "I'll go the other way, and we'll see what this place looks like."

"Sounds good enough," Karen said. She started to move off toward the towering mountain that looked down at the ship from the left, while I made my way over the heaps of rock to the cliff at the right.

I kept up a running conversation with her over the suitphones as we went.

"How's it look from there?" I asked.

"Pretty much the same," she said. "There's a long plain, and then this mountain. Twenty-five, thirty thousand feet high, I'd say. I can't see the top of it."

"Nice," I said. "Things are dull here. The cliff looks down on a valley, and there's a sign of something that might have been a river once, before Lanargon tore loose from its sun. But there's no sign of life anywhere."

"Do you think this might be the wrong place? Some other dark planet that no one knows about?"

"I don't think so," I said, as I scaled up a jagged precipice and heaved myself onto a small plateau. "They're probably all on the other side of this planet. It's a big place, you know. I'm sure that—"

I stopped, chilled, and whirled at the sound of the terrible scream that ripped through my suitphones at that moment. I paused, not knowing in which direction I should run, and then, as Karen's scream burst forth again, I began to race wildly through the twisting outcrops toward her.

"Mike! Mike! They're here!"

"I'm coming," I told her, and kept on running. A moment later, the ship came into sight, and I passed it and headed in the direction Karen had taken. It led through a dropping path into the plain that approached the mountain, and I dashed out toward her.

I saw her a moment later. She was standing on the top of a rock out-crop about ten feet high, kicking savagely at ten or twelve space-suited figures who were attempting to climb up and reach her. We had found the planet—but its inhabitants had gotten to us first.

I leaped forward and shouted my encouragement as I came. The next minute, I was at the base of the plateau, piling into the gang of aliens. They were husky, sturdy creatures, humanoid in shape, clad in dark spacesuits that made them almost invisible in the faint starlight.

I dragged one of them away from the path leading to the top of the plateau and crashed my gloved fist into his stomach. He bounded back without showing that the blow had hurt him, and made a signal to the others.

Immediately they split into two groups, working with calm, cold efficiency. Five or six of them continued to try to reach Karen, and the rest turned on me. I found myself surrounded by half a dozen aliens.

I struck out at the first one and saw him go reeling into the arms of one of his comrades, but then another hit me a stunning blow from behind. I staggered forward, felt another fist drive into my stomach. The flexible material of my suit yielded, and I gasped for breath.

Pulling away, I caught one alien by the arm and swung him down, but two more hit me at once. A gloved hand bashed into the yielding plastic of my face mask, and I went flying down on my back. I felt someone pommeling me viciously for a few moments, and then I stopped feeling anything.

※

When I awoke, Karen and the ship and the aliens were gone, and I was alone on the plain, sprawled out with my arms wrapped fondly around a small boulder that I had been using as a pillow.

The aliens had seen us, had come, had taken Karen, and had left for—where? What had they done with Karen? I hurled the questions at myself, angry for having allowed us to separate even for the moment.

I picked myself up, and took a few unsteady trial steps. I ached all over from my beating, but I managed to shake off the dizziness and keep on going. I had to find Karen, wherever she was, get her back to Earth somehow. I didn't know how I was going to do it.

Lanargon was a big planet. There was no light to guide me. And the ship was gone.

Evidently they had left me for dead and taken Karen and the ship back to wherever it was they had come from. I started walking, not knowing and not caring which direction I might be heading in, simply putting one foot after another in the blind energy of complete despair. I headed down the long sweeping plain, walking nowhere on this world of perpetual nightfall, a dull pain throbbing all over my body.

I don't have any idea how long I walked before the light appeared. All I know is I had been marching mechanically without so much as noticing where I was going, moving up one outcrop and down the next—and then, I became conscious of a glimmer of light in the distance. It was faint, but impossible to mistake against the inky Lanargon bleakness.

Suddenly I returned to life. I started to trot animatedly toward the source of light, hoping wildly it might be a signal beam of some sort sent up by Karen. As I drew near, though, I discovered what it was.

It was a small party of aliens, gathered together at the edge of a sprawling range of low-lying hills. There were about five of them, and in their midst was a portable generator which threw off just enough light to illuminate their camp. I guessed that they were another party out searching for us who were not aware that the other group had already achieved its mission.

I approached them in a wide semi-circle, swinging around from the left so I would be above them on the foothills. I could see now that they had a small vehicle of some sort, and that they were dismantling their camp and loading the equipment they had with them into the vehicle. I revised my earlier guess; this was a search-party who knew that the quarry had been snared, and which was preparing to return to home base.

I drew closer to them, close enough now to see that they were nearing the end of their task. I would have to move quickly.

I made my way down the side of the hill, deciding which one of the aliens was to be my victim. By the time I was on the plain, I had my man. He was busy about a hundred feet away, dismantling a wireless transmitter of some sort. The groundcar cut him off from the other four neatly. But I had to get him the first time; any struggle and I'd find myself fighting off all five of them within an instant.

I picked up a jagged triangular rock and squeezed it lovingly as I edged across the plain. The alien was bending over, doing something to the base of the transmitter.

After glancing around to make sure I was unobserved, I raised my hand high and brought the rock down against the back of the alien's head. He fell forward without a sound and sprawled out grotesquely on the transmitter.

"Sleep tight," I murmured, as I dragged him further into the shadows. Working quickly, I peeled his spacesuit from him, tossed the body to one side—what it looked like, in the airless void that was Lanargon's cloak, was stomach-turning—and stepped smoothly into the suit, pulling it on over my own. The aliens were big men; I was able to fit, suit and all, into the alien suit without trouble.

I returned to the transmitter and pulled it free of the ground. Another of the aliens appeared and waved to me, as if signalling that I should hurry up. I waved back, picked up the transmitter, and walked over to join the group.

※

They were about to get into their vehicle as I drew near. I kept my head down, didn't say anything, and climbed aboard, dragging the transmitter up with me. I stood in the corner of the car as it sped over the ground, holding my breath and hoping against hope that none of them would say anything to me.

None of them did. And, some twenty minutes later, the crystal dome of a huge city appeared in view. It arched high above the plain, and within I could see the busyness of a great city—the home of the marauders.

The car sped through the airlock and into the domed city. My breath left me as I contemplated the magnitude of the alien city, by far the largest dome in the universe. It must have contained a population of millions or of tens of millions.

As we moved rapidly deeper into the city, I heard my companions behind me slipping out of their spacesuits. In a moment, they stood revealed—tall, muscular humanoids whose chief alien distinction was the network of fine blue veins criss-crossing the golden skin of their hard, cold faces, and the two sinewy tentacles which sprouted from their sides just below their arms.

I began to sweat. No doubt they would wonder shortly why I was remaining in my suit now that we were inside the city. I couldn't very well explain that if I removed the suit, my own spacesuit would be revealed beneath.

I felt a rough hand on my shoulder—and then, immensely more horrible, something which was not a hand spun me around. I faced one of the aliens, looked straight into the cold eyes of one of the creatures of Lanargon.

He snapped something at me, two short sentences in a harsh-sounding, unfamiliar language. I glared blankly at him, and he repeated his question.

Again I made no reply, and he peered closely, staring into the misty faceglass of my spacesuit. He must have seen what he was looking for, because a moment later he had called two of his companions over to see me. I heard them discussing the situation excitedly.

Apparently they didn't know what to make of my presence. A live Earthman somehow smuggled into their car? It bewildered them, just for a split second.

A split second was just enough. I smashed a fist into the nearest alien just as he had made up his mind to grab me, and sent him pirouetting back against his two friends. They wobbled around in the speedily-moving truck for a couple of seconds, and I lifted the transmitter I had brought in and hurled it at them.

They bounced back against the wall. A fourth alien appeared and I felt the cold grip of his tentacle for a moment. I slashed out with the side of my hand and knocked the tentacle away. Then I had opened the door of the car, and, without looking at the ground below, leaped out.

I hit the ground as it came up to meet me. My spaceboots absorbed most of the shock, but it still rippled through me like a junior-grade lightning bolt as I hit. I sank to my knees for a second, then elbowed up and started to run.

I was free and at large—in the domed city of the Lanargon marauders. Somewhere in this sprawling citadel was Karen. I began to run down a side street, as an alarm sounded somewhere behind me.

※

It was a completely alien city. I crouched in a pit of shadows beneath a building of dizzying height and looked around, struck by the utter strangeness of the sunless city.

The dome reached high into the airless sky, and outside it I could see the blank wall of space. The buildings were delicate, airy things, with networks of web hanging from one to the next. I saw aliens crawling over these webs spider-fashion to get from one building to another.

The air seemed warm—at least, the aliens I saw moving through the streets were dressed skimpily—and the many spiky trees with blue leaves glittering in the brightness of the air were thriving as if it were a tropical climate.

The buildings were arranged in concentric circles, I saw; apparently they radiated outward from the atomic pile that would undoubtedly be the heart of such a dome. It was a giant, incredible, artificial city, probably built with the slave labor of the millions of prisoners taken during the years of Lanargon raids.

I was safe so long as I remained crouching where I was. But I knew I would never rescue Karen that way, though.

The first step was to find a weapon. I noticed that the aliens of both sexes went about armed, and that seemed my easiest chance. I edged out of my hiding place and moved toward the street, waiting for a pedestrian to come by alone.

It took three nerve-wracking minutes—and when one came, it was a female. She was over six feet tall, with a magnificent body only nominally covered by her brief clothing, and strapped to her hip was a gem-studded blaster. I stepped out behind her as she went past.

"I hate to do this to a lady," I said apologetically, as I clubbed down on the back of her neck and grabbed the blaster from its holster in the same motion. She started to crumple before I had the gun out.

I hauled her back into the shadows and left her lying there. I still had no idea where to go, but now I was armed. The blaster was an efficient and murderous-looking weapon, and I wouldn't have to rely on my fists alone any longer.

I strapped on the blaster and glanced warily around. No one in sight. I knew I'd look tremendously conspicuous in this spacesuit, but I would have to chance it. I'd look even more conspicuous walking around without it.

Karen was here someplace, I told myself—but I realized I had only a fool's chance of finding her. I was ready to give her up for lost, if I could carry out a bigger project: that of getting to the atomic reactor that was the core of this city and destroying it. I felt completely nerveless. I had a job, and I was going to do it. Life without Karen wouldn't mean much any more—but I could redeem it if I could take all of Lanargon with us.

I walked inward, toward the center of the city.

❋

People stared curiously at me, wondering why I was wearing a spacesuit, no doubt, but no one said anything. I continued trudging along the yielding permoplast streets, and after a block or two I found what I was looking for—a Lanargon slave.

He was obviously an Earthman, in his early thirties, which meant he had been grabbed in the raid of 3175. He was wearing only a loincloth, no blaster, and so his slave status was apparent.

I followed him for about thirty paces, until we reached the corner. Then I edged in behind him and said quietly, "Turn left at this corner, will you?"

He glanced back, saw what must have been an imposing spacesuited figure, and obeyed without questioning. "Who are you?" he asked when we had rounded the corner.

"An Earthman," I said. "You can help me."

Quickly I explained the course of events from the time Lanargon first had showed up in the mass detector to Karen's kidnapping.

"I've heard about that," he said. "I saw the girl and the ship arrive."

"Where are they?" I asked immediately.

"The girl's been taken to the Central Temple. I'm a slave there. The ship's been brought into the dome too, and it's not far from the Temple either. The Lanargon scientists want to study it and see if they're missing any wrinkles."

"What Temple? What are they going to do to Karen?"

The slave looked at me pityingly for a long moment. "The Temple is the place all the power of the dome comes from. The aliens worship it as a shrine. They're going to sacrifice your wife to their god. Their god's a pool of live radiation."

"What?"

He nodded. "They do it every year, usually with a female slave. I heard them talking. I'm in the High Priest's retinue, and I found about it. The ceremony's scheduled to take place this afternoon."

I gripped his hand. "Fellow, I don't even know your name, but I love you. Can you get me there? We don't have much time." I didn't know what I was going to do, but I was going to do something. I was sure of that.

He glanced uneasily up and down the street. "It's worth a try," he said. "This hellhole deserves to be blasted wide open. And I think I see the man who's going to do it."

He led me along at a rapid pace toward the heart of the city. After a while, I saw a huge conical building loom up before me. And—outside it—was my ship!

"There it is!" I said. "That must be the Temple."

"That's right. And your ship. Now, if there were only some way of finding your wife and getting clear—"

I looked at him. "Wait a minute," I said. "There are thousands, maybe millions of you slaves on Lanargon. Innocent people. Suppose I do succeed? Suppose I blasted the dome down? You'd all die."

The slave smiled bitterly. "Don't get guilt-feelings over that," he said. He lifted his arm and showed me a metallic bulge along his side. "See this? It's a compact transistor wave-generator embedded in my flesh. Removing it means death. And if we get further than a dozen miles from the Dome, it kills us automatically. It's very efficient—and it means that no slave can ever leave Lanargon alive."

The enormity of it chilled me. "That helps to keep you in line neatly, doesn't it?" I said.

He nodded. "They can also kill us within the city. If a slave steps out of line, it's the easiest thing to raise the frequency generated by this device to a lethal pitch. They'll allow a slave to go almost anywhere, because he can't possibly do any harm—not when his life can be snuffed out by any master in an instant."

A sudden burst of thought illuminated my mind. "If that's true, I think I know how I can carry this thing off. Let's go someplace where I can get out of all these spacesuits and into a slave's loincloth!"

✺

The slave—his name was Dave Andrews—took me to his quarters, a miserable room not far from the Temple. There, I stripped out of both spacesuits and donned one of his loincloths.

"You look a little pale," he commented. "But otherwise I guess you can pass, if no one looks too closely for the generator that isn't planted in your side."

I looked ruefully at my discarded blaster. "I'm going to feel lonely without that thing on my hip."

Andrews shrugged. "No slave would dare carry one. You'll just have to do without until this is all over."

"All right," I said. "Let's get going. The sacrifice should be starting soon, shouldn't it?" The image of Karen's body plummeting into a lake of neutrons drifted into my mind, and I winced.

"Within the hour," he said.

Together we crossed the plaza that led to the massive Temple. No one seemed to notice us; apparently slaves were utterly beneath contempt in Lanargon. At the Temple door, a cross-hatched alien face confronted us, saw that we were slaves, and let us through.

"I'll have to help out at the ceremony," Andrews said. "You can come along. It'll give you your chance of getting close to the High Priest. And remember the way you came. You'll have to get out of here and into your ship later."

"Don't worry," I said stolidly. "I'll manage. I've never wanted to destroy anything so much before in my life."

We entered an elevator which was already occupied by a gigantic alien in luminescent yellow robes. I saw Andrews bend and touch his forehead to the floor without a moment's hesitation, and, much as it went against the grain, I did the same.

"The High Priest," he explained softly.

I nodded. I had guessed as much.

We rode the elevator to the sixty-first floor. As we got out, the priest said, "Bring the sacrifice to the Hall of the God, slaves."

We bowed again, and turned off down a long aisle. My heart leaped as Andrews entered a room guarded by two aliens and said, "High Priest requests delivery of the sacrifice to the Hall of the God."

One of the aliens nodded curtly and pointed toward an inner door. Andrews opened it and said quickly, "Prisoner, we have come to take you to the God." He stepped inside and clapped a hand over her mouth, stifling the cry than broke from her as she recognized me in the guise of a slave.

We closed the door, shutting out the alien guards.

"Karen," I said.

Andrews turned away and I folded her in my arms. She was quivering from anxiety and terror, though I saw her making an effort to recover her nerves. She couldn't. I didn't blame her as she broke down and started to sob.

A gong sounded loudly.

Gently, Andrews said, "We'll have to go."

"Mike? Mike—are they going to do this thing to me?"

I looked at her. She was wearing what was probably the sacrificial gown, a clinging, translucent thing through which I could easily see her naked body beneath. "Don't worry," I said. "I'll get us out of it."

✹

We led her along the hall, Andrews grasping one arm and I the other, while one of the alien guards walked before us and one behind. We walked for what seemed to be miles through the temple building, until we reached a door some twenty feet high. It swung open as we approached.

I gasped. We stood at the entrance to a great amphitheatre, with an immense dais and rows of seats stretching off into the misty distance. And—between the dais and the seats—there was an open pit that seemed to reach down into the bowels of the planet. I looked down and reeled dizzily at the sight of that bright lake of radiation hundreds of feet below—the lake into which Karen's naked body was soon to be hurled.

"You lead her up there," Andrews whispered to me. "Give her to the High Priest. From there it's up to you. I'm going to go back and get an elevator ready in case you do get out of it alive. Move as fast as you can when you get away."

I nodded imperceptibly and marched forward with Karen. The great hall was filled—packed with row on row of uncountable aliens, sitting in quiet anticipation of the sacrifice to be performed before their eyes. Television cameras blinked down like unmoving eyes, telling me that the rest of the aliens were undoubtedly watching too.

I saw the robed figure of the High Priest, stark and majestic on the dais. He was intoning prayers to which the aliens responded antiphonally. A gong sounded repeatedly somewhere in the distance, and flames licked up from the abyss below.

He gestured for the sacrifice to be brought forward. I tightened my grip on Karen's arm and started to walk up the long row of steps that led to the dais. The chanting of the multitude rose to an agonizing volume, a savage beat of barbaric fury echoing round and round the great hall.

I was at the heart of it now—the center of life of the race that set itself against all mankind. I clenched and unclenched my fists in antic- ipation as I traversed the long span of steps.

I handed over Karen. The priest took her and in one swift motion ripped away her thin gown, revealing her naked to the crowd. She began to cry. I muttered a silent curse. Hatred was a red haze before my eyes.

He took her in his giant hands and grasped her around the waist with those two slimy tentacles. The gong sounded furiously, and he responded to it with booming incantations. He lifted Karen's unprotest- ing body high over his head, prepared to hurl it into the open abyss—

And I charged forward and snatched her from him just as he was about to release her. We stood there, he and I, on the dais, while a shocked multitude waited for him to strike me dead.

✸

I saw him lower his arm to his side and press a button in his robe— presumably the button that would activate the death-dealing device embedded in my body. Only I wore no such thing. He stared at me in an agony of exasperation as I unbelievably refused to die.

Then I advanced toward him. No one dared move. He bellowed something, and guards broke from their lethargy and started racing up the dais—but it was a long way to go.

He shouted and leaped at me. I felt his powerful hands encircling me and shoving me toward the abyss. I broke loose, hearing Karen's screaming as a dim noise in the background, and shoved backward. He reeled and groped for the blaster at his side. Before he could use it, I dropkicked it from his hand and sent it flying in a gleaming arc up, out, and into the pit.

He turned in utter dismay and watched it disappear. His face was a mask of despair and sheer horror. The guards were drawing near us, now.

I moved in close and unleashed a barrage of punches. He countered with wild swipes of his tentacles. I could hear Karen yelling clearly now, "They're coming! They're coming!"

With coolness born of complete desperation, I reached out and seized him around the waist. I strained to lift the three-hundred pound body from the ground, pulled, yanked, and heaved him high out over the abyss, a pinwheeling figure of arms and legs and tentacles. He screamed all the way down.

I turned and saw Karen crouching behind me, scooped her up, and we began to run. "This way!" I heard a slave cry, and he pushed the guard nearest him down into the abyss as well. A moment later he had crumpled into death himself, but he had saved us—whoever he was. We plunged through the door and out into the corridor.

Everywhere we saw slaves battling with the alien masters. They were dying, of course—as fast as the aliens could kill them—but they were clearing a path to the elevator for us. Andrews was waiting there.

Tears were in his eyes. "Great," he said, "Wonderful! But now get into your ship and get out of here *fast!*"

We made our way through a confused mob of aliens and slaves. The stunned aliens seemed helpless with their High Priest dead. We pushed through them, the three of us, and cut through to the ship. We paused for a moment at the base of the catwalk. I glanced at Andrews.

"I'm not coming," he said, forestalling my question. "There's no point to it. I'm a dead man the second I leave the Dome. Go on— get going."

"We'll never forget you," I said. I boosted Karen up the catwalk and followed behind her. We made it inside safely, and the hatch clanged closed.

"Get into your acceleration cradle," I shouted, and leaped for the control panel. I set up a manual pattern for blastoff.

Out the viewport I could see the aliens coming to life, moving toward us in a mighty horde. I finished fumbling with the controls and heaved downward on the blasting stud just as a couple of them began to scale the fins of the ship.

The ship leaped skyward in an instant. In three seconds, we burst through the dome and out into space. Acceleration hit me like a gigantic fist, and I slumped over and blacked out.

❋

The next thing I knew Karen was bending over me and lifting me to my feet. "We're safe," she said.

I rubbed my head and nodded. "And we took them all with us. It must have been something down there when the ship broke through the dome and sent their atmosphere whipping out into space. It's a lousy way to die—but they deserved it. All but those poor slaves. They were dead either way, though."

"Come look out the port," Karen said.

I did. I stared down at the bright, boiling radioactive fury that lit up the blackness of space where the dark planet should have been.

"It must have been that blaster," I said after a long pause. "The one I kicked into the radiation lake. When it reached the reactor at the bottom, it must have blown the roof off."

"They must have been destroyed in an instant."

I looked at the beacon outside the viewport. "It's the end of the dark planet," I said slowly. "We've touched off a chain reaction that will last forever."

"Forever," she repeated. "It's all over now."

"I don't think we'll ever forget Lanargon," I said. "But I'd like to know what the galaxy's astronomers are going to say when they notice a brand-new sun in this part of the cosmos."

"They'll have all sorts of wild guesses. But we can tell them the right answer, can't we?"

"Yes," I said. I glanced once more at the fissioning hell that had been Lanargon, shuddered, and set our course for Earth.

COSMIC KILL
(1957)

In the 1950s magazine covers were printed well ahead of the interiors of the magazines, done in batches of, I think, four at a time. This was a matter of economics—using one large plate to print four covers at once was much cheaper than printing them one by one. But sometimes the practice created problems.

For example, the April, 1957 cover of Amazing Stories was printed in the fall of 1956 with a group of others, well ahead of its publication date, bearing this announcement above the name of the magazine:

BEGINNING—COSMIC KILL—2-part serial of thundering impact

"Cosmic Kill" was supposed to be a sequel to a short novel that Amazing had published six years before—"Empire of Evil," by Robert Arnette. The readers had supposedly been clamoring for a follow-up to that great story all that time, and now, finally, it was going to be published.

The trouble was that the actual author behind the "Arnette" pseudonym on "Empire of Evil" was Paul W. Fairman, and Fairman, having recently become the editor of Amazing and Fantastic, suddenly found that he didn't have time to write a two-part serial of thundering impact. By December, 1956 publication day was nearing, though, for the April issue, due out in February, and a serial had to be found for it. So Paul Fairman phoned me one December morning and asked if I would mind very much writing a two-part serial called "Cosmic Kill," a sequel to something of his from 1951— and deliver it the following week, because it had to be on the newsstands two months from then.

Sure, I said. Nothing to it.

That night I dug out the January, 1951 Amazing *and read "Empire of Evil," which turned out to be a wild and woolly thing starring blue Mercurians with green blood, savage Martian hill men that had nasty tusks, and Venusians with big black tails. Even back then we knew that there weren't any Mercurians, Martians, or Venusians, of course. That didn't really matter to me at the moment. What did matter was that I had to put together a story of some sort, more or less overnight, that was in some way connected to its predecessor, and Fairman had either killed off or married off nearly all the characters in the original piece.*

Well, never mind that, either. He had left one or two surviving villains, and I invented a couple of new characters to set out after them, and in short order I had put together a plot. It wasn't going to be a literary masterpiece; it was just going to be a sequel, written to order, to Fairman's slapdash space-opera, which had been goofy to the point of incoherence. But—what the hell—no one was going to know I had written it, after all. And I reminded myself that plenty of my illustrious colleagues had written pulp-magazine extravaganzas just as goofy in their younger days. Here was my revered Henry Kuttner's novelet from Marvel Science Stories *of 1939, "The Time Trap," with this contents-page description: "Unleashed atomic force hurled Kent Mason into civilization's dawn-era, to be wooed by the Silver Princess who'd journeyed from 2150 A.D., and to become the laboratory pawn of Greddar Klon—who'd been projected from five hundred centuries beyond Mason's time sector!" Kuttner had put his own name on that one. And here in the same issue was future Grand Master Jack Williamson with "The Dead Spot"—"With his sigma-field that speeded evolution to the limit imposed by actual destruction of germ cells, plus his technique of building synthetic life, Dr. Clyburt Hope set out to create a new race—and return America's golden harvest land into a gray cancer of leprous doom!"*

The reputations of Kuttner and Williamson had survived their writing such silly stories. So would mine. But would I survive writing a 20,000-word novella in two days, which is what Fairman was expecting me to do?

Here my collaborator Randall Garrett came to my aid. I have never been much of a user of stimulants—I don't even drink coffee. Garrett, though, said that my predicament could be solved with the help of something called benzedrine—we would call it "speed," today—which he happened to take to control his weight. A little benzedrine would hop up my metabolism to the point where writing 40 pages in a one-day sitting would be no problem at all.

So he came over to my West End Avenue place and gave me a few little green pills, and the next day I wrote the first half of "Cosmic Kill," and the day after that I wrote the second half. I went out of my way to mimic the style of the original story, using all sorts of substitutes for "he said" that were never part of my own style—"he snapped," "he wheezed," "she wailed" and peppering the pages with adverbial modifiers—"he continued inexorably," "he said appreciatively," "he remarked casually." The next day I took the whole 80-page shebang down to Paul Fairman's office and it went straight to the printer. It was just in time for serialization in the April and May, 1957 issues of Amazing, my one and only appearance under the byline of Robert Arnette. And on the seventh day I rested, you betcha.

The funny thing is that Cosmic Kill isn't really so bad. I had to read it for the first time in 48 years for this collection, and I was impressed with the way it zips swiftly along from one dire situation to another without pausing for breath, exactly as its author did back there in December, 1956. Treat it as the curio it is: the one and only example of Silverberg writing a story on speed.

I.

Lon Archman waited tensely for the Martian to come nearer: Around him, the ancient world's hell-winds whined piercingly. Archman shivered involuntarily and squeezed tighter on the butt of the zam-gun.

One shot. He had one shot left. And if the Martian were to fire before he did—

The wind picked up the red sand and tossed it at him as he crouched behind the twisted gabron-weed. The Martian advanced steadily, its heavy body swung forward in a low crouch. It was still out of range of the zam-gun. Archman didn't dare fire yet, not with only one charge left.

A gust of devilish wind blew more sand in the Earthman's face. He spat and dug at his eyes. A little undercurrent of fear beat in the back of his mind. He shoved the emotion away. Fear and Lon Archman didn't mix.

But where the blazes was that Martian?

Ah—there. Stooping now behind the clump of gabron-weed. Inching forward on his belly toward Archman now. Archman could almost see the hill-creature's tusks glinting in the dim light. His finger wavered on the zam-gun's trigger. Again a gust of wind tossed sand in his eyes.

That was the Martian's big advantage, he thought. The Martian had a transparent eyelid that kept the damned sand out; Archman was blinded by the stinging red stuff more often than not.

Well, I've got an advantage too. I'm an agent of Universal Intelligence, and that's just a dumb Martian hillman out there trying to kill me.

A torrent of sand swept down over them again. Archman fumbled on the desert floor for a moment and grabbed a heavy lichen-encrusted rock. He heaved it as far as he could—forty feet, in Mars' low grav. It kicked up a cloud of sand.

The Martian squealed in triumph and fired. Archman grinned, cupped his hands, threw his voice forty feet. The rock seemed to scream in mortal agony, ending in a choking gasp of death.

The Martian rose confidently from his hiding place to survey the smoking remains of Archman. The Earthman waited until the Martian's tusked head and shoulders were visible, then jammed down on the zam-gun's firing stud.

It was his last shot—but his aim was good. The Martian gasped as the force-beam hit him, and slowly toppled to his native soil, his massive body burned to a hard black crust. Archman kept the beam on him until it flickered out, then thrust the now-useless zam-gun in his belt-sash and stood up.

He had won.

He took three steps forward on the crunching sand—and suddenly bleak Mars dissolved and he was back in the secret offices of Universal Intelligence, on Earth. He heard the wry voice of Blake Wentworth, Chief of Intelligence, saying, "The next time you fight on Mars, Archman, it'll be for keeps."

※

The shock of transition numbed Archman for a second, but he bounced out of his freeze lightning-fast. Eyeing Wentworth he said, "You mean I passed your test?"

The Intelligence Chief toyed with his double chin, scowled, referred to the sheet of paper he held in his hand. "You did. You passed *this* test. But that doesn't mean you would have survived the same situation on Mars."

"How so?"

"After killing the Martian you rose without looking behind you. How did you know there wasn't another Martian back there waiting to pot you the second you stood up?"

"Well, I—" Archman reddened, realizing he had no excuse. He had committed an inexcusable blunder. "I didn't know, Chief. I fouled up. I guess you'll have to look for someone else for the job of killing Darrien."

He started to leave the office.

"Like hell I will," Wentworth snapped. "You're the man I want!"

"But—"

"You went through the series of test conflicts with 97.003 percent of success. The next best man in Intelligence scored 89.62. That's not good enough. We figured 95% would be the kind of score a man would need in order to get to Mars, find Darrien, and kill him. You exceeded that mark by better than two percent. As for your blunder at the end—well, it doesn't change things. It simply means you may not come back alive after the conclusion of your mission. But we don't worry about that in Intelligence. Do we, Archman?"

"No, sir."

"Good. Let's get out of this testing lab, then, and into my office. I want to fill you in on the details of the job before I let you go."

Wentworth led the way to an inner office and dropped down behind a desk specially contoured to admit his vast bulk. He mopped away sweat and stared levelly at the waiting Archman.

"How much do you know about Darrien, Lon?"

"That he's an Earthman who hates Earth. That he's one of the System's most brilliant men—and its most brilliant criminal as well. He tried to overthrow the government twice, and the public screamed for his execution—but instead the High Council sent him to the penal colony on Venusia, in deference to his extraordinary mind."

"Yes," wheezed Wentworth. "The most disastrous move so far this century. I did my best to have that reptile executed, but the Council ignored me. So they sent him to Venusia—and in that cesspool he gathered a network of criminals around him and established his empire. An Empire we succeeded in destroying thanks to the heroic work of Tanton."

Archman nodded solemnly. Everyone in Intelligence knew of Tanton, the semi-legendary blue Mercurian who had given his life to destroy Darrien's vile empire. "But Darrien escaped, sir. Even as Space Fleet Three was bombarding Venusia, he and his closest henchmen got away on gravplates and escaped to Mars."

"Yes," said Wentworth, "To Mars. Where in the past five years he's proceeded to establish a new empire twice as deadly and vicious as the one on Venus. We know he's gathering strength for an attack on Earth—for an attack on the planet that cast him out, on the planet he hates more than anything in the cosmos."

"Why don't we just send a fleet up there and blast him out the way we did the last time?" Archman asked.

"Three reasons. One is the Clanton Space Mine, the umbrella of force-rays that surrounds his den on Mars and makes it invulnerable to attack—"

"But Davison has worked out a nullifier to the Clanton Mine, sir! That's no reason—"

"*Two,*" continued Wentworth inexorably, "Even though we can break down his barrier, our hands are tied. We can't come down to the level of worms, Archman. Darrien hasn't done anything—*yet.* We know he's going to attack Earth with all he's got, any day or week or month now—as soon as he's ready. But until he does so, we're helpless against him. Earth doesn't fight preventive wars. We'd have a black eye with the whole galaxy if we declared war on Darrien after all our high-toned declarations.

"And Three, Intelligence doesn't like to make the same mistake a second time. We bombed Darrien once, and he got away. This time, we're going to make sure we get him."

"By sending me, you mean?"

"Yes. Your job is to infiltrate into Darrien's city, find him, and kill him. It won't be easy. We know Darrien has several doubles, orthysynthetic duplicate robots. You'll have to watch out for those. You won't got two chances to kill the real Darrien."

"I understand, sir."

"And one other thing—this whole expedition of yours is strictly unofficial and illegal."

"Sir?"

"You heard me. You won't be on Mars as a representative of Universal Intelligence. You're there on your own, as Lon Archman, Killer. Your job is to get Darrien without implicating Earth. Knock him off and the whole empire collapses. But you're on your own, Archman. And you probably won't come back."

"I understand, sir. I understood that when I volunteered for this job."

"Good. You leave for Mars tonight."

☀

A pair of black-tailed Venusians were sitting at the bar with a white-skinned Earth girl between them, as Hendrin the Mercurian entered. He had been on Mars only an hour, and wanted a drink to warm his gullet before he went any further. This was a cold planet; despite his thick shell-like hide, Hendrin didn't overmuch care for the Martian weather.

"I'll have a double bizant," he snapped, spinning a silver three-creda piece on the shining counter. One of the Venusians looked up at that. The whip-like black tail twitched.

"You must have a powerful thirst, Mercurian!"

Hendrin glanced at him scornfully. "I'm just warming up for some serious drinking, friend. Bizant sets the blood flowing; it's just a starter."

The drink arrived, and he downed it in a quick gulp. That was good, he thought. "I'll have another...and after it, a shot of dolbrouk as a chaser."

"That's more like it," said the Venusian appreciatively. "You're a man after my own heart." To prove it, he downed his own drink—a mug of fiery brez. Roaring, he slapped his companion's back and pinched the arm of the silent Earth girl huddled between them.

Ideas started to form in Hendrin's head. He was alone on a strange planet, and a big job faced him. These two Venusians were well along in their cups—and they wore the tight gray britches and red tunic of Darrien's brigades. That was good.

As for the girl—well, she might help in the plan too. She was young and frightened-looking; probably she'd been caught in a recent raiding-party. Her clothes hung in tatters. Hendrin appreciatively observed the occasional bare patch of white thigh, the soft curve of breast, visible through the rents. Yes, she might do too. It depended on how drunk these Venusians were.

The Mercurian left his place at the bar and walked over to the carousing Venusians. "You sound like my type of men," he told them. "Got some time?"

"All the time in the universe!"

"Good enough. Let's take a booth in the back and see how much good brew we can pour into ourselves." Hendrin jingled his pocket. "There's plenty of cash here—cash I might part with for the company of two such as you!"

The Venusians exchanged glances, which Hendrin did not miss. They thought he was a sucker ready to be exploited. Well, the Mercurian thought, we'll see who gets exploited. And as for the money—that was his master's. He had an unlimited expense account for this mission. And he intended to use it to the utmost.

"Come, wench," said one Venusian thickly. " Let's join this gentleman at a booth."

✸

Hendrin jammed his bulk into one corner of the booth, and one of the Venusians sat by his side. Across from him sat the other Venusian and the girl. Her eyes were red and raw, and her throat showed the mark of a recent rope.

Chuckling, Hendrin said, "Where'd you get the girl?"

"Planetoid Eleven," one of the Venusians told him. "We were on a raiding party for Darrien, and found her in one of the colonies. A nice one, is she not?"

"I've seen better," remarked Hendrin casually. "She looks sullen and angry."

"They all do. But they warm up, once they see they've no alternative. How about some drinks?"

Hendrin ordered a round of brez for all three, and tossed the barkeep another three-creda coin. The drinks arrived. The Venusian nearest him reached clumsily for his and spilled three or four drops

"Oopsh…waste of good liquor. Sorry."

"Don't shed tears," Hendrin said. "There's more where that came from."

"Sure thing. Well, here's to us all—Darrien too, damn his ugly skin!"

They drank. Then they drank some more. Hendrin matched them drink for drink, and paid for most—but his hard-shelled body quickly converted the alcohol to energy, while the Venusians grew less and less sure of their speech, wobblier and wobblier in coordination.

Plans took rapid shape in the Mercurian's mind. He was here on a dangerous mission, and he knew the moment he ceased to think fast would be the moment he ceased to think.

Krodrang, Overlord of Mercury, had sent him here—Krodrang who had been content to rule the tiny planet without territorial ambitions for decades, but who suddenly had been consumed by the ambition to rule the universe as well. He had summoned Hendrin, his best agent, to the throne-room.

"Hendrin, I want you to go to Mars. Join Darrien's army. Get close to Darrien. And when you get the chance, steal his secrets. The Clanton Mine, the orthysynthetic duplicate robots, anything else. Bribe his henchmen. Steal his mistress. Do whatever you can—but I must have Darrien's secrets! And when you have them—kill him. Then I shall rule the system supreme."

"Yes, Majesty."

In Hendrin's personal opinion the Overlord was taken with the madness of extreme age. But it was not Hendrin's place to question. He was loyal—and so he accepted the job without demur.

Now he was here. He needed some means of access to Darrien.

Pointing at the girl, he said, "What do you plan to do with her? She looks weak for a slave."

"Weak! Nonsense. She's as strong as an Earthman. They come that way, out in those colonies. We plan to bring her to Dorvis Graal, Darrien's Viceroy. Dorvis Graal will buy her and make her a slave to Darrien—or possibly a mistress."

Hendrin's black eyes narrowed "How much will Dorvis Graal pay?"

"A hundred credas platinum, if we're lucky."

The Mercurian surveyed the girl out of one eye. She was undeniably lovely, and there was something else—a smoking defiance, perhaps—that might make her an appealing challenge for a jaded tyrant. "Will ye take a hundred fifty from me?"

"From *you*, Mercurian?"

"A hundred-eighty, then.",

The girl looked up scornfully. Her breasts heaved as she said, "You alien pigs buy and sell us as if we're cattle. But just wait! Wait until—"

One Venusian reached out and slapped her. She sank back into silence. "A hundred-eighty, you say?"

Hendrin nodded. "She might keep me pleasant company on the cold nights of this accursed planet."

"I doubt it," said the soberer of the two Venusians. "She looks mean. But we'd never get a hundred-eighty from Dorvis Graal. You can have her. Got the cash?"

Hendrin dropped four coins into the Venusian's leathery palm.

"Done!" the Venusian cried. "The girl is yours!"

The Mercurian nodded approvingly. The first step on the road to Darrien's chambers had been paved. He reached across the table and imprisoned the girl's wrist in one of his huge paws, and smiled coldly as defiance flared on her face. The girl had spirit. Darrien might be interested.

☀

Lon Archman shivered as the bitter Martian winds swept around him. It was just as it had been in the drug-induced tests Wentworth had run back in the Universal Intelligence office, with one little difference.

This was no dream. This was the real thing.

All he could see of Mars was the wide, flat, far-ranging plain of red sand, broken here and there by a rock outcrop or a twisted gabron-weed. In the distance he could see Canalopolis, the city Darrien had taken over and made the headquarters for his empire.

He started to walk.

After about fifteen minutes he saw his first sign of life—a guard, in the grey-and-red uniform of Darrien's men, pacing back and forth in the sand outside Canalopolis. He was an Earthman. He wore the leather harness that marked the renegade. Archman's lips pursed coldly as he watched the Earthman pace to and fro. Cautiously the Intelligence agent edged up on the renegade. He couldn't use his zam-gun; he needed the renegade's uniform. It would have to be a surprise attack.

Remembering what had happened in the final test on Earth, Archman glanced in all directions. Then he sprang forward, running full tilt at the unseeing renegade.

The man grunted and staggered forward as Archman cracked into him. Lon snatched the renegade's zam-gun and tossed it to one side. Then he grabbed the man by the scruff of his tunic and yanked him around.

He was a scrawny, hard-eyed fellow with fleshless cheeks and thin lips—probably a cheap crook who thought he stood better pickings serving Darrien than making a go of it on Earth. Archman hit him.. The renegade doubled in pain, and Archman hit him again—hard. The man crumpled like a wet paper doll.

Again the Intelligence man glanced warily around. He was a quick learner, and he wanted to improve that 97.003% score to 100%. 100%

118

meant survival on this mission, and Archman wasn't particularly anxious to die.

No one was in sight. He stripped off the unconscious guard's clothing, then peeled out of his own. The chill Martian winds whipped against his nakedness. Hastily he donned the guard's uniform. Now he was wearing the uniform of Darrien's brigade of filthy renegades.

Drawing his zam-gun, he incinerated his own clothing. The wind carried the particles away, and there was no trace. Then he glanced at the naked, unconscious renegade, already turning blue, frozen cold. Without remorse Archman killed him, lifted the headless body, carried it fifty feet to a sand dune, shoved it out of sight.

Within minutes the man would be buried by tons of sand. Archman had considered this first step carefully, had originally planned to exchange clothing with the guard and assume his identity. But that was risky. This was safer. Men often got lost in the Martian desert and vanished in the sand. When the time came for changing of the guard, that would be what they would report of this man.

So far, so good. Archman tightened the uniform at the waist until it was a convincing fit. Then he began to trot over the shifting sand toward the city ahead.

About ten minutes later he was inside Canalopolis. The guards at the gate, seeing him in Darrien's uniform, passed him without question.

The city was old—old and filthy, like all of Mars. Crowded streets loomed before him, streets thick with shops and bars and dark alleys, lurking strangers ready to rob or gamble or sell women. It wasn't a pleasant place. Archman smiled grimly. This was a fitting planet for Darrien to have set up his empire. Dirty and dark, justice-hating like Darrien himself.

Well, Archman thought, I've got to begin somewhere. Getting to Darrien would be a slow process—especially if he wanted to live through it.

The city's streets were thronged with aliens of all sorts: bushy-tailed Venusians, swaggering boldly with their deadly stingers at the end of their black tails; blue Mercurians, almost impregnable inside their thick shells; occasionally a Plutonian, looking like a fish with legs with their finned hands; and, of course, the vicious, powerful Martians, all of them showing their sneering tusks.

Here and there there was an Earthman, like Darrien himself a renegade. Archman hated those worst of all, for they were betraying their home world.

He stood still and looked around. Far ahead of him, in the middle of the city, rose a vaulting palace sculptured from shimmering Martian quartz. That was undoubtedly Darrien's headquarters. Surrounding it were smaller buildings, barracks-like—and then the rest of the city sprawled around it. Darrien had built himself a neat little fortress, thought Archman.

He wasn't at all sure how he was going to reach Darrien. But that would come in time. The first action, he thought, would be to get a couple of drinks under his belt and to have a look around the town.

A sign in three languages beckoned to him: BAR.

He cut his way through the milling traffic and entered. It was a long, low-ceilinged room which stank of five planets' liquor. A Martian bartender stood before a formidable array of exotic drinks; along the bar, men of five worlds slumped in varying degrees of drunkenness. Farther back, lit by a couple of dusty, sputtering levon-tubes, there were some secluded booths.

Archman stiffened suddenly. In one of the booths was a sight that brought quick anger to him—anger that he just as quickly forced to subside.

A blue Mercurian was leaning over, pawing a near-nude, sobbing Earth-girl. There were two Venusians in the booth with them, both slumped over the table, lying in utter stupor face-down in little pools of slops.

An Earth-girl? Here? And what the hell was that hardshell doing pawing her?

Archman's first thoughts were murderous. But then he realized such a situation gave him a chance to make a few contacts on this unfriendly planet. He shouldered past a couple of drozky-winos at the bar, choking back his disgust, and moved toward the booth in the back.

✸

The levon-tube was sputtering noisily, going *griz-griz* every few seconds. Energy leakage, thought Archman. He reached the booth, and the Mercurian left the girl alone and looked up inquisitively at him.

"Hello, Mercurian. Nice bit of flesh you've got there."

"Isn't she, though? I just bought her off these sots you see before you." The Mercurian indicated the drunken Venusians, and laughed. "We ought to cut their tails off before they wake!"

Archman eyed the alien stonily. "Drunk they may be, but they wear Darrien's uniform—which is more than you can say, stranger."

"I'm here to join up, though. Don't leap to conclusions. I'm as loyal to Darrien as you are, maybe more so."

"Sorry," Archman apologized. "Mind if I sit down?"

"Go right ahead. Dump one of the tailed ones on the floor. They're so drunk they'll never feel it."

Casually Archman shoved one of the Venusians by the shoulder. The alien stirred, moaned, and without complaining slid into a little heap on the floor. Archman took his seat, feeling the girl's warmness next to him.

"My name's Archman," he said. "Yours?"

"Hendrin. Just arrived from Mercury. A fine wench, isn't she?"

Archman studied the girl appreciatively. Her face was set in sullen defiance, and despite her near-nudity she had a firm dignity about her that the Earthman liked. She seemed to be staring right through the Mercurian rather than at him, and the fact that her breasts were nearly bare and her lovely legs unclad hardly disturbed her.

"Where are you from, lass?"

"Is it your business—traitor?"

Archman recoiled. "Harsh words, pretty one. But perhaps we've met somewhere on Earth. I'm curious."

"I'm not from Earth. I was a colonist on Planetoid Eleven until—until—"

"An attractive bit of property," Archman told the Mercurian. "You capture her yourself?"

Hendrin shook his domed head. "No. I bought her from these Venusians here. I mean to sell her to our lord Darrien, for use as a plaything."

Archman smiled casually. "I could almost use one like her myself. Would you take a hundred credas for her?"

"I paid a hundred-eighty."

"Two hundred, then?"

"Not for a thousand," said the Mercurian firmly. "This girl is for Darrien himself."

"Beasts," the girl muttered.

The Mercurian slapped her with a clawed fist. A little trickle of blood seeped from the corner of her mouth, and Archman had to force himself to watch coldly.

"You won't sell, eh?" Archman said. That was unfortunate, he thought. Having merchandise such as this to offer might conceivably get him close to Darrien quickly. And the girl was just that—merchandise. As an Intelligence agent went, Archman knew that all lives including his own were expendable in the struggle to assassinate Darrien.

"I sure won't," said the Mercurian exultantly. "Why, Darrien will go wild when he sees this one! What do I need your money for, against the power he can offer for her?"

"What if he simply takes her away from you?"

"Darrien wouldn't do that. Darrien's smart; he knows how to keep the loyalty of his men." The Mercurian rose, clutching the girl's wrist. "Come, lovely. We go to seek Darrien now, before anything might happen to her. And as for you, Earthman, it was good to make your acquaintance—and perhaps we shall meet again some day."

"Perhaps," Archman said tightly. He sat back and watched as the Mercurian, gloating, led his prize away. A flash of thighs, the bright warmness of a breast, and then girl and captor were gone.

This is a filthy business, Archman thought bitterly.

But the Mercurian was on his way to Darrien. It would be useful, reflected the Earthman, to follow along and find out just what happened. At this stage of the enterprise, any trail could be taken.

❋

Hendrin the Mercurian moved at a steady rate through the streets of Canalopolis, dragging the sobbing girl roughly along.

"You don't have to pull me," she said icily, struggling with her free hand to pull together the tatters of her clothing. "I don't want my arm yanked out. I'll come willingly."

"Then walk faster," Hendrin grunted. He peered ahead, toward the rosy bulk of Darrien's palace, as a structure of intrigue began to form in his mind. Using the girl as a pawn, he could gain access to Darrien.

That alone wouldn't help. In all probability he'd see not the real Darrien, but an orthysynthetic duplicate of the shrewd leader. One false move and Hendrin would find himself brainburned and tossed out as carrion for the sandwolves.

This had to be done carefully, very carefully. But Hendrin felt no fear. Overlord Krodrang had hand-picked him from the ranks of his secret operatives, and Hendrin was confident he could fulfill his monarch's commands.

"Why do you have to do this to me?" the girl asked suddenly. "Why couldn't I have been left on Planetoid Eleven with my parents, in peace, instead of being dragged here, to be paraded nude through the streets of this awful city and—" She gasped for breath.

"Easy, girl, easy. That's a great many words for your soft throat to spew out so quickly."

"I don't want your lying gentleness!" she snapped. "Why am I being sold to Darrien? And what will he do to me?"

"As for the former, I'm afraid I'll have to beg off. I'm selling you for money—"

"But those Venusians said you bid more for me than Darrien would have paid!"

"They were drunk. They didn't recognize a prize specimen when they see one."

"*Prize specimen!*" She spat the words back at him. "To you aliens I'm just a prize specimen, is that it?"

"I'm afraid so," Hendrin said lightly. "As for what Darrien will do to you—come now, milady, that ought to be obvious!"

"It is," she said glumly. "But why does life have to be this way? That Earthman, back in the bar—doesn't he have any loyalty to someone of his own world?"

"Apparently not. But enough of this talk; what's your name?"

"Elissa Hall."

"A pretty name, though a trifle too smooth for my taste. How old are you, Elissa?"

"Nineteen."

"Umm. Darrien will be interested, I'm sure."

"You're the most cold-blooded creature I've ever met," she said.

Hendrin chuckled dryly. "I doubt it. I'm a kindly old saint compared with Darrien. I'm just doing my job, lady; don't make it hard for me."

She didn't answer. Hendrin rotated one eye until he had a good view of her. She had blonde hair cut in bangs, blue eyes, a pert nose, warm-looking lips. Her figure was excellent. Some other time, perhaps, Hendrin might have had some sport with her first and scarcely found it dull. But not now. Like all his people, the Mercurian was cold and businesslike when it came to a job. And—much as he would have liked the idea—it didn't fit into the strategy.

"Halt and state name," snapped a guard suddenly, presenting a zam-gun. He was a Martian, grinning ferociously.

"Hendrin's my name. I'm a member of Darrien's raiders, and I'm bringing this girl to sell to him."

The Martian studied Elissa brazenly, then said, "Very well. You can pass. Take her to Dorvis Graal's office, and he'll talk to you."

Hendrin nodded and moved ahead past the guard and into the compound of buildings surrounding Darrien's lofty palace.

＊

Dorvis Graal, Darrien's Viceroy and the Chief of Canalopolis' Security Police, was a Venusian. He looked up from a cluttered desk as Hendrin and the girl entered. There was a bleak, crafty glint in his faceted eyes; his beak of a nose seemed to jab forward at the Mercurian, and the deadly stinging-tail went *flick-flick* ominously.

"Who are you, Mercurian?"

"The name is Hendrin. I've recently joined Darrien's forces."

"Odd. I don't remember seeing a dossier on you."

Hendrin shrugged. "This red tape is beyond me. All I know is I signed on to fight for Darrien, and I have something I think might interest him."

"You mean the girl?" Dorvis Graal said. He squinted at her. "She's an Earth colonist, isn't she?"

"From Planetoid Eleven. I think our lord Darrien might be interested in her."

Dorvis Graal chuckled harshly. "Possibly he will—but if he is, there'll be the devil to pay when Meryola, Darrien's mistress, finds out!"

"That's Darrien's problem," the blue Mercurian said. "But I'm in need of cash. How can I get to see Darrien?"

"Darrien wouldn't bother with you. But let me think about this for a moment. What would you consider a fair price for the wench?"

"Two hundred credas and a captaincy in Darrien's forces."

The Venusian smiled derisively. "Mars has two moons, as well. Why not ask for one of those?"

"I've named my price," said Hendrin.

"Let me look at the girl," Dorvis Graal rose, flicking his bushy tail from side to side, and stepped forward. "These rags obscure the view," he said, ripping away what remained of Elissa's clothing. Her body, thus revealed, was pure white for a moment—until suffused by a bright pink blush. She started to cover herself with her hands, but Dorvis Graal calmly slapped her wrists away from her body. "I can't see if you do that," he said.

After a lengthy appraisal he looked up. "A fair wench," he remarked. "Perhaps Darrien will expend a hundred credas or so. Certainly no more."

"And the captaincy?"

"I can always ask," said the Venusian mockingly.

Hendrin frowned. "What do you mean, *you* can ask? Don't I get to talk to Darrien?"

"I'll handle the transaction," said Dorvis Graal. "Darrien doesn't care to be bothered by every Mercurian who wanders by with a bare-bottomed beauty he's picked up in a raid. You wait here, and I'll show him the girl."

"Sorry," Hendrin said quickly. He threw his cloak over the girl's shoulders. "Either I see Darrien myself or it's no deal. I'll keep the girl myself rather than let myself be cheated out of her."

Dorvis Graal's whip-like tail went rigid with anger for an instant—but then, as he saw Hendrin apparently meant what he said, he relaxed. "Just a minute, there."

Hendrin and the girl were nearly at the door. "What?"

"I'll let you in," he said. "I'll let you see Darrien and take him the girl. It's rare to let a common soldier in, but in this case perhaps it can be done."

"And how much do I bribe you?"

"Crudely put," said the Venusian. "But I ask no money of you. Simply that—if Darrien, for some reason, should not care to buy the girl, *I* get her. Free."

Hendrin scowled, but his active mind had already jumped to that conclusion. It was too bad for the girl, of course, but what of that? At least he'd definitely get to see Darrien this way—which was his whole plan. And the chance of Darrien's turning down the girl was slim.

"Fair enough," he said aloud. The girl uttered a little gasp of mingled shame and rage at this latest bargain. "How do I reach Darrien?"

"I'll give you a pass to the tunnel leading to the throne-room. The rest is up to you. But remember this: you won't live long if you try to cheat me."

"I'm a man of my word," Hendrin said, meaning it. He accepted the pass from Dorvis Graal, grinned wolfishly, and seized the girl's arm. "Which way do I go?"

"The tunnel entrance is down there," Dorvis Graal said, pointing. "And here's hoping Darrien isn't in a buying mood today." He leered suggestively as Hendrin led the girl away.

Lon Archman watched, puzzled as the Mercurian and the girl disappeared into Dorvis Graal's office. He had followed them this far without difficulty—but now that he was within Darrien's compound, he had no idea where he was heading now. His body writhed impatiently, longing for action, but his mind kept careful check, holding him back. This was a game that had to be played cautiously.

The Mercurian was selling the girl to Darrien. That seemed like a good dodge, thought Archman—except where was he going to get another girl to take to the tyrant? He'd have to find some other way of working himself into the palace. It was too late to overpower the Mercurian and take the girl from the Planetoids to Darrien himself.

Or was it? He wondered...

Suddenly the door of Dorvis Graal's office opened and Hendrin and the girl stepped out into the street again. Archman noticed that the girl no longer wore her tattered clothes; she had been stripped bare in the Viceroy's office, it seemed. Now she wore the Mercurian's cloak loosely around her shoulders, but it concealed little.

And Hendrin was clutching some sort of paper in his hand. A pass?

Yes. It had to be a pass. A pass to see Darrien!

A plan formed itself instantly in Archman's mind, and he broke from the shadows and dashed toward Dorvis Graal's office just as the girl and Mercurian disappeared into another door.

A figure stepped forward to intercept him after he had run no more than a dozen paces. Archman felt a stiff-armed fist hurl him back, and he stared into the barrel of a cocked zam-gun.

"Where are you heading so fast?" The speaker was a Martian guard.

"I have to see Dorvis Graal. It's on a matter of high treason! Darrien's in danger of an assassin!"

"*What?*" The Martian's expression shifted from one of menacing hostility to keen interest. "Are you lying?"

"Of course not, you fool. Now get out of my way and let me get to the Viceroy before it's too late!"

The zam-gun was holstered and Archman burst past. He reached Dorvis Graal's office, flung open the door, and bowed humbly to the glittering-eyed Venusian, who looked up in some astonishment.

"Who are you? What's the meaning of this?"

"I'm Lon Archman of Darrien's brigade. Quick, sir—have a Mercurian and a girl been through here in the last minute or so?"

"Yes, but—say, what business is this of yours?"

"That Mercurian's an *assassin!*" Archman got as much excitement into his voice as he could manage. "I've been following him all morning, but he shook me just outside the entrance to the compound. He intends to kill Darrien!"

A mixture of emotions played suddenly over the Viceroy's face—greed, fear, curiosity, disbelief. "Indeed? Well, that can easily be stopped. He's in the tunnel, on the way to Darrien. I'll have the tunnel guards intercept him and send him up to Froljak the Interrogator for some questioning. Thanks for your information, Archman."

"May I go after him, sir?"

"What?"

"Into the tunnel. I want to kill that Mercurian, sir. Myself. I don't want your tunnel guards to do it."

"They're not going to kill him," Dorvis Graal said impatiently. "They'll just hold him for questioning, and if you're telling the truth that he's an assassin—"

Archman scowled. This wasn't getting him into the tunnel, where he wanted to go. "Let me go after him, sir," he pleaded. "As a reward. A reward for telling you. I want to be in on the capture."

Dorvis Graal seemed to relent. It was pretty flimsy, Archman thought, but maybe—

Yes. "Here's a pass to the tunnel," the Viceroy said. "Get going, now—and report back to me when it's all over."

"Yes, sir. Thanks!"

Archman seized the pass and streaked for the tunnel at top speed.

After he had left, Dorvis Graal lifted the speaking-tube that gave him instant contact with the tunnel guards.

"Holgo?"

"Yes, sir?"

"Has a Mercurian passed through the tunnels yet? He's got a naked wench with him."

"Yes, sir. He and the girl came by this way two minutes ago. He had a pass, so I let him through. Is there anything wrong?"

"No—no, not at all," Dorvis Graal said. Craftily he reasoned that even if the Mercurian reached Darrien safely, which he seemed likely to do, he'd probably not be facing the leader himself but only an expendable orthysynthetic duplicate. There was always time to catch him, if he really were the assassin.

And as for the Earthman—well, just to be safe Dorvis Graal decided to pick him up. He had seemed just a little too eager to get into the tunnel.

Into the tube he said, "There's an Earthman coming into the tunnel now. He's also got a pass, but I want you to pick him up and hold him for questioning. Got that?"

"Yes, sir."

Dorvis Graal broke the contact and sat back. He wondered which one was lying, the Mercurian or the Earthman—or both. And just what *would* happen if an assassin reached Darrien.

Perhaps, Dorvis Graal thought, it might mean *I'd* reach power. Perhaps.

He sat back, an amused smile on his cold face, and contemplated the possibilities.

❀

Hendrin reached the end of the long corridor and folded Dorvis Graal's pass in his pocket. He would probably need it to get out again.

He turned to the girl. "Pull the cloak tight around you, lass. I don't want Darrien to see your nakedness until the proper moment. And try to brighten up and look more desirable."

"Why should I?" she sniffled. "Why should I care what I look like?"

Patiently the Mercurian said, "Because if Darrien doesn't buy you I have to give you to that Venusian out there. And, believe me, you'll be a lot better off with Darrien than in the arms of that foul-smelling tailed one out there. So cheer up; it's the lesser of the two evils." He closed the cloak around her and together they advanced toward Darrien's throne room.

A stony-faced Martian guard stood outside the throne room. "What want you with Darrien?"

"I bring him a girl." Hendrin pointed to Elissa, then showed the guard Dorvis Graal's pass. "The Viceroy himself sent me to Darrien."

"You can pass, then," grunted the Martian. He opened the door and Hendrin stepped in.

It was a scene of utter magnificence. The vast room was lined from wall to wall with a fantastically costly yangskin rug, except in the very center, where a depression had been scooped out and a small pool created. In the pool two nude earthgirls swam, writhing sinuously for Darrien's delight.

Darrien. Hendrin's eyes slowly turned toward the throne at the side of the vast room. It was a bright platinum pedestal upon which Darrien and his mistress sat. Hendrin studied them while waiting to be noticed.

So that's Darrien—or his double. The galaxy's most brilliant and most evil man sat tensely on his throne, beady eyes darting here and there, radiating an unmistakably malevolent intelligence. Darrien was a small, shrunken man, his face a complex network of wrinkles and valleys. Darrien or his double, Hendrin reminded himself again. The possibility was slim that Darrien himself was here; more likely he was elsewhere in the palace, operating the dummy on the throne by a remote-control device he himself had conceived.

And at Darrien's side, the lovely Meryola, Darrien's mistress. She was clad in filmy vizosheen that revealed more than it hid, and the Mercurian was startled at the beauty revealed. It was known that Meryola's beauty was enhanced by drugs from Darrien's secret laboratories, but even so she was ravishing in her own right.

Hendrin had to admire Darrien. After the destruction of Venusia five years ago, a lesser man might have drifted into despair—but not Darrien. Goaded by the fierce rage and desire for vengeance that burnt within him, he had simply moved on to Mars and established here a kingdom twice as magnificent as that the Earthmen had destroyed on Venus.

He was talking now to a pair of bushy-tailed Venusians who stood before the throne. Lieutenants, obviously, receiving some sort of instructions. Hendrin made a mental note to find out who they were later.

Finally Darrien was through. The tyrant looked up and fixed Hendrin in his piercing gaze.

"Who are you, Mercurian, and what do you want here?"

Darrien's voice was astonishingly deep and forceful for a man so puny in body. For a moment Hendrin was shaken by the man's commanding tones.

Then he said, "I be Hendrin, sire, of your majesty's legions. I bring with me a girl whom perhaps—"

"I might purchase," snapped Darrien. "That fool Dorvis Graal! He knows well that I can't be troubled with such petty things."

"Begging your pardon, sir," Hendrin said with glib humility, "but the Viceroy said that this girl was of such surpassing beauty that he couldn't set a proper price himself, and sent me to you with her."

Hendrin noticed an interesting series of reactions taking place on the face of the tyrant's mistress. Meryola had been staring curiously at the girl, who stood slumped beneath the shapeless cloak. As Hendrin spoke, Meryola seemed to stiffen as if fearing a rival; her breasts, half-visible through her gauzy garment, rose and fell faster, and her eyes flashed. Hendrin smiled inwardly. There were possibilities here.

Darrien was frowning, bringing even more wrinkles to his face. Finally he said, "Well, then, let's see this paragon of yours. Unveil her—but if she is not all you say, both of you shall die, and Dorvis Graal in the bargain!"

Hendrin approached the girl. "Three lives depend on your beauty, now—including your own."

"Why should I want to live?" she murmured.

Hendrin ignored it and ripped away the cloak. Elissa stood before Darrien totally nude. To his relief Hendrin saw the girl was cooperating; she stood tall and proud, her breasts outthrust, her pale body quivering as if with desire. Darrien stared at her for a long moment. Meryola, by his side, seemed ready to explode.

At length Darrien said, "You may live. She is a lovely creature. Cover her again, so all eyes may not see her."

Hendrin obediently tossed the cloak over her shoulders and bowed to Darrien.

"Name your price."

"Two hundred credas—and a captaincy in your forces."

He held his breath. Darrien turned to Elissa.

"How old are you, girl?"

"Nineteen."

"Has this Mercurian laid lustful hands on you?"

"I've never been with any man, sire," the girl said, blushing.

"Umm." To Hendrin Darrien said, "The captaincy is yours, and *five* hundred credas. Come, girl; let me show you where your quarters will be."

❋

Darrien rose from the throne, and Hendrin was surprised to see the man was a dwarf, no more than four feet high. He strode rapidly down the pedestal to Elissa's side. She was more than a foot taller than he.

He led her away. Hendrin, his head bowed, glanced up slowly and saw Meryola fuming on the throne. Now was the time to act, he thought. Now.

"Your Highness!" he whispered.

She looked down at him. "I should have you flayed," she said harshly. "Do you know what you've done?"

"I fear I've brought your Highness a rival," Hendrin said. "For this I beg your pardon; I had no way of knowing Darrien sought concubines for himself. And I sorely needed the money."

"Enough," Meryola said. Her face was black with anger, but still radiant. "Out of my sight, and let me deal with the problem you've brought me."

"A moment, milady. May I speak?"

"Speak," she said impatiently.

He stared at her smouldering gray-flecked eyes. "Milady, I wish to undo the damage I've caused you this day."

"How could you do that?"

Hendrin thought quickly. "If you'll go to my lord Darrien and occupy his attention for the next hour, I'll slip within and find the girl. You need only sign an order testifying that she's a traitor to Darrien, and I'll convey her to the dungeons—where she'll die before Darrien knows she's missing."

Meryola glanced at him curiously. "You're a strange one, Hendrin the Mercurian. First you bring this ravishing creature to Darrien—then, when his back is turned, you offer to remove her again. Odd loyalty, Mercurian!"

Hendrin saw that he had blundered. "I but meant, milady, that I had no idea my act would have such consequences. I want the chance to redeem myself—for to bring a shadow between Darrien and Meryola would be to weaken all of our hopes."

"Nicely spoken," Meryola said, and Hendrin realized he had recovered control. He looked at her bluntly now, saw tiny crows' feet beginning to show at the edges of her eyes. She was a lovely creature, but an aging one. He knew that she would be ultimately of great use to him.

"Very well," she said. "I'll endeavor to separate Darrien from his new plaything—and while I'm amusing our lord, get you inside and take the girl away. I'll double his five hundred credas if he never sees her again."

"I thank you," Hendrin said. The Mercurian offered her his arm as she dismounted from the throne. He felt a current of anticipation tingling in him. He was on his way, now. Already he had won Darrien's approval—and, if he could only manage to convey the girl to the dungeons without Darrien's discovering who had done it, he would be in the favor of the tyrant's mistress as well. It was a good combination.

Legend had it that only Meryola knew when Darrien himself sat on the throne and when a duplicate. He would need her help when the time comes.

Exultantly he thought: *Oh, Krodrang, Krodrang, you sent the right man for this job!*

Quietly he slipped from the throne room in search of Elissa, feeling very proud of himself.

◉

The entrance to the tunnel was guarded by two Venusians and a fin-handed Plutonian. Lon Archman approached and said, "Is this the way to Darrien's throne room?"

"It is. What would you want there?"

Archman flashed the Viceroy's pass. "This is all the explanation you should need."

They stepped aside and allowed him through. The corridor was long and winding and lit by the bright glow of levon tubes. There was no sign of the Mercurian or the girl up ahead.

That was all right, Archman thought. He had no particular interest in them, so long as he were inside the Palace itself. And his ruse had worked, evidently; here he was, with a pass to the throne room.

Trotting, he rounded a bend in the corridor and halted suddenly. Three Martians blocked his way, forming a solid bar across the tunnel.

"Stay right there, Earthman."

"I've got a pass from Dorvis Graal," he snapped impatiently. "Let me go." He smelled the foul musk of the Martians as they clustered around him.

"Hand over the pass," ordered the foremost of the trio.

Suspiciously Archman gave him the slip. The Martian read it, nodded complacently, and ripped the pass into a dozen pieces, which he scattered in the air.

"Hey! You can't do that! Dorvis Graal—"

"Dorvis Graal himself has just phoned me to revoke your pass," the Martian informed him. "You're to be held for questioning as a possible assassin."

Grimly Archman saw what had happened. His 97.003% rating had fooled him into thinking he was some sort of superman. Naturally, the Viceroy had been suspicious of the strange-faced, over-eager Earthman with the wild story, and had ordered his pickup. Possibly the Mercurian and the girl were safely within, or else they had been picked up too. It didn't make any difference. The wily Viceroy was cautiously taking no chances in the affair.

Almost instantly Archman's zam-gun was in his hand, and a second later the Martian's tusked face was a blossoming nightmare, features disappearing in a crackle of atomized dust. The man sagged to the floor. Archman turned to the other two, but they had moved already. A club descended on his arm with stunning force and the zam-gun dropped from his numbed fingers. He struck out with his fist, feeling a stiff jolt of pain run through him as he connected.

"Dorvis Graal said not to kill him," said one of the Martians.

Archman whirled, trying to keep eyes on both of them at once, but it was impossible. As one rocked back from the force of the Earthman's blow, the other drew near. Archman felt hot breath behind him, turned—

And a copperwood club cracked soundly against the side of his head. He fought desperately for consciousness, realizing too late that he had blundered terribly. Then the club hit him again and a searing tide of pain swept up around him, blotting out tunnel and Martians and everything.

Hendrin confronted the shivering Elissa. She stood before a mirror clad only in a single sheer garment Darrien had given her.

"Come with me," he whispered. "Now, before Darrien comes back!"

"Where will you take me?"

"Away from here. I'll hide you in the dungeons until it's safe to get you out. Now that I've been paid, I don't feel any need to give you to Darrien—and the tyrant's mistress will pay me double to get you out."

She smiled acidly. "I see. I suppose I'll then be subject to your tender mercies again—until the next time you decide to sell me. Sorry, but I'm not going. I'll take my chances here. Darrien probably takes good care of his women."

"Meryola will kill you!"

"Possibly. But how long could I live with you outside? No, I'll stay here, now that you've sold me."

Hendrin cursed and pulled her to him. He hit her once, carefully, on the chin. She shuddered and went sprawling backward; he caught her—she was surprisingly light—and tossed her over his shoulder. Footsteps were audible at the door.

He glanced around, found a rear exit, and slipped through. A staircase beckoned. The Mercurian, bearing his unconscious burden, ran.

●

Through a dim haze of pain Lon Archman heard voices. Someone was saying, in a Martian's guttural tones, "Put this one in a cell, will you?"

Another voice, with a Plutonian's liquid accents, said, "Strange the dungeons should be so busy at this hour. But a few moments ago a Mercurian brought an Earthgirl here to be kept safe—a would-be assassin, I'm told."

"As is this one. Here, lock him up. Dorvis Graal will be here to interrogate him later, and I suppose there'll be the usual consequences."

"That means two executions tomorrow," said the Plutonian gleefully. "Two?"

"Yes. The Lady Meryola sent me instructions just before you came that the Earthgirl is to die in the morning, without fail. Now the Earthman comes." The jailer chuckled. "I think I'll put 'em in the same cell. Let 'em enjoy their last night alive!"

Archman dizzily felt himself being thrown roughly into a cold room, heard a door clang shut behind him. He opened one eye painfully. Someone was sobbing elsewhere in the cell.

He looked. It was the Earthgirl, the one the Mercurian had been with. She lay in a crumpled, pathetic little heap in the far corner of the cell, sobbing. After a moment she looked up.

"It's you—the Earthman!"

He nodded. "We've met before."

A spasm of sobbing shook her.

"Ease up," Archman said soothingly, despite the pain that flashed up and down his own battered body. "Stop crying!"

"Stop crying? Why? Why, when they're going to kill us both tomorrow?"

END OF PART ONE

||

Synopsis of what has gone before:

LON ARCHMAN of Universal Intelligence has been sent to Mars on the difficult task of assassinating DARRIEN, the shrewd madman who threatens Earth. Darrien had established an empire on Venus, destroyed five years earlier by Earth spaceships—but Darrien had fled to Mars and built an empire of even greater strength. It is Archman's job to find Darrien and kill him—a job complicated by the fact that Darrien is known to utilize several orthysynthetic duplicate robots indistinguishable from himself.

At the same time, HENDRIN, a blue Mercurian in the pay of Krodrang, Overlord of Mercury, has arrived on Mars for similar reasons: to kill Darrien and transfer his secret weapons to Mercury. When Archman first encounters the Mercurian, Hendrin is with a captive Earthgirl, ELISSA HALL, whom he has purchased from a pair of drunken Venusian soldiers. Hendrin means to sell the girl to Darrien and thus gain access to the palace. Archman decides to follow Hendrin.

The Mercurian persuades DORVIS GRAAL, Darrien's viceroy, to give him a pass to Darrien. Archman, using the device of accusing Hendrin of being an assassin, likewise gets past the Viceroy—but this time Dorvis Graal has doubts, and orders pickup of both Hendrin and Archman for questioning.

Archman is caught in the tunnel that leads to Darrien's palace. Hendrin and Elissa get through and the Mercurian shows the girl to Darrien, who is immediately taken by her beauty and buys her.

However, MERYOLA, Darrien's mistress, is jealous of the newcomer. She bribes Hendrin to spirit Elissa away from Darrien and hide her in the dungeons of the palace.

Archman and Elissa, who had met briefly before, now meet again—in the same cell. And all signs point to their executions the following morning.

※

In the darkness of the cell, Archman eyed the shadow-etched figure of the girl uneasily. He was twenty-three; he had spent six years in Universal Intelligence, including his training period. That made him capable of handling tusked Martians and finny Plutonians with ease, but a sobbing Earthgirl? There were no rules in the book for that.

Suddenly the girl sat up, and Archman saw her wipe her eyes. "Why am I crying?" she asked. "I should be happy. Tomorrow they're going to kill me—and that's the greatest favor I could wish for."

"Don't talk like that!"

"Why not? Ever since Darrien's raiders grabbed me on Planetoid Eleven, I've just been bought and sold, over and over, bargained for, used as a pawn in one maneuver after another. Do you think I care if they kill me now?"

Archman was silent. Flickering rays of light from somewhere outside bobbed at random in the cell, illuminating the girl's almost bare form from time to time. He wanted to talk gently to her, to take her in his arms, to comfort her—

But he couldn't. He was a trained assassin, not a smooth-talking romancer. The words wouldn't come, and he crouched back on his heels, feeling the throbbing pain from his beating and the even sharper pain of not being able to speak.

It was the girl who broke the silence. She said, "And what of you? You're a renegade, a traitor to your home world. How will you feel when you die tomorrow? Clean?"

"You don't understand," Archman said tightly. "I'm not—" He paused. He didn't dare to reveal the true nature of his mission.

Or did he? What difference did it make? In an hour or so, he would be taken to the Interrogator—and most assuredly they would pry from his unwilling subconscious the truth. Why not tell the girl now and at least go to death without *her* hating him? The conflict within him was brief and searing.

"You're not what?" she asked sarcastically.

"I'm not a renegade," he said, his voice leaden. "You don't understand me. You don't know me."

"I know that you're a cold-blooded calculating murderer. Do I need to know anything else, Archman?"

He drew close to her and stared evenly at her. In a harsh whisper he said, "I'm an Intelligence agent. I'm here to assassinate Darrien."

There, he thought. He'd made his confession to her. It didn't matter if the cell were tapped, though he doubted it—the Interrogator would dredge the information from him soon enough.

She met his gaze. "Oh," she said simply.

"That changes things, doesn't it? I mean—you don't hate me any more, do you?"

She laughed—a cold tinkle of a sound. "Hate you? Do you expect me to *love* you, simply because you're on the same side I am? You're still cold-blooded. You're still a killer. And I hate killers!"

"But—" He let his voice die away, realizing it was hopeless. The girl was embittered; he'd never convince her that he was anything but a killing machine, and it didn't matter which side he was on. He rose and walked to the far corner of the cell.

After a few moments he said, "I don't even know your name."

"Do you care?"

"You're my cellmate on the last night of my life. I'd like to know."

"Elissa. Elissa Hall."

He wanted to say, *it's a pretty name,* but his tongue was tied by shame and anger. Bitterly he stared at the blank wall of the cell, reflecting that this was an ironic situation. Here he was, locked in a cell with a practically nude girl, and—

He stiffened. "Do you hear something?"

"No."

"I do. Listen."

"Yes," she said a moment later. "I hear it!"

Footsteps. The footsteps of the Interrogator.

❋

Cautiously, the blue Mercurian touched the stud of the door-communicator outside Meryola's suite.

"Who's there?" The voice was languid, vibrant.

"Hendrin. The Mercurian."

"Come in, won't you?"

The door slid aside and Hendrin entered. Meryola's chamber was as luxuriously-appointed a suite as he had ever seen. Clinging damasks, woven with elaborate designs and figures, draped themselves artistically over the windows, a subtle fragrance lingered in the air, and, from above, warm jampulla-rays glowed, heating and sterilizing the air, preserving Meryola's beauty.

As for Meryola herself, she lay nude on a plush yangskin rug, bronzing herself beneath a raylamp. As Hendrin entered, she rose coyly, stretched, and without sign of embarrassment casually donned a filmy robe. She approached Hendrin, and the usually unemotional Mercurian found himself strangely moved by her beauty.

"Well?" Her tone was business-like now.

"You ask of the girl?"

"Of what else?"

Hendrin smiled. "The girl has been disposed of. She lies in the dungeon below."

"Has anyone seen you take her there? The mistress of the wardrobe, perhaps? That one's loyal to Darrien, and hates me; I suspect she was once Darrien's woman, before she aged." A shadow of anger passed over Meryola's lovely face, as if she were contemplating a fate in store for herself.

"No one saw me, your Highness. I induced her to leave the wardrobe-room and took her there by the back stairs. I handed her over to the jailer with orders to keep her imprisoned indefinitely. I gave him a hundred credas."

Meryola nodded approvingly. She crossed the room, moving with the grace of a Mercurian sun-tiger, and snatched a speaking-tube from the wall.

"Dungeons," she ordered.

A moment later Hendrin heard a voice respond, and Meryola said, "Was an Earthgirl brought to you just now by a large Mercurian? Good. The girl is to die at once; these are my orders. No, fool, no written confirmation is needed. The girl's a traitor to Darrien; what more do you need but my word? Very well."

She broke the contact and turned back to Hendrin. "She dies at once, Mercurian. You've been faithful. Faithful, and shrewd—for Darrien pays you to bring the girl here, and Meryola pays you to take her away."

She opened a drawer, took out a small leather pouch, handed it to Hendrin. Tactfully he accepted it without opening it and slipped it into his sash.

"Your servant, milady."

Inwardly he felt mildly regretful; the girl *had* come in for raw treatment. But soon she'd be out of her misery. In a way, it was unfortunate; with the girl alive he might have had further power over Meryola. Still, he had gained access to the palace, which was a basic objective, and he had won the gratitude of Darrien's mistress, which was the second step. As for the third—

"Lord Darrien will be angry when he finds the girl is missing, milady. There's no chance he'll accuse me—"

"Of course not. He'll be angry for a moment or two, but I think I'll be able to console him." She yawned delicately, and for an instant her gown fluttered open. She did not hurry to close it. Hendrin wondered if, perhaps, she longed for some variety after five years of Darrien's embraces.

"Our master must be pleased to have one so fair as you," the blue Mercurian said. He moved a little closer to Meryola, and she did not seem to object. "Legend has it that he trusts you with his innermost secrets—such as the identity of his robot duplicates."

Meryola chuckled archly. "So the galaxy knows of the orthysynthetics, eh? Darrien's Achilles heel, so to speak. I thought it was a secret."

"It is as widely known as your loveliness," Hendrin said. He was nearly touching Meryola by now.

Frowning curiously, she reached out and touched his bare shoulder. She rubbed her forefinger over the Mercurian's hard shell and commented, "You blue ones are far from thin-skinned, I see."

"Our planet's climate is a rigorous one, milady. The shell is needed."

"So I would imagine. Rough-feeling stuff, isn't it? I wonder what the feel of it against my whole body would be like...."

Smiling, Hendrin said, "If milady would know—"

She edged closer to him. He felt a quiver of triumph; through Meryola, he could learn the secret of Darrien's robot duplicates. He extended his massive arms and gently caressed her shoulders.

She seemed to melt into him. The Mercurian started to fold her in his arms. Then his hypersensitive ears picked up the sound of relays clicking in the door.

In one quick motion he had pushed her away and bent stiffly, kneeling in an attitude of utter devotion. It was none too soon. Before she had a chance to register surprise, the door opened.

Darrien entered.

❋

Lon Archman crouched in the far corner of the cell, listening to the talk going on outside.

A cold Martian voice was saying, "There's an Earthman here. Dorvis Graal wants him brought to Froljak the Interrogator for some questions."

"Certainly." It was the Plutonian jailer who spoke. "And how about the girl? Do you want her too?"

"Girl? What girl? My orders say only to get the Earthman. I don't know anything about a girl."

"Very well. I'll give you the man only." The Plutonian giggled thickly. "And when Froljak's through with him, I guess you can bring the shattered shell back to me and I'll put it out of its misery. Froljak is very thorough."

"Yes," the Martian said ominously. "Take me to the cell."

Suddenly Archman was conscious of the girl's warmth against him, of her breasts and thighs clinging to him.

"They're going to take you away!" she said. "They're going to leave me here alone."

"A moment ago you said you hated me," Archman reminded her bluntly.

She ignored him. "I don't want to die," she sobbed. "Don't let them kill me."

"You'll be on your own now. I'm going to be Interrogated." He shuddered slightly. The capital "I" on "Interrogated" was all too meaningful. It was an inquisition he would never survive.

"Is this the cell?" the Martian asked, outside.

"That's right. They're both in there."

The cell door began to open. Elissa huddled sobbing on the floor. Archman realized he had been a fool to give up so easily, to even allow the thought of death to enter his mind while he still lived.

"When the Martian comes in," he whispered, "throw yourself at his feet. Beg for mercy; do anything. Just distract him."

Her sobbing stopped, and she nodded.

Archman flattened himself against the wall. The Martian, a burly, broad-shouldered, heavy-tusked specimen, entered the cell.

"Come, Earthman. Time for some questions."

Elissa rose and leaped forward. She threw herself at the Martian, grovelling before him, clasping his ankles appealingly.

"What? Who are you?"

"Don't let them kill me! Please—I don't want to die! I'll do anything! Just get me out of here!"

The Martian frowned. "This must be the Earthgirl," he muttered. To Elissa he said, I'm not here for you. I want the Earthman. Is he here?"

"Don't let them kill me!" Elissa wailed again, wrapping herself around the Martians legs.

Archman sprang.

He hit the Martian squarely amidships, and the evil-smelling breath left the alien in one grunted gust. At the same moment Elissa's supplication turned into an attack; with all her strength she tugged at the surprised Martian, knocked him off balance.

The zam-gun flared and ashed a chunk of the wall. Archman drove a fist into the Martian's corded belly, and the alien staggered. Archman hit him again, and smashed upward from the floor to shatter a tusk. A gout of Martian blood spurted.

The Martian thrashed about wildly; Archman saw a blow catch Elissa and hurl her heavily against the wall. He redoubled his own efforts and within moments had efficiently reduced the Martian to a sagging mass of semi-conscious flesh, nothing more. He seized the zam-gun.

"Elissa! Come on!"

But the girl was slumped unconscious on the floor. He took a hesitant step toward her, then whirled as a voice behind him cried, "What's all the noise around here?"

It was the Plutonian jailer. And the door was beginning to close.

Nimbly Archman leaped through, as the micronite door clanged shut on the girl and the unconscious Martian. The Plutonian had done whatever had to be done to close the cell door. Now he was fumbling for a weapon.

The fish-man's wide mouth bobbed in astonishment as Archman sprang toward him.

"The Earthman! How—who—"

Viciously Archman jabbed the zam-gun between the spread lips and fired. The Plutonian died without a whimper, his head incinerated instantly.

Archman turned back to the door. He heard Elissa's faint cries within.

But there was no sign of a lever. How did the door open? He ran up and down the length of the cell block, looking for some control that would release the girl.

There was none.

"Step back from the door. I'm going to try to blast it open."

He turned the zam-gun to full force and cut loose. The micronite door glowed briefly, but that was all. A mere zam-gun wouldn't break through.

Angrily Archman kicked at the door, and a hollow boom resounded. Time was running short, and the girl was irretrievably locked in. The door obviously worked on some secret principle known only to the jailers, and there was no chance for him to discover the secret now.

"Elissa—can you hear me?"

"Yes." Faintly.

"There's no way I can get you out. I can't stay here; there's certain to be someone here before long."

"Go, then. Leave me here. There's no sense in both of us being trapped."

He smiled. There seemed to be a warmth in her voice that had been absent before. "Good girl," he said. "Sorry—but—"

"That's all right. You'd better hurry!"

Archman turned, stepped over the fallen form of the Plutonian jailer, and dashed the length of the dungeon, toward the winding stairs that led upward. He had no idea where he was heading, only knew he had to escape.

The stairs were dark; visibility was poor. He ran at top speed, zam-gun holstered but ready to fly into action at an instant's notice.

He rounded a curve in the staircase and started on the next flight. Suddenly a massive figure stepped out of the shadows on the landing, and before Archman could do anything he felt himself enmeshed in a giant's grip.

✺

Hendrin froze in the kneeling position, waiting for Darrien to enter the room.

The diminutive tyrant wore a loose saffron robe, and he was frowning grimly. Hendrin wondered if this were the *real* Darrien, or the duplicate he had seen before—or perhaps another duplicate entirely.

"You keep strange company, Meryola," Darrien said icily. "I thought to find you alone."

Hendrin rose and faced Darrien. "Sire—"

"Oh! The Mercurian who bought me the fair wench! I'm glad to see you here too. I have a question for the two of you."

"Which is?" Meryola asked.

Instead of answering, Darrien paced jerkily around the chamber, peering here and there. Finally he looked up.

"The girl," he boomed. "Elissa. What have you done with her?"

Hendrin stared blankly at Darrien, grateful for the hard mask of a Mercurian's face that kept him from betraying his emotions. As for Meryola, she merely sneered.

"Your new plaything, Darrien? I haven't seen her since this Mercurian unveiled her before you."

"Hmm. Hendrin, what were you doing here, anyway?"

The Mercurian tensed. "Milady wished to speak to me," he said, throwing the ball to her. In a situation like this it didn't pay to be a gentleman. "I was about to receive her commands when you entered, sire."

"Well, Meryola?"

She favored Hendrin with a black look and said, "I was about to send the Mercurian on an errand to the perfumers' shop. My stocks are running low."

Darrien chuckled. "Clever, but you've done better, I fear. There are plenty of wenches around who'll run your errands—and your supply of perfumes was replenished but yesterday." The little man's eyes burnt brightly with the flame of his malevolent intelligence. "I don't know why you try to fool me, Meryola, but I'll be charitable and accept your word for more than it's worth."

He fixed both of them with a cold stare. "I suspect you two of a conspiracy against Elissa—and you, Mercurian, are particularly suspect. Meryola, you'll pay if the girl's been harmed. And, Hendrin—I want the girl back."

"Sire, I—"

"No discussion! Mercurian, bring back the girl before nightfall, or you'll die!"

Darrien scowled blackly at both of them, then turned sharply on his heel and stalked out. Despite his four feet of height, he seemed an awesome, commanding figure.

The door closed loudly.

"I didn't expect that," Meryola said. "But I should have. Darrien is almost impossible to deceive."

"What do we do now?" Hendrin said. "The girl, milady—"

"The girl is in the dungeons, awaiting execution. She'll be dead before Darrien discovers where she is."

Hendrin rubbed his dome-like head. "You heard what Darrien said, though. Either I produce the girl or I die. Do you think he'll go through with it?"

"Darrien always means what he says. Unfortunately for you, so do I." She stared coldly at him. "The girl is in the dungeons. Leave her there. If you *do* produce the girl alive *I'll* have you killed."

Hendrin nodded unhappily. "Milady—"

"No more, now. Get away from me before Darrien returns. I want to take his mind off Elissa until the execution's past. Then it will be too late for him to complain. Leave me."

Baffled, Hendrin turned away and passed through the door into the hallway, which was dimly lit with levon-tubes. He leaned against the wall for a moment, brooding.

Events had taken a deadly turn. He had interposed himself between Darrien and Meryola, and now he was doomed either way. If he failed to restore Elissa to Darrien, the tyrant would kill him—but if he did bring back the Earthgirl, Meryola would have him executed. He was caught either way.

For once his nimble mind was snared. He shook his head moodily.

The girl was in the dungeon. The shadow of a plan began to form in his mind—a plan that might carry him on to success. He would need help, though. He would need an accomplice for this; it was too risky a maneuver to attempt to carry off himself.

The first step, he thought, would be to free the girl. That was all-important. With her dead, there was no chance for success.

Quickly he found the hall that led toward the stairs, and entered the gloomy, dark stairwell. He started downward, downward, around the winding metal staircase, heading for the dungeons where he had left the girl.

There was a sound as of distant thunder coming from below. Someone running up the stairs, Hendrin wondered? He paused, listening.

The noise grew louder. Yes. Someone was coming.

Cautiously he stepped back into the shadows of the landing, and peered downward waiting to see who was coming.

He could see, on the winding levels below, the figure—the figure of an Earthman. *By Hargo,* he thought. *It's the one who tried to buy the girl from me—Archman! What's he doing here?*

Then the Mercurian thought: *He's shifty. Perhaps I can use him.*

He ducked back into the shadows and waited. A moment later Archman, breathless, came racing up the stairs. Hendrin let him round the bend, then stepped out of the darkness and seized the Earthman firmly.

※

Lon Archman stiffened tensely as the unknown attacker's arms tightened about his chest. He struggled to free his hands, to get at the zam-gun, but it was impossible. The assailant held his arms pinioned in an unbreakable hold.

He squirmed and kicked backward; his foot encountered a hard surface.

A deep voice said, "Hold still, Archman! I don't mean to hurt you."

"Who are you?"

"Hendrin. The Mercurian. Where are you heading?"

"None of your business," Archman said. "Let go of me."

To his surprise, the blue alien said, "All right." Archman found himself free. He stepped away and turned, one hand on his zam-gun.

The Mercurian was making no attempt at an attack. "I want to talk to you," Hendrin said.

"Talk away," Archman snapped.

"Where are you coming from? What are you doing in the palace, anyway?"

"I'm coming from the dungeons, where I was tossed by some of Darrien's tunnel guards. I'm escaping. Understand that? And as soon as I'm through telling you this, I'm going to blast a hole in you so you don't carry the word back to your master Darrien."

Surprise and shock were evident on the Mercurian's face. "Escaping? From Darrien?"

"Yes."

"Strange. From our brief meeting I thought you were loyal. Who are you, Archman?"

"That doesn't much concern you." He gestured impatiently with the zam-gun, but he was reluctant to blast the Mercurian down. It seemed that the blue man was concealing something that could be important.

There was a curious expression on the Mercurian's hard-shelled face, as well. Archman looked warily around; no one was in sight. He wondered just how loyal to Darrien the Mercurian was...and if Hendrin could be used to further his own ends.

"I've just been talking to that girl you brought in here," he said. "What's she doing in the dungeons? I thought you were going to sell her to Darrien."

"I did. Darrien's mistress Meryola had a fit of jealousy and ordered the girl killed, while Darrien's back was turned."

"I see!" Archman now understood a number of things. "All's not well between Darrien and his mistress, then?" He grinned. "And you're the cause of the trouble, I'll bet."

"Exactly," said the Mercurian. "You say the girl's still in the dungeons alive?"

Archman nodded. "For the time being. She's locked in, but the jailer's dead. I killed him when I escaped."

"Hmm. I'm in a funny fix—Darrien wants me to get the girl back for him, or else he'll kill me—but if I return the girl Meryola kills me. It's a tight squeeze for me."

"I'll say." Plans were forming rapidly in Archman's mind. If he could get the girl out of the dungeon, and somehow manipulate her and this Mercurian, who was undeniably in a bad situation—

"Earthman, can I trust you to keep your tongue quiet?" Hendrin asked suddenly.

"Maybe. Maybe not."

"I'll have to take my chances then. But you're a renegade; I'll assume your highest loyalty isn't to Darrien but to yourself. Am I right?"

"You could be," Archman admitted.

"Okay. How would you like to have that girl for yourself, plus half a million credas? It can be arranged, if you'll play along with me."

Archman allowed a crafty glint of greediness to shine in his eyes, and said, "You kidding?"

"Mercurians generally play for keeps. I'm telling the truth. Are you interested? The girl, and half a million platinum credas."

"Who foots the bill?"

There was a long pause. Then Hendrin said, "Krodrang. The Overlord of Mercury. I'm in his pay."

A tremor of astonishment rocked Archman, nearly throwing him off guard. He mastered himself and said, "I thought you were one of Darrien's men. What's this about Krodrang?"

Lowering his voice and peering cautiously around the stairs, the Mercurian said: "Krodrang is one who would usurp the power of Darrien. I'm on Mars for the purpose of killing Darrien and stealing his power. If you'll play along with me, I'll see to it that you get the girl—and Krodrang is not a poor man."

Archman was totally amazed. So there were *two* assassins out for Darrien's neck! *Well,* he thought, *between us we ought to get him.*

But as he stared at the Mercurian, he knew that killing Darrien would not end the job. Hendrin would have to go, too—or else he'd get back to Krodrang with the plans for the Clanton Mine, the orthysynthetic robots, and other of Darrien's secrets, and Earth would face attack from Mercury.

It would take delicate handling. But for the moment Archman had an ally working toward the same end he was.

"Well?" Hendrin asked. "What do you say?"

"Kill Darrien and collect from Krodrang, eh? It sounds good to me. Only—how are you going to get at Darrien? Those orthysynthetic robots—"

"Meryola knows which of the Darriens is real and which a robot. And she's scared stiff that the Earthgirl's going to replace her in Darrien's affections. I've got an idea," Hendrin said, "We can play Darrien and Meryola off against each other and get everything we want from them. It's tricky, but I think you're a good man, Earthman—and I *know* I am."

He had the Mercurian's characteristic lack of modesty, Archman thought. The Earthman wondered how far he could trust the blueskin.

It looked good. As long as the Mercurian thought that Archman was simply a mercenary selling out to the highest bidder and not a dedicated Earthman with a stake of his own in killing Darrien, all would be well.

"Where do we begin?" Archman asked.

"We begin by shaking hands. From now on we're in league to assassinate the tyrant Darrien, you and I."

"Done!" Archman gripped the Mercurian's rough paw tightly.

"All right," Hendrin said. "Let's get down to the dungeon and free Elissa. Then I'll explain the plan I've got in mind."

❀

In the musty, dank darkness of the dungeon level, Archman said, "She's in that cell—the third one from the left. But I don't know how to open it. There's a Martian in there with her."

"How did that happen?"

"They came to get me—Dorvis Graal wanted to question me on some silly matter, which is why I was being held here. I decided to make a break for it. The door was closing as I ran out. The girl and the Martian were trapped inside."

"And you couldn't get them out?"

"No," Archman said. "I couldn't figure out how to open the door again. I tried, but it was no go, so I started up the stairs. Then you caught me."

The Mercurian nodded. Suddenly he stumbled and grunted a sharp Mercurian curse.

"What happened?"

"Tripped on something." He looked down and said, "By the fins I'd say it's a Plutonian. His head's been blown off with a zam-gun."

"That's the jailer," Archman said. "I killed him when I escaped."

"He would have known how to open this damned lock, too. Well, I guess it couldn't be helped. Did you try blasting this door open with your gun?"

"Wouldn't work. The door heated up, but that was all."

Again the Mercurian grunted. He began to grope along the wall, feeling his way, looking for a switch. Archman joined him, even though in the murky darkness he could scarcely see. The Mercurian's eyes were much sharper. A Mercurian needed extraordinary eyes: they had to filter out the fantastic glare of the sun in one hemisphere, and yet be able to see in the inky gloom of Mercury's nightside.

"These doors work by concealed relays," Archman said. "There ought to be a switch that trips the works and pulls back the door. That Plutonian knew where it was."

"And so do I," Hendrin exclaimed. He extended a clawed hand into one of the darkest corners of the cell block and said, "There are four controls here. I guess it's one for each of these cells. I'm going to pull the third from the left, and you get ready in case that Martian makes trouble."

"Right."

Archman drew his zam-gun and stood guard. No sound came from within; he hoped Elissa was all right. She'd been left alone with that Martian for nearly twenty minutes now. Quite possibly the tusked creature had recovered consciousness by now. Archman hoped not.

"Here goes," Hendrin said.

He yanked the switch. The relays clicked and the door slid open.

❋

Archman half expected the Martian to come charging out as soon as the door opened. He expected to be fighting for his life. He expected almost anything but what he actually saw.

The Martian was lying where he had left him, sprawled in the middle of the cell. Elissa, clad only in her single filmy garment, was squatting by the Martian's head.

As the door opened, the Martian stirred. Elissa coolly reached out, grabbed a handful of the alien's wiry skull-hair, and cracked the

Martian's head soundly against the concrete floor of the cell. The Martian subsided.

Elissa looked up, saw Archman. "Oh—it's you."

"Yes. I came back to free you," he said. "I see you've been having no trouble with your friend here."

She laughed a little hysterically. "No. Every time he started to wake up, I banged his head against the floor. But I didn't know how long I could keep on doing it."

"You don't need to any more," said Hendrin, appearing suddenly. "Archman, you'd better tie the Martian up so he doesn't give us any more trouble."

At the sight of the hulking Mercurian, Elissa uttered a little gasp. *"You—!"*

"What am I going to tie him in?" Archman asked.

"You might tear my robe up into strips," Elissa suggested, bitter sarcasm in her voice. "I've been wearing clothing for almost an hour anyway."

"That's an idea," said the Mercurian coolly. "Yes—use her robe, Archman."

The Earthman chuckled. "I don't think she intended you to take her seriously, Hendrin. I'll use my shirt instead."

"As you please," the Mercurian said.

Elissa glared defiantly at both of them. "Who are you going to sell me to now?" she asked. "You, Hendrin—you've parlayed me into quite a fortune by now, haven't you?"

Archman realized that he had told the girl his true identity. Cold sweat covered him at the recollection. If she should give him away—

To prevent that he said quickly, "Say, Hendrin, the girl's had a raw deal. I suggest we tell her what part she plays in this enterprise right now."

"Very well. I'm sorry for the mistreatment I've given you," Hendrin told her. "Unfortunately you became part of a plan. I'm on Mars for the purpose of assassinating Darrien. I'm in the pay of Krodrang of Mercury."

"And I'm assisting him," Archman said hastily, nudging Elissa to warn her not to ask any questions. "We're both working to assassinate Darrien. You can help us, Elissa."

"How?"

"Hendrin will explain," Archman said.

"I'll help you only at one condition—that you free me once whatever plan you have is carried out."

Hendrin glanced at Archman, who nodded. "Very well," Hendrin lied. "You receive your freedom once the job is done." He smiled surreptitiously at Archman as if to tell him, *The girl will be yours.*

Archman rose. "There. He's tied. All right, Hendrin: explain this plan of yours, and then let's get out of here."

He faced the Mercurian eagerly, wondering just what the blue man had devised. Archman was a shrewd opportunist; he *had* to be, to handle his job. Right now he was willing to pose as Hendrin's stooge or as anything else, for the sake of killing Darrien. Afterward, he knew he could settle the score with Krodrang's minion.

"Here's what I have in mind," Hendrin said. "Darrien and Meryola are at odds over this girl, right? Very well, then. I'll take Elissa back to Darrien—"

"No!" This from the girl.

"Just for a few minutes, Elissa. To continue: I'll take the girl to Darrien, and tell him that Meryola ordered her killed, and I'll make up enough other stories so Darrien will send out an order to execute Meryola. I think he's sufficiently smitten by Elissa to do that.

"Meanwhile, you, Archman—you go to Meryola and tell her what I've done. Tell her Darrien is going to have her killed, and suggest to her that if she wants to stay alive she'd better get to Darrien first. After that, it's simple. She'll tell you how to kill Darrien; you do it, we rescue Elissa, get Meryola out of the way somehow, and the job is done. Neat?"

"I couldn't have planned it better myself," Archman said admiringly. It was so: this was exactly as he would have handled the situation. He felt a moment of regret that he and Hendrin were working for opposite masters; what a valuable man the Mercurian would be in Intelligence!

But Hendrin would have to die too, for Earth's sake. He was a clever man. But so was Darrien, Archman thought. And Darrien would have to die.

"What about me?" Elissa asked. "Are you sure you'll get me out of this all right?"

Archman took her hand in his, and was gratified that she didn't pull away. "Elissa, we're asking you to be a pawn one last time. One more sale—and then we'll rid the universe of Darrien. Will you cooperate?"

She hesitated for a moment. Then she smiled wanly. "I'm with you," she said.

Hendrin waited nervously outside the throneroom with the girl. "You say Darrien's in there, but not Meryola?" he asked the unsmiling guard.

"Just Darrien," the guard replied.

"The stars are with us," Hendrin muttered. He took the girl's arm and they went in.

Together they dropped on their knees. "Sire!"

Darrien rose from the throne, and an expression of joy lit his warped little face. "Well, Mercurian! You've brought the girl—and saved your life."

"I did it not to save my life but my honor," Hendrin said unctuously. "Your Majesty had accused me of acting in bad faith—but I've proved my loyalty by recovering the girl for you."

Darrien came waddling toward them on his absurdly tiny legs and looked Elissa up and down. "You've been in the dungeons, my dear. I can tell by the soot clinging to your fair skin. But by whose order were you sent there?"

Hendrin glanced at the courtiers, who maintained a discreet distance but still were within hearing. "Sire, may I talk to you a moment privately?"

"About what?"

"About the girl...and Meryola."

Darrien's sharp eyes flashed. "Come with me, then. Your words may be of value to me."

The dwarfish tyrant led Hendrin into a smaller but equally luxurious room that adjoined the throne room. Hendrin stared down at the tiny Darrien, nearly half his height. Within that swollen skull, the Mercurian thought, lay the galaxy's keenest and most fiendish mind. Could Darrien be manipulated? That was yet to be seen.

One thing was certain: this was not the real Darrien before him. The tyrant would not be so foolish as to invite a massive Mercurian into a small closed room like this; it would amount to an invitation to assassinate him.

"Sire, the girl Elissa was in the dungeons at the direct order of the lady Meryola."

"I suspected as much," Darrien muttered.

"And when I arrived there, I found that the jailer was about to carry out an order of execution on Elissa, also at your lady's behest."

"*What!*"

Hendrin nodded. "So strong was the order that I was forced to kill the jailer, a worthless Plutonian, to prevent him from carrying out the execution."

"This is very interesting," Darrien mused. "Meryola rightly senses a rival—and has taken steps to eliminate her. Steps which you have circumvented, Hendrin." Gratitude shone in Darrien's crafty eyes.

"I have further news for you, Sire. When you came upon me in Meryola's chambers earlier today—it was not an errand of perfumery that brought me there."

"I hardly thought it might be."

"On the contrary—your lady was pleading with me—to *assassinate* you!"

Darrien—or the Darrien-robot—turned several shades paler. Hendrin reflected that the robot, if this were one, was an extraordinarily sensitive device.

"She said this to you?" Darrien asked. "She threatened my life?"

"She offered me five thousand credas. Naturally, I refused. Then she offered me her body as well—and at this point you entered the room."

Darrien scowled. "My life is worth only five thousand credas to her, eh? But tell me—had I not entered the room, Mercurian, would you have accepted her second offer?"

"I was sorely tempted," Hendrin said, grinning. "But pretty women are easily come by—while *you* are unique."

"Mere flattery. But you're right; Meryola has outlived her worth to me, and I see now that I'll have to dispose of her quickly." Darrien reached for the speaking-tube at his elbow. "I'll order her execution at once—and many thanks to you for this information, friend Hendrin."

※

Archman paused for a moment outside the door of Meryola's private chamber, preparing his plan of attack and reviewing the whole operation so far.

He'd been in and out of trouble—but Darrien was going to die. The mission would be accomplished. And Lon Archman would survive it.

He had a double motive for survival now. One was the simple one of wanting to stay alive; two was the fact that he now thought he had someone to stay alive *for.* Perhaps.

He knocked gently at the door.

"Who's there?"

"You don't know me, but I'm a friend. I've come to warn you."

A panel in the door opened and Archman found himself staring at a dark-hued eye. "Who are you from, Earthman? What do you want?"

"Please let me in. Your life depends on my seeing you."

A moment passed—then the door opened.

"Are you the lady Meryola?"

"I am."

She was breathtakingly lovely. She wore but the merest of wraps, and firm breasts, white thighs, were partially visible. There was a soft, clinging sexuality about her, and yet also a streak of hardness, of cold-ness, that Archman was able to appreciate. He also saw she was no longer very young.

She was holding a zam-gun squarely before his navel. "Come in, Earthman, and tell me what you will."

Archman stepped inside her chambers. She was nearly as tall as he, and her beauty temporarily stunned him.

"Well?"

"Do you know Hendrin the Mercurian, milady?"

"Indeed. Are you from him?"

"Not at all. But I know Hendrin well. He's a cheating rogue willing to sell out to any bidder."

"This is hardly news," Meryola said. "What of Hendrin."

He eyed her almost insultingly before answering. Meryola was indeed a desirable creature, he thought—but for one night only. Archman mentally compared her with Elissa Hall, who was nearly as beautiful, though not half so flashy. It wasn't difficult to see why Darrien preferred Elissa's innocence to this aging, shrewd beauty.

He smiled. "At this very moment," he said, "Hendrin is with our master Darrien. He has brought him the girl Elissa, and they are together now."

"It's a lie! Elissa's in the dungeons!"

"Would you care to call your jailers, milady?"

She stared suspiciously at him and picked up the speaking-tube. After nearly a minute had passed, she looked back at Archman. "The line is dead, Earthman."

"As is your jailer. Hendrin freed the girl and took her to Darrien. And one other fact might interest you: Darrien has tired of you. He has made out the order for your death."

"*Lies!*"

Archman shrugged. "Lies, then. But within the hour the knife will be at your throat. He vastly prefers the younger girl. Believe me or not, at your peril. But if you choose to believe me, I can save your life."

"How, schemer?"

He moved closer to her, until he was almost dizzied by her subtle perfume. "You hold the secret of Darrien's robots. Reveal it to me, and I'll destroy Darrien. Then, perhaps, another Earthman will claim your favors. Surely you would not object to ruling with *me.*"

She laughed, a harsh, indrawn laugh, and it seemed to Archman that the cat's claws had left their furry sheath. "You? So that's your motive—you ask me to yield Darrien's secret in order to place yourself on the throne. Sorry, but I'm not that foolish. You're an enterprising rascal, whoever you are, but—"

Suddenly the door burst open. Three Martians, their tusks gleaming, their thick lips drawn back in anticipation of murder, came running in.

"Darrien's assassins!" Archman cried. He had his zam-gun drawn in an instant.

The first Martian died a second later, complete astonishment on his face. A bolt from Meryola's gun did away with the second, while a third spurt finished the remaining one. Archman leaped nimbly over the bodies and fastened the bolt on the door.

Then he stooped and snatched a sheet of paper from the sash of one of the fallen Martians. He read it out loud: "To Grojrakh, Chief of the Guards: My displeasure has fallen upon the lady Meryola, and you are to despatch her at once by any means of execution that seems convenient. D."

"Let me see that!"

He handed her the paper. She read it, then cursed and crumpled the sheet. "The pig! The pig!" To Archman she said, "You told the truth, then. Pardon me for mistrusting you—"

"It was only to be expected. But time grows short."

"Right." Her eyes flashed with the fury of vengeance. "Listen, then: none of the Darriens you have seen is the real one. There are three orthysynthetics which he uses in turn. Darrien himself spends nearly all his time in a secluded chamber on the Fifth Level."

"Is the room guarded heavily?"

"It's guarded not at all. Only I know how to reach it, and so he sees no reason to post a guard. Well, we'll give him cause to regret that. Come!"

"Down this hallway and to the left," Meryola said.

This was the moment, Archman thought. It was the culmination of his plan, and the ending of a phase of history that traced its roots to a politician's pompous words years ago—"*Let Venus be our penal colony*—"

So they had planted the seeds of evil on Venus, and they had banished Darrien there to reap them. And with the destruction of Darrien's empire on Venus, they had permitted Darrien to escape and found yet another den of evil.

The end was near, now. With Darrien dead the mightiest enemy of justice in the galaxy would have been blotted out. And Darrien *would* die—betrayed by his own mistress.

They reached the door.

It was a plain door, without the baroque ornamentation that characterized the rest of the palace. And behind that door—Darrien.

"Ready?" Meryola asked.

Archman nodded. He gripped the zam-gun tightly in one hand, pressed gently against the door with the other, and heaved.

The door opened.

"There's Darrien!" Meryola cried. She raised her zam-gun—but Archman caught her arm.

Darrien was there, all right, crouching in a corner of the room, his wrinkled face pale with shock. He wore a strange headset, evidently the means with which he controlled the orthysynthetics. And he held as a shield before him—

Elissa.

This was one pleasure the tyrant had not been willing to experience vicariously through his robots, evidently. Tears streaked the girl's eyes; she struggled to escape Darrien's grasp, without success. Her flesh was bloodless where his fingers held her. There was no sign of Hendrin.

"Let me shoot them," Meryola said, striving to pull her arm free of Archman's grip.

"The girl hasn't done anything. She's just a pawn."

"Go ahead, Archman," Darrien taunted. "Shoot us. Or let dear Meryola do it."

Meryola wrenched violently; Archman performed the difficult maneuver of keeping his own gun trained on Darrien while yanking Meryola's away from her. With two guns, now, he confronted the struggling pair at the far end of the little room.

"Shoot, Archman!" Elissa cried desperately. "I don't matter! Kill Darrien while you have the chance."

Sweat beaded Archman's face. Meryola flailed at him, trying to recover her weapon and put an end to her lord and her rival at once.

The Earthman held his ground while indecision rocked him. His code up to now had been, the ends justify the means. But could he shoot Elissa in cold blood for the sake of blotting out Darrien?

His finger shook on the triggers. *Kill them,* the Intelligence agent in him urged. But he couldn't.

"The Earthman has gone cowardly at the finish," Darrien said mockingly. "He holds fire for the sake of this lovely wench."

"Damn you, Darrien. I—"

Meryola screamed. The door burst open, and Hendrin rushed in. Right behind the Mercurian, coming from the opposite direction, came one of Darrien's orthysynthetic duplicates—Darrien's identical twin in all respects, probably summoned by Darrien by remote control.

And the orthysynthetic carried a drawn zam-gun.

❋

What happened next took but a moment—a fraction of a moment, or even less.

Meryola took advantage of Archman's astonishment to seize one of his two zam-guns. But instead of firing at Darrien, she gunned down Hendrin!

The Mercurian looked incredulous as the zam-gun's full charge seared into his thick hide, crashing through vital organs with unstoppable fury.

Meryola laughed as the blue Mercurian fell. "Traitor! Double-dealer! How—"

The sentence was never finished. The zam-gum in the hand of Darrien's double spoke, and Meryola pitched forward atop Hendrin, her beauty replaced by charred black crust.

Archman snapped from his moment of shock, and his gun concluded the fast-action exchange. He put a bolt of force squarely between the orthysynthetic's eyes, and a third body dropped to the floor.

From behind him came a cry. "Archman! Now! Now!"

He whirled and saw, to his astonishment, that Elissa had succeeded in breaking partially loose from Darrien. Archman's thoughts went back to that moment in Blake Wentworth's office when, in a drug-induced illusion, he had won the right to participate in this mission by gunning down a Martian across the vast distances of the red desert. His marksmanship now would count in reality.

His finger tightened on the zam-gun.

"You wouldn't dare shoot, Earthman!" Darrien said sneeringly. "You'll kill the girl!"

"For once you're wrong, Darrien," Archman said. He sucked in his breath and fired.

A half-inch to the right and his bolt would have killed Elissa Hall. But Archman's aim was true. Darrien screamed harshly. Archman fired again, and the tyrant fell.

✸

He found himself quivering all over from the strain and tension of the last few moments. He looked around at the grisly interior of the room. There lay Hendrin, the shrewd Mercurian, who had played one side too many and would never live to collect his pay from Krodrang. There, Meryola, whose beauty had faded. There, the Darrien-robot. And there, Darrien himself, his foul career cut short at last.

"It's over," he said tiredly. He looked at Elissa Hall, whose lovely face was pale with fear. "It's all over. Darrien's dead, and the mop-up can begin."

"Your aim was good, Archman. But you could have fired at Darrien before. My life doesn't matter, does it?"

His eyes met hers. "It does—but you won't believe that, will you? You think I'm just a killer. All right. That's all I am. Let's get out of here."

"No—wait." Suddenly she was clinging to him. "I—I've been cruel to you, Archman—but I saw just then that I was wrong. You're not just the murderer I thought you were. You—you were doing your job, that's all."

He pulled her close, and smiled. He was thinking of Intelligence Chief Wentworth, back on Earth. Wentworth had rated Archman's capabilities at 97.003%. But Wentworth had been wrong.

Archman had done the job. That was 100% efficiency. But he had Elissa now, too. Score another 100%. He gently drew her lips to his, knowing now that this mission had been successful beyond all expectations.

NEW YEAR'S EVE—2000 A.D.
(1957)

My meeting with William L. Hamling of Imagination and Imaginative Tales at the 1955 Cleveland s-f convention had led almost immediately to yet another steady writing contract for me. Hamling, a dapper, youthful-looking Chicagoan who, like me, had loved science fiction since his teens, had been Ray Palmer's managing editor for the Ziff-Davis science-fiction magazines in the late 1940s, and when the Ziff-Davis company moved its editorial offices to New York in 1950 Hamling remained in Chicago, starting his own Chicago-based publishing outfit, Imagination, his first title, was a decent enough lower-echelon s-f magazine, but not even such major names as Robert A. Heinlein and James Blish could get its sales figures up much beyond the break-even point, and in the summer of 1955 Hamling decided to emulate his friend Howard Browne of Amazing and revert to the tried-and-true Ziff-Davis formula of uncomplicated action fiction written to order by a team of staffers. The lead stories for the book would be done by such veteran pulp-magazine stars as Edmond Hamilton and Dwight V. Swain. For the shorter material he turned to the same quartet that was producing most of Browne's fiction: Lesser, Fairman, Garrett, and Silverberg. Evidently he figured that our capacity for turning out s-f adventure stories to order was infinitely expandible, and, as it happened, he was right. On January 16, 1956, I got this note from my agent, Scott Meredith:

"We sent one of your yarns to Bill Hamling. While he couldn't use this yarn, he's going to write you directly to tell you what he wants in the way of plotting, etc. He does like your stuff and will want to see a lot more of it *in the future. You'll know better what to expect when you get his letter, and then you can get right to work."*

Hamling's letter followed a month or so later. What he wanted was short, punchy stories with strong conflicts, lots of color and action, and straightforward resolutions. And he made a very explicit offer: the Garrett-Silverberg team was invited to deliver 50,000 words of fiction a month, all lengths from short-shorts up to 7500 words or so, and we would be paid $500 for each monthly package.

At that point we were each writing a couple of stories a month for Browne and doing our novelet series for Campbell, and I was sending out solo stories to such editors as Lowndes, Shaw, and Gold as well. And I was still a Columbia undergraduate, starting the second half of my senior year. But college would soon be behind me and by this time I had dauntless confidence in my own prolificity. We accepted the deal. The first package, six stories, went off to Hamling in June, 1956. Early in July we sent him five more, and toward the end of that month another six, and seven in August before I took time off to get married. And so it went, month after month. The $500 checks—$5000 or thereabouts in modern purchasing power—arrived punctually and we split them fifty-fifty regardless of who had written the stories in each package.

I could not tell you, this long after the fact, which of us actually wrote most of these stories. As I look at them now, some seem to be entirely Randall's work, some appear to be exclusively mine, and others must have been true collaborations, begun by one of us and finished later the same day by the other. The names under which the stories appeared provide no clue, because Hamling ignored the pseudonyms we put on the manuscripts ("T. H. Ryders," "William Leigh," "Eric Rodman," "Ray McKenzie," etc.) and randomly stuck bylines of his own choosing on them—"Warren Kastel," "S. M. Tenneshaw," "Ivar Jorgensen," and many another. Sometimes he would put my own name on a story, and sometimes Garrett's, and in several cases stories written entirely by Garrett appeared under my name and stories written entirely by me appeared under his. Some of these switched stories I can still identify: I know my own stylistic touches, and I also know the areas where Garrett's superior knowledge of chemistry and physics figured in the plot of a "Silverberg" story that I could not possibly have written then. But it's a hopeless job to correct the Silverberg and Garrett bibliographies now to indicate that on occasions we found ourselves using each other's names as pseudonyms.

The little story here, "New Year's Eve—2000 A.D.," from the September, 1957 issue of Imaginative Tales—*came out under the "Ivar Jorgensen" name. That byline was originally the property of Paul W. Fairman but was transformed by Browne and then Hamling into a communal pseudonym. This one was wholly my work. I know that not only because such very short stories as these were almost always written by one or the other of us, not both, but also because I am the sort of pedantic guy who believed that the twenty-first century would not begin until January 1, 2001, as one poor sap tries to argue in this story. (I knew better, when the twenty-first century really did come around a few years ago, than to waste breath voicing that point of view.) I think the story is an amusing artifact. I was wrong about the date of the first lunar voyage by 31 years, but I was right on the nose about the premature celebration of the new century at the dawning of Y2K.*

George Carhew glanced at his watch. The time was 11:21. He looked around at the rest of the guests at the party and said, "Hey! Thirty-nine more minutes and we enter the Twenty-First Century!"

Abel Marsh squinted sourly at Carhew. "How many times do I have to tell you, George, that the new century won't begin for another *year*? 2001 is the first year of the Twenty-First Century, not 2000. You'll have to wait till next year to celebrate that."

"Don't be so damned picayune," Carhew snapped. "In half an hour it'll be the year 2000. Why *shouldn't* it be a new century?"

"Because—"

"Oh, don't fight over it, boys," cooed Maritta Lewis, giggling happily. She was a tall brunette with wide eyes and full lips; she wore a clinging synthoplast off-the-bosom blouse and a sprayon skirt that molded her hips and long legs. "It's whatever century you want it to be, tonight! Twentieth! Twenty-first! Don't get an ulcer, dad. Live it up!"

She climbed out of the web-chair she had been decorating and crossed to the bar. "Come on, you two grouches. What kind of drinks can I get you?"

"Dial me a Four Planets," Carhew said.

"Okay, spaceman. How about you, Abel?"

"Old-fashioned whiskey sour for me. None of these futuristic drinks." He grinned. "I still believe its the twentieth century, you see."

Maritta dialed the drinks and carried them back across the room to the two men, narrowly avoiding spilling them when a wildly dancing couple pranced past.

Carhew took his drink, observing the firm swell of the girl's breasts before him. "Care to dance, Maritta?"

"Why, sure," she said.

He sipped at the hopefully-named Four Planets, then put it on the low ebony table near him and stood. Maritta seemed to float into his arms. She wore some new scent, pungent and desirable.

Carhew drew her tightly to him, and the music billowed loudly around them. They danced silently for a while.

"You seem moody, George," she said after a few moments. Something troubling you?"

"No," he said, but from the tone of his voice it might as well have been *Yes*.

"You worry too much, you know? I've only known you for an evening, and I can see you're a worrier. You and that man you came in with—that Abel. Both of you stiff and tense, and snapping at each other about nothing at all. Imagine, quarrelling over whether next year is the Twentieth or the Twenty-first Century!"

"Which reminds me—" Carhew glanced at his watch. "It's 11:40. Twenty minutes to midnight."

"You're changing the subject. Why don't you come down to Dr. Bellison's when the holiday is over."

Carhew stiffened suddenly. *"Bellison! That quack? That mystic—!"*

"You don't understand," she said softly. "You're like all the rest. But you haven't experienced Relativistic Release, that's all. You ought to come down sometime. It'll do you a world of good."

❋

Feeling chilled, Carhew stared at the girl in his arms. Heldwig Bellison's Relativistic Release philosophy was something new, something that had come spiralling out of Central Europe via jetcopter in 1998 and was busily infecting all of America now.

He didn't know too much about it. It was, he knew, a hedonistic cult, devoted sheerly to pleasure—to drug-taking and strange sexual orgies and things like that. It seemed to Carhew, in the room's half-light, that the girl's eyes were dilated from drugs, and that her face bore the signs of dissipation. He shuddered.

No wonder she was so gay, so buoyant! Suddenly he no longer felt like dancing with her. He moved mechanically until the dance was over, then left the floor and headed for his seat.

"You still haven't answered me, George. Will you come down to the clinic when the holiday's over?"

He sipped at his drink. "Don't ask me now, Maritta. Wait till later— till I'm really drunk. Then ask me. After midnight. Maybe by then I'll be anxious to see Dr. Bellison. Who knows?"

She giggled. "You're funny, George. And Abel, too. What do you two do for a living?"

Carhew exchanged a glance with dour Abel Marsh. Marsh shook his head imperceptibly.

"We're...designers," he said. "Draftsmen. Sort of engineers."

"Sounds frightfully dull."

Carhew was glad she didn't intend to pursue the line of questioning too much further. "It is," he said.

He raised the Four Planets to his lips and drained it.

"Be a good girl, will you, and get me another drink?"

"Sure. One Four Planets, coming up."

"No," he said. "This time I'll have a screwdriver—with lots of vodka."

"Switching drinks in midstream, eh? Okay, if you want to live dangerously!"

Carhew studied the girl's trim form as she crossed the room to the bar. She was a lovely, langorous creature; it was a pity she belonged to that horrid cult. Carhew wondered how many men she had had already. He and Marsh had had time for very few dates in the past three years; he knew little about women. Tonight was their first really free night since 1998.

And even tonight, tension hung over them. An unanswered question remained to be answered.

Carhew glanced at his watch. "Eleven forty-nine," he said. "Eleven more minutes."

"Eleven minutes to A.D. 2000," Marsh said.

"Eleven minutes to the Twenty-First Century."

"Twentieth."

"Twenty-first!"

"Twentieth!"

Maritta reappeared with the drinks.

"Are you two still bickering over that silly business?" she asked. "You're like a couple of babies. Here's your drink, George."

Carhew took the drink from her and gulped at it, almost greedily. The vodka affected him rapidly; he felt his head starting to spin.

"Well," he said "Twentieth or Twenty-first....doesn't matter much....anyone got the time?"

"Eleven fifty-one," Marsh said.

"That means—nine more minutes." Carhew finished his drink. "I think I'll have another one," he said.

*

This time he weaved his way across the room to the bar and dialed his own—a martini, this time.

He sensed warmth behind him, and turned to see Maritta pressing gently against him. "You'll get sick if you keep switching drinks," she said.

"Maybe I want to get sick," he said. "Maybe I see this whole sick crazy drug-ridden world and I want to get just as sick as it is." *I'm getting sober,* he thought. *Don't want to do that.*

He made out the time dimly. Eleven fifty-five. Five more minutes. Five minutes to the Year 2000. Dull tension started to mount inside him.

"You look awfully worried," Maritta said. "I really think you should see Doctor—"

"Told you not to ask me that until after midnight. Wait till I'm good'n drunk. Maybe I'll say yes then."

He finished his cocktail, laughed crazily, and let the glass fall to the floor. It crashed against the leg of an iron table, and shattered, tinkling. "Too bad," he said. "Guess I broke the glass. Guess so."

"You're drunk," she said.

"Good. But not drunk enough."

The room was starting to blur around him now; couples whirled by in a wild dance, and he could hardly see. From somewhere, the music began again.

"Let's dance," he suggested, and staggered forward into the girl's arms.

They danced. While they spun around the room, someone turned on a radio. The announcer's voice said, "Ladies and gentlemen, the time is now Eleven Fifty-Nine. In just one minute, the world will welcome a new year—and a new century, some claim, though purists insist that—"

Yeah, he thought. *Purists like Marsh.*

Somewhere inside his mind he was conscious that he ought to be at the window, looking out, when midnight came. He had one minute. Less than that, now. Fifty seconds. Forty-five. Forty.

Maritta's lips touched his in a lingering kiss. He felt her body straining against his, while somewhere within him his mind went on counting. Thirty-five. Thirty. Twenty-five.

Twenty.

"Excuse me," he said thickly. "Gotta go look out the window."

Fifteen.

He sensed Abel Marsh standing next to him, pressing the button that would clear the opaqued window and make it possible for them to look out.

Ten. Nine. Eight.

The window cleared. Outside the night was black except for a few billion city lights and the round silver dollar up above that was the moon.

Seven. Six.

A current of excitement started to build up in Carhew. He saw the girl clinging to his arm. The three of them stared outward at the silent skies.

Five. Four. Three. Two.

ONE!

"It's twelve midnight," the announcer said. "We enter the Year 2000!"

Suddenly a bolt of light split the sky—a shaft of white flame that leaped up from the Earth and sprang through the heavens, lighting up the entire city and probably half the continent. A burning, searing bolt of light.

Carhew felt suddenly sober. He looked at Marsh.

Behind them, the radio blared: "We bring you now a special announcement relayed from White Sands Rocket Base. One minute ago, at the stroke of midnight, the Rocket Ship *Moonflight* made a successful blastoff. It was the first time in the history of humanity that man has broken forth from the bonds of Earth in a manned spaceship. We expect to bring you further bulletins throughout the night. Landing on the moon itself is scheduled for eight A.M. on New Year's Day."

Carhew was smiling. He looked at Abel Marsh, his fellow engineer on the project. "Well, we made it," he said hoarsely. "The ship took off."

"Happy New Year!" someone yelled. "Happy New Century!"

It didn't matter much now, Carhew thought, which century this was. Not now. Twentieth or twenty-first, it made no difference.

All that counted was that this was the Age of Space.

THE ANDROID KILL
(1957)

Here, from the November, 1957 Imaginative Tales, is one of the stories from the batch that Garrett and I sent to Bill Hamling in October, 1956. This is another one that I'm pretty sure I wrote entirely on my own.

It's an okay little chase story, but its big significance for me is that Hamling published it under the byline of "Alexander Blade," the first time one of my stories had appeared that way. As I mentioned in the introduction to "Guardian of the Crystal Gate," such powerful Alexander Blade stories as "The Brain" (Amazing, October 1948) and "Dynasty of the Devil" (Amazing, June 1949) had wowed me back when I was still too young to shave. Now, a mere nine years later, right around the time I was contemplating growing the beard that has been my trademark for the past forty-some years, I had become Alexander Blade myself!

I was crazy to leave Laura here alone for a minute, I was thinking, as the space-liner roared through the atmosphere toward the spaceport at Rigel City. Even though the mighty ship was travelling at a thousand miles an hour, I kept urging it onward, down toward the port. I had to get there on time. Had to.

I kept picturing the way the riot-torn city must look, now that the long-festering hatred for synthetic android men had burst loose into a full-scale android kill. Clay Armistead had finally stirred up the riot his

167

sick mind craved. And I had picked this week to make a business trip and leave my wife alone—alone, in the heart of the riot.

I counted the seconds until the spaceship would land. I had cut short my business trip the second I had heard of the riots, had caught the first liner back to Rigel City to find Laura and get her out of danger's path.

The ship landed. *"Unfasten deceleration cradles,"* came the impersonal order from the loudspeakers, but I had already done that. I raced down the companionway, past a startled stewardess, shoved my way through a little knot of uniformed baggage-androids and grabbed my suitcase. There wasn't any time to waste.

Quickly, the moment the catwalk for passengers was open, I dashed through the hatch and out into the bright, warm air of Rigel City. The giant sun was high above; it was a pleasant spring day.

And then all the pleasantness vanished. I saw the mob, pushing and shouting and shoving, at the far end of the landing field. It was an ugly sight. They looked like so many buzzing bees, each of them inflamed with killing-lust and brutality.

I passed through the checkout-desk in record time and on through the Administration Building, listening to the sounds of the mob. Somehow, they had smelled out the fact that there were androids aboard the starship that had just arrived, and they were determined to get them.

Well, that wasn't my worry. I was concerned only with Laura.

A sleek taxi pulled up in front of me and waited, its turboelectric engine throbbing quietly. The driver was a human; I was startled not to see the familiar red star on his forehead. He looked at me coldly, without the politeness of the android cabby.

"Where to, fellow?"

"Twenty-fourth and Coolidge," I said, and started to get in. "On the double."

"Sorry, Mac. Coolidge is out of bounds. I'd be crazy to take my hack through there. I'll drop you at Winchester. Okay?"

I frowned, then nodded. It meant a ten-minute walk, but it was better than nothing. "Good enough," I said, and started for a second time to enter.

I got one leg inside the cab. Then a hand grabbed me from behind, pulled me out, and I was swung around.

"Where the hell you think you're going—you damned *android?*"

For a second, I was too startled even to get angry. There were three men facing me—cold-eyed, hard-faced men with hatred naked in their features. I recognized them, contorted though their faces were.

Clay Armistead—the chief rabble-rouser, a burly, squat, ugly man who had been spreading lies about the synthetic men for years.

Roger Dubrow, tall, athletic, Armistead's partner in their food-store business and his partner in villainy as well, it seemed.

Dave Hawks, a local tough just riding along for the fun.

"Android?" I said. "Is this a game, Armistead? You've known me for ten years. I'm no more of an android than you are. Let go of me!"

I wrenched my arm free and turned to my taxi—but the driver shook his head nervously and stepped on the accelerator. *He* wasn't looking for trouble.

"Come here, android," Hawks said. "C'mere and lemme rough you up." He snatched at my suitcase, grabbed it away, tossed it to one side.

"Hold it, Hawks." I looked from one face to the next. They looked alike—cold, menacing, ugly: "You know as well as I do that androids have red stars on their foreheads. Stop this nonsense, and go play your games elsewhere."

I still couldn't take them seriously. It was impossible for an android to masquerade as a human, and they knew it. Why were they accusing me, then? It was fantastic.

"Those red stars can be obliterated, Preston," Armistead said, in a cold, tight voice. "It's a secret the androids have kept for years. But now we know. We know you're synthetic, Preston. And we're going to get you!"

It was incredible. It was unbelievable. But it was happening, here in my own city, on the world where I'd lived all my thirty years. And suddenly, I was fighting for my life against three of my neighbors who were positive I was a synthetic man!

Out of the corner of my eye, I saw Dave Hawks moving on me. The sounds of the mob were chillingly close, and I knew I'd be in for trouble for sure if the entire swarm got here while the three ringleaders were working someone over. I'd be ripped to pieces before I knew what was happening.

Hawks closed and swung. His punch landed above my eye. I blinked away the pain and crashed a fist into his midsection. At the same time, Dubrow joined in. Armistead held back and watched.

An open-handed blow from Dubrow knocked me sprawling.

"Look at the android," Dubrow gloated. "Look at him flat on his back!"

I kicked upward viciously and sent Dubrow over backward screaming in pain. Hawks dove savagely, and we went rolling over and over. I
was getting numb from the fighting; all I wanted to do was find Laura
and get out of this madhouse, and instead—

"Finish him off!" Armistead hissed. "The cops are coming!"

Sirens wailed. The Rigel City police—badly outnumbered, unable
to handle the rioting in its full intensity—had heard of the outbreak at
the spaceport and were on their way. Dubrow and Hawks clung to me,
their fists pounding into me. I struck back, blindly, clawing, scratching,
kicking. Blood trickled down my face—*real* blood. Human blood. But
they didn't care.

"Come on, android! Fight!" A palm crashed into my cheek; another into my throat. Choking, gasping, I rose to my feet with desperate
determination. My clothes were in tatters, my suitcase gone.

I grabbed Hawks, swung the burly man around, sent him crashing
into Dubrow and Armistead. Without waiting to see what would happen,
I began to run. Just run, blindly, without direction. Running away. I was
running for my life, and I still didn't quite believe it was all happening.

❂

I ran. I ran through the tangled mob of people, through the screaming, yelling, hysterical android-hating people of Rigel City. Bullets whined
overhead, and here and there I could see the bright flash of a disruptor-
pistol warning the outraged crowd back. There was no stopping them.

I kept running. I reached the fence that bordered the spaceport, ran
until I found an exit gate. There was a guard patrolling it, but I went by
so fast he didn't know what had happened.

My heart was pounding and my lungs seemed to be quivering
under the strain. And right down in my stomach was a cold hard knot
of fear. Not so much for myself directly—I was too numb for that. But
I was afraid for Laura.

"Do you *have* to go to Trantor, darling?" she had asked. "I'll miss you."

"I'll miss you too, darling," and it had been the truth. "But we can't
afford both to go—and I can't afford *not* to go. You know that."

"I know, all right. But still—"

I had left her behind, and had been gone eight days. Only eight
days—but in that time, Clay Armistead had fanned the smoldering
human-android antagonism into a full-scale android kill.

The streets were nearly deserted as I raced into the heart of Rigel City. Up ahead, I could see fires burning—fires, no doubt, coming from shops of android shopkeepers. We had tried to live side by side, androids and men, identical in everything except birth, but it seemed doomed to failure.

I kept running, my legs moving almost mechanically. I passed one of the burning stores. It was John Nealy's beauty parlor, and in the smoke and fiery shadows I could see figures moving about.

Someone emerged, face covered with soot. It was Lloyd Garber, a sedate, wealthy accountant—now wildeyed with fury. He saw me.

"Hey, Preston! Come give us a hand!"

I stopped. "Are you mixed up in this too, Garber?"

"We've got Nealy in here," Garber said, ignoring my question. "We're making him watch while we burn his store. We need some help."

As Garber spoke, an expensive hairdrying machine came hurtling through the open door. There was a scream of anguish from within, and I thought I recognized the voice of android John Nealy, ladies' hairdresser extraordinary. Androids tended to go into unmasculine businesses like that, I thought. Maybe that was why people like Clay Armistead hated them so.

I paused, wondering if I should take time out to help Nealy, when another soot-smeared figure emerged from the store. He was so blackened I couldn't recognize him, but he waved his arm as soon as he saw me.

"Hey, Garber—there's Cleve Preston!"

"Yeah, I know," Garber replied. "I was just—"

"Didn't you hear what Armistead said? Preston's an android! He's been hiding the red star all his life!"

"*What?* But I—"

I didn't stick around to see what would happen. Nealy would have to fend for himself. I dodged around the corner and ran as fast as I could. Footsteps pursued me for a while, and then I was alone. I kept on running.

It was a nightmare. The city was totally gripped by the android kill. How many of the inoffensive synthetic men were dead already I had no way of knowing—but I was sure Armistead and his men would not rest until every red-starred forehead had felt the boot.

And why me? Why had Armistead suddenly decided *I* was an android, and made me the object of hatred along with the true synthetics? For a dizzy moment I nearly began to feel like an android myself.

There had been other android kills before, on other planets, in other cities. I had read about them; I had sympathized with the persecuted underdogs, had felt gratitude that it wasn't happening here, to me and my family.

But now it *had* happened here—and it was happening to me. I was one of the hunted now, and a chill gripped me as I tried not to think of Laura's probable fate.

Blind, unreasoning hatred was on the loose in Rigel City. And there was nothing I could do but run.

✸

I reached my home about an hour later—or rather, what *had* been my home.

In the slanting late-afternoon shadows, it was a sight that nearly made me cry. I had bought an inexpensive but attractive bubble-home six years before, when Laura and I were married. It hadn't been much, but it had been ours. It *had* been.

Now, it looked as if it had been in the path of a juggernaut. The door was smashed in, the interior charred and seared, the furnishings torn, books and drapes and chairs floating in puddles of dirty water. I moved from room to room, numb, too numb to cry.

Chalked on the wall of the room that had been my study was a simple, crude message:

ANDROIDS DON'T DESERVE TO LIVE LIKE THIS
—C.A.

C.A.—Clay Armistead! And again the accusation of android.

My home destroyed, my wife kidnapped or dead, I walked dazedly down the steps to the street and slouched at the edge of the curb. Night was coming now, and the four moons glittered coldly above, shining without sympathy. There was no sympathy in the world, I thought—only hatred.

I had lost everything I loved within eight days. In the distance, I heard the sound of shouting and killing. It was quiet here, in the residential district of Rigel City, but I could imagine what it must have been like the day they did *this* to my home.

As I sat slouched there, a voice from above me said, "It's a tough break, Preston."

I spun to my feet instantly and turned to face the speaker. It was Ken Carpenter, my next-door neighbor, who stood above me. I reached out and grabbed him by the throat.

"Go ahead, Carpenter—call me an android too! Pull out a gun and kill me! You can't take anything else from me!"

"Whoa!" Carpenter said, in a choked voice. "Easy, Cleve. I had nothing to do with this."

Suspiciously, I released my grip. He rubbed his throat for a moment or two. "You're pretty quick on the trigger, aren't you?"

"I have to be," I said. "In the last couple of hours I've learned it's the only way to stay alive."

"I guess you're right," Carpenter said. "I don't blame you for wanting to kill, either." He shook his head sadly. "I watched the whole thing, Cleve. It was awful."

His face was red, and he couldn't meet my eyes. "You helped, didn't you?" I asked. I wasn't even angry.

He said nothing, but words weren't necessary. I could see the guilt unconcealed on his face.

After a pause he spoke. "I had to," he said hoarsely. "They—they came here. Armistead asked me to help." He lowered his head. "They would have done the same thing to my house if I refused. I—I had to, Cleve."

"Okay," I said. "You've got a wife and family too. I won't hold any grudge." It was the truth. I probably would have done the same thing. If Carpenter had made any move to save my house, he would only have brought destruction needlessly on his own head.

I moistened dry lips. "Tell me where Laura is," I said.

"Armistead took her away," Carpenter said quietly.

"Took her away? Where?"

"Just before they burned your house," said Carpenter. "Armistead went in himself and came out with your wife. They put her in a car and drove away with her."

"They didn't hurt her?"

Carpenter shook his head. "She gave them quite a fight, but I didn't see them hurt her. They just took her away."

"You know they're calling me an android, don't you?" I asked.

He nodded. "Armistead started spreading that around yesterday afternoon. There was a big gang outside your house and they took Laura away. I went outside to find out what was happening, and Armistead said they were going to burn your place because you're an android." He looked at me suspiciously for a second. "It's not true, is it? I mean—"

"No, it's not true!" I said angrily. "How did all this start? This riot, I mean."

"Well, you know how it's been between humans and androids here—sort of an uneasy truce for years. And you know how Armistead feels about equal rights for them. Well, two days ago an android murdered Mary Cartwright."

"What?"

Mary was another neighbor of ours, a young housewife from down the block. She was a good friend of Laura's; they spent a lot of time together.

"But Mary was in favor of android equality," I said in confusion. "Why would—"

Carpenter shrugged. "It happened, that's all. It was a particularly vicious murder. As soon as word got around, Armistead got up and said it was time we got rid of the androids in Rigel City, before they killed the rest of us."

I was stunned. The androids were peaceful, likable folk, who kept to themselves and were well aware of the consequences of an act such as this. "How do they know it was an android?" I asked. "Are they sure?"

"Positive. The android was caught in the act."

"By whom?"

"Armistead. He—"

"That's enough," I said in sudden disgust. The whole crude plot was painfully obvious now. Armistead had had Mary Cartwright murdered by his own henchmen, and had framed an android. He had then used this "evidence" as provocation to touch off an android kill—and the reign of terror was still going on. The municipal authorities were probably paralyzed; the police force was pitifully inadequate, and in all likelihood half of them had joined the rioters anyway.

Anti-android hatred was an easy thing to stir up. The synthetic men and women were too handsome, too intelligent, too perfect—too easy to envy and to hate. The three centuries since their development had been marked by a steady history of riots such as this one.

Only now it was here, right here, and I was caught up in the middle of it.

And Laura? Where was she?

Suddenly I felt the desire to wring Clay Armistead's thick neck.

✦

I started to walk, without knowing where I was going. I just felt that I had to get moving, to walk off the overpowering frustration and fear and hate I was feeling.

Half an hour later, I found myself in a part of Rigel City I had never been in before—the oldest part of town, almost a slum. Here things were quiet. There was no sign of the rioters. Maybe the riot was dying down finally; maybe all the androids were dead or in hiding.

It was now night. The air was becoming chilly, and I felt cold and alone.

A figure moved in front of me. Someone was lurking in the shadows. Instantly, I went on guard.

The prowler was circling toward me in the dimness, and I saw the gleam of a knife suddenly against the dull black of the night. I poised myself and waited for the attack. I was becoming accustomed to violence as the normal activity of life.

Curiously, the man in the shadows remained there. We froze, boxing each other in uneasily, each waiting for the other to spring. Finally he stepped forward, knife upraised.

I moved forward to meet him, and as the knife descended my hand shot up to intercept the other's arm. I clamped my hand around his wrist and held him there. We stared into each other's faces.

In the flickering light of the four moons I could see him plainly. His features were even and regular, and he would have been handsome but for the raw, jagged gash across one cheek. Imprinted in the center of his forehead was a neat, five-pointed red star.

He was an android.

"You're Cleve Preston, aren't you?" he asked.

I nodded.

"You can let go of me, then. I won't stab you." There was something in his voice that made me trust him, and I let go. He sheathed the knife and looked curiously at me. "So you're one of us! I heard Armistead shouting it."

"Sorry," I said. "You're wrong. I'm no more of an android than Armistead is. He's just framing me for some motive of his own."

"But—"

As the knife started to raise again, I quickly said, "But I'm on your side! I'm being hunted like an android, and so I'm fighting like one. I'm with you, whoever you are."

"George Huntley," the android said. "I thought you were a human—I mean, one of the rioters. I couldn't take any chances. I've been hiding in the back alleys here ever since the thing started."

"I understand."

"They took your wife, didn't they?" he asked suddenly.

"How did you know?"

"I saw them," he said. "She's in Armistead's headquarters. His supermarket. That's the headquarters for the whole thing, you know."

The supermarket was in the heart of town, about half an hour's quick walk further on. "The place must be guarded," I said. "Can we get in?"

"They'll kill you on sight!" Huntley said.

"I have to get in there," I told him. "My wife is in there. Do you understand that? My *wife.*"

"Yes, but—all right, come on! You and me—we'll go in there and get your wife!"

❋

It was a strange alliance—a human being everyone accused of being an android, and a genuine android whose life was forfeit if he got caught. I stood a chance—just a chance.

We arrived at Armistead's supermarket near midnight, approaching it cautiously from the rear. There was a crowd milling around outside, talking and strutting, probably busy telling each other about their day's exploits in killing and looting. I shuddered as I saw them—complacent, proud of their day's work.

"How are we going to get inside?" I asked. "There must be a hundred of them."

He rubbed his forehead nervously, fingering the damning star. Unconsciously, he seemed to be rubbing some of the grime away so the mark of his non-humanity stood out more clearly. "Don't worry," he said. "There's a side window. You go in, and I'll follow you."

"How about the alarm?"

"You want your wife?" the android asked.

"I want to stay alive," I said.

"You will," Huntley said, and prodded me to keep heading forward. After a few minutes he said, "I'd like your wife to get free too."

"What business is it of yours?"

He looked at me squarely. "Androids have brothers," he said. "Vat-mates, really, but we feel a pretty close affection. My brother was the android who supposedly murdered Mary Cartwright. Armistead's butchers cut him down before he could deny it."

"Sorry to hear that," I said.

"You know something else? Your wife was the only witness to the murder of Mary Cartwright."

Suddenly I went stiff all over. The puzzle came clear now. Laura had seen the killing, had seen the android murdered too. Perhaps it had happened in our house, our backyard. No wonder Armistead had her put away for safe keeping—it was a miracle he hadn't just killed her. That also explained why *I* was being hunted—to get me out of the way, to keep me from reaching her and exposing the truth.

"Now you see?" the android asked.

"I see," I said. "If we can get Laura out, it'll clear your brother's name. It'll—"

"Stop talking," he said. "It's time for action."

We were practically at the back of the sprawling supermarket building now. We stood at the first-floor window for a second, and I looked back at Huntley.

"Well?"

"Smash the window and go in," Huntley said. "I'll take care of the alarm. There's nothing to worry about."

"I don't understand," I said. "How—"

"*Go on!*"

I grabbed a stone and smashed in the window. The bells began to ring. And then I saw how the android George Huntley had been planning to take care of the alarm.

❋

He gave me a shove that knocked me halfway through the window. I turned and saw him starting to run. For a second I felt betrayed—then horrified.

He was running toward the front of the building, straight toward the crowd of android killers standing out there. And he was shouting, "Come get me! Catch me if you can!"

He had deliberately sacrificed himself. I heard them yelling, heard the sound of footsteps as they started to pursue him, ignoring the alarm.

I had no further time to waste. I leaped over the sill, found the alarm switch, threw it. The supermarket became still.

I began to pick my way through the darkened storeroom, through the heaps of baskets and crates, toward Armistead's office. I was confident that I would find Armistead there.

I did.

He was sitting with his back to the door, talking on the phone.

"What's that? Crazy android ran right past the store and they're all chasing him? I was wondering about that. The alarm bell just went off here, and it must have been the same guy. Musta broke a window in back first."

He kept on talking. I stopped listening. I was looking at Laura.

She sat tied up in one corner of the room, her eyes wide with astonishment at the sight of me. She seemed to be in pretty good shape. Her blouse was torn, her skirt was slashed to the thigh, and I could see bruises and scratches that made me wince. But they hadn't hurt her. That was all that mattered. Home, books, furniture—as long as they hadn't hurt Laura, what did the other things matter?

"Hello, Armistead," I said. I stepped inside and slammed the door. "I came to pay you a little visit."

He whirled, threw down the phone, and came toward me all in the same motion. He was a thick-bodied, ugly man, and there was strength in his arms and legs. He charged. I waited for him, and hit him in the face. Blood trickled out over his split lip, making him look even uglier.

"Goddamn android," he muttered.

I laughed. "You're starting to believe your own lies, Armistead. And that's bad." I hit him again. His eyes blazed, and he struck out at me wildly. He was strong, but he wasn't used to fighting. He was a talker. He let other people do his fighting for him.

For a minute I felt that I really *was* an android—or, at least, that I was fighting for all the synthetic men who had died since the first one had left the laboratory three centuries ago. My fists ploughed into Armistead's belly, and he rocked on his feet. His eyes started to look glassy.

He got in one more punch, a solid one that closed my already-battered eye. And then I moved in on him.

"That's for Centaurus," I said, and hit him. "That's for Rigel. That's for Procyon." I went on, naming all the places where there had been anti-android rioting. By the time I was finished, Armistead lay in a huddled, sobbing heap on the floor.

I untied Laura, kissed her, and trussed Armistead up against the chair.

"It's good to see you, honey," I told her.

"I thought you'd never come back," she said.

I turned to Armistead and snapped on the portable tape-recorder on his desk. "Okay, Armistead. I want a full confession of the way you provoked this riot. Begin with the way you had Mary Cartwright killed, and keep moving from there." I hit him again, just by way of loosening his tongue.

From somewhere in the front of the supermarket, I heard someone yell, "Hey, Armistead! We got another!"

The "other" must have been Huntley. I clamped my lips together. Armistead was beginning to speak, slowly, unwillingly. The whole dirty story was going down on tape.

Any minute, the townspeople would be in here to report the happy news to Armistead. But I was going to have a full confession by that time, and I was going to make them listen to every bit of it. I was going to make sure that George Huntley's sacrifice hadn't been in vain.

THE HUNTERS OF CUTWOLD
(1957)

Harlan Ellison, who had been living next door to me in the summer of 1955 as my writing career suddenly and spectacularly took off, had a somewhat slower start himself, but by the middle of 1956 he, too, was selling stories about as fast as he could write them. Just as I had been, he was an avid science-fiction reader who longed to have his own stories published in the magazines he had read in his teens, and very quickly he joined Howard Browne's team of staffers at Amazing *and placed material with three or four other titles.*

But he had a knack for writing crime stories too—tales of juvenile-delinquent kid-gangs were a specialty of his—and in the summer of 1956 he struck up a relationship with two new magazines that published that sort of thing, Trapped *and* Guilty. *They paid an extravagant two cents a word, twice as much as what most of the science-fiction magazines we were selling to then would pay, and their editor, one W. W. Scott, seemed willing to buy as many stories as Harlan could bring them. Harlan was good enough to let me in on this bonanza, and, busy as I was meeting my monthly quota at* Amazing *and* Imagination, *I started doing crime stories too. My records show the sale of "Get Out and Stay Out" to* Guilty *in June, 1956, and "Clinging Vine" to* Trapped *a couple of weeks later.*

And then W. W. Scott announced that he had been asked to edit a science-fiction magazine too, Super-Science Fiction, *and Harlan and I suddenly had the inside track on a lucrative new market.*

Scott—"Scottie," everybody called him, except a few who called him "Bill"—was a short, cheerfully cantankerous old guy who would have fit right into a 1930s Hollywood movie about newspapermen, which was what I think he had been before he drifted into magazine editing. His office was tiny and crammed with weary-looking manuscripts that such agents as Scott Meredith, delighted to find a possible new market for ancient stuff that had been rejected everywhere, sent over by the ton. His voice was a high-pitched cackle; he had a full set of top and bottom dentures, which he didn't always bother to wear; and I never saw him without his green eyeshade, which evidently he regarded as an essential part of the editorial costume. To us—and we both were barely past 21—he looked to be seventy or eighty years old, but probably he was 55 or thereabouts. He freely admitted to us that he knew next to nothing about science fiction and cared even less, and invited us to bring him as much material as we could manage.

We certainly did. Getting an open invitation like that from a two-cents-a-word market was like being handed the key to Fort Knox. In late June I wrote "Collecting Team" for him, which he published as "Catch 'em All Alive" in the first issue—December, 1956 of Super-Science. (Under its original title it has been reprinted dozens of times in school readers.) I also did a batch of science fillers for Scottie to use in rounding off blank pages—little essays on space exploration, computer research, and an interesting new drug called LSD. Harlan had a story in that first issue, too, and two in the second one. (I was too busy to do anything but science fillers for that issue.) The third issue had one Ellison and one Silverberg story; the fourth, two of mine, one of his. And so it went, month after month. As I got into the swing of it, I began doing longer pieces for the magazine. A 12,000-word story—and I was writing at least one for almost every issue from the fifth number on—paid $240, more than the monthly rent on my West End Avenue apartment, and I could turn one out in two working days.

By 1957, Harlan had moved along to an army base, having been careless enough to let himself get drafted, and the job of filling the pages of Super-Science Fiction, Trapped, and Guilty devolved almost entirely on me. Just as well, too, because I didn't have good personal chemistry with Paul Fairman of Amazing and Fantastic and he had begun to cut back on buying stories from me. Around the same time, Bill Hamling found that the sales figures of Imagination and Imaginative Tales were trending sharply downward, leading him to buy fewer stories from his staff and soon afterward to kill both magazines. My writing partnership with Randall Garrett had ended, too, at the urging of my wife, Barbara, who disliked Garrett intensely and didn't want him coming around to see me. Faced with the loss of my two most reliable markets and the separation from my collaborator,

THE HUNTERS OF CUTWOLD

I needed to be fast on my feet if I wanted to go on earning a decent living as a writer, and so I made myself very useful to W. W. Scott indeed. For Trapped *and* Guilty *I wrote bushels of crime stories ("Mobster on the Make," "Russian Roulette," "Murder for Money," etc., etc., etc.) and for* Super-Science Fiction *I did two or three stories an issue under a wide assortment of pseudonyms. At two cents a word for lots and lots of words I could support myself very nicely from that one market.*

"The Hunters of Cutwold," which I wrote in April, 1957 for the December, 1957 Super-Science Fiction *under the pseudonym of Calvin M. Knox, is typical of the many novelets I did for Scottie: stories set on alien planets with vivid scenery, involving hard-bitten characters who sometimes arrived at bleak ends. I suspect I derived the manner and some of the content from the South Sea stories of Joseph Conrad and W. Somerset Maugham, both favorite writers of mine. Scholars who have been writing theses on such Conrad-influenced novels of mine as* Downward to the Earth *and* Hot Sky at Midnight, *published at much later stages of my career, please take note.*

I t was morning on Cutwold, fifth planet in the Caveer system. And there would be betrayal by nightfall, Brannon knew. He knew it the way he knew the golden-green sun would rise, or the twin, blank-faced moons. He knew it ahead of time, half-sensing it with the shadowy precognitory sense that made him so terribly valuable as a guide in the deadly forests of Cutwold.

He crouched in the sandy loam outside his cabin, staring down the yet-unpaved street, a lean tanned figure with thin sharp-curving lips and deepset sepia eyes that had seen too much of the galaxy and of men. He was waiting for the betrayal to begin.

He did not have to wait long.

The morning had started like all the others: at dawn Caveer broke through the haze, showering its eight worlds with golden-green brightness, and moments later on Cutwold the dawnbirds set up their keening icy shriek as if in antiphonal response. Brannon always rose when the dawnbirds' cry was heard; his day began and ended early.

It was eleven years since he had drifted to Cutwold when the money ran out. For eleven years he had led hunting parties through the vine-tangled Cutwold forests, keeping them from death by his strange foresight. He had made some friends in his eleven years on Cutwold, few of them human.

It was eleven days since he had last had any money. This was the off season for hunting. The tourists stayed away, amusing themselves on the pleasure-worlds of Winter V or losing themselves in dream-fantasy on the cloud-veiled planets in Procyon's system. And on Cutwold the guides grew thin, and lived off jungle vines and small animals if they had not saved any money.

Brannon had not saved. But when the dawnbirds woke him that morning, something in their shrill sound told him that before noon he would be offered work, if he wanted it…and if his conscience could let him accept.

He waited.

At quarter past ten, when hunger started to grab Brannon's vitals in a cold grasp, Murdoch came down the road. He paused for a moment where Brannon crouched, looking down at him, shading his eyes from the brightness of the sun.

"You're Kly Brannon, aren't you?"

"I am. Hello, Murdoch."

The other stared. He was tall, taller even than Brannon, with shadows shading his craggy face. Strange suns had turned Murdoch's face a leathery brown, and his eyebrows were a solid thick worm above his dark eyes, meeting. He said, "How did you know my name?"

"I guessed," Brannon said. He came slowly to his feet and met Murdoch's eyes, an inch or two above his own. He moistened his lips. "I don't want the job, Murdoch."

Somewhere in the thick jungle a scornful giant toad wheezed mockingly. Murdoch said, "I haven't said anything about any jobs yet."

"You will. I'm not interested."

Calmly, Murdoch drew a cigarette-pack from his waistpouch. He tapped the side of the pack; the magnetic field sent a cigarette popping three-quarters of the way out of the little jeweled-metal box. "Have one?"

Brannon shook his head. "Thanks. No."

Murdoch took the extended cigarette himself, flicked the igniting capsule on its tip, and made an elaborate ceremony out of placing it in his mouth. He puffed. After a long moment he said, "There's ten thousand units cold cash in it for you, Brannon. That's the standard guide fee multiplied by ten. Let's go inside your shack and talk about it, shall we?"

Brannon led the way. The shack was dark and musty; it hadn't been cleaned in more than a week. Brannon's few possessions lay scattered about carelessly. He had left Dezjon VI in a hurry, eleven years before, leaving behind everything he owned save the clothes on his back. He hadn't bothered to accumulate any property since then; it was nothing but a weight around a man's neck.

He nudged the switch and the dangling solitary illuminator glowed luminously. Brannon sprawled down on an overstuffed pneumochair that had long since lost its buoyancy, and gestured for his visitor to take a chair.

"Okay," Brannon said finally. "What's the deal?"

※

Murdoch waited a long moment before speaking. A gray cloud of cigarette smoke crept about his face, softening the harsh angularity of his features. At length he said, "I have been told that a race calling themselves the Nurillins lives on this planet. You know anything about them?"

Brannon flinched, even though his extra sense had warned him this was coming. His eyes slitted. "The Nurillins are out of my line. I only hunt animals."

Sighing, Murdoch said, "The Extraterrestrial Life Treaty of 2977 specifically designates one hundred eighty-six life forms as intelligent species and therefore not to be hunted, on pain of punishment. The Treaty Supplement of 3011 lists sixty-one additional life forms which are prohibited to game hunters. I have both those lists with me. You won't find the Nurillins of Cutwold named anywhere on either."

Brannon shoved away the two brown paper-covered documents Murdoch held out to him. "I don't want to see the list. I know the Nurillins aren't on them. But that doesn't mean they aren't people. They ran away into the interior of the forests when humans settled on Cutwold. When the survey team made up the lists, they didn't have any Nurillins to judge by. Naturally they weren't included."

Murdoch nodded. "And thus they are free game to any hunters. I've brought a party of nine to Cutwold, Brannon. They're interested in hunting Nurillins. They say you're the only man on Cutwold who knows where the Nurillins are." Murdoch drew a thick bankroll from his pouch and held it by the tips of finger and thumb. "Ever see this much money before, Brannon?"

"Ten thousand? Not all in one lump. But it's too much. All you need to offer is thirty pieces of silver."

Murdoch whitened. "If that's the way you feel about this job, you—"

"The Nurillins are human beings," Brannon said tiredly. Sweat streamed down his body. "I happened to stumble over their hiding-place one day. I've gone back there a few times. They're my friends. Am I supposed to sell them for ten thousand units—or ten million?"

"Yes," Murdoch said. He extended the bankroll. "Until the Galactic Government declares them otherwise, they're fit and legitimate quarry for hunting parties, without fear of legal trouble. Well, my clients want to hunt them. And I happen to know both that you're the only man who can find them for us, and that you don't have a cent. What do you say?"

"No."

"Don't be stubborn, Brannon. I've brought nine people to Cutwold at my own expense. I don't get a cent back unless I deliver the goods. I could make it hard for you if you keep on refusing."

"I keep on refusing."

Murdoch shook his head and ran lean strong fingers through the blue-died matting of close-cropped hair that covered it. He looked peeved, more than angry. He jammed the bankroll into Brannon's uneager hand. "I want nine Nurillin heads—no more, no less. You're the man who can lead us to them. But let me warn you, Brannon: if we have to go out into that jungle ourselves, without you, and if we happen to come across your precious Nurillins ourselves, we're not just going to settle for nine heads. We'll wipe out the whole damned tribe of them. You know what a thermoton bomb can do to animals in a jungle?"

Brannon's mind had already pictured the fierce white brightness of the all-consuming flash. "I know," he said hoarsely. His eyes met Murdoch's: metal against metal. After a long silence Brannon said, "Okay. You win. Get your party together and I'll lead them."

News travelled fast on Cutwold. It was noon by the time Brannon reached the main settlement, noon by the time he had rid his mind of the jangling discord of Murdoch's stony presence.

He came down the lonely road into the Terran settlement alone, and blankfaced men turned to look at him and looked away again, knowing he carried a hundred hundred-unit bills tucked carelessly in his hip pocket, and hating him for it. The road at noon was sunbaked and hot: squat diamond-backed reptiles with swollen heads hopped across the path, inches from Brannon's feet.

There were perhaps fifty thousand Terrans on Cutwold, located in six settlements scattered over the face of the planet. It was a warm and fertile planet, good mostly for farming and hunting, weak on minerals. Once there had been a few thousand Nurillins living where the Terrans now lived; remnants of a dying race, they had fled silently into the darkly warm depths of the forest when the first brawling Earthman arrived.

Kly Brannon had discovered the Nurillins. Everyone knew that. Whether it had been through some trick of his extra sense or by sheer blind luck, no one knew. But now everyone also knew that Brannon had sold the Nurillins out to a hard-faced man named Murdoch for a roll of bills. They could see it in Brannon's eyes, as he came down out of the lonely glade where he had built his shack.

He was supposed to meet Murdoch and his nine nimrods at two-thirty. That left Brannon a couple of hours and a half yet to soak the bitterness out of himself. He stopped in at a shingled hut labelled VUORNIK'S BAR.

Vuornik himself was tending bar, a sour-faced Terran with the pasty puffy flesh of a man who spent his time indoors. Seven or eight settlers were in the bar. They turned as Brannon kicked open the door, and swivelled their heads away again as they saw who it was.

"Morning, Vuornik. Long time no see."

The barkeep swabbed a clean place at the bar for Brannon and rumbled, "Nothing on the cuff today, Brannon. You know the rules here. I can't stretch your credit any."

"I didn't say a word about credit. Here, Vuornik. Suppose you give me a double khalla, straight, and honest change for this bill."

With elegant precision Brannon peeled a hundred off the roll Murdoch had given him, and laid it in the outstretched, grasping, fleshy palm of the barkeep. Vuornik stared at the bill strangely, rubbing it between the folds of flesh at the base of his thumb. After a moment he poured Brannon a drink. Then he went to the till, drew forth a fifty, two twenties, a five, and four singles, shuffled them into a neat stack, and handed them to Brannon.

"You ain't got anything smaller than hundreds?" Vuornik asked.

"All I have is hundreds," said Brannon. "Ninety-nine of them plus change."

"So you took the job, then," Vuornik said.

Brannon shrugged. "You told me no more drinks on the cuff. A man gets thirsty without money, Vuornik."

He raised the mug and sipped some of the thin greenish liquor. It had a hard cutting edge to it that stung his throat and slammed into his stomach solidly. He winced, then drank again. The raw drink eased some of the *other* pain—the pain of betrayal.

He thought of the gentle golden-skinned people of the forest, and wondered which nine of them would die beneath the blazing fury of hunters guns.

A hand touched his shoulder. Brannon had anticipated it, but he hadn't moved. He turned, quite calmly, not at all surprised to find a knife six inches from his throat.

❋

Barney Karris stood there, eyes bleared, face covered by two days' stubble. He looked wobbly, all of him but the hand that held the knife. That was straight, without a tremor.

"Hello, Barney," Brannon said evenly, staring at the knife. "How's the hunting been doing?"

"It's been doing lousy, and you know it. I know where you got all that cash from."

From behind the bar, Vuornik said, "Put that sticker away, Barney."

Karris ignored that. He said, "You sold out the Nurillins, didn't you? Murdoch was around; he talked to me. He got your address from me. But I didn't think you'd—"

Vuornik said, "Barney, I don't want any trouble in my bar. You want to fight with Brannon, you get the hell outside to do it. Put that knife out of sight or so help me I'll blast you down where you stand."

"Take it easy," Brannon murmured quietly. "There won't be any trouble." To Karris he said, "You want my money, Barney? That why you pulled the knife?"

"I wouldn't touch that filthy money! Judas! Judas!" Karris' redrimmed eyes glared wildly. "You'd sell us all out! Aren't you human, Brannon?"

"Yes," Brannon said. "I am. That's why I took the money. If you were in my place you'd have taken it, too, Barney."

Karris scowled and feinted with the knife, but Brannon's extra sense gave him ample warning. He ducked beneath the feint, pinwheeled, and shot his right arm up, nailing Karris in the armpit just where the fleshy part of the arm joined the body. Knuckles smashed into nerves; a current of numbness coursed down Karris' arm and the knife dropped clatteringly to the floor.

Karris brought his left arm around in a wild desperate swipe. Brannon met the attack, edged off to the side, caught the arm, twisted it. Karris screamed. Brannon let go of him, spun him around, hit him along the cheekbone with the side of his hand. Karris started to sag. Brannon cracked another edgewise blow into the side of Karris' throat and he toppled. He landed heavily, like a vegetable sack.

Stooping, Brannon picked up the knife and jammed it three inches into the wood of the bar. He finished his drink in two big searing gulps.

The bar was very quiet. Vuornik was staring at him in terror, his pasty face dead white. The other eight men sat frozen where they were. Karris lay on the floor, not getting up, breathing harshly, stertorously, half-sobbing.

"Get this and get it straight," Brannon said, breaking the frigid silence. "I took Murdoch's job because I *had* to. You don't have to love me for it. But just keep your mouths shut when I'm around."

No one spoke. Brannon set his mug down with exaggerated care on the bar, stepped over the prostrate Karris, and headed for the door. As he started to push it open, Karris half-rose.

"You bastard," he said bitterly. "You Judas."

Brannon shrugged. "You heard what I said, Barney. Keep your mouth shut, and keep out of my way."

He shoved the door open and stepped outside. It was only twelve-thirty. He had two hours to kill yet before his appointment with Murdoch.

❁

He spent two hours sitting on a windswept rock overlooking the wild valley of the Chalba River, letting the east wind rip warmly over his face, blowing with it the fertile smell of rotting vegetation and dead reptiles lying belly-upmost in tidal pools of the distant sea.

Finally he rose and made his way back toward civilization, back toward the built-up end of the settlement near the spaceport, where Murdoch was waiting for him.

When Brannon entered the hotel room, it was Murdoch's face he saw first. Then he saw the other nine. They were grouped in a loose semicircle staring toward the door, staring at Brannon as if he were some sort of wild alien form of life that had just burst into the room.

Murdoch said, "I want you all to meet Kly Brannon. He's going to be our guide. He's spent eleven years hunting on Cutwold—really knows the place. Brannon, let me introduce you to the clients."

Brannon was introduced. He eyed each of them in turn.

There were four couples, one single man. All were Terrans. All looked wealthy, all looked bored. Typical tourist-type hunters, Brannon thought in weary contempt.

At the far left was Leopold Damon and his wife. Damon was fat and bald and looked to be on his second or third rejuvenation; his wife was about his age, puffy-eyed, ugly. They were probably tougher than they looked.

Next to them sat the Saul Marshalls. Marshall was a thin dried-out man with glittering eyes and a hooked ascetic nose. His wife was warmer-looking, a smiling brunette of thirty or so.

At their right was Clyde Llewellyn and his wife. Llewellyn was mild, diffident-looking, a slim redhaired man who seemed about as fierce as a bank clerk. His wife—Brannon blinked—his wife was a long, luxurious, cat-like creature with wide bare shoulders, long black hair, and magnificent breasts concealed only by sprayon patches the size of a one-unit coin.

The fourth couple consisted of Mr. and Mrs. Fredrik Rhawn, two sleek socialites, flawless of face and form, who seemed to have been turned out on a machine lathe. Next to them sat the loner, Rod Napoli, a burly, immensely broad man with thick features and gigantic hands.

"Mr. Napoli lost his wife on our previous tour," Murdoch said discreetly. "It—ah—explains the uneven number we have."

"I see," Brannon said. Napoli didn't look particularly bereaved. He sat inhaling huge gulps of air at each breath, looking like a highly efficient killing machine and nothing else.

"Well, now you've met everyone," said Murdoch. "I want you to know that this group is experienced in the ways of hunting, and that you're not just guiding a group of silly amateurs." His eyes narrowed. "Our goal, as you know, is the Nurillin."

"I know," Brannon returned acidly. "That's already been made clear."

"When would you like to start?" Murdoch asked.

"Now," said Brannon.

"Now?"

"Now?" said Fredrik Rhawn, half-rising. "So soon? But we just had lunch. I mean, couldn't we hold this thing over till tomorrow?"

"I'd like to get started," Brannon said stubbornly. He added silently, *the quicker the better. I want to get this thing over with.*

Rhawn's wife murmured something to him, and he said, "All right. It's foolish of me to hold everyone back, isn't it? We're ready to go any time."

"Good," Murdoch said. He glanced at Brannon. "Our equipment is packed and ready. We're at your disposal."

"Let's go, then," Brannon said.

* * *

Brannon estimated privately that the trip would take two days of solid march. He had found the Nurillins after only little more than a day's journey out of the settlement, but that was when he was alone and moving at a good pace.

They left the settlement single file at three-thirty that afternoon, Brannon in the lead, followed by Napoli, who lugged along the handtruck carrying their supplies and provisions, and then, in order, the Rhawns, the Damons, the Marshalls, and the Llewellyns, with Murdoch last of all, just back of radiant Marya Llewellyn.

Two days. As Brannon pushed on slowly through the thick forest, slashing down the clinging vines as he went, the thought of spending two days with these people was intolerable, the thought of the quest they were on impossible to carry in his mind. When he thought of the soft-voiced Nurrillins and the few happy days he had spent with them, and now realized that he was bringing nine trophy-happy tourists through the woods to their secret hiding place—

He shook his head. Behind him, Napoli said, "Something wrong?"

"Damned fly buzzing in my ears. They'll eat you alive if you let them."

Napoli chuckled. They moved on.

Brannon was sure the tourists knew what the Nurillins were. That just added an extra twist to it. Murder was punishable by life imprisonment, which in these days of hundred-fifty-year lifespans was ten times as dreadful as capital punishment. Since detection was almost unavoidable, people rarely murdered.

But *legal* murder—ah, that was another thing. All the thrill of destroying a thinking, breathing, intelligent creature, with none of the drawbacks. In the early days of stellar expansion, the natives of a thousand worlds had been hewn down mercilessly by wealthy Terrans who regarded the strange life forms as "just animals."

To stop that, the Extraterrestrial Life Treaty of 2977 had been promulgated, and its supplement. From then on, none of the creatures listed could be shot for game. But there still were other worlds, newer worlds, worlds which had been missed in the survey. And races such as the Nurillins, with but a handful of members. The Nurillins had retreated when the Terrans came, and so they had been missed by the Treaty-makers.

And so they were still free game for the guns of Rod Napoli and Leopold Damon and anyone else willing to pay for their pleasure. Brannon scowled.

A vine tumbled down out of nowhere and splashed itself stickily across his face. He slashed it out of the way with his machete and pushed on.

He knew the forest well. His plan was to take the most circuitous route possible, in hopes that Murdoch would never be able to find his way to the Nurillins again. Accordingly he struck out between two vast cholla-trees, signalling for the others to follow him.

Suddenly Murdoch called out, "Hold it up there, Brannon! Mrs. Damon wants to rest."

"But—"

"*Hold it,*" Murdoch snapped. There was urgency in the hunt director's voice. Brannon stopped.

He turned and saw Mrs. Damon sitting on a coarse-grained gray rock at the side of the footpath, massaging her feet. Brannon smiled and revised his estimate upward. It was going to take *three* days to get there, if this kept on happening with any regularity.

Murdoch said, "Brannon, could I see you for a minute as long as we've stopped?"

"Sure," Brannon said. "What is it?"

Murdoch had drawn away from the others somewhat and stood at a distance, with Marya Llewellyn. Her husband was paying no attention; he had joined the group that stood around Mrs. Damon. Brannon sauntered over Murdoch.

"Are you taking us in the right direction?" Murdoch asked abruptly.

Surprised—for his foresight did not work all the time—Brannon glanced at Marya Llewellyn. The girl was staring at him out of dark pools of eyes, darker even than her jet hair. She wore only shorts and the sprayon patches over her breasts; she looked at him accusingly and said, "I don't think we're heading the right way."

"How would *you* know?" Brannon snapped.

Murdoch smiled coldly. "You're not the only one with heightened sensory powers, Brannon. Mrs. Llewellyn has a peculiar and very useful gift of knowing when she's going toward a goal and when she isn't. She says the route you just took doesn't feel right. She says it doesn't lead straight to the Nurillins."

"She's right," Brannon admitted. "What of it? I promised I'd get you there, and I will. Does it make any difference if I take a slightly roundabout route? *I'm* the guide, don't forget."

"I haven't forgotten it. And I'll let you continue on this path another hour or so, provided we don't get any further off the course. But I thought I'd warn you that Marya here will be able to detect it any time you try to fool us. Any time you deliberately try to get us lost, she'll tell me about it."

Brannon looked stonily at her. He said nothing.

"Losing your charges in the jungle is attempted murder," Murdoch went on. "I'd feel entirely justified in shooting you down if necessary."

Brannon's jaws tightened. "For the benefit of you and your little bloodhound here, I'm doing my best. I'll get you to the Nurillins. And if it's okay with Mrs. Damon, I'd like to get moving again right now."

❂

An hour later, they were still moving. Dark shadows were scudding across the sky now, and the forest was thickening into jungle—jungle where death might wait behind any tree or under any pebble. But still Brannon kept moving.

Knowing that Marya Llewellyn had some strange way of sensing direction didn't alter his plans any. He had intended from the first, whatever Murdoch's suspicions were, to lead the party sooner or later to the Nurillins. Brannon had been around; he never deluded himself with false hopes. Murdoch had hired him to lead them there, and Murdoch would not settle for less.

The nine tourists said little as they proceeded. They were lost in the strangeness of Cutwold.

Cutwold—or Caveer V, as the starcharts called it—was a warm, almost tropical world, heavily forested, heavily inhabited by life of all sorts. Once in its history it had spawned an intelligent species, the Nurillins. But they had been too gentle for Cutwold, and when Brannon had discovered them they were in the final throes before race extinction, with perhaps ten generations remaining to them if they kept out of man's way.

The forest was speaking, now. Crying abuse at the man who led ten others on a mission of murder.

The giant frogs, those cynical toothy amphibians half the size of a man, were honking scornfully from either side of the path. Further back originated the deep moaning bellow of the groundsnakes, and Brannon heard also the endless yipping of the little blue dogs that raged through the forest in murderous packs. He sensed nervousness spreading over his charges as night approached.

Above, Caveer, the golden-green sun that Brannon, in a forgotten past, had said was the loveliest he had ever seen, was dropping toward the horizon. Jonquil, first of the identical featureless moons of Cutwold, glimmered palely in the still-blue sky; Daffodil yet lay hidden in the nestling clouds of day, but soon would break forth and with its sister spiral across the night sky.

Then was the time of fear, in the forest—when the moons were bright.

Brannon plodded methodically forward through the darkening forest, dragging his ten charges along as if they were tied to his back. Somewhere ahead lay the refuge of the unsuspecting Nurillins; somewhere ahead lay a soft-eyed alien girl who had spoken kindly to him once long ago, and who now would receive her reward.

Karris' accusing words burned his soul.

Judas. Judas.

It wasn't so, Brannon protested silently. It wasn't so. If they only could see *why* he was doing this—

They couldn't. To them he was a Judas, and Judas he would remain.

He stopped, suddenly. His jungle-sensitive ears, aided by the vague blur of a foresight in his mind, picked up the sound of feet drumming against forest soil. Hundreds of feet.

"What's the trouble?" Murdoch asked.

"Pack of wild dogs coming this way," said Brannon. "Let's pull into a tight circle and wait them out."

"No!" Mrs. Marshall gasped suddenly. "No!"

Her ascetic-faced husband turned to her, skin drawn so tight over his face he looked mummified. He slapped her, once; a white blotch appeared on her face, rapidly turning red. "Keep quiet," he said.

"That goes for all of you," snapped Brannon. "They won't bother us if they have some other quarry. Stay still, try not to move—and if any of you lose your heads and fire into the pack, you won't live to fire a second time."

He listened, tensely. First came the thump-*thump* of some large beast, then the pat-*pat*-pat of dogs, hundreds of them, in fierce pursuit.

"Here they come," Brannon said.

※

The quarry came first, bursting out of the thick wall of vegetation that hemmed in the pathway on both sides. It was a Cutwold bull, eleven feet through the withers, a monster of a taurine with yellow curved horns two feet long jutting from its skull.

Now the bubbly slaver of fear covered its fierce jaws, and the thick black hide was slashed in a dozen places, blood oozing out steadily. The vanguard of the attacking force rode with the bull: two small blue dogs who clung to the animal's hind legs, snapping furiously, hoping to slice through the hamstring tendon and bring the bull crashing to the ground.

The pack is hungry tonight, Brannon thought.

He had only a moment's glimpse of the bull; then it was gone, blasting its way through the yielding underbrush, and only the sound of its snorting bleats of terror remained. But then came the pursuers.

Brannon had learned to fear the blue dogs of Cutwold more than the poison-trees or the velvet snakes or any of the other deadly jungle creatures he knew. The dogs were built low to the ground; they were whippet-like creatures whose claws could rend even the armor-thick leather of the giant bull, whose teeth bit the toughest meat, whose appetites never reached satiety. They burst into the clearing and streamed across the road so fast one dog appeared to melt into its successor, forming an unending lake of blue, a blur broken only by the glinting of their red eyes and snapping teeth.

Brannon remained quite still, standing with his group. The women were frozen, fearstruck; Napoli was staring at the dog horde with keen interest, but the other men appeared uneasy. Brannon counted minutes: *one, two, three...*

The numbers of dogs thinned until it was possible to see daylight between them. Off in the distance a cry of chilling intensity resounded: the bull had been brought to earth. Good, Brannon thought. The dogs would feed tonight, and for a while at least would keep away.

One last dog burst through the trampled brush. And paused.

And turned inquisitively, guided by who knew what mad impulse, to sniff at the clustered huddle of human beings standing silently in the jungle path.

It bared its teeth. It drew near. The rest of the pack was out of sight, almost inaudible. Suddenly Clyde Llewellyn lowered his heavy-cycle gun and sent three bullets smashing through the dog's body and skull, even as Brannon reached out to prevent it.

The dog fell. Savagely Brannon smashed Llewellyn to the ground with one backhanded swipe. "You idiot! Want to kill us all?"

The mildness vanished from the little man's face as he picked himself up. He started to go for his gun; Brannon tensed, but this time it was Murdoch who caught hold of Llewellyn. He shook him twice, slapped him.

"We've got to get moving now," Brannon said. "The dogs are blood-crazy tonight. They'll be back here any minute, as soon as the wind drifts the scent to them." He pointed up the road. "Go on! Start running, and don't stop!"

"What about you?" Murdoch asked.

"I'll back you up. Get going."

He watched as they ran ahead. As they passed out of sight, Brannon lifted the dead dog and heaved it as far in the opposite direction as he could. The yipping grew louder; the pack was returning.

They came a moment later, muzzles coated with red, smelling new blood. Brannon crouched beside the thick trunk of a quaa-tree, waiting. The dogs paused in the clearing, sniffed the air, and, ignoring Brannon, set off toward their dead companion.

Brannon turned and ran up ahead, rejoining the others.

They were waiting for him.

"The dogs are off our trail," he said. He looked at the sullen-faced Llewellyn. A bruise was starting to swell on the side of his face. "You're lucky I didn't shoot you down as you deserved," Brannon told him.

"Don't talk like that to my clients," said Murdoch.

"Your client nearly got us all killed. I specifically told you all to hold fire."

"I didn't like the looks of that dog," said Llewellyn. "He looked dangerous."

"One dog isn't half as dangerous as a pack. And one live dog won't draw a pack; a dead one will, when the blood gets into the air."

"Is the whole trip going to be like this?" Mrs. Rhawn asked suddenly. "Dangerous?"

Brannon took a deep breath before replying. "Mrs. Rhawn, you're on Cutwold to commit murder, whether you know it or not. The animals you're hunting are people, just like you and me. Murder is never easy. There's always danger. It's the price you pay for your sport."

Around the circle, faces whitened. Murdoch was taut with anger. Brannon looked inquisitively at him, but no reply was forthcoming.

Then he glanced upward. Both moons were high above, now, and the sun was barely visible, a lime-colored flicker hovering above the horizon, half intersected by the vaulting trees. It was getting late. It was almost time to make camp for the night.

"Let's move along," Brannon said.

✦

For half an hour more they hacked their way deeper into the jungle, until it was obviously too dark to travel further that day. Brannon marched at the head of the file, eyes keen for danger, ears listening, mind shrouded in black thoughts.

Behind him came the others. *Nine thrill-killers,* he thought. Nine allegedly civilized human beings who were spending fabulous sums for the privilege of gunning down other beings coolly and consciencelessly.

It would be so easy, Brannon told himself, to lose these nine and their coordinator in the jungle—despite Marya Llewellyn. There were so many pitfalls to right and left of the main path: the carnivorous trees that waited, leaves quivering, for something meaty to trap their tropisms and plunge into a network of catch-claws. The giant toads whose tongues could flick out and snarl themselves around a man's throat in an unbreakable lariat's grip. All Brannon needed to do was lead them a short distance from the beaten path—

But that was the coward's solution. No, he told himself. He would bring them to their destination, for only that would fully serve his purpose.

Above, a nightbird squawked in the sky, calling, *"Keek! Keek! Keek!"*

On Cutwold day was heralded by the dawnbirds, night by the nightbirds. It was a system more efficient than clocks. Brannon said, "Okay. We stop here. Drop your packs and let's set up the shelter."

Under Murdoch's direction the plastic tent-bubble went up within minutes, puffing out of the extrusion panel carried for the purpose. Brannon patrolled the area, burning a wide swath around the camp with his flamer, as a signal to wildlife to stay away during the night. Unless they were ravenous, they would respect the singed circle of vegetation.

He left a fire outside the tent hatch that would last all night. Then he crawled inside. The others were already within their sleeping packs, though none were asleep. Brannon ventured a private guess that few of them would sleep soundly this night. The jungle was noisy—noisier, perhaps, for those with this sort of hunt in mind.

The Rhawns were talking in low whispers. Brannon caught Mrs. Rhawn saying, "...I don't think I trust that guide too much. He looks so strange, and *tense.*"

Her husband glanced at Brannon, who was staring at the ground. "Hush! I think he can hear us."

Smiling, Brannon looked away. The others were gathering in for the night, trying to sleep. Brannon stepped outside, peered at the now almost entirely dark sky. The two moons hung overhead like two lanterns, casting shadows through the trees.

An animal was prowling outside the singed circle, sniffing the ground, staring strangely at the intruders who had broken the jungle peace.

He turned away and returned to the tent, found an unoccupied corner, and slouched to the ground. He was thinking.

Thinking of a stubblefaced man in a bar who had cried *Judas* at him, and of ten thousand Galactic Currency Units that was his fee for this trip, and of a time three years before when he had gone off into the jungle on a solitary quest, and found—

The Nurillins.

❀

It had been a warm day in the twelfth month of Brannon's eighth year on Cutwold. He had been without work for three weeks, without money for two, and had gone on a foraging mission into the jungle.

At least foraging had been the ostensible reason. Actually he was searching—searching for something deeper than he could understand, out there. He needed to get away from the men of the settlement; that much he knew. So he struck out on his own, deep into the jungle.

The first day had been routine. He covered his usual quota of hiking miles, shot three small succulent birds and roasted them for his meal, dined on the sweet stems of kyril-shoots and the slightly bitter wine of the domran plant. At nightfall he camped and slept, and when the keening shriek of the dawnbirds woke him he rose and continued on, travelling unknowingly and uncaringly the same route that three years later he would cover with a party of wealthy killers.

Then he had no idea where he was going. He put one foot before the other and forged on, pausing now and then to stare at some strange plant or to avoid some deadly little reptile or insect.

Somewhere on that second day, he ran into trouble.

It began with the *thrum-thrum* of a giant toad in a thicket of blue-leaved shrubs. Brannon turned, reaching for his gun—and as he turned, a sudden thrumming came from the other side of the path, as well. He whirled—and found he was caught between two of the great squat amphibians!

He took two half-running steps before a sticky tongue lashed out and caught him round the middle. The thicket parted, and he saw his captor, vast mouth yawning, bulging yellow eyes alight with anticipation. Brannon clawed desperately at the gummy pink ribbon that held him fast, but there was no escaping it. He dug his feet deep in the rich soil, braced himself—

The other toad appeared. And snared him as well.

He stood immobile, tugged in two directions at once, with two gaping toad-mouths waiting to receive him the moment the other yielded. The pressure round his middle was unbearable; he started to wish that one or the other would release him, so death would come.

But before death would be devouring. The victorious toad would digest him alive.

Then suddenly he heard a bright chirping sound, unlike any animal call he had ever known. There was a whistling in the underbrush and then a lithe golden form was at his side. Brannon's dark eyes were choked with tears of pain; he could barely see.

But the strange figure smiled at him and tapped each of the straining toads gently between the protruding eyes, and spoke three liquid alien words. And one toad, then the other, released him.

The tongues ripped away, taking with them clothing, skin, flesh. Brannon stood tottering for a moment, looking down at the red rawness of his waist, sucking in air to fill the lungs from which all air had been squeezed by the constricting tongues.

The alien girl—Brannon saw her as that now—gave one further command. The toads uttered thrums of disgust, turned, flopped heavily away into the darkness of the deeper jungle.

Brannon looked at the alien. "Thanks," he said. "Whoever—*whatever* you are."

And plunged forward, dropping heavily on his face in the warm jungle soil.

※

He woke, later. When he could speak the language, he learned that it was four days later.

He was in a hut, somewhere. Golden alien figures moved about him. They were slim, humanoid in appearance, but hairless. Their skulls were bald shining domes of yellow; their eyes, dark green, were somehow sad.

Brannon looked down at himself. He was swathed in bandages where the tongues of the giant toads had ripped away the flesh. Someone bent above him, holding a cup to his lips.

He drank. It was broth, warm, nourishing. The girl who held it was the one who had rescued him in the forest. She smiled at him.

"Lethii," she said, pointing to herself.

Uncertainly Brannon touched his chest. "Brannon."

She repeated it. "Brannon." She grinned at him.

He grinned back.

That was the beginning.

He stayed there three weeks, among the Nurillins. He discovered that there were perhaps three thousand of them, no more; once, they had had great cities throughout Cutwold, but that had been many thousands of years before, and the jungle had long since reclaimed them.

The girl named Lethii was his guide. She nursed him to health, kept constant company with him when he was well enough to walk, taught him the language. It was a smooth and flowing language, not difficult to learn.

"The toads are our steeds," she told him one day. "My people trained them long ago to respond to our commands. When I heard you screaming for help I was bewildered, for I knew the toads never attacked any of us."

"I didn't know I was screaming," Brannon said.

"You were. The touch of a toad's tongue is agony. I heard your voice and saw you, and knew that the toads had attacked you because you were—not of us."

Brannon nodded, "And I never will be."

But at times during the weeks that passed he thought he *had* become one of them. He learned the Nurillin history—how they had been great once, and now were dying away, and how when the Terran scout ships had come the Nurillins had realized the planet was no longer theirs, and had moved off into the jungle to hide and wait for the end.

He felt himself growing a strange sort of love for the girl Lethii— not a sexual sort of love, for that was impossible and even inconceivable between their species and his, but something else just as real. Brannon had never felt that sort of emotion again.

He met others, and came to know them—Darhuing, master of the curious Nurillin musical instruments; Vroyain, whose subtle and complex poetry bewildered and troubled Brannon. Mirchod, the hunter, who showed Brannon many ways of the jungle he had not known before.

But Brannon sensed strain in the village, finally, when he knew the people well enough to understand them. And so when six weeks had passed he said to Lethii, "I'm well now. I'll have to rejoin my people."

"Will you come back?"

"Yes," he said. "I'll come back."

❂

He came back twice more—once half a year later, once a year after that. They had welcomed him gladly, had grieved at his leave-taking.

Now a year and a half had slipped by since the last visit, and Brannon was returning once again. But this time he was bringing death.

Above the tent a bird shrieked, the long low wail of a dawnbird, and Brannon realized night had gone. He had dreamed of the Nurillins. He had remembered the three visits past, the visits now to be blotted out by bloodshed.

He got to his feet and stood looking down at the ten sleepers.

It was possible to kill them all, one by one, as they slept. No one would find them. Brannon would return alone, and no one would question him. The Nurillins would remain untroubled where they dwelt.

He shook his head.

His decision had been made; he would abide by it. He nudged Murdoch. The dark-faced man blinked and was awake in an instant, staring up at Brannon.

"Time to get up," Brannon said. "It's dawn. You can't sleep all day."

Murdoch got to his feet, nodding. "Time to get up," he repeated loudly. "Everybody up!"

The hunters awoke, grumbling and complaining.

"Will we reach the Nurillins today, Mr. Brannon?" asked Saul Marshall's wife. "I'm stiff all over from sleeping on the ground."

"Did you sleep?" said Mrs. Damon. "I couldn't. I was up every moment of the night. Those birds, and the animals I kept hearing—!"

"Yes," said Rhawn's wife. "I hope we'll get there today. Another night sleeping out would really be too much."

Brannon very carefully erased the scowl of contempt before it had fully formed on his face. He said, "There's a very good chance we may get there before nightfall tonight. If all of you hurry up, that is. We're not getting any closer while we sit around in camp."

It was a telling point. Breakfast was perfunctory, just a handful of food-tabs and a once-over with a molecular rinse. Within an hour, the camp had been broken up, the plastic tent dissolved, the equipment repacked and reshouldered.

While Brannon waited for the Damons and the Rhawns to ready themselves for the day's march, he walked over to Murdoch, who was talking with Marya Llewellyn.

She looked incredibly fresh and lovely, as if she had slept in a germicidal incubator all night rather than in a jungle tent. Her skimpy clothes were barely creased.

"Well?" Brannon asked. "Am I taking you the right way?"

Murdoch glared at him. "We trust you, Brannon. You don't have to act this way about it."

"You trust me? You didn't yesterday."

"Marya says you're leading us toward the Nurillins. Well, you ought to be. We're paying you enough."

Brannon glanced at Marya Llewellyn. "Are you from Earth, Mrs. Llewellyn?"

"Originally. I live on Vega VII now."

That explained the deep tan, the air of health. "Have you done much hunting before?" Brannon asked.

"Mrs. Llewellyn has been on four hunting tours of mine," Murdoch said. "In fact, she met her husband on a tour. We were hunting in the Djibnar system then." He grinned at her, and she returned the grin. Brannon wondered whether any sort of relationship existed between these two besides that of hunter and hunt director. Probably, he thought. Not that it mattered any to him.

"We're ready," Mrs. Damon called cheerily.

Brannon turned. She was plump, good-natured looking. A grandmotherly type. Out here, hunting intelligent beings? He shrugged. Strange kill-lusts lay beneath placid exteriors; he had found that out long before. He wondered how much these people were paying Murdoch for the privilege of committing legal murder. Thousands, probably.

Brannon surveyed the group of them. Only big Napoli was a familiar type: he was a legitimate sportsman, as could be seen by the way he handled his gear and himself in the jungle. As for the rest of them, these hunters, they were a cross-section—but they all shared one characteristic. All had a curious intent glint in their eyes. The glint of killers. The glint of people who had come halfway across the galaxy to cleanse their minds and souls by emptying the chambers of their guns into the innocent golden bodies of the Nurillins.

He moistened his lips. "Let's go," he said crisply. "There's a lot of hiking yet ahead."

❋

There wasn't much doubt in Brannon's mind that he would reach the Nurillins' village safely with his ten charges. The half-comprehended sense that had been with him so long guided him through the thick jungle.

Sometimes stray thoughts popped into his mind: *a man named Murdoch will come to you this morning and offer you a job.*

Other times, it would be more subtle: a shadowy wordless feeling that to take a given path would be unwise, that danger lurked somewhere.

Still other times he felt nothing at all. Fortunately this happened infrequently.

Brannon knew without knowing that the party would reach the Nurillin village on time. It was only a matter of picking one foot up and slogging it back down a yard further ahead, of mechanically marching on and on and on through the endless jungle that made up so much of the planet Cutwold.

Overhead Caveer climbed toward noon height, sending down cascades of golden-green radiance. Rhawn's wife asked once, "How soon will we be out of this dreadful jungle?"

Rhawn said, "Darling, be patient. This is one of the last places in the universe where we can do something like this. What an experience it'll be to tell about! When we're vacationing again next season, won't we be envied so!"

"I suppose you're right, dear."

Brannon's lips firmed grimly. *I suppose you're right, dear.*

He could picture them gossiping now—of the time they came across the secret village of aliens on Cutwold, and killed them for trophies because the Galactic Government had not said it was illegal. As these rich socialites roved from pleasure-spot to pleasure-spot, they would repeat the story, boasting of the time they had killed on Cutwold.

"You look angry," a soft voice said. "I wish I knew why you always look so angry."

Brannon had known a moment in advance: Marya Llewellyn had left her place in line and had come to his side. He glanced down at her. "Angry? Me?"

"Don't try to hide it, Brannon. Your face is dark and bitter. You're strange, Brannon."

He shrugged. "It comes from long years in the outworld, Mrs. Llewellyn. Men get strange out here."

"Call me Marya, won't you?" Her voice was low. "Do you think we'll reach the Nurillins' village today?"

"Hard to tell. We're making a good pace, but if Mrs. Damon gets tired and has to rest, or if a herd of thunderbeasts decides to cut across our path, there'll be delays. We may have to camp out again tonight. I can't help it if we do."

Her warm body brushed against his. "I won't mind. If we *do* camp out—tonight, when everyone's asleep—let's stay awake, Brannon. Just the two of us."

For a moment he failed to see what she meant. Then he did, and he scowled and quickened his pace. One betrayal was bad enough...but not two. He thought of golden Lethii, and the harsh angles of his face deepened.

He looked back. Llewellyn was marching on, not knowing or not caring about his wife's behavior. The others showed some sign of strain, all but stony-faced Murdoch bringing up the rear and the tireless Napoli.

"I'm exhausted," Mrs. Damon said. "Can we rest a while, Mr. Brannon?"

"No," he said, surprising her. "This is dangerous country we're passing through. These shining-leaved bushes here—they're nesting places for the giant scorpions. We have to keep moving. I want to reach the village before nightfall if possible."

At his side Marya Llewellyn emitted a little gasp. "You said that deliberately!"

"Maybe. Maybe I'm turning you down because I'm afraid of getting mixed up in a quarrel."

"My husband's a silly fool. He won't cause us any trouble."

"I wasn't talking about your husband. I was talking about Murdoch."

For a second he thought she would spring at him and rake his eyes with her enamelled fingernails. But color returned to her suddenly pale face after a moment. She glared at him in open hatred and dropped back into formation, leaving him alone at the head of the line.

Brannon shook his head. He felt sudden fatigue, but forced himself to accelerate the pace.

❋

Noon passed. A flock of scaly air-lizards passed by and showered them with nauseous droppings at twelve-thirty; Brannon brought one down with a quick shot of his handgun and showed the grisly beast to the group. Marshall photographed it. He had been taking photographs steadily.

After a brief rest at one, they moved on. Brannon set a sturdy pace, determined not to spend another night in the jungle before reaching the village. At two, they paused by a waterhole to splash cooling water on their parched faces.

"How about a swim?" Marya asked. She began to strip.

"I wouldn't advise it," said Brannon. "These waterholes are populated. Tadpoles the size of your thumb that'll eat your toes off while you swim and work their way up your body in two minutes."

"Oh," she said faintly. There was no swimming.

They moved on. And at three-thirty Brannon paused, signalling for quiet, and listened to the jungle noises.

To the steady *thrum...thrum...thrum* of the giant toads. To the sound that meant they had reached the Nurillins' village.

Brannon narrowed his eyes. He turned to Murdoch and said, "All right, we're here. The Nurillins live just up ahead. From now on it's your show, Murdoch."

The hunt leader nodded. "Right. Listen to me, all of you. You're to fire one shot at a time, at only one of the beasts."

The beasts, Brannon thought broodingly, thinking of Vroyain the poet. *The beasts.*

"When you've brought down your mark," Murdoch went on, "get to one side and wait. As soon as each of you has dropped one, we're finished. We'll collect the trophies and return to the settlement. Aim for the heart, or else you may spoil the head and ruin the trophy. Brannon, are these creatures dangerous in anyway?"

"No," Brannon said quietly. *Thrum...thrum...* "They're not dangerous. But keep an eye out for the giant toads. They can kill."

"That's your job," Murdoch said. "You and I will cover the group while the kill is going on." He looked around. "Is everything understood? Good. Let's go."

✸

They headed forward, moving cautiously now, guns drawn and ready. The thrumming of the toads grew more intense. Brannon saw landmarks he had seen before. The village was not far. They were virtually at the point now where he had been attacked by the toads, before Lethii had rescued him.

Thrum...thrum...

The sudden croaking sounds were loud—and a toad burst from the underbrush, a Nurillin mounted astride the ugly creature. Brannon stared at the Nurillin but did not recognize him.

"That one's mine," Napoli said before anyone else of the group was aware of what was happening. The burly huntsman lowered his rifle and pumped one shot through the Nurillin's heart.

Brannon winced. That was the first one.

The Nurillin dropped from his mount, a look of astonishment frozen on his face. The toad uttered three defiant bellows and waddled forward, mouth opening, deadly tongue coiling in readiness as Napoli went to claim his kill.

"Watch out for the frog," Brannon warned.

Napoli laughed. And then the tongue flicked out and wrapped itself around the big man's bull-like neck and throat. Napoli gagged and clawed at his throat, trying to say the word "Help" and failing.

Brannon's first shot severed the outstretched pink tongue, breaking the link between the toad and Napoli. His second shot ripped a gaping hole in the toad's pouting throat. Napoli reeled away, gasping for air, and ripped the tongue away from his skin. It came away bloody; a line of red circled his neck like the mark of a noose.

"I thought I could outmaneuver him," Napoli said. "But that tongue moved like lightning."

"I warned you," Brannon said. Napoli knelt by the dead Nurillin.

"This one's mine," he repeated. "I got mine."

They moved on, rounding a bend in the path, coming now to the outskirts of the village itself. Four male Nurillins were coming toward them, their green eyes sharp with accusation. Again, Brannon did not know any of them. He was thankful for that much.

"What were those shots?" asked one of them, in the Nurillin tongue. Brannon was the only one who could understand, and he could make no reply.

It was Marshall's wife who spoke first. "Why, they're just like *people!*" she said in wonderment.

"Of course," her husband snapped dourly. "That's why we're here." He lowered his gun to firing level and sent the rightmost Nurillin sprawling with a quick shot. The other three turned to flee, but were dropped rapidly with bullets from the guns of Rhawn, his wife, and— of all people—grandmotherly Mrs. Damon.

That makes five, Brannon thought. *Five corpses.*

Four more and it would all be over.

Trickles of alien blood stained the forest sand now. The four dead Nurillins lay with limbs grotesquely tangled, and the four successful huntsmen were beaming with pride.

And more Nurillins were coming. Many of them. Brannon shuddered.

"Here comes a batch of them," Murdoch shouted. "Be ready to move fast."

"They won't hurt you," said Brannon. "They don't understand violence. That's why they ran away."

❋

They came, though, to see what the disturbance was. Brannon turned and saw Llewellyn levelling for a distance shot, his mild face bright with killing fever, his eyes fixed. He fired, and brought down Darhuing the musician. The Nurillin toppled out of the front row of the advancing aliens.

"I'd like another one," Napoli said. "Let me get another one."

"No!" Brannon said.

"He's right," said Murdoch. "Just one each. Just one."

Marshall's wife picked off her trophy before the aliens reached the glade. The second to die was a stranger to Brannon. The others scattered, ducking into the underbrush on both sides of the road—but not before Leopold Damon had fired. His shot caught a Nurillin slightly above the heart and sent the alien spinning backward ten feet.

Eight were dead, now. And only one Nurillin had not sought hiding. Lethii.

She came forward slowly, staring without comprehension at the little knot of gunbearing Earthmen.

"Brannon," she said. "Brannon. What are you doing?" The liquid syllables of the alien tongue seemed harsh and accusing.

"I—I—"

She stood slim and unafraid near two fallen Nurillins and stared bitterly at Brannon. "You have come back...but your friends kill!"

"I had to do it," Brannon said. "It was for your sake. For your tribe's sake. For my sake."

"How can that be? You brought these people here to kill us—and you say it's good?"

She doesn't understand, Brannon thought drearily. "I can't explain," he said.

"Listen! He's speaking her language!" Mrs. Damon exclaimed.

"Watch out, Brannon," said Marya Llewellyn suddenly. She laughed in derision.

"No," Brannon said. But for once his foresight failed him. Before he could turn, before he could deflect Marya's aim, she had fired, still laughing.

Lethii stared at him gravely, reproachfully, for a fragment of a second. Then she put her hand to her chest and fell, headlong into the dust.

❁

The journey back to the settlement seemed to take forever. Brannon led the way, eyes fixed ahead of him, never looking back, never speaking.

Behind came the nine, each with a trophy, each with the deep satisfaction of knowing he had murdered an intelligent being and would go scot-free.

Brannon was remembering. Remembering the look on nine Nurillin faces as they fell to the ground, remembering especially that of the ninth victim. Lethii. It had *had* to be her, of course. Her, out of the three thousand. That was necessarily part of the betrayal.

It took a day and a half to reach the main settlement again; Brannon did not sleep in the tent with the others, but remained outside, sitting near the fire with his hands locked across his knees, thinking. Just thinking.

It was late in the afternoon when the group stumbled out of the edge of the jungle and found themselves back in civilization. They stood together in a nervous little group.

Murdoch said, "I want to thank you, Brannon. You got us there, and you got us back, and that's more than I sometimes thought you were going to do."

"Don't thank me, Murdoch. Just get going. Get off Cutwold as fast as you can, and take your nine killers with you."

Murdoch flinched. "They weren't *people*, those aliens. You still can't understand that. The Treaty doesn't say anything about them, and so they're just animals."

"Go on," Brannon said hoarsely. "Go. Fast."

He looked at them—puffed up with pride they were, at having gone into the jungle and come out alive. It would have been so easy to kill them in the jungle, Brannon thought wearily. Marya Llewellyn was looking blackly at him, her body held high, inviting him. She had known about Lethii. That was why she had waited, and fired last, killing her.

"We want to say goodbye, Mr. Brannon," gushed Mrs. Damon. "You were just wonderful."

"Don't bother," Brannon said. He spat at their feet. Then he turned and slowly ambled away, not looking back.

He came into Vuornik's Bar. They were all there, Vuornik, and Barney Karris, and the eight or nine other regular barflies. They were all staring at him. They knew, all of them. They knew.

"Hello, Judas," Karris said acidly. A knife glinted in his belt. He was ready to defend himself.

But Brannon didn't feel like fighting. He slouched down next to the bar and said, "Give me the usual, Vuornik. Double khalla, straight."

"I don't know as I want to serve you in my place, Brannon. I don't know."

Brannon took one of Murdoch's bills from his back pocket and dropped it on the bar. "There's my money. My money's good. *Give me that drink, Vuornik!*"

His tone left little doubts. Vuornik said nervously, "Okay, Brannon. Don't fly up in an uproar." He poured the drink.

Brannon sipped it numbly, hoping it would wipe away the pain and the guilt. It didn't. *Judas,* he thought. *Judas.*

He wasn't any Judas. He had done what was right.

If he hadn't led Murdoch to the Nurillins, Murdoch would have gone himself. Sooner or later he would have found them. He would have destroyed them all…not just these nine.

But now there had been a hunt. Nine trophies had been brought back. Murdoch's nine hunters would boast, and the Nurillins would no longer be a secret. Soon, someone high in government circles would learn that there was a species in the galaxy still unprotected from hunters. Survey ships would come, and the Nurillins would be declared untouchable.

It had had to happen. But there would be no more hunting parties to the interior of Cutwold, now that the galaxy knew the Nurillins existed. They would be safe from now on, Brannon hoped. Safe at the cost of nine lives…and one man's soul.

No one would ever forgive him on Cutwold. He would never forgive himself. *But he had done the right thing. He hadn't had any choice.*

He finished his drink and scooped up his change and walked slowly across the barroom, out into the open. The sun was setting. It was a lovely sight—but Brannon couldn't appreciate it now.

"So long, Judas," came Karris' voice drifting after him out of the bar. "So long, Judas."

COME INTO MY BRAIN
(1958)

This was practically the last story I wrote under my monthly contract deal for Bill Hamling's Imagination. *I turned it in in March, 1957—it was called "Into the Unknown," then, and the byline I put on it was "Ray McKenzie"—but Hamling, who was gradually working off his inventory all through 1957 as he wound down his magazines, didn't find a slot for it until the June, 1958 number, the third issue from the end. It was Hamling who gave it the title it bears here, and he replaced my "McKenzie" pseudonym with the time-honored monicker of "Alexander Blade."*

Dane Harrell held the thought-helmet tightly between his hands, and, before putting it on, glanced over at the bound, writhing alien sitting opposite him. The alien snarled defiantly at him.

"You're sure you want to go through with this?" asked Dr. Phelps.

Harrell nodded. "I volunteered, didn't I? I said I'd take a look inside this buzzard's brain, and I'm going to do it. If I don't come up in half an hour, come get me."

"Right."

Harrell slipped the cool bulk of the thought-helmet over his head and signalled to the scientist, who pulled the actuator switch. Harrell shuddered as psionic current surged through him; he stiffened, wriggled, and felt himself glide out of his body, hover incorporeally in the air between his now soulless shell and the alien bound opposite.

Remember, you volunteered, he told himself.

He hung for a moment outside the alien's skull; then he drifted downward and in. He had entered the alien's mind. Whether he would emerge alive, and with the troop-deployment data—well, that was another matter entirely.

*

The patrol-ships of the Terran outpost on Planetoid 113 had discovered the alien scout a week before. The Dimellian spy was lurking about the outermost reaches of the Terran safety zone when he was caught.

It wasn't often that Earth captured a Dimellian alive, and so the Outpost resolved to comb as much information from the alien as possible. The Earth-Dimell war was four years old; neither side had succeeded in scoring a decisive victory over the other. It was believed that Dimell was massing its fleets for an all-out attack on Earth itself; confirmation of this from the captured scout would make Terran defensive tactics considerably more sound.

But the Dimellian resisted all forms of brainwashing, until Phelps, the Base Psych-man, came forth with the experimental thought-helmet. Volunteers were requested; Harrell spoke up first. Now, wearing the thought-helmet, he plunged deep into the unknown areas of the Dimellian's mind, hoping to emerge with high-order military secrets.

His first impression was of thick grey murk—so thick it could be cut. Using a swimming motion, Harrell drifted downward, toward the light in the distance. It was a long way down; he floated, eerily, in free-fall.

Finally he touched ground. It yielded under him spongily, but it was solid. He looked around. The place was alien: coarse crumbly red soil, giant spike-leaved trees that shot up hundreds of feet overhead, brutal-looking birds squawking and chattering in the low branches.

It looked just like the tridim solidos of Dimell he had seen. Well, why not? Why shouldn't the inside of a man's mind—or an alien's, for that matter, resemble his home world?

Cautiously, Harrell started to walk. Mountains rose in the dim distance, and he could see, glittering on a mountaintop far beyond him, the white bulk of an armored castle. Of course! His imaginative mind realized at once that there was where the Dimellian guarded the precious secrets; up there, on the mountain, was his goal.

He started to walk.

Low-hanging vines obscured his way; he conjured up a machete and cut them down. The weapon felt firm and real in his hand—but he paused to realize that not even the hand was real; all this was but an imaginative projection.

The castle was further away than he had thought, he saw, after he had walked for perhaps fifteen minutes. There was no telling duration inside the alien's skull, either. Or distance. The castle seemed just as distant now as when he had begun, and his fifteen-minute journey through the jungle had tired him.

Suddenly demonic laughter sounded up ahead in the jungle. Harsh, ugly laughter.

And the Dimellian appeared, slashing his way through the vines with swashbuckling abandon.

"Get out of my mind, Earthman!"

*

The Dimellian was larger than life, and twice as ugly. It was an idealized, self-glorified mental image Harrell faced.

The captured Dimellian was about five feet tall, thick-shouldered, with sturdy, corded arms and supplementary tentacles sprouting from its shoulders; its skin was green and leathery, dotted with toad-like warts.

Harrell now saw a creature close to nine feet tall, swaggering, with a mighty barrel of a chest and a huge broadsword clutched in one of its arms. The tentacles writhed purposefully.

"You know why I'm here, alien. I want to know certain facts. And I'm not getting out of your mind until I've wrung them from you."

The alien's lipless mouth curved upward in a bleak smile. "Big words, little Earthman. But first you'll have to vanquish *me*."

And the Dimellian stepped forward.

Harrell met the downcrashing blow of the alien's broadsword fully; the shock of impact sent numbing shivers up his arm as far as his shoulder, but he held on and turned aside the blow. It wasn't fair; the Dimellian had a vaster reach than he could ever hope for—

No! He saw there was no reason why he couldn't control the size of his own mental image. Instantly he was ten feet high, and advancing remorselessly toward the alien.

Swords clashed clangorously; the forest-birds screamed. Harrell drove the alien back...back...

And the Dimellian was eleven feet high.

"We can keep this up forever," Harrell said. "Getting larger and larger. This is only a mental conflict." He shot up until he again towered a foot above the alien's head. He swung downward twohandedly with the machete—

The alien vanished.

And reappeared five feet to the right, grinning evilly. "Enough of this foolishness, Earthman. Physical conflict will be endless stalemate, since we're only mental projections, both of us. You're beaten; there's no possible way you can defeat me, or I defeat you. Don't waste your time and mine. Get out of my mind!"

Harrell shook his head doggedly. "I'm in here to do a job, and I'm not leaving until I've done it." He sprang forward, sword high, and thrust down at the grinning Dimellian.

Again the Dimellian sidestepped. Harrell's sword cut air.

"Don't tire yourself out, Earthman," the alien said mockingly, and vanished.

❋

Harrell stood alone in the heart of the steaming jungle, leaning on his sword. Maybe they were only mental projections, he thought, but a mental projection could still get thoroughly drenched with its own mental sweat.

The castle still gleamed enigmatically on the distant mountain. He couldn't get there by walking—at least, it hadn't seemed to draw any nearer during his jaunt through the jungle. And hand-to-hand combat with the alien was fruitless, it appeared. A fight in which both participants could change size at will, vanish, reappear, and do other such things was as pointless as a game of poker with every card wild.

But there had to be a way. Mental attack? Perhaps *that* would crumble the alien's defenses.

He sent out a beam of thought, directed up at the castle. *Can you hear me, alien?*

Mental laughter echoed mockingly back. *Of course, Earthman. What troubles you?*

Harrell made no reply. He stood silently, concentrating, marshalling his powers. Then he hurled a bolt of mental energy with all his strength toward the mocking voice.

The jungle shuddered as it struck home. The ground lurched wildly, like an animal's back; trees tumbled, the sky bent. Harrell saw he had scored a hit; the alien's concentration had wavered, distorting the scenery.

But there was quick recovery. Again the mocking laughter. Harrell knew that the alien had shrugged off the blow.

And then the counterblow.

It caught Harrell unawares and sent him spinning back a dozen feet, to land in a tangled heap beneath a dangling nest of vines. His head rocked, seemed ready to split apart. He sensed the alien readying a second offensive drive, and set up counterscreens.

This time he was ready. He diverted the attack easily, and shook his head to clear it. The score was even: one stunning blow apiece. But he had recovered, and so had the alien.

Harrell aimed another blow, and felt the alien sweep it aside. Back came the answering barrage of mental force; Harrell blocked it.

Stalemate again, the alien said.

We're evenly matched, Harrell replied. *But I'll beat you.* He looked up at the far-off castle on the mountainside. *I'll beat you yet.*

That remains to be proven, troublesome Earthman.

❋

Harrell tramped on through the jungle of the alien's mind for a while, and then, realizing he was getting no closer to the all-important castle on the hill, stopped by a brook to wipe away his perspiration. It was hot on this accursed world—hot, muggy, dank.

He kneeled over the water's surface. It looked pure, cool. A sudden thought struck him, and he peeled a strip from his shirt and dipped it in the water.

The plasticloth blackened and charred. He let it drop, and the "water" quickly finished the job. Pool? No; he thought. Concentrated sulphuric acid, or something else as destructive.

Grinning grimly at his narrow escape, he wiped his perspiration with another strip torn from his sleeve, and kept going. Several hours, at least, had passed since he had entered the strange world within the alien's mind.

That meant one of two things: either the time-scale in here was different, somehow, from that outside, or that his half-hour limit had elapsed in the outer world and Dr. Phelps was unsuccessful in bringing him back.

That was a nice thought. Suppose he was stuck here indefinitely, inside the mind of an alien being, in this muggy jungle full of sulphuric-acid brooks? A nice fate that was.

Well, he thought, *I asked for it.*

The stalemate couldn't continue indefinitely. If he had swallowed some of the acid he thought was water, that would have ended the contest without doubt; he wouldn't have had time to cope with the searing fluid.

The answer lay there—*surprise.* Both he and the alien were mental entities who could do battle as they pleased—but in this conflict, it was necessary to take the opponent by surprise, before he could counterthrust or vanish.

He began to see a solution.

Up ahead lay the castle—unreachable, through some trick of the alien's. Very well. Harrell's brows drew together in concentration for a moment; his mind formed a strategy—and formed men to carry it out.

There were six of him, suddenly.

❖

Six identical Harrells—identical in size, shape, form, purpose. They would attack the Dimellian simultaneously. Or, at least, five of them would, creating a diversionary action while the sixth—Harrell-original—made a frontal assault on the castle.

Harrell-original faced his five duplicates and briefly instructed each in his job. They were like puppets.

"Harrell-one, you' re to attack in conjunction with Harrell-two, on the mental level. Take turns heaving mental bolts at the alien. While one of you is recharging, the other is to unload. That won't give him time to get any sort of defense organized, and certainly no counter-attack.

"Harrell-three and Harrell-four, you're to attack physically, one armed with sword and one with blaster, from opposite sides at once. *That* ought to keep him busy, while he's fighting off the rest of you.

"Harrell-five, your job is to serve as frontrunner—to find the Dimellian and engage him in conversation while the other four are getting ready to attack. Make him angry; get him concerned about what you're saying. And the second his defenses drop an inch, the other four of you jump in. All of you got that?"

They nodded in unison.

"Good. Meantime I'll make an assault on the castle, and maybe I can get through with you five running interference for me."

He dismissed them, and they set out in different directions. He didn't want the Dimellian to find out what was up; if the alien saw the strategy and had time to create duplicates of its own, the conflict would end in stalemate almost certainly.

Harrell waited, while his five duplicates went into action.

Through the mental link with Harrell-five, he listened as his duplicate said, "The time has come to finish you off, alien. I'm glad I found you. That acid trick almost got me, but not quite."

"A pity," the alien replied. "I was hoping the ruse would finish you. It's becoming quite irritating, having you in here. You're starting to bore me."

"Just you wait, you overstuffed wart-hog. I'll have those tentacles of yours clipped soon enough."

"Empty words, Earthman. You've run out of strategies; your best course is to get out of my mind and forget this entire silly affair."

"Oh, no. I'll have those secrets pried out of you quicker than you think."

"How?"

"I'm not giving away *my* secrets, alien. I'm here after yours."

Harrell readied himself. He gave the signal: *now.*

Harrell-one and Harrell-three appeared. Harrell-one loosed a bombardment of mental force that shook the alien; Harrell-three dashed forward, wielding a machete.

Harrell-two and Harrell-four went into action, Harrell-two following up with a second mental bolt, Harrell-four firing a blaster. The bedeviled alien looked from side to side, not knowing where to defend himself first.

The scenery began to rock. The alien was going down.

Harrell took to the air.

Levitating easily above the jungle, he found the castle and zeroed in on it. As he dropped downward, it changed—from a vaulting proud collection of spires and battlements to a blocky square building, and from that into an armored box with a padlock.

The Dimellian stood before it, struggling with the five duplicate Harrells.

Harrell stepped past—*through*—the writhing group. The Dimellian's defenses were down. The secrets were unguarded.

He wrenched the padlock off with a contemptuous twist of his hand. The box sprang open. Inside lay documents, neatly typed, ready for his eye.

The alien uttered a mighty howl. The forest dissolved; the universe swirled around Harrell's head. The last thing he heard was the terrible shrieking of the alien.

❋

He woke. It seemed to be months later.

Dr. Phelps stood by his side, staring at him solicitously. The alien, still bound, sat slumped over, heavy head lolling against one shoulder.

Harrell took two or three deep breaths, clearing his head. He grinned. "I've got them," he said. "Information on troop movements, plan of battle, even the line of journey across space. This was a top-flight officer we captured—and a rugged battler."

"Good work," the psychman said. "I was worried at first. You had some expressions of real terror on your face when you put the helmet on. But then the alien let out an awful scream and slumped over."

"Dead?"

"I'm afraid so."

Harrell grinned weakly. "I guess I was just too many for him. The shock of having the core of his mind penetrated—" Tiredly he said, "Doc, how come you didn't get me out at the half-hour mark?"

"Eh?"

"I told you to pull me out after half an hour had gone by. Why didn't you? I was in there half a day at least—and I might have stayed there forever."

The psychman was looking at him strangely. "Half a day, you say? No, Lieutenant Harrell. The total time elapsed, from the moment you donned the helmet to the instant the alien screamed—why, it was less than ten seconds!"

CASTAWAYS OF SPACE
(1958)

Typical W.W. Scott material: an exotic world, some disreputable characters engaged in interstellar hanky-panky, a bit of a twist ending. I wrote it in January, 1958 and gave it the rather flat-footed title of "Pursuit," which Scottie changed to the more vivid "Castaways of Space," and so be it. It ran in the October, 1958 issue of Super-Science Fiction *under the byline of "Dan Malcolm," which I had begun using frequently for Scottie now. There were two other items of mine in the same issue, one under my more famil-iar pseudonym, "Calvin M. Knox," and the other under my own name. That one was "Gorgon Planet," the very first short story I had ever sold (to the Scottish magazine,* Nebula, *in 1954), which I dug out now and sold again to Scottie for five times as much as* Nebula *had paid. He didn't like my title and put what he thought was a much better one on it: "The Fight With the Gorgon." Sometimes Scottie was right about title changes, and sometimes, well, not.*

Lieutenant McDermott was having a couple of drinks in the Nine Planets Bar on Albireo XII when his wristband bleeped, telling him to report to Patrol headquarters for assignment. McDermott scowled. This was his time off and he didn't give a damn what Headquarters said. He cupped his hand tightly around the drinkflask and took a long slug. The wristband bleeped again, impatiently.

McDermott waited a minute or two and finished his drink. Then he switched the band to audio and said in a sour tone, "McDermott reporting. What is it?"

The thin, edgy voice of the Officer of the Day said, "Job for you, Mac. There's been a kidnapping and we want you to do the chasing."

"I'm off duty. Get Squires."

"Squires is in sick-bay having his head sewed back on," was the acid reply. "Get out of that bar and get yourself down here in five minutes or—"

The threat was unvoiced, but McDermott didn't need much persuasion. He knew his status as a Galaxy Patrol Corpsman was shaky enough, and a couple more black marks would finish him completely. He didn't like that idea. Getting booted out of the crime-prevention unit would mean he would have to go back to working for a living, and at his age that wasn't nice to think about.

"Okay," he rumbled. "Be right there."

He pulled a platinoid five-credit coin from his pocket, fingered its embossed surface lovingly for a moment, and spun it down on the counter. The bartender slid two small coppers back at him in change. Pocketing them, McDermott grinned apologetically at the gray-skinned Denebian floozie he had been making plans about until the call to HQ, and shouldered his way out of the bar. He walked pretty well, considering there was nearly five credits' worth of straight Sirian rum under his belt.

McDermott held his liquor pretty well. He was a big man, six-three and two hundred sixty pounds, and there was plenty of alcohol-absorbing bulk there to gobble up the stuff as he poured it down his throat.

His car, with the official nova-emblem of the Galaxy Patrol Corps, was sitting outside the bar. He tumbled into it, jabbed the start-button fiercely, and shot away from the curb. The trip to Headquarters took him twenty minutes, which was pretty good time considering that the building was halfway across town.

Sergeant Thom was at the night desk, a wizened little Aldebaranian who looked up as McDermott came through the door and said, "Better leg it upstairs, Mac. Davis is on tonight and he wants you fast."

"He's waited this long," McDermott said. "He can wait a little longer. No sense rushing around."

❋

McDermott took the gravtube upstairs and entered the Officer of the Day's cubbyhole without knocking. The O.D. was Captain Davis, a forty-year veteran of the Corps who lived a model life himself and who had several times expressed himself rather harshly on the subject of McDermott's drinking.

Now he looked at McDermott with an expression of repugnance on his face and said in his tight little voice, "I'm sorry to have found it necessary to pull you off your free time, Lieutenant."

McDermott said nothing. Davis went on, "A matter has come up and at the moment you're the only man at this base who can handle it. A girl named Nancy Hollis has been kidnapped—an Earthgirl, visiting this world on a tour with her parents. The father is a big-wheel diplomat making a galactic junket. She was plucked out of her hotel room and carted away in a Model XV-108 ship by a man identified only as Blaine Hassolt of this city. Know him?"

McDermott shook his head.

Davis shrugged. "Well, no matter. The girl left a scribbled note and we got on the trail pretty fast after the snatch. Hassolt was heading outsystem with her and we slapped a spy-vector on the ship. We followed it as far as we could. It disappeared pretty fast and as far as we can compute it crashlanded on Breckmyer IV. We saw the ship in orbit around that world and we saw a small lifeship detach from the main and skedaddle down to the planetary surface. Lifeships land but they don't take off. That means Hassolt and the girl are somewhere on Breckmyer IV. Get out there and find them, Mac."

Moistening his lips, McDermott said, "You're sure it's Breckmyer IV?"

"Yes."

"Oh."

McDermott knew that planet. It was a stinking hot one, whose moderate zones were intolerable and whose tropical zones were sheer hell. It was inhabited by primitive humanoids and there were no Terran settlements anywhere on the planet. He was being handed a lousy job, maybe even a suicide job. But the kidnapped girl's father was a big-wheel diplomat, and policy dictated making at least a token effort to get her off Breckmyer IV, if she had survived the landing. The Corps *had* to send someone down there to look around—and the least valuable member of the local base was a rumsoaked Corpsman named McDermott.

"You'll leave at once," Davis told him. "You won't stop at your bar for booze. You won't stop to take a shave. You won't stop to do any old damn thing."

"Yes, sir," McDermott said stonily.

"We're fueling up a ship for you at the Corps port. It'll be ready for blasting in fifteen minutes. Heaven help you if you're late."

"I'll be there on time, sir."

"You'd better be."

❋

McDermott got to the spaceport in time for the blasting. He had made one tiny stop, at an all-night package store just outside the space-port area, but Davis didn't have to know that. And the mass margin of the ship was a thousand pounds; nobody would mind if he brought a small brown bag containing a couple of bottles on board.

The ship was all ready for him. Under the floodlights the service flunkies bustled around, piping in fuel and checking the instruments. McDermott wondered why they were going to so much trouble. This was a sacrifice flight anyway; he wasn't going to find that girl in the jun-gle, and he'd be damned lucky if he ever got back alive after making a landing on Breckmyer IV.

But he didn't say anything. The groundside flunkies looked at him with the worship and wonder in their eyes, the way they looked at any full-fledged Corpsman no matter how seedy he was, how disreputable. As far as they were concerned, McDermott was a Corpsman, and the glamor of that rank eclipsed completely any incidental. deficiencies of personality he might possibly have.

He climbed into the control cabin of the ship. It was an XV-110, a four-man ship with auxiliary boost. That would make landing and tak-ing off on rough terrain easier, and there would be room for him to bring back both Hassolt and the girl if he could find them.

McDermott stowed his three bottles of rum in the gravholder near the pilot's chair, headed to the galley, and found a nipple-top in the gal-ley stores. He opened one of the bottles, fastened the nipple to it, and took a quick slug. Then he strapped himself in for blastoff position while the count-down went on outside.

"Ready for blast, Lieutenant McDermott."

"Ready," he snapped back.

The automatic pilot was ready to function too. A glittering metallic tape dangled loosely from the mouth of the computer. McDermott knew that the tape would guide him faithfully through the hyperwarp across the eighteen light-years that separated him at the moment from Breckmyer IV. The trip would take a day and a half, ship time. If he budgeted himself properly, those three rum bottles would see him through the round trip.

If there was a round trip.

"Blasting in eight seconds, Lieutenant."

"Check."

He touched his fingers to the control board and switched on the activator for the autopilot. From here on he was just so much baggage. The ship would fly itself without any help from him.

Reaching out, he made sure his precious rum was secure against blastoff. He leaned back, waiting. He knew no one gave much of a damn whether he reached Breckmyer IV safely or not, whether he found the girl safe and sound, whether he got back to the Albireo base. He was being sent out just for the sake of appearances. The Corps was making a gesture. Look here, Mr. Hollis, we're trying to rescue your daughter.

McDermott scowled bitterly. The last number of the count-down sounded. The ship rocked back and forth a moment and shot away into space. Eleven seconds after the moment of blastoff, the autopilot activated the spacewarp generator, and so far as observers on Albireo XII were concerned McDermott and his ship had ceased to exist.

*

A day and a half later, the autopilot yanked the ship out of warp, and in full color on the ship's screen was the system of Breckmyer—the big golden-yellow sun surrounded by its thirteen planets. McDermott had finished one full bottle of his rum, and the benippled second bottle was drained almost to its Plimsoll line, but he had had time to look up the Breckmyer system in the ship's ephemeris anyhow.

Of the thirteen planets, only one was suitable for intelligent life, and that was the fourth. The first three were far too hot; the fifth through eighth were too big, and the outer planets were too cold.

The fourth, though, was inhabited—by tribal-organized humanoids of a Class III-a civilization. There were no cities and no industries. It was a primitive hunting-and-agricultural world with a mean temperature of 85 in the temperate zones and 120 in the tropics. McDermott meant to avoid the tropics. If Hassolt and the girl had landed there, McDermott didn't intend to search very intensely for them. Not when the temperature was quite capable of climbing to 150 or 160 in the shade—and a hot, muggy, humid 160 at that.

He guided the ship on manual into an orbit round the fourth planet at a distance of three hundred thousand feet. That far up, the mass-detector would function. He could vector in on the crashed ship and find its whereabouts.

Snapping on the detector, he threw the ship into a steady orbit and waited. An hour later came the beep-beeping of a find; and, tuning the fine control on his detector plate, he discovered that he had indeed located the kidnap ship.

It had crashed in the temperate zone, for which McDermott uttered fervent blessings. The little lifeship had landed no more than a couple of miles from the stolen vessel. Presumably Hassolt and Nancy Hollis were somewhere in the neighborhood.

His subradio came to life and Captain Davis' thin voice said, "Come in, McDermott. Come in."

"McDermott here, sir."

"Any luck? Are you in orbit around the planet yet?"

"I'm in orbit," McDermott confirmed. "And I've found the ship, all right. It's down below me. I'm making ready for a landing now."

"Good luck," Davis said, and there wasn't much friendliness in his voice. "The girl's father sends his best wishes to you. He says he'll take good care of you if you bring his daughter back safely."

"Members of the Corps are not allowed to accept emoluments in the course of duty," McDermott recited tiredly, knowing that Davis was just testing him. "If I can find the girl I'll bring her back."

"You'd better," Davis said coldly. "There'll be all kinds of trouble if Senator Hollis' daughter doesn't get found."

The contact died. McDermott shrugged his shoulders and took another quick pull of the rum. It warmed his insides and buoyed him with confidence. Moving rapidly, he set up a landing orbit that would put his ship down not far from the crashed vessel.

He threw the relays back. Slowly his ship left its orbit and began to head groundward.

<hr />

The landing was a good one. McDermott had been in the Corps for fifteen years, and in that time you learned how to make a good landing in a spaceship. You have to learn, because the ones who didn't learn didn't last for fifteen years.

He fined the ship into a pinpoint area a mile or so broad, which is pretty much of a pinpoint from three hundred thousand feet up. Then he brought her down, aiming for the flattest spot, and by skilful use of the auxiliary boost managed to land the ship smoothly without crisping. more than a few thousand square feet of the jungle with the exhaust of his jets.

His jungle kit was all ready for him—medications, a Turner blastgun, a machete, a compass, and such things. He slung it over his back and slithered down the dragwalk to ground level. He leaned against the ship and pushed, but it didn't rock. It was standing steady, its weight cutting a few inches into the ground. Good landing, he told himself. Hope takeoff is just as good.

The thermometer in his wrist-unit read 94 degrees, humidity 89 percent. It was clammily moist as he started out on his mission. His mass-detector told him that the crashed spaceship lay two and a half miles to the west, and he figured he had better start out from there in his search for Hassolt and Nancy Hollis. The lifeship was somewhere further to the west; his portable detector was not powerful enough to locate it more definitely.

He began to walk.

McDermott was wearing regulation alien-planet costume: high boots and leatheroid trousers, thick teflon jacket, sun helmet. Because Breckmyer IV was a reasonably Earthtype planet, he did not need a breathing-mask.

The jungle all about was thick and luxurious. The plants went in for color here. Stout corrugated-boled palmtrees rose all about him, and their heavy fronds, dangling almost to the jungle floor, were a blue-green hue ringed with notches of red. Creeping and clinging yellow vines writhed from tree to tree, while a carpet of flaming red grass was underfoot. The vegetation seemed to be sweating; beaded drops of moisture lay quivering on every succulent leaf.

McDermott walked. He had to cut his way through the overhanging thicket of vines with backhand sweeps of his machete every five or six steps, and though he was a big man and a powerful one he was covered with sweat himself before he had travelled a quarter of a mile through the heavy vegetation. He resisted the temptation to strip away his jacket and shirt. The forest was full of droning, buzzing insects with hungry little beaks, and the less bare skin he exposed the better.

He had seen what jungle insects could do to a man. He had seen swollen and bloated corpses, victims of the cholla-fly of Procyon IX, killed by a single sting. And though it was oven-hot here, McDermott kept his uniform on until it stuck to his body in a hundred places. Dead men didn't perspire, but he preferred to perspire.

Jungle creatures hooted mocking cries all around. Once, twice he thought he saw a lithe figure shaped like a man peer at him from between two trees and slip silently off into the darkness, but he wasn't sure. He shrugged his shoulders and kept going. He wasn't interested in the native life. They were pretty skilled with poisoned blowdarts on Breckmyer IV, he had been told. He felt an uncomfortable twitch between his shoulderblades, and pressed grimly on, cursing the man who had sent him out here to sweat.

An hour later he reached the wrecked spaceship. It had oxidized pretty badly in the atmosphere on the way down, and there wasn't much left of it. Certainly it could never take off. Hassolt would probably beg him to take him back to civilization, if he was still alive.

The lifeship had landed a mile further west, and that meant nearly thirty minutes of weary slogging. McDermott's breath was coming fast and he had to stop every few minutes to rest and mop the sticky sweat out of his eyes; it rolled down into his thick brows and dripped maddeningly onto his cheeks.

The lifeship sat on its tail in a little clearing. It had landed well. McDermott looked at it. The lifeships were hardly bigger than bathtubs—rocket-equipped bathtubs. They were big enough for two people, three if they were willing to crowd together, and they were capable of coming down through a planetary atmosphere and making a safe landing. That was all. They could not be used for taking off again, but they would get their occupants safely down.

McDermott stood by the lifeship a moment, looking around. The grass was pretty well trampled here; a good sign of a village in the neighborhood. Most likely Hassolt and the girl were in the village.

He started to walk again. In ten minutes the village appeared, a nest of randomly-arranged huts on high stilts, circling loosely around the banks of a jungle stream. Advancing cautiously, McDermott saw a few of the natives, slim catlike humanoid creatures whose bodies were covered with a soft yellow fur. He made sure his blastgun was where he could reach it, and activated his verbal translator.

He stepped forward into the village.

✸

Two or three of the natives edged out from their huts and came to meet him, padding silently over the beaten-down grass. There was no fear in their gleaming blue eyes, only curiosity.

McDermott started to say, "I'm looking for a couple of my people who crashlanded here."

Then he stopped.

An Earthman was coming out of the biggest and most magnificent hut in the village. He was grinning. He was a tall man, though not as tall as McDermott was, and his face was very thin, with hard angling cheekbones. He was wearing lustrous robes made from the hide of some jungle animal, thick, handsome robes. On his head he wore a kind of crown made from ivory.

"Are you Blaine Hassolt?" McDermott demanded.

The other nodded with easy familiarity. He spoke in a pleasant drawling voice. "I'm Hassolt, yes. And you've come to get me and bring me back?"

McDermott nodded.

Hassolt laughed. "How thoughtful of you!"

McDermott said, scowling, "I don't give a damn if you rot here or not, Hassolt. I'm here to get the girl. You can come back and stand trial or you can stay here in the jungle."

One of Hassolt's eyebrows rose quizzically. "I take it you're a Corpsman?"

"You take it right."

"Ah. How nice. There was a time when I was actually praying that we were being followed by a Corpsman—that was the time when the controls blanked out, and I had to crashland. I was very worried then. I was afraid we'd be cast away forever on some dangerous planet."

"You like it this hot?" McDermott asked.

"I don't mind. I live a good life here," Hassolt stretched lazily. "The natives seem to have made me their king, Lieutenant. I rather like the idea."

McDermott's eyes widened. "And how about the girl—Nancy Hollis?"

"She's here too," Hassolt said. "Would you like to see her?"

"Where is she?"

Instead of answering Hassolt turned and whistled at the big hut. "Nancy! Nancy, come out here a moment! We've got a visitor."

A moment passed; then, a girl appeared from the hut. She, too, wore robes and a crown; underneath the robes her body was bare, oddly pale, and she made ineffectual attempts to conceal herself as she saw McDermott. She was about nineteen or so, pretty in a pale sort of way, with short-cropped brown hair and an appealing face.

"I'm Lieutenant McDermott of the Corps, Miss Hollis," McDermott said. "We put a spy-vector on Hassolt's ship and traced you here. I've come to take you back."

"Oh, have you?," Hassolt said before the girl could speak. "You haven't consulted *me* in this matter. You realize you propose to rob this tribe of its beloved queen."

McDermott's scowl tightened. He gestured with the blastgun and raised it to firing level. "I have a ship about three miles from here," he said. "Suppose you start walking now. In an hour or two we can be there, and in a day and a half we'll all be back safe and sound on Albireo XII."

"I don't want to be rescued," Hassolt said deliberately. "I like it here."

"What you like doesn't matter. Miss Hollis, this man forcibly abducted you, didn't he?"

She nodded.

"Okay," McDermott said. He nodded over his shoulder in the direction of the ship. "Let's go, Hassolt."

"Put the gun down, McDermott," Hassolt said quietly.

"Don't make trouble or I'll gun you down right now," McDermott snapped. "I'm more interested in rescuing Miss Hollis than I am in dragging you back to court."

"Miss Hollis will stay right here. So will I. Put the gun down. McDermott, there are four natives standing in a ring, thirty feet behind you, and each one is holding a blowdart pipe. All I have to do is lift my hand and you'll be riddled with darts. It's a quick death, but it isn't a nice one."

McDermott's broad back began to itch. Sweat rolled in rivers down his face. He cautiously glanced around to his left.

Hassolt was right. Four slim catlike beings stood in a semicircle behind him, blowpipe poised at lips. McDermott paused a moment, sweating, and then let his gun drop to the ground.

"Kick it toward me," Hassolt ordered.

McDermott shoved it with his foot toward the other. Hassolt hastily scooped it up, stowed it in his sash, and gestured to the aliens. Two of them slipped up behind McDermott and relieved him of his machete. He was now unarmed. He felt like an idiot.

Hassolt grinned and said, "Make yourself at home and keep out of trouble, McDermott. And remember that my bodyguards will be watching you all the time."

He turned and walked away, heading back toward the hut.

❋

McDermott stared after him; finally he muttered a brief curse and looked at the girl.

"I'm sorry I got you into this," she said.

"It's not your fault, Miss. It's mine. My fault for joining the Corps and my fault for taking this assignment and my fault for not shooting Hassolt the second I saw him."

"It would have done no good. The natives would have killed you immediately."

He looked around at the village. Two or three natives skulked in the distance, ready to transfix him with darts if he showed any sign of trouble.

He said, "How did all this happen? I mean, Hassolt being king and everything?"

She shrugged. "I hardly know. I met him one afternoon at the Terran Club and he bought me a couple of drinks—I thought he was interesting, you know. So we went for a drive in his car, and next thing I knew he was forcing me aboard a ship and blasting off."

McDermott looked at her. "With what purpose in mind?"

"Ransom," she said. "He told me all about it as soon as we were in space. He was heading for the Aldebaran system, where he'd cable my father for money. If Dad came through, he was going to turn me over to the authorities and vanish. If Dad refused to pay, he'd—take me with him as his mistress. But we were only a little distance from Albireo when I grabbed control of the ship and tried to head it back. I didn't succeed."

"But you did foul up the controls so thoroughly that Hassolt had to abandon his original idea and crashland the ship here?"

"Yes. We came down in the lifeship and the natives found us. Hassolt had a translator with him, and it turned out they wanted us to be their king and queen, or something like that. So we've been king and queen for the past few days. The natives do everything Hassolt says."

"Do they obey you, too?"

"Sometimes. But I'm definitely second-fiddle to him."

McDermott chewed at his lip and wished he had brought his remaining bottle of rum along. It was a nasty position. Far from being anxious to be rescued, Hassolt was probably delighted to live on Breckmyer IV. He wasn't willing to leave, and he wasn't willing to let Nancy Hollis go either. Nor was he going to let McDermott escape alive and possibly bring a stronger Corps force to rescue the girl.

He eyed the blowpipers speculatively. Unarmed as he was, he didn't dare risk trying to escape, with or without the girl. The ship was too far from the village, and beyond a doubt the natives would know shortcuts and could easily head him off at Hassolt's command.

Sneaking up behind Hassolt was equally impossible. As king, Hassolt was thoroughly guarded. Belting him from behind and making a run for the ship with the girl would be sheer suicide.

McDermott sat down by a grassy rise in the turf.

"What are you going to do?" the girl asked. She was looking at him in the starry-eyed way that teenage girls were likely to look at Corpsmen who came to rescue them from alien planets. She didn't seem to realize that this particular Corpsman was average, overweight, and didn't have the foggiest idea of how to rescue either her or himself.

"Nothing," McDermott said. "Nothing but wait. Maybe some other ship will come after *me*. But I doubt it."

❉

McDermott spent the next few hours wandering around the village. Evidently some sort of council meeting was going on in Hassolt's hut; McDermott heard the sounds of alien words from time to time.

The blowpipers ringed in the village. There was no way out. He wondered if Hassolt intended to keep him prisoner indefinitely.

No, that was unlikely. McDermott, as a Corpsman, was a potential danger to Hassolt at all times. Hassolt undoubtedly would get rid of him as soon as the business at hand was taken care of.

And the girl was looking at him so damned *hopefully*. As if she pegged her life on a serene inner confidence that the Corpsman was going to engineer her rescue somehow:

Somehow.

The afternoon was growing late and the big golden sun was sinking in the distance when one of the aliens came noiselessly up to them, and proferred each of them a bowl of some sort of liquid.

"What is it?" McDermott asked, sniffing the contents of the bowl suspiciously.

"Something alcoholic," she said. "They make it out of fermented vegetable mash. Hassolt drinks it and says it's okay."

McDermott grinned and sampled it. It was sweet and musky-tasting, not at all bad. And potent. Two bowlsful this size could probably keep a man in a pleasant alcoholic stupor half a day.

He finished the bowl off hurriedly and realized that the girl was looking at him in surprise and—was that disgust? Her image of him as a super-boyscout was fading fast, he thought. He had guzzled the liquor just a bit too greedily.

"Good," he said.

"Glad you like it."

He started to make some reply, but he heard an approaching footfall behind him, and turned. It was Hassolt. He was holding McDermott's blastgun tightly in his hand and his face had lost the sophisticated, mocking look it had had earlier. He seemed drained of blood now, a pale, white sickly color. It was pretty plain that Hassolt had just had a considerable shock. Something that had rippled him to the core.

He said, in a voice that was harsh and breathy, "McDermott, how far is your ship from here?"

McDermott grinned. "Three miles. Three and a half, maybe. More or less due east."

Hassolt waggled the blastgun. "Come on: Take me to it."

"Right now?"

"Right now."

McDermott stared levelly at the kidnapper for an instant, and let some of the euphoria induced by the alien drink leave his mind. Narrowing his eyes in unbelief, he said, "Are you serious?"

"Stop wasting time. I want you to take me to the ship *now*."

The girl was staring in bewilderment at him. McDermott said, "You sure got tired of the kinging business fast, Hassolt. You loved it here two hours ago."

"I didn't know two hours ago what I know now. You know what they do to their king and queen at the end of the year? They throw them into a live volcano! It's their way of showing thanks to the volcano-god for having brought them safely through the year. Then they pick a new king and queen."

McDermott started to chuckle. "So it's the old savage story, huh? Treat you like a king for a year and chuck you to the lava!"

"I happened to come along a few days after the old king and queen had been sacrificed," Hassolt said. "Usually they choose the new ones from their tribe, but they prefer to have strangers. Like the girl and me."

McDermott continued chuckling. "But what's your hurry? If the new year's only a few days old, you have plenty of time."

"I don't care to stick around. Take me to your ship now, McDermott."

"Suppose I don't?"

Hassolt stared meaningfully at the gun. McDermott said calmly, "If you shoot me, I can't guide you to the ship, can I?"

Tightly Hassolt said, "In that case I'd find it myself. You can either take me there and stay alive, or refuse and die. Take your choice."

McDermott shrugged. "You have me there. I'll take you."

"Let's go, then. Now."

"It's late. Can't you wait till morning? It'll be dark by the time we get there."

"Now," Hassolt said.

"How about the girl?"

"She stays here," Hassolt said. "I just want to get away myself. The two of you can stay here. I'm not going to take any more chances. That she-devil wrecked the other ship."

"So I guide you to my ship and let you blast off, and I stay here and face the music?"

"You'll have the girl. Come on now," Hassolt said. His face was drawn and terror-pale.

"Okay," McDermott said. "I'll take you to the ship."

He could understand Hassolt's jittery impatience. The natives might not like their king taking a runout powder, and Hassolt intended to get out while he still could. His ransom project didn't matter, now; having found out what the real function of the king was on this planet, he wanted off in a hurry, at any cost.

Which, McDermott reflected, leaves me and the girl here. And I'm the substitute king.

And a boiling volcano waiting for me at the end of my year-long reign, he thought.

They left the girl behind in the village and slipped off into the thick jungle as the first shadows of night began to descend. McDermott led, and Hassolt, following behind him, made it plain that he was keeping the gun not very far from the small of McDermott's back all the time. The Corpsman hacked stolidly forward into the jungle, retracing his steps.

"It was only three miles, you say?"

"Maybe four," McDermott replied. "Don't worry, Hassolt. I'll take you to the ship. I'd rather be a live coward than a dead hero."

They pressed on. After a while they passed the lifeship and the wreckage of the mother ship, and McDermott knew they were on the right path. The sun dropped below the horizon; the sky darkened, and two small jagged moons, bright and pitted, drifted into the sky. The air was cooler now. McDermott thought of the girls back at the village. And of the volcano.

"You thought you had a pretty good deal, eh, Hassolt? Servants and food and booze and a girl, all set up for the rest of your life. You don't think you might have gotten tired of it after a while?"

"Shut up."

"But then they let you know what was waiting for you, and you decided to run out. Lucky for you that I came along with my nice shiny ship," McDermott said. He was thirsting for a drink of any kind.

Half an hour later, they reached the ship. McDermott turned and saw Hassolt staring at it almost lovingly. He said, "You know how to operate it?"

"I'll manage. You come aboard and show me."

They boarded the ship, which stood silently in the forest as night descended. Hassolt prowled around, looking at the controls. It was obvious to McDermott that the kidnapper was not familiar with the XV-110 model.

He turned to Hassolt and said, "Look here—you don't know how to run this ship and I do. Why don't you let me stay on board as pilot?"

Hassolt chuckled. "You think I'm crazy? Take a Corpsman aboard? Look, that girl wrecked the other ship, and I'm going to travel in this one alone. Show me which button to push and then clear off."

"That's definite, huh?"

"Yeah."

"Okay. Come here."

He led Hassolt to the control panel and gave him a brief rundown on the operation of the ship. The beady-eyed kidnapper took it all in with deep interest.

The rum-bottle was still sitting in the grav-holder next to the pilot's seat, where McDermott had left it for consumption on the return journey. In the darkened ship, it looked like some control lever to the left of the chair.

"Now, this lever over here," McDermott said.

He grasped the bottle firmly as if it were a control. Suddenly he ripped it from its holder and in the same motion swung it back into Hassolt's skull. The bottle broke with a loud crack, and Hassolt dropped to the ground as if poleaxed. McDermott bent over him and took the blastgun gun from his hands. Hassolt was still breathing.

Tenderly he scooped Hassolt up and dragged him out of the ship, across the clearing, and propped him up against a tree outside of the firing-range. Then McDermott stood for a long moment, thinking.

It was dark now. Jungle-beasts honked and hooted in the night. It was a seven-mile hike round trip back to the village to get the girl, and when he got there he probably would be swarmed over immediately and held. By now the natives probably had discovered that their king and the newcomer had vanished. They wouldn't let him slip out of sight a second time.

McDermott shook his head regretfully. He climbed back into the ship and readied it for blastoff.

Too bad about the girl, he thought. But it was suicide to go back to get her.

He thought: it wouldn't be such a bad life—for a while. He'd be waited on hand and foot, and there'd be plenty of that pungent liquor, and of course he would have the girl. But at the end of the year there would be the volcano waiting for both of them.

Better that one of us should escape, he thought. Too bad about the girl. I'll tell Davis that the lifeship blew up on landing, and that both of them were killed and their bodies beyond salvage.

You ought to go back and get her, something said inside him. But he shook his head and began setting up the blasting pattern. If he went back, he'd never get a second chance to escape. *No boy-scout stuff, McDermott; you're too old for that. Pull out while you can.*

And Hassolt and the girl would meet the volcano in a year. He shrugged sadly and jabbed down on the button that activated the jets.

The ship sprang away from Breckmyer IV. McDermott felt a pang of sadness for the girl, and then forgot her. The rescue mission had failed; leave it at that. His chief regret was that he had needed to use the bottle of rum to club down Hassolt. It was the last bottle. It was going to be a long dry voyage back to Albireo, McDermott thought mournfully.

EXILED FROM EARTH
(1958)

*Though most of the stories I wrote for Super-Science were done to order
and formula, sometimes I used W.W. Scott as a salvage market for material I had originally aimed at one of the upper-level magazines. He didn't
mind that it didn't fit his usual action-adventure mode, so long as I didn't do
it too often and the story had, at least, some science-fictional color. He and
I were pretty much dependent on each other now, he for the material I supplied so effortlessly, I for those resonant two-cents-a-word checks. March
1958 alone saw me sell him two s-f stories, "The Traders" and "The Aliens
Were Haters," and five crime pieces, "Doublecrosser's Daughter," "Deadly
Widow," "Rollercoaster Ride," "Let Him Sweat," and "The Ace of Spades
Means Death," plus some batches of science fillers. The pay came to over a
thousand dollars, a regal sum in preinflation 1958 money. How I thought
up all the story ideas, God alone knows: I can only tell you that when I sat
down each morning and put paper in the typewriter, a story would be there
waiting to be written.*

*In this case the story that had been waiting to be written, in mid-
October of 1957, involved an old actor out in the stars who wanted to go
back to Earth and play Hamlet one last time—something that I thought
Horace Gold of Galaxy might be interested in, for a cent a word more than
Scottie would pay. I called it "You Can't Go Back." Horace didn't fancy it.
Neither did Bob Mills, who had replaced Tony Boucher as the editor of
Fantasy and Science Fiction. So early in April of 1958, I took it down to
Scottie. He bought it unhesitatingly, changed its title on the spot to "Exiled
from Earth," and ran it under the byline of "Richard F. Watson" in the*

December, 1958 issue of Super-Science, *where it kept company with my other two recent submissions, "The Aliens Were Haters" (under my own name) and "The Traders" (as Calvin M. Knox). Scottie renamed the latter story "The Unique and Terrible Compulsion." As I said earlier, some of his title changes were improvements, but not all.*

The night old Howard Brian got his impossible yen to return to Earth, we were playing to an almost-full house at Smit's Terran Theater on Salvor. A crowd like that one really warms a director's heart. Five hundred solemn-mouthed, rubber-faced green Salvori had filed into the little drab auditorium back of the circus aviary, that night. They had plunked down two credits apiece to watch my small troupe of exiled Terran actors perform.

We were doing *King Lear* that night—or rather, a boiled-down half-hour condensation of it. I say with I hope pardonable pride that it wasn't too bad a job. The circus management limits my company to half an hour per show, so we won't steal time from the other attractions.

A nuisance, but what could we do? With Earth under inflexible Neopuritan sway, we had to go elsewhere and take whatever bookings we could. I cut *Lear* down to size by pasting together a string of the best speeches, and to Sheol with the plot. Plot didn't matter here, anyway; the Salvori didn't understand a word of the show.

But they insisted on style, and so did I. Technique! Impeccable timing. Smit's Players were just about the sole exponents of the Terran drama in this sector of the outworlds, and I wanted each and every performance to be worthy of the world that kind cast us so sternly forth.

I sat in the back of the theater unnoticed and watched old Howard Brian, in the title role, bringing the show to its close. Howard was the veteran of my troupe, a tall, still majestic figure at seventy-three. I didn't know then that this was to be the night of his crackup.

He was holding dead Cordelia in his arms and glaring round as if his eyes were neutron-smitters. Spittle flecked his gray beard.

"*Howl, howl, howl, howl! Oh, you are men of stones:*
Had I your tongues and eyes, I'd use them so
That heaven's vaults should crack. She's gone forever.
I know when one is dead, and when one lives;

She's dead as earth. Lend me a looking-glass;
If that her breath will mist or stain the stone,
Why then she lives."

As Howard reached that tingling line, *She's dead as earth,* I glanced at my watch. In three minutes *Lear* would be over, and the circus attendants would clear the auditorium for the next show, the popular Damooran hypnotists. Silently I slipped from my seat, edged through the brightly-lit theater—Salvori simply can't stand the dark—and made my way past a row of weeping aliens toward the dressing-room, to be on hand to congratulate my cast.

I got there during the final speech, and counted the curtain-calls: five, six, seven. Applause from outside still boomed as Howard Brian entered the dressing-room, with the rest of the cast following him. Howard's seamed face was beaded with sweat. Genuine tears glittered in his faded eyes. *Genuine.* The mark of a great actor.

I came forward and seized his hand. "Marvelous job tonight, old man. The Greenies loved every second of it. They were spellbound."

"To hell with the Greenies," Howard said in a suddenly hoarse voice. "I'm through, Erik. Let someone else play Lear for your gaggle of gawping green-faced goggle-eyed aliens in this stale-sawdust circus."

I grinned at the old man. I had seen him in this crochety bitter mood before. We all were subject to it, when we thought of Earth. "Come off it, Howard!" I chuckled. "You don't mean to tell me you're retiring again? Why, you're in your prime. You never were better than—"

"No!" Howard plopped heavily into a chair and let his gaudy regal robes swirl around him. He looked very much the confused, defeated Lear at that moment. "Finished," he breathed. "I'm going back to Earth, Erik. *La comeddia è finita.*"

"Hey!" I shouted to the rest of the company. "Listen to old Uncle Vanya here! He's going back to Earth! He says he's tired of playing Lear for the Greenies!"

Joanne, my Goneril, chuckled, and then Ludwig, the Gloucester, picked it up, and a couple of others joined in—but it was an awkward, quickly dying chuckle. I saw the weary, wounded look on old Howard's face. I grinned apologetically and snapped, "Okay! Out of costume double fast, everyone. Cast party in twenty minutes! *Kethii* and roast *dwaarn* for everybody!"

"Erik, can I talk to you in your office?" Howard murmured to me.

"Sure. Come on. Talk it all out, Howard."

I led the gaunt old actor into the red-walled cubicle I laughingly call my office, and dialed two filtered rums, Terran style. Howard gulped his drink greedily, pushed away the empty glass, burped. He transfixed me with his long gray beard and glittering eye and said, "I need eleven hundred credits to get back to Earth. The one-way fare's five thousand. I've saved thirty-nine hundred."

"And you're going to toss your life's savings into one trip?" I shook my head emphatically. "Snap out of it, Howard! You're not on stage now. You aren't Lear—not a doddering old man ready to die."

"I know that. I'm still young—*inside.* Erik, I want to play Hamlet in New York. I want it more than anything else there is. So I've decided to go back to New York, to play Hamlet."

"Oh," I said softly. "Oh, I see."

Draining my glass, I stared reflectively at Howard Brian. I understood for the first time what had happened to the old actor. Howard was obviously insane.

The last time anyone had played Hamlet in New York, I knew, it had been the late Dover Hollis, at the climax of his magnificent career. Hollis had played the gloomy prince at the Odeon on February 21, 2167. Thirty-one years ago. The next day, the Neopuritan majority in Congress succeeded in ramming through its anti-sin legislation, and as part of the omnibus bill the theaters were closed. Play-producing became a felonious act. Members of the histrionic professions overnight lost what minute respectability they had managed to attain. We were all scamps and scoundrels once again, as in the earliest days of the theater.

I remembered Dover Hollis' 2167 *Hamlet* vividly, because I had been in it. I was eighteen, and I played Marcellus. Not too well, mind you; I never was much of an actor.

Howard Brian had been in that company too, and a more villainous Claudius had never been seen on America's shores. Howard had been signed on to do Hamlet, but when Dover Hollis requested a chance to play the part Howard had graciously moved aside. And thereby lost his only chance to play the Dane. He was to have reclaimed his role a week later, when Hollis returned to London—but, a week later, the padlocks were on the theater doors.

I said to Howard, "You can't go back to Earth. You know that, don't you?"

He shook his head obstinately. "They're casting for *Hamlet* at the Odeon again. I'm not too old, Erik. Bernhard played it, and she was an old *woman,* with a wooden leg, yet. I want to go."

I sighed. "Howard, listen to me: you accepted free transportation from the Neopuritan government, like all the rest of us, on the condition that you didn't try to return. They shipped you to the outworlds. You can't go back."

"Maybe they're out of power. Maybe the Supreme Court overthrew the legislation. Maybe—"

"Maybe nothing. You read *Outworld Variety,* the same as the rest of us. You know how things stand on Earth. The Supreme Court is twelve to three Neopuritan, and the three old holdouts are at death's door. Congress is Neopuritan. A whole new generation of solemn little idiots has grown up under a Neopuritan president. It's the same all over the world." I shook my head. "There isn't any going back. The time is out of joint, Howard. Earth doesn't want actors or dancers or singers or other sinful people. Until the pendulum swings back again, Earth just wants to atone. They're having a gloom orgy."

"Give me another drink, Erik," Howard said hollowly. I dialed it for him. He slurped half of it down and said, "I didn't ask you for a sermon. I just want eleven hundred credits. You can spare it."

"That's questionable. But the money's irrelevant, anyway. You couldn't get back to Earth."

"Will you let me try?"

His dry cheeks were quivering, and tears were forming in his eyes. I saw he was in the grip of an obsession that could have only one possible end, and I knew then that I had lost my best actor. I said, "What do you want me to do?"

"Guarantee me the money. Then get me a visa and book passage for me. I'll take care of the rest."

I was silent.

He said, "We've been together thirty years, Erik. I remember when you were a kid actor who didn't know blank verse from a blank check. But you grew up into the best director I ever worked with."

"Thanks, Howard."

"No. No thanks needed. I did my best for you, even on this rotten backwater. Remember my Prince Hal? And I did Falstaff too, ten years later. And Willy Loman, and Mark Diamond, and the whole Ibsen cycle."

"You were great," I said. "You still are."

"We never did *Hamlet,* though. You said you couldn't bear to condense it for the Greenies. Well, now's my chance. Send me to Earth.

Lend me the dough, see the Consul for me, fix things up. Will you do that for me, Erik?"

I drew in my breath sharply. I realized I had no choice. From this night on, Howard would be no good to me as an actor; I might just as well try to let him die happy.

"Okay," I said. "I'll see what I can do for you."

"You're a prince, Erik! An ace among men and the director of directors. You—"

I cut him off. "It's time for the cast party. We don't want to miss out on that sweet burbling *kethii.*"

As usual, we were very very gay that night, with the desperate gaiety of a bunch of actors stranded in a dismal alien world where we were appreciated for the way we did things but not for what we did. We were just another act in Goznor's Circus, and there wasn't one of us who didn't know it.

I woke the next morning with a *kethii* head, which is one way of saying that my eyeballs were popping. The odor of slops got me up. My flat is in the Dillborr quarter of Salvor City, and Dillborr is the rough Salvori equivalent for Pigtown. But Earthmen actors are severely restricted as to living quarters on worlds like Salvor.

I dressed and ran myself through the reassembler until my molecules were suitably vitalized and I felt able to greet the morning. Ordinarily I'd have slept till noon, getting up just in time to make the afternoon rehearsal, but this day I was up early. And I had told the cast that I was so pleased with *Lear* I was cancelling the regular daytime runthrough, and would see them all at the usual evening check-in time of 1900.

I had plenty of work to do this day.

I knew it was a futile cause; Howard had as much chance of getting back to Earth as he did of riding a sled through a supernova and coming out uncooked. But I had promised him I'd see what I could do, and I was damned well going to try.

First thing, I phoned the office of Transgalactic Spacelines, downtown in the plusher section of Salvor City. A Neopuritan gal appeared on the screen, her face painted chalk-white, her lips black, her eyes frowning in the zombie way considered so virtuous on Earth. She recognized me immediately, and I could almost hear the wheels in her brain grinding out the label: *Sinful actor person.*

I said, "Good morning, sweetheart. Is Mr. Dudley in the office yet?"

"Mr. Dudley is here," she said in a voice as warm as stalactites and about as soft. "Do you have an appointment to talk to him?"

"Do I *need* one?"

"Mr. Dudley is very busy this morning."

"Look," I said, "tell him Erik Smit wants to talk to him. That's your job, and it's sinful of you to try to act as a screen for him." I saw the retort corning, and quickly added, "It's also sinful to make nasty remarks to possible customers. Put Dudley on, will you?"

Dudley was the manager of the local branch of the spaceline. I knew him well; he was a staunch Neopuritan with secret longings, and more than once he had crept into our theater in disguise to watch the show. I knew about it and kept quiet. I wondered what Miss Iceberg would say if she knew some of the things her boss had done—and some he would like to do, if he dared.

The screen imploded swoopingly and Dudley appeared. He was a heavy-set man with pink ruddy cheeks; the Neopuritan pallor did not set well on him. "Good morning, Mr. Smit," he said formally.

"Morning, Walter. Can you give me some information?"

"Maybe. What kind, Erik?"

"Travel information. When's the next scheduled Salvor-Earth voyage?"

He frowned curiously. "The *Oliver Cromwell's* booking in here on the First of Ninemonth—that's next Twoday—and is pulling out on the Third. Why?"

"Never mind that" I said. "Second-class fare to Earth is still five thousand credits, isn't it?"

"Yes, but—"

"Do you have a vacancy on the Earthbound leg of the journey?"

He said nothing for a moment: Then: "Yes, yes, we have some openings. But—this can't be for *you*, Erik. You know the law. And—"

"It isn't for me," I said. "It's for Howard Brian. He wants to play Hamlet in New York."

A smile appeared on Dudley's pudgy face. "He's a little out of date for that, unless there's been a revolution I haven't heard about."

"He's gone a little soft in the head. But he wants to die on Earth, and I'm going do my best to get him there. Five thousand credits, you say?" I paused. "Could I get him aboard that ship for seventy-five hundred?"

Anger flickered momentarily in Dudley's eyes as his Neopuritan streak came to life. Controlling himself, he said, "It's pointless to offer bribes, Erik. I understand the problem, but there's absolutely nothing you or I or anyone can do. Earth's closed to anyone who signed the Amnesty of 2168."

"Eight thousand," I said. "Eighty-five hundred."

"You don't understand, Erik. Or you *won't* understand. Look here: Howard would need an entrance visa to get onto Earth. No visa, no landing. You know that, I know that, he knows it. Sure, I could put him aboard that ship, if you could find a spaceport man who'd take a bribe—and I doubt that you could. But he'd never get off the ship at the other end."

"At least he'd be closer to Earth than he is now."

"It won't work. You know what side I'm on personally, Erik. But it's impossible to board a Transgalactic Line ship without proper papers, and Howard can't ever get those papers. He *can't* go back, Erik. Sorry."

I looked at the face framed in the screen and narrowly avoided bashing in the glass. It would only have netted me some bloody knuckles and a hundred credit repair bill, but I would have felt better about things. Instead I said, "You know, your own behavior hasn't been strictly Neopuritan. I might write some notes—"

It was a low blow, but he ducked. He looked sad as he said, "You couldn't prove anything, Erik. And blackmail isn't becoming on you."

He was right. "Okay, Walter. Hope I didn't take up valuable time."

"Not at all. I only wish—"

"I know. Drop around to the circus some time soon. Howard's playing *Lear.* You'd better see it now, while you have the chance."

I blanked the screen.

I sat on the edge of my hammock and cursed the fact that we'd all been born a century too late—or maybe too early. 21st Century Earth had been a glorious larking place, or so I had heard. Games and gaiety and champagne, no international tensions, no ulcers. But I had been born in the 22nd Century, when the boom came swinging back the other way. A reaction took place; people woke from a pleasant dream and turned real life into a straight-laced nightmare.

Which was why we had chosen between going to prison, entering mundane professions, and accepting the new Neopuritan government's free offer to take ourselves far from Earth and never come back. We'd been on Salvor thirty years now. The youngest of us was middle-aged.

But makeup does wonders, and anyway the Salvori didn't care if Romeo happened to be fifty-seven and slightly paunchy.

I clenched my hands. I had been a wide-eyed kid when the Neopuritans lowered the boom, and I jumped at the chance to see the outworlds free. Now I was forty-nine, balding, a permanent exile. I vowed I was going to work like the deuce to help Howard Brian. It was a small rebellion, but a heartfelt one.

I called my bank and had them flash my bankbook on the screen. It showed a balance of Cr. 13,586—not a devil of a lot for thirty years' work. I scribbled a draft for six thousand in cash, dropped it in the similarizer plate, and waited. They verified, and moments later a nice wad of Interstellar Galactic Credits landed in the receiving slot.

I got dressed in my Sevenday best, locked up the place, and caught a transport downtown to the spaceport terminal. As an Earthman, of course, I rode in the back of the transport, and stood.

A coach was just leaving the terminal for the spaceport. By noon I found myself forty miles outside Salvor City, standing at the edge of the sprawling maze of buildings and landing-areas that is Salvor Spaceport. I hadn't been out here since that day in 2168 when the liner *John Calvin* deposited me and eighty-seven other Terran actors, dancers, strippers, and miscellaneous deported sinners, and a bleak-faced official advised us to behave ourselves, for we were now subject to the laws of Salvor.

I made my way through the confusing network of port buildings to the customs shed. My 6000-credit wad felt pleasantly thick in my pocket. Customs was crowded with aliens of various hues and shapes who were departing on a Mullinor-bound liner and who were getting a routine check-through. Since Mullinor is under Terran administration, not only were the Salvori officials running the check but a few black-uniformed employees of Transgalactic Spacelines were on hand as well. I picked out the least hostile-looking of those, and, palming a twenty-credit piece, sidled up to him.

He was checking through the passports of the departing travellers. I tapped him on the shoulder and slipped the bright, round double stellar into his hand at the same time.

"Pardon me, friend. Might I have a minute's conversation with you in privacy?"

He glanced at me with contempt in his Neopuritan eyes and handed me back the big coin. "I'll be through with this job in fifteen minutes. Wait for me in Depot A, if there's any information you want."

Now, it might have been that one of his superiors was watching, and that he didn't want to be seen taking a gratuity in public. But I knew that was a mighty shaky theory for explaining his refusal. I didn't have much hope, but I hied myself to Depot A and waited there for half an hour.

Finally he came along, walking briskly and whistling a hymn. He said, "Do you wish to see me?"

"Yes."

I explained the whole thing: who I was and who Howard was, and why it was so important to let Howard get aboard the ship for Earth. I let him know that there would be two or three thousand credits in it for him if he arranged things so Howard Brian could board the *Oliver Cromwell* next Twoday. At least, I finished, he would die with Earth in sight, even though he might not be permitted to disembark.

I stood there waiting hopefully for an answer and watched his already frosty gaze drop to about three degrees Kelvin. He said, "By the law, Mr. Smit, I should turn you in for attempting to bribe a customs official. But in your case justice should be tempered by mercy. I pity you. Please leave."

"Dammit, I'll give you *five* thousand!"

He smiled condescendingly. "Obviously you can't see that my soul is not for sale—not for five thousand or five billion credits. The law prohibits allowing individuals without visas to board interstellar ships. I ask you to leave before I must report you."

I left. I saw I was making a head-first assault on a moral code which by its very nature was well-nigh impregnable, and all I was getting out of it was a headache.

Bribery was no good. These people took a masochistic pride in their underpaid incorruptibility: I was forced back on my last resort.

I went to see the Terran Consul. The legal above-board approach was my one slim hope.

Archibald von Junzt McDermott was his name, and he was a tall and angular person clad entirely in black, with a bit of white lace at his throat. It was his duty to comfort, aid, and abet Terran citizens on Salvor. Of course, I was no longer a Terran citizen—that was part of the Amnesty too—but I was of Terran birth, at least.

He wore the full Neopuritan makeup, bleached face, cropped hair, blackened lips; he hardly seemed like a comforting type to me. He sat stiffly erect behind his desk and let me squirm and fidget a while before he said, "You realize, of course, that such a request is impossible to grant. Utterly."

Quietly I said, "I'm asking for a relaxation of the rules on behalf of one very sick old man who will probably die of joy the moment Earth comes into sight, and who is guaranteed not to touch off a revolution, promote licentiousness, seduce maidens, or otherwise upset the aims and standards of Neopuritan Earth."

"'There can be no relaxation of the rules," Consul McDermott repeated stonily.

"Can't you look the other way *once?* Don't you know what pity is, Consul?"

"I know the meaning of the word well. I feel deep pity for you now, Mr. Smit. You have no spine. You are afraid to face the world as it is. You're a weakling, Mr. Smit, and I offer you my pity."

"Damned decent of you," I snorted. "You won't grant Howard Brian a visa to Earth, then?"

"Definitely not. We're neither cruel nor vindictive, Mr. Smit. But the standards of society must be upheld. And I cannot find it within my heart to encourage immorality."

"Okay," I said. I stood up and flashed a withering glare at him—a glare of pure hate that would have been a credit to the starchiest Neopuritan preacher in the universe.

Then I turned and walked out.

❋

It was 1800 when I got back to my flat, and that left me an hour to relax before I had to get down to the theater to set things up for the 2030 performance. I got out of my stiff dress clothes and into my work outfit, and spent a little time on my forthcoming condensation of *Medea* while waiting for the hour to pass. I felt sour with defeat.

The visiphone chime sounded. I activated the receiver and John Ludwig's face appeared, half in makeup for his role of Gloucester.

"What is it, Johnny?"

"Erik, can you get right down to the theater? Howard's had a sort of stroke. We'll have to call off tonight's performance."

"I'll decide that," I said. "I'll be right down."

They had fixed up a rough sort of bed for him in the main dressing-room, and he was stretched out, looking pale and lean and lonely;

gobbets of sweat stood out on his forehead. The whole company was standing around, plus a couple of tentacled Arcturan acrobats and the three Damooran hypnotists whose act follows our show each night.

Ludwig said, "He got here early and started making up for *Lear.* Then he just seemed to cave in. He's been asking for you, Erik."

I went over to him and took his cool wrist and said, "Howard? You hear me, Howard?"

He didn't open his eyes, but he said, "Well, how did it go? Did you book the trip for me?"

I took a deep breath. I felt cold and miserable inside, and I glanced around at the tense ring of faces before I told the lie. "Yeah," I said. "Sure, Howard. I fixed it all up. Leave it to old Erik. Everything's fine."

A pathetic trusting childlike smile slowly blossomed on his face. I scowled and snapped to a couple of others, "Carry him into my office. Then get finished making up for tonight's show."

Ludwig protested, "But Howard doesn't have an understudy. How can we—"

"Don't worry," I barked. *"I'll* play Lear tonight, if Howard's out."

I supervised as they carried Howard, bed and all, through the corridor into my office. Then, sweating nervously, I collared the three Damoorans and said, "Are you boys doing anything for the next half hour or so?"

"We're free," they said in unison. They looked like a trio of tall, red, flashy animated corkscrews with bulbous eyes in their forehead. They weren't pretty, but they were masters of their trade and fine showmen. They hung around Goznor's Circus all the time, even when they weren't on.

I explained very carefully to them just what I wanted them to do. It was an idea I'd held in reserve, in case all else failed. They were dubious, but liberal application of platinum double stellar coins persuaded them to give in. They vanished into my office and shut the door behind them. While I was waiting, I found Howard's makeup kit and started turning myself into King Lear.

Perhaps fifteen minutes later the Damoorans filed out again, and nodded to me. "You had better go in there, now. He's on Earth. It was a very good trip."

I tiptoed into the office. Howard lay sprawled on the bed, eyes screwed tight shut, mouth moving slowly. His skin was a frightening waxy white. I put an ear near his lips to hear what he was mumbling.

"I cannot live to hear the news from England,

But I do prophesy the election lights
On Fortinbras; he has my dying voice:
So tell him, with the occurents, more and less,
Which have solicited—the rest is silence."

My mind filled in the stage direction: *Dies.* Act Five, Scene Two. Hamlet's last speech.

Bravo, I thought. I looked down at Howard Brian. His voice had ceased, and his throat was still. His part was played. Howard Brian had acted Hamlet at last, and it was his finest moment on Broadway.

He was smiling even in death.

The Damoorans had done their job well. For thirty years I had watched them perform, and I had faith in their illusion-creating ability. Howard had probably lived months in these last fifteen minutes. The long journey to Earth, the tickertape parade down Fifth Avenue, the thronged opening-night house, deafening applause. Certainly the Damoorans had manufactured good notices for him in the late editions.

Anyway, it was over. Howard Brian had cheated them after all. He had returned to Earth for his swansong performance.

I shook a little as I left the office and shut the door behind me. The on-stage bell sounded. I heard Kent and Gloucester begin their scene.

I went out there as Lear and maybe I did a good job. The cast told me later that I did, and the Salvori loved it. It didn't matter. Howard would have wanted the show to go on.

But I couldn't help thinking, during the solemn aftershow moments when they carried Howard out, that my turn was coming. You can't go back to Earth; but someday in the next twenty years I was going to want to go back with all my heart, as Howard had wanted. The thought worried me. I only hoped there'd be a few Damoorans around, when my time came.

SECOND START
(1959)

Here's a story written in July, 1958 and published in the February, 1959 issue of Super-Science Fiction *that is the most interesting rediscovery I made while choosing material for this collection.*

As usual, W.W. Scott retitled it for publication—he called it "Re-Conditioned Human." But when I leafed through the magazine, I needed to read only the first paragraph to realize what I had stumbled upon:

> *"The name they gave me at the Rehabilitation Center was Paul Macy. It was as good as any other, I guess. The name I was born with was Nat Hamlin, but when you become a Rehab you have to give up your name."*

Paul Macy, who was called Nat Hamlin before being sentenced to rehabilitation for his crimes, is the protagonist of a novel of mine called The Second Trip, *which was first published in 1972. I wrote it in November, 1970, one of the strongest periods of my writing career. The Second Trip is one of my best books. (The novel just preceding it was the Nebula-winning* A Time of Changes; *the one just after it was* The Book of Skulls.) *I rarely re-read my own books, but I happened to read* The Second Trip *a few months ago, in connection with a new edition, for the first time in more than three decades. Coming to it after so many years, I had forgotten most of its details and I was able to read it almost as an outsider, caught up in the narrative as though encountering it for the first time. I have to tell you that I was quite impressed.*

Another thing that I had forgotten over the years, it seems, is that back there in 1970 I had based The Second Trip *on an earlier story, already twelve years old, that I had written one busy morning for Super-Science Fiction. Not only had I forgotten that* The Second Trip *had grown out of the earlier story, I had entirely forgotten the whole existence of the earlier story itself, and great was my astonishment when I encountered Paul Macy/Nat Hamlin in that 1959 magazine.*

Anyone interested in studying the evolution of a writer would do well to compare the story and the novel that grew out of it. The story is set in a universe of easy travel between stars, many centuries from now. The novel is set on Earth in the year 2011. The former identity of the Macy of the story is an interstellar jewel thief and smuggler, whose old confederates in crime want to force him back into their syndicate. The former identity of the Macy of the novel is a brilliant sculptor who happens also to be a psychopath, and who struggles to regain control of his body after it has been given to a newly created personality. In concept, in handling, in everything, the two works could not have been more different—and yet one plainly grew out of the other, twelve years later. The evidence of the characters' names is there to prove that. The story is the work of a young man of 23, turning out material as fast as possible to fill the pages of a minor science-fiction magazine. The novel is the work of a mature writer of 35, who was devoting all the skill and energy at his command to the creation of a group of novels that would establish him as one of the leading s-f writers of his day. Reading the two works just a few months apart, as I did last year, was an extraordinary revelatory experience for me.

———————

The name they gave me at the Rehabilitation Center on Earth was Paul Macy. It was as good as any other, I guess. The name I was born with was Nat Hamlin, but when you become a Rehab you have to give up your name.

I didn't mind that. What I did mind was the idea of having my face changed, since I was pretty well content with my looks the way they were. They gave me the option of choosing either a refacing job or else getting outside the Four Parsec Zone and staying there, and I opted to keep my face and leave Earth. This was how I happened to settle on Palmyra, which is Lambda Scorpii IX, 205 light-years from Earth. I met Ellen on Palmyra. And Dan Helgerson met me. I didn't figure to run into Helgerson there, but it's a smaller universe than you think.

Helgerson was a sometime business associate of Nat Hamlin's—the *late* Nat Hamlin, because that was the way I thought of my former identity. Hamlin had been in the jewel-trading business. Also the jewel-stealing business, the jewelry-fencing business, and the jewelry-smuggling business, and toward the end of his varied career, after he had made contact with an enterprising Sirian who owned a fusion forge, the jewel-making business.

Hamlin was quite a guy. If it had to do with pretty pebbles, and if it happened to be illegal, you could bet Hamlin was mixed up in it. That was why the Galactic Crime Commission finally had to crack down, grab Hamlin, and feed him through the psychic meatgrinder that is the Rehabilitation Center. What came out on the other end, purged of his anti-social impulses and stuff like that, was Paul Macy.

Me.

Naturally they confiscated Hamlin's wealth, which included a cache of gold in Chicago, a cache of pure iron on Grammas VI, a cache of tungsten on Sirius XIX, and a cache here and there of whatever was most precious to a particular planet. Hamlin had been a smart operator. He had been worth a couple of billions when they caught him. After they finished turning him into me, they gave me five thousand bucks in Galactic scrip—not a hell of a lot of money by Nat Hamlin's standards—he used to carry that much as pocket-change for tips—but more than enough for Paul Macy to use in starting his new life.

The Rehab people found me a good job on Palmyra, as a minor executive in a canning factory. It was the sort of job where I could make use of Nat Hamlin's organizational abilities, channelling them constructively into the cause of faster and more efficient squid-canning. Canned squid is Palmyra's big industry. The fishermen bring them in from the wine-colored sea in the billions, and we ship them all over the universe.

I got good pay from the canning people and I found a nice bachelor home on the outskirts of Palmyra City. I found a nice girl, too—Ellen Bryce was her name, Earthborn, 24, soft violet hair and softer green eyes. She worked in the shipping department of our place. I started noticing her around, and then I started dating her, and then before I knew it I was starting to think of getting married.

But then one night after I left my office I stopped into the bar on the corner for a vraffa martini as a bracer, and I saw Dan Helgerson sitting at one of the tables.

I tried to pretend I didn't see him. I hunched down at the bar and sipped at my cocktail.

But out of the corner of my eye I saw him get up and start sauntering over to me. Wildly I hoped I was mistaken, that this was not Helgerson but someone else.

It was Helgerson, all right. And when he slid in next to me, clapped me on the back, and said, "Hello, Nat. Long time no see," I knew I was in trouble.

My hand tightened on the stem of my cocktail glass. I looked up at Helgerson and tried to keep my face blank, unrecognizing.

"There must be some mistake. My name isn't Nat."

"Come off it, pal. You're Nat Hamlin or I'm drunker than I think I am. And I don't get that drunk on one shot of booril."

"My name is Paul Macy," I said in a tight voice. "I don't know you."

Helgerson chuckled thickly. "You're a damn good actor, Nat. Always were. But don't push a joke too far. I've been looking for you for weeks."

"Looking for me?"

"There's a privacy booth over there, Nat. Suppose we go over and talk in there. I've got a proposition you might want to hear."

I felt a muscle twanging in my cheek. I said, "Look, fellow, my name is Macy, not Nat Hamlin. I'm not interested in any propositions you might have."

I shook my head. "No, Helgerson. Just keep away and leave me alone."

A slow smile rippled out over Helgerson's face. "If your name is Macy and you don't know me, how come you know my name? I don't remember introducing myself."

It was like a kick in the ribs. I had blundered; it had been an accident. But it had happened before I could stop it. The Rehab treatment had altered Hamlin's personality, but it hadn't wiped out his old memories. As Paul Macy, I had no business knowing Helgerson's name— but I did.

I scowled and said, "Okay. Let's go over to the privacy booth and I'll fill you in on the news."

Scooping up my half-finished drink, I followed Helgerson across the room to the privacy booth. On the way I glanced at my watch. It was quarter after five. Ellen was expecting me at half past six at her place, for dinner. I had been figuring on a leisurely shower and shave first, but if it took too long to get rid of Helgerson I would probably have to skip everything and go straight out to Ellen's.

He slipped a coin into the slot and the crackling blue privacy field built up around us, shielding our little booth in an electronic curtain impervious to spybeams and eavesdroppers. He said, "Okay, Nat. What's this Paul Macy bit? Some new dodge?"

"No. No dodge."

I reached into my breast pocket, and Helgerson's jowly face twitched in momentary alarm, as if he half expected me to yank out a blaster. Instead I drew out my wallet and silently handed him my identity card— not the blue one that everyone has to carry, but the other one, the yellow card they had given me when I left the Rehabilitation Center.

He read both sides of it and when he handed it back to me his face was a lot different.

"So they got Nat Hamlin. Whaddya know. And they left your face alone?"

"I took the Four Parsec option. As long as I keep away from Earth I can wear my old face. I figured it was safe, on Palmyra. Nobody in our line operated on Palmyra."

"We do now."

It was my turn to twitch in alarm. "How?"

"We're setting up an import chain. The Palmyrans are getting interested in owning pretty jewelry. They weren't, before, but we've been working on them. It's a virgin market, Nat."

"My name is Macy."

"Sorry. Anyway, we're setting up a pipeline. And you're the key man."

The muscle in my cheek twanged again. "I'm not in the business any more, Helgerson."

"Listen to me, Nat—Macy, whatever you call yourself. I've checked up on you ever since I heard you were here. You got a good position—you're respected—trusted. I figured you were setting something up for yourself. But I guess it was just because you were a Rehab. Well, anyway, it's a natural. We could send the stones in wrapped up in those squid-cans—call them market returns, code the wrappers. All you have to do is grab the loaded cans and turn them over to me. I'll guarantee you three quarters of a million a year for it."

I felt sick. I wanted to get out of that booth fast. "I'm not in the business," I said bleakly.

"Eight hundred thousand. Nat, this setup is a peach!"

"I told you—"

"I'll go as high as a million."

"Look," I said. "I'm a Rehab. That means I've been through the Center, analyzed, monkeyed-with, headshrunk, rearranged. There isn't a criminal molecule left in me. I can't do it even if I wanted to. And I don't want to."

He smiled pityingly. "Don't give me that crap, Nat. If you wanted to bad enough, you could break your conditioning. It's been done before."

"Maybe it has. But I don't want to. Not even for a billion a year."

"Nat—"

"The name is Macy. And I'm not interested." I looked at my watch. It was getting late. I didn't want to talk to Helgerson any more. Ellen was expecting me. I reached out and yanked the shutoff lever, and the privacy field died away with a faint whuffling sound. Helgerson was glaring at me and I glared back. "The answer is no. Finally and absolutely. And don't bother me any more, Helgerson. I'll run you in for violating the Rehab Code if you do."

I got up and strode toward the door. Helgerson yelled something after me, but I was too angry to listen.

❋

It was quarter of seven when I got to Ellen's, which meant I was fifteen minutes late, and I hadn't had time for that shower and shave, either. But Ellen didn't make any acid remarks. That was how she differed from most of the women I knew; she could forgive and forget, and without making a fuss about it.

She was wearing a sprayed-on strylon dress that covered her body with a layer of plastic two molecules thick—enough to keep her within the bounds of maidenly decency, but also revealing enough to make her quite an eyeful. I held her against me for a minute or two, as if her nearness could drain away the inner tension Helgerson had provoked in me. It didn't, but it was pleasant anyway.

Then she broke away, with the excuse that dinner would be spoiled. She had made roast seafowl with a garnishment of starflower sprouts, and cool white wine from Mellibor to wash it all down. We ate quietly; I was troubled over the Helgerson business. If a bunch of my old pals set up the trade on Palmyra, it was going to make life very hard for me here. Bitterly I asked myself why they had had to come here; I had had eight months of peace, but now it was to be shattered.

We dumped the dishes into the autowash. Ellen nuzzled against me playfully and said, "You're quiet tonight, Paul. Worried. What's bothering you?"

I tried to wear a cheerful grin. "Nothing much."

I shrugged. "Plant business," I lied. Telling even a small lie like that gave me a twinge of remorse, thanks to the built-in conscience the Rehab Center had given me. My conditioning didn't prevent me from telling lies, but it made sure that I felt the effects of even a small one. "We had some trouble come up today. Nothing serious."

"Shake it off, then! Let's go for a drive, yes?"

We rode to the roof, where I had parked my aircar, and for the next two hours we soared through the Palmyran night. I drove out over the ocean, glittering with the reflection of a million stars and a quartet of bright moons, and then swooped down over the coastal plains, still mostly untouched by man's hand. We said little, satisfied just to have each other near. When I was with Ellen I was glad I had been Rehabbed; Nat Hamlin had never trusted another human being, and so Nat Hamlin had never been in love. I had not only a different name but a different set of emotions, and that made all the difference in the universe.

It was nearly eleven when I brought the aircar lightly to rest on the roof of Ellen's building. Our goodnights took half an hour, but they weren't the sort of goodnights Nat Hamlin would have appreciated, because Paul Macy didn't play the game as close as his predecessor in our body did. Ellen was passionate within bounds; she wanted to be my wife, not my mistress, and she knew the best way of achieving that goal. Which was all right with me. I could be patient a while longer.

I left her at half past eleven and drove home in a pleasantly euphoric state, having nearly forgotten about the ominous popping-up of Dan Helgerson. But when I entered my place, a little after midnight, I saw the red light on my autosec lit up.

I nudged the acknowledger to let the machine know I was home, and it said, "Mr. Helgerson called while you were out, sir. He left his number. Shall I call him back?"

"No. I'm tired and I don't want to speak to him."

"He said it was urgent, sir," the autosec protested gently. "He said, quote, it would be too bad for you if you didn't call him."

There was a sour taste in my mouth and a knot of tension formed in my chest. I sighed. "All right. Call him back."

❋

Helgerson's fleshy face formed in the depths of the screen. He wore an ugly smile. "Glad you decided to call back, Nat. You ran out on me so fast before that I didn't have time to tell you all I wanted to tell you."

"Well, spill it out now. Quick. It's late and I don't want to waste any more time on you than I have to."

"I'll come right to the point," Helgerson said. "We want you to join our syndicate. You're the key man; the whole thing revolves around your coming in. And if—"

"I told you I'm playing it straight. I'm not Nat Hamlin any more."

"And if you turn down the offer," Helgerson went on, ignoring the interruption, "we're going to have to take steps to make you join us."

I was quiet for a moment. "What sort of steps?"

"You have a girlfriend, Hamlin. I hear you're pretty high on her. Plan to marry her, maybe. I've checked up a lot about you. How would your girlfriend react if she found out you were a Rehab?"

"She—I—" I closed my mouth and felt black anger ripple up through me. And with it came the sick feeling my conditioning supplied, to keep me from doing anything violent. I wanted to do something violent right then. I said instead, "People don't discriminate against Rehabs. The Code says they're to be treated as completely new individuals. Paul Macy didn't commit Nat Hamlin's crimes."

"That's what the Code says, yeah. But nobody really trusts a Rehab, deep down. There's always the lingering suspicion that he might backslide."

"Ellen would trust me even if she knew."

"Maybe she would, maybe she wouldn't. How about the people you work with? They don't know, either—only the top bosses. And your friends. What's going to happen if they suddenly find out you've been holding out on them, that you're really a Rehab?"

I knew what would happen, and I felt bitter-tasting fear. Legally a Rehab is an innocent man and should be subject to no prejudice—but in practice there's a certain coldness between most people and Rehabs, a lack of trust that goes deeper than the legal codes. My nice neat life on Palmyra would be smashed if Helgerson spread the word about.

But I *couldn't* go in with him on the deal.

I said, "You wouldn't pull a thing like that."

"Not if you wised up and let me go back into business with you, Nat. You can overcome your conditioning if you fight it hard enough. Think it over, Nat. I'll phone you tomorrow night. If the answer's still no, the whole planet will know about you the next morning."

The screen went blank.

＊

I paced up and down my room for three hours, cursing Helgerson out and getting my blood pressure up. I realized I was boxed in.

Sure, I could break my conditioning and go back to Helgerson. It probably would mean a total nervous breakdown inside of a month and a permanent case of the shakes, but I could do it. I didn't *want* to do it, though. They had fixed me so I *liked* being honest. Besides, a backsliding Rehab doesn't get a third chance. If I got caught, it would mean total personality demolition—the death sentence for Macy-Hamlin. They would wipe out my mind and build a wholly new identity into my body, one that would have to be taught how to read and write and tie his shoelaces all over again.

No. Joining Helgerson was impossible.

But the alternative was having word of my Rehab status spread all over the place. Maybe Ellen would stick with me after she knew, maybe not; but either way I could never be happy on Palmyra again. The rumor would spread, and I couldn't deny it, which would confirm it. And suddenly I would find myself persona non grata at a lot of places where I was welcomed right now.

I chewed it all out inside myself and saw the only thing I could do, under the circumstances. I couldn't let Ellen find out about me from Helgerson. I would have to tell her myself. I had been meaning to tell her for months, but kept putting it off, postponing it, being afraid of her reaction. The time had come to let her know.

I activated the autosec and told it to phone Ellen. The time was past three in the morning, but I didn't care.

Her head and shoulders appeared on the screen, blinking, sleep-fogged, lovely. "What is it, Paul?"

"I've got to see you, Ellen. Got to talk to you."

"Right now."

"Right now," I said.

I braced myself for the deluge, but it didn't come. She shrugged, smiled, said, "You must have a good reason for it, darling. I'll have coffee ready when you get here."

* * *

The trip took me twenty minutes. I was jittery and tense, and words rolled around crazily in my mind, ways of explaining, ways to tell what I had to tell. Ellen kissed me warmly as I came in. She was wearing a filmy sort of gown and she was still squint-eyed from sleep.

She put a cup of coffee in my hand and I sat down facing her and I said, "Ellen, what I'm going to tell you is something you should have known from the start. I want you to hear me out from beginning to end without interrupting."

I told her the whole thing: how Nat Hamlin had thrived for thirteen years as a top interstellar jewel smuggler, how he had been wanted by half the worlds of the galaxy, how he had finally been caught and Rehabbed into me. I explained why I had taken the Palmyra option, how I had rebuilt my life, how I had begun with a fresh slate. I also told her how much I loved and needed her.

Then I went into the Helgerson episode, and his threat. "That's why I came here, Ellen. To tell you before he had the chance to. But everything's ruined for me here anyway. I can't stop him from exposing me. I'll leave Palmyra tomorrow, go back to Earth, tell them I've changed my mind and want a refacing job done. That way none of Hamlin's old pals can pop up this way again. And I'll find some other world somewhere and start over a second time. That's all, Ellen."

Her expression hadn't changed during the whole long narration. Now that she saw I was finished she said, "I wish you could find some way of avoiding the refacing, Paul. I like your face the way it is."

The implications of what she had said didn't register for a moment. Then I gaped foolishly and gasped, "You—you'll come with me?"

"Of course, silly. You should have told me before—but it doesn't make any difference. I love Paul Macy. Nat Hamlin's dead, so far as I'm concerned."

A floodtide of warmth and happiness swept over me. She trusted me! She—loved me! I had been an idiot not to see the depth of that love, to know that I could have told her the truth all along. "You—aren't like the others, Ellen. The fact that I'm a Rehab doesn't matter to you."

There was an odd expression on her face as she said, "Of course it doesn't matter."

She got up and took her purse from a dresser drawer. She fumbled through the purse, found something, brought it over and handed it to me. "You're not the only one with a past, darling."

I was holding a yellow identity card in my hand. It told me that the girl who was known as Ellen Bryce had been born Joan Gardner, until her sentence two years ago. The card didn't tell me what the sentence had been for, and I didn't want to know. But it did tell me that Ellen was a Rehab too.

✸

The last barriers of mutual mistrust were down between us. Ellen cried, and maybe I cried a little too, and then we laughed at how silly we had both been to keep our big secrets from each other. I figure half the pain in this universe is brought about by people who hide things unnecessarily and then brood over what they've hidden. But we didn't have any more secrets from each other. Dan Helgerson couldn't hurt us now.

He couldn't do anything to what we had between us. If Rehabs don't trust each other, how can they expect the rest of the world to trust them? I didn't care what Joan Gardner had done in her twenty-two years of life. Maybe she had chopped her parents into hamburger; maybe she had been the most active call-girl in the galaxy. What did that matter? Joan Gardner was dead, and Ellen Bryce was the girl I held in my arms that night.

It was ridiculous for me to go home that night, and I stayed till dawn and Ellen made breakfast for us. We talked and planned and wondered, and between us we not only set the date but figured out what I was going to do about Helgerson and his threat.

When Helgerson called the next day to find out my answer, I said, "You win. I'll come in with you at a million a year."

"I knew you'd smarten up, Nat. We need you and you need us. It's a good deal. You always had an eye for a good deal."

"When do I begin?"

"Right away. Suppose you come on over here for lunch and a drink, and I'll give you a month's advance as a binder." He quoted an address on Palmyra City's swank South Side. "You won't regret doing this, Nat. We'll keep it quiet and the Rehab boys won't ever find out you're breaking your conditioning."

"Sure. I'll be right over."

I hung up and reeled dizzily against the wall while the shock of the conversation left me. Rehab conditioning is no joke. Not only do they erase the neuroses that led you to become a criminal in the first place, but they stick in a few mental blocks that make it tough to go back to your old ways. I was fighting those blocks now. Waves of pain rolled through me. It was double-edged pain, too—for not only was I fighting the Rehab conditioning, I was also going against an older, still-active block I had about turning stoolpigeon. Nat Hamlin had been vividly expressive on the subject of stoolies. Paul Macy still found the idea repugnant. But I didn't have any choice. And Helgerson was going to be in for a surprise.

When the pain spasms were gone, I picked up the phone again and asked for the Rehab desk of the local Crime Commission office. The face of Commissioner Blair, the man who had placed me on Palmyra, appeared on the screen: relaxed, pink-cheeked, smiling.

"Hello, there, Paul. What's up?"

"You know Dan Helgerson, Commissioner?"

His brows furrowed. "The name doesn't register."

I said, "You can check him against your master lists later. He's wanted for jewel swindles on fifty worlds or so. He was one of Nat Hamlin's old buddies."

"And what about him, Paul?"

I winced at the inner pain. I said, "Helgerson's on Palmyra, Commissioner. He's been in touch with me and he's trying to blackmail me into setting up a jewel-smuggling ring here. He says if I don't come across, he'll spread the word that I'm a Rehab." I saw the alarm and anger appear on Blair's face. "I told him I agreed to his terms, and he's expecting me for lunch today. But of course—I can't really go back into partnership with him—"

"Naturally not. Give me the address of the place where he's expecting you, and we'll pick him up. If he's wanted as you say, we can book him on that charge—and even if he isn't, we can grab him on Invasion of Privacy. A Rehab's entitled to live in peace. You don't have to wear the mark of Cain on your forehead for the things Nat Hamlin did."

I was weak-kneed and sweat-soaked by the time I hung up. But I was smiling in satisfaction. Dan Helgerson was going to be awfully surprised when the police and not me showed up at his hotel.

Nat Hamlin had had two attributes for which he was admired throughout the galaxy by his fellow crooks. He never doublecrossed a buddy and he declared repeatedly that he would rather cut his throat than turn stoolie. Helgerson had given his address because he knew he could trust Nat Hamlin.

But Helgerson had made a big mistake. He underestimated the Rehab conditioning. He wasn't dealing with Nat Hamlin at all. He was dealing with a guy named Paul Macy, and Macy wasn't hampered by any of Hamlin's attributes.

❋

The trial was a closed-chamber affair that took eight hours. Helgerson sat across the room, glaring at me in anger and disbelief. Even then, he couldn't believe that Nat Hamlin had called copper on him.

The central office of the Galactic Crime Commission sent in a full dossier on Helgerson by ultrafax, and the judge read through it, heard my testimony, and quickly sentenced Helgerson to be remanded to Earth for Rehabilitation. The case didn't make the Palmyra papers, because my identity as a Rehab had to be kept quiet.

Ellen and I were married the next day; I got a leave of absence and we departed on our honeymoon. The first stop was Earth, where I visited the Rehab Center and asked for a minor refacing—just enough to keep other buddies of Nat Hamlin's from recognizing me. They altered my hair color from black to reddish-brown, thinned out my nose, widened my mouth, shortened my jaw, and gave me a mustache. Ellen had designed the new face herself. It looked pretty much like the old me, but there were minor differences. When we got back to Palmyra, it wouldn't be hard for Ellen to explain that I had had an aircar crackup and had needed some plastic surgery.

From Earth we went on to Durrinor, the playground-world, and our three months there were as close to Eden as I expect to get. The time came, finally, sadly, to return to Palmyra. We had a private cabin aboard the spaceship; we still thought of ourselves as honeymooners, and intended to keep on thinking of ourselves that way for the rest of our lives.

The first night on board the spaceliner we had just finished getting settled and unpacked in our stateroom when the doorchime sounded. I opened the door. My jaw slid down an inch or two.

Dan Helgerson was standing outside the door, and he was wearing the blue-and-gold uniform of a crewman. He smiled pleasantly. "Good evening, sir. Welcome aboard the *Queen of the Stars*. I hope you enjoy your trip, sir." Then his expression changed as he recognized me behind the minor changes. "Ah—you're Nat—Nat Hamlin—"

"No," I said. "Paul Macy, just as it says on the doorplate, Dan."

He shook his head. "Not Dan. The name is Joseph, sir. Joseph Elson. I'm your purser, and it'll be my pleasure to serve you during this trip. If you need me, just ring. Thank you—Mr. Macy."

"Thank you—Joseph."

We smiled at each other, and he shut the door. Joseph Elson, eh? Well, Joseph Elson it was, then. I hoped I wouldn't accidentally call him Dan during the course of the trip. A Rehab deserves that much courtesy, after all.

MOURNFUL MONSTER
(1959)

1958 was a bad year for the science-fiction magazines. Their sales had been dropping ever since the peak year of 1953, when an all-time record 39 different titles were published (and helped to kill each other off by overcrowding the newsstands.) In 1958 the American News Company, the main magazine distributor, abruptly went out of business, taking with it a lot of magazines that it had been financing through advances against earnings. And the continued boom in paperback publishing was squeezing the surviving all-fiction magazines into a marginal existence.

Many of the s-f magazines I had been writing for in the previous four years began to shut up shop or to cut back drastically on frequency of publication, and I was beginning to feel uneasy about my ability to earn a living through the sort of mass production of stories that had carried me through those years. In particular I worried about W.W. Scott's Super-Science, which had become my mainstay. It was a poky little magazine at best, which probably had never shown much of a profit, and I wondered how much longer I was going to be able to sell it all those $240 novelets.

Against this gloomy background the sudden upsurge of monster fiction provided one commercial bright spot. In the late 1950s a magazine called Famous Monsters of Filmland, which specialized in photo-essays on classic Hollywood horror movies of the "Frankenstein" and "Wolf-Man" sort, had shot up overnight to a huge circulation. A couple of the science-fiction editors, desperately trying to find something that worked, experimented with converting their magazines to vehicles for horror fiction. Thus Larry Shaw's Infinity *and* Science Fiction Adventures, *for which I had been a steady contributor, vanished and were replaced by two titles called* Monster Parade *and* Monsters and Things. *(I wrote for them too.) And over at Super-Science Fiction, Scottie concluded that the only way to save his magazine was to convert it to a book of monster stories also. Word went out to all the regular contributors, of whom I was the most productive, that all material purchased thenceforth would have to have some monster angle in it. I didn't find that difficult, since most of the stories I was doing for him were space adventures featuring fearsome alien beings, and I would simply need to make the aliens a little bigger and more fearsome.*

Strangely, Scottie didn't change the title of the magazine. This was odd, because the presence of "Science" in it wasn't something likely to appeal to horror fans. Instead he plastered the words SPECIAL MONSTER ISSUE! in big yellow letters above the name of the magazine on the April, 1959 issue, commissioned a painting that featured a gigantic and notably hideous creature sweeping a couple of space-suited humans up in its claws, and retitled every story in inventory to give it a monster-oriented twist: "The Huge and Hideous Beasts," for example, or "The Abominable Creature." (His gift for the utterly flat-footed title may have stood him in good stead here.)

The lead story for the issue was one that I was writing in July, 1958, just as the change in policy went into effect. Evidently I found it necessary to restructure the story midway through for the sake of monsterizing it, because on my frayed and tattered carbon copy of the manuscript I find a penciled note in my own handwriting indicating a switch in the plot as of page 26: "They are continuing along when they see a huge monster looming ahead. They lay low, but the monster pursues them. They hear it crackling along behind them. They trip it, but it claws its way out of the trap and comes at them." And so on to the end of the story as you will see it here. Whatever non-monster denouement I might originally have had in mind is lost forever in the mists of time.

I turned the story in with the title I had originally given it, "Five Against the Jungle," a nice old-fashioned pulp title which of course was not right for the revamped Super-Science, so Scottie changed it to "Mournful Monster." By so doing, he gave away, to some extent, the fact that it wasn't really a horror story—that the monster, while appropriately monstrous, was actually a sympathetic figure. But so, after all, was Frankenstein's monster, and that didn't harm the commercial appeal of the movie. The prime subtext of the whole monster genre, I decided, must really be existential alienation.

I t was almost time for the regular midweek flight to leave. On the airstrip, the technicians were giving the two-engine jet a last-minute checkup. In fifteen minutes, according to the chalked announcement on the bulletin board, the flight would depart—making the two-thousand-mile voyage across the trackless, unexplored wilderness that lay between the Terran colonies of Marleyville and New Lisbon, on the recently settled planet of Loki in the Procyon system.

In the Marleyville airport building, Dr. David Marshall was having one last drink for the road, and trying unsuccessfully to catch the attention of the strikingly beautiful girl in the violet synthofab dress. Marshall, an anthropologist specializing in non-human cultures, was on his way to New Lisbon to interview a few wrinkled old hunters who claimed to have valuable information for him. He was trying to prove that an intelligent non-human race still existed somewhere on Loki, and he had been told at Marleyville that several veteran hunters in New Lisbon had insisted they knew where the hidden race lived.

"Now boarding for the flight to New Lisbon," came the tinny announcement from the loudspeaker. "Passengers for New Lisbon please report to the plane on the field."

Marshall gulped the remainder of his drink, picked up his small portfolio, and headed through the swinging door to the airfield. Stepping out of the aircooled building into the noonday heat was like walking into a steambath. The climate on Loki ranged from subtropical to utterly unbearable. Humans had been able to settle in coastal areas only, in the temperate zone. There was one Earth colony here, Marleyville, forty years old and with a population of about eighteen thousand. Far across the continent, on the western coast, was the other major colony, New Lisbon, with some twenty thousand people. Half a dozen other smaller colonies were scattered up and down each coast, but few humans had ventured into the torrid interior of the continent. It was one vast unexplored jungle.

And as for the other continents of the planet, they were totally unsuited for human life. Temperatures in the equatorial regions of Loki ranged as high as 180 degrees. In the cooler areas of high and low latitude, a more tolerable range of 70-100 prevailed. The polar regions were more comfortable so far as climate went, but they were barren and worthless as places to farm and mine.

"Last call for New Lisbon plane," the announcer called. Marshall trotted up the ramp, smiled at the stewardess, and took a seat. The plane was an old and rickety one. It had seen many years' service, Marshall thought. Loki Airlines had a "fleet" of just one plane, purchased at great expense from the highly industrialized neighbor world of Thor. There was not much traffic between Marleyville and New Lisbon. Once a week, the old jet plane made a round trip across the jungle for the benefit of those people—never more than a dozen or so each time—who had some reason for travelling to another colony.

The plane seated about forty, but no more than fifteen were aboard. The attractive girl in the violet dress was sitting a few rows ahead of Marshall. With so many empty seats in the plane, he did not have any valid excuse for sitting down next to her. Which was unfortunate, he thought with mild regret.

He glanced around. People sat scatteredly here and there in the plane. The stewardess came by and pleasantly told him to fasten his seat belt. A few moments later, the twin jet engines rumbled into life. The plane rolled slowly out onto the runway. Within instants, it was aloft, streaking eastward on the five-hour journey to distant New Lisbon.

*

The accident happened in the second hour of the flight. Marshall had been dividing his time between staring out the window at the bright green blur that was the ground eighteen thousand feet below, and reading. He had brought an anthropological journal with him to read, but he found it difficult to concentrate. He would much rather have preferred to be talking to the girl in the violet dress.

He was wondering whether he would have any luck in New Lisbon. This was the final year of his research grant; in a few months his money would run out, and he would have to return to Earth and take a job teaching at some university. He hoped there would be some clue waiting at the other colony.

The only way an anthropologist could win prestige and acclaim these days was by doing an intensive report on some unknown alien race. The trouble was, most of the planets of the galaxy had been pretty well covered by now. He had his choice of venturing onto some distant and dangerous world or of repeating someone else's work.

But there was a rumor that somewhere on Loki lived the remnants of an almost-extinct alien race. Marshall had pegged his hopes on finding that race. He had arrived in Marleyville a week ago and had spoken to some of the old settlers. Yes, they knew the rumors, they told him; no, they couldn't offer any concrete information. But there were some early settlers in New Lisbon who might be able to help. So Marshall was on his way to New Lisbon. And if he drew a blank there, it was back to Earth.

His thoughts were running in that depressing channel, and he decided to try to get some sleep instead of doing still more brooding and worrying. He nudged the seat-stud, guiding the seat back into a more comfortable position, and closed his eyes.

An instant later a shriek sounded in the ship.

Marshall snapped to attention. He glanced across the cabin and saw what the cause of the shriek had been. Great reddish gouts of flame were streaking from the engine on the opposite wing. Moments later the ship yawed violently to one side. Over the public address system came the pilot's voice: "Please fasten seat belts. Remain seated."

An excited buzz of conversation rippled through the ship. Marshall felt strangely calm and detached. So this was what it was like to become involved in an aircraft accident!

His ears stung suddenly as the ship lost altitude. It was dropping in a long, slow glide toward the ground. Shockwaves ran through the passenger cabin as the smoking jet engine exploded. Above everything came the tight, tense voice of the pilot: "We are making an emergency landing. Remain calm. Do not leave your seats until the instruction is given."

The ship was swooping toward the jungle in an erratic wobbling glide now. Cries of panic were audible. With one engine completely gone, the pilot was having obvious trouble controlling the ship. It came stuttering down through the atmosphere. Marshall could make out individual features of the landscape now. He saw jungle, wild, fierce-looking, untamed.

"Prepare for landing!" came the pilot's words. Marshall gripped his chair's arms tightly. A second later the ship thundered to the ground, accompanied by the crashing sound of falling trees. Marshall glanced out the window. They had crashlanded in the thick of the jungle, pancaking down on top of the trees and flattening them.

He ripped off his safety belt. No time to stop to think—had to get out of the plane. He fumbled for his portfolio, picked it up, saw something else under the seat. In big red letters it said SURVIVAL KIT. Marshall grabbed it.

Passengers were rising from their seats. Some were stunned, unconscious, perhaps dead from the violent impact of landing. Marshall stepped out into the aisle. Words met his eyes—EMERGENCY EXIT. His hands closed on a metal handle. He thrust downward, out.

The door opened. He tumbled out, dropping eight or nine feet to the soft, spongy forest floor. He knew he had to run, run fast.

He ran—helter-skelter, tripping and stumbling over the hidden vines. Sweat poured down his body. Time seemed to stand still. He wondered how many other passengers would escape in time from the doomed ship.

The explosion, when it came, seemed to fill the universe. A colossal boom unfolded behind him. The jungle heat rose to searing intensity for a moment. Marshall fell flat, shielding his head against metal fragments with his arms. He lay sprawled face-down in the thick vegetation, panting breathlessly, while fury raged a few hundred yards behind him. He did not look. He uttered a prayer of thankfulness for his lucky escape.

And then he realized he had very little to be thankful for. He was alive, true. But he was alive in the middle of a trackless jungle, with civilization a thousand miles away at the nearest. Desperately, he hoped that there had been other survivors.

❂

He waited for a few minutes after the blast had subsided. Then he rose unsteadily. The ship was a charred ruin, a blistered hulk. Fragments of the fuselage lay scattered over a wide area. One had landed only a few dozen feet from where he lay.

He started to walk toward the wreckage.

Figures lay huddled in the grass. Marshall reached the first. He was a man in his fifties, heavy-set and balding, who was clambering to his feet. Marshall helped him up. The older man's face was pale and sweat-beaded, and his lips were quivering. For a moment neither said anything.

Then Marshall said, in a voice that was surprisingly steady, "Come. We'd better look for other survivors."

The second to be found was the girl in the violet dress. She was sitting upright, fighting to control her tears. Marshall felt a sudden surge of joy when he saw that she was still alive. She had not completely escaped the fury of the blast, though; her dress was scorched, her eyebrows singed, the ends of her hair crisped. She seemed otherwise unharmed.

Not far from her lay two more people—a couple, who got shakily to their feet as Marshall approached them. Like the others, they were pale and close to the borderline of hysteria.

Five survivors. That was all. Marshall found six charred bodies near the plane—passengers who had succeeded in escaping from the ship, but who had been only a few feet away at the time of the blast. None of the bodies was recognizable. He turned away, slowly, shoulders slumping. Five survivors out of twenty. And they were lost in the heart of the jungle.

"We're all that's left," he said in a quiet voice.

The girl in the violet dress—her beauty oddly enhanced by the tattered appearance of her clothing and the smudges of soot on her face—murmured, "It's horrible! Going along so well—and in just a couple of moments—"

"It was an old plane," muttered the older man bitterly. "An antique. It was criminal to let such a plane be used commercially."

"Talking like that isn't going to help us now," said the remaining man, who stood close to his wife.

"Nothing's going to help us now," said the girl in the violet dress. "We're in the middle of nowhere without any way of getting help. It would have been better to be blown up than to survive like this—"

"No," Marshall said. He held up the small square box labelled SURVIVAL KIT. "Did any of you bring your survival kits out of the plane? No? Well, luckily, I grabbed up mine before I escaped. Maybe there's something in here to help us."

They crowded close around as he opened the kit. He called off the contents. "Water purifier....compass....a flare-gun and a couple of flares....a blaster with auxiliary charges....a handbook of survival techniques. That's about it."

"We'll never make it," the girl in the violet dress said softly. "A thousand miles back to Marleyville, a thousand miles ahead to New Lisbon. And no roads, no maps. We might as well use that blaster on ourselves."

"No!" Marshall snapped. Staring at the stunned, defeated faces of the other four, he realized that he would have to assume the leadership of the little group. "We're *not* giving up," he said sharply. "We can't let ourselves give up. We're going ahead—ahead to New Lisbon!"

❋

The first thing to do, Marshall thought, was to get organized. He led them a few hundred yards through the low underbrush, to the side of a small stream. Strange forest birds, angry over the sudden noisy invasion of their domain, cackled shrilly in the heavy-leaved trees above them. Marshall took a seat on a blunt boulder at the edge of the stream and said, "Now, then. We're going to make a trek through this jungle and we're going to reach New Lisbon alive. All clear?"

No one answered.

Marshall said, "Good. That means we all have to work together, if we're going to survive. I hope you understand the meaning of cooperation. No bickering, no selfishness, no defeatism. Let's get acquainted, first. My name is David Marshall. I'm from Earth. I'm a graduate student of anthropology—came to Loki to do anthropological research toward my doctorate in alien cultures."

He glanced inquisitively at the girl in the violet dress. She said in a faltering voice, "My name is Lois Chalmers. I'm—I'm the daughter of the governor of the New Lisbon colony."

Marshall's eyes widened slightly. Governor Alfred Chalmers was one of the most important men in the entire Procyon system. Her presence here meant that there would surely be an attempt to find the survivors of the crash.

Marshall next looked toward the married couple. The man, who was short, thickset, and muscular, said, "I'm Clyde Garvey. This is my wife Estelle. We're second-generation colonists at Marleyville. We were going to take a vacation in New Lisbon."

The remaining member of the little band was the middle-aged man. He spoke now. "My name is Kyle, Nathan Kyle. I'm from Earth. I have large business investments on Loki, both at Marleyville and New Lisbon."

"All right," Marshall said. "We all know who everybody else is, now." He looked up at the sky. It was mid-afternoon, and only the overhanging roof of leaves shielded the forest floor from the fiercely blazing sun. "We were just about at the halfway point of the trip when we crashed. That means it's just as far to Marleyville as it is to New Lisbon. Probably we're slightly closer to New Lisbon. We might as well head in that direction."

"Maybe it's better to stay right where we are," Nathan Kyle suggested. "They're certain to search for survivors. If we stay near the wreckage—"

"They could search this jungle for a hundred years and never cover the whole territory," Marshall said. "Don't forget that the only transcontinental plane on this world just crashed. All they have is a handful of short-range copters and light planes—not sufficient to venture this deep into the jungle. No; our only hope is to head for New Lisbon. Maybe when we get close enough, we'll be spotted by a search-party."

"What will we eat?" Estelle Garvey wanted to know.

"We'll hunt the native wildlife," Marshall told her. "And supplement that with edible vegetation. Don't worry about the food angle."

"How long will it take to reach New Lisbon?" Kyle asked.

Marshall shrugged. "We'll march by day, camp by night. If we can average ten miles a day through the jungle, it'll take about three months to reach safety."

"Three months—!"

"I'm afraid so. But at least we'll get there alive."

"Nice to know *you're* so confident, Marshall," Kyle said bleakly. "Three months on foot through a jungle thick with all sorts of dangers—"

"Don't give up before we've started," Marshall said. He studied the survival kit compass for a moment, frowning. "We want to head due east. That way. If we start right away, we can probably cover five or six miles before nightfall. But let's eat and freshen up first."

❋

The blaster supplied in the survival kit had one hundred shots in it, plus an extra hundred in the refill. Marshall was a fair shot, but he knew he would have to do better than fair if they were to survive the trip. Every shot would have to count.

He and Garvey struck out into the forest while Kyle and the women remained behind to fashion water-canteens out of some gourds that grew near the water's edge. The two men entered the darkest part of the jungle, where the treetops were linked a hundred feet above the forest floor by a thick meshwork of entangled vines that all but prevented sunlight from penetrating.

They moved slowly, trying to avoid making noise. Garvey heard a threshing in the underbrush and touched Marshall's arm. They froze; a second later a strange creature emerged from a thicket a few feet from them. It was vaguely deerlike, a lithe, graceful beast whose hide was a delicate grayish-purple in color. In place of horns, three fleshy tendrils sprouted from its forehead.

The animal studied the two men with grave curiosity. Evidently it had never seen human beings before, and did not know whether or not to be afraid. Slowly the forehead-tendrils rose in the air, until they stood erect like three pencils on the beast's head.

Marshall lifted the blaster. Alarmed at the sudden motion, the animal gathered its legs and prepared to bound off into the darkness. Marshall fired quickly. A bolt of energy spurted from the blaster; he aimed for the chest, but his aim was high, and he caught the beast in the throat instead. The animal blinked once in surprise, then slipped to the mossy carpet of the forest.

Marshall and Garvey carried their prey back to the stream slung between them. The women had worked efficiently while they were gone, Marshall saw. Five gourds lay ranged neatly along the stream's bank, each one carefully hollowed out. Kyle was busy with the water purifier.

Marshall and Garvey dumped the deer-like creature in the middle of the clearing. "Our first meal," Marshall said. "I hope there aren't any vegetarians among us."

⁕

It was a messy business, skinning the animal and preparing it for cooking. Marshall drew that job, and performed it with the small knife from the survival kit. Garvey and his wife built the fire, while Kyle cut down a green branch to use as a spit.

The cooking job was extremely amateur, and the meat, when they finally served it, was half raw and half scorched. None of them seemed to have much of an appetite, but they forced themselves to eat, and washed it down with the purified water. After the meal, Marshall carefully wrapped up the remainder of the meat in the animal's own hide, tying the bundle together with vines. They filled their gourd canteens and plugged them shut.

No one said much. A tremendous task faced them—a trek across half a continent, through unknown jungle. All five seemed subdued by the enormity of the job that confronted them.

They started out, hacking their way through the intertwined brambles, following the compass on an easterly course. The stream followed right along with them, which made things a little easier. It was always good to know that your water supply was heading in the same general direction you were going.

Loki's day was twenty-eight hours long. Marshall's wristwatch was an Earthtype standard one, so it was of little use to him, but Garvey wore a watch which gave the time as half past three in the afternoon, Loki time—

Marleyville time. But they were a thousand miles east of Marleyville, and heading further east with every step. Marshall did not attempt to adjust the time to the longitude. Life was complicated enough as it was, just then.

If Garvey's watch were right, though, they had about six more hours of marching time before nightfall would arrive. If they could average a mile an hour while walking, Marshall thought, it might be possible to reach New Lisbon in eighty or ninety days. If they lived that long, he added grimly.

The stream widened out after a while, becoming a fairly broad little river. Water beasts were slumbering near the bank. Marshall approached to look at them. They were reptiles, sleek velvet-brown creatures twenty feet long, with tails that switched ominously from side to side and toothy mouths that yawned hungrily at the little party of Terrans. But the animals made no attempt to come up on shore and attack. They simply glared, beady-eyed, at the Earthman.

After more than an hour of steady marching Lois Chalmers asked for a few minutes to rest, and they halted. She pulled off the stylish pumps she was wearing, and stared ruefully at her swollen feet.

"These shoes of mine just aren't intended for jungle treks," she said mournfully. "But I can't walk barefoot in the jungle, I suppose."

Garvey said, "If you'd like, I'll make you some sandals out of bark and vines."

The girl brightened. "Oh, would you!"

So there was a fifteen-minute half while Garvey fashioned crude sandals for her. During the wait, Marshall ventured down to the river-bank again. The big sleeping reptiles lay sunning themselves on the mud by the side of the water. Marshall saw golden shapes gliding through the water. Fish. Another source of food, he thought, and one that would not consume the precious blaster-charges. They would need to make hooks from slivers of bone, and fishing-line from the sinews of animals. He smiled to himself as the idea occurred. David Marshall, late of the University of Chicago, had no business knowing anything about such primitive things as home-made fishing equipment.

But a man had to survive, he thought. And to survive you had to use your brains.

He peered at the slowly-moving fish below in the water, and nodded to himself. The first opportunity they had, they would improvise some fishing equipment.

The river narrowed to a stream again, later on, and veered sharply off to the south. The party continued on the eastward path, even though they were no longer with a water supply: The afternoon darkened into night, and the jungle heat subsided.

As dusk began to gather around them, Marshall said, "We'd better stop now. Make camp here, continue in the morning. We'll get into trouble if we try to hike in the dark."

They settled in a small clearing fenced in by vaulting trees whose trunks were the thickness of a dozen men. The forest grew dark rapidly; Loki's three gleaming moons could be seen bobbing intermittently above the trees, and a sprinkling of stars brightened the night.

Marshall said, "We'll stand watch in shifts through the night. Kyle, you take first watch. Then Lois. I'll hold down the middle slot. Mrs. Garvey, you follow me, and your husband can have the last shift. Two hours apiece ought to do it."

He opened the survival kit and handed the blaster and flare gun to Kyle. The businessman frowned and said, "What am I supposed to do?"

"Stay awake, mostly, and keep an eye out for visiting animals. And if you happen to hear an airplane overhead, shoot off one of the flares so they'll be able to find us."

"Do you think they'll send a plane this far?" Lois asked.

Marshall shook his head. "Frankly, no. But it can't do any harm to be prepared."

He and Garvey built a fire while the others collected a woodpile to use as fuel through the night. They remained close together; Marshall chose a clump of grass as his bed, while the Garveys huddled in each other's arms not far away and Lois bedded down on the other side of the fire. Kyle, as first watch, sat near the fire.

Marshall did not find it easy to fall asleep. His senses were troubled by new sensations—the *chickk-chickk* of the jungle insects, the far-off hooting of night-flying birds, the occasional unnerving trumpet-call of some huge wandering animal settling down for the night. The flickering of the campfire bothered him no matter how tightly he clamped his eyelids together. He remained awake a long while squirming and shifting position, his mind full of a million thoughts and plans. He was still half awake and dimly aware of what was happening when Kyle's shift ended, for he heard the financier talking to Lois, waking her up. But some time after that he dozed off, because he was soundly asleep when Lois came to fetch him for his shift on patrol.

He was dreaming of some pleasant tropical isle where there was nothing to do but sleep on the beach, swim, make love, and sip mild drinks. He felt the girl's hand on his shoulder, but she had to shake him several times before he woke.

Finally he rolled over and blinked at her. "What's the matter?"

"Your turn," the girl whispered.

"Turn?" he repeated vaguely. Then he came fully awake. "Oh. I see." He got to his feet and glanced at his watch. It read two o'clock. He made a rough computation into Loki time and decided that it was about six and a half hours before dawn.

He looked around. The Garveys and Kyle were sound asleep; Kyle was even snoring. The fire was getting a bit low. Marshall added some logs to it.

"Was there any trouble?" he asked.

"No," Lois said. "Nothing happened. Good night."

"Good night," he replied.

She crossed the clearing and settled down to sleep. Marshall squatted by the fire and stared upward. A great white bird had settled on a tree-limb above him, and the huge creature was staring down at the camp with serene indifference. For a moment Marshall seriously considered shooting the big bird with the blaster he held; it would probably provide them with enough meat for several days. But he held back, reluctant to kill anything quite so beautiful. They still had some of the deer meat left, and there was no need to kill again just yet. After a short while the bird took wing, and flew off into the darkness with solemn dignity.

Marshall paced round the camp. An hour slipped by. He looked around, saw the girl Lois sitting up, her head propped against her hand, watching him. He walked over to her.

"Why are you up?"

"I can't sleep. I'm wide awake again," she whispered. "Mind if I keep you company?"

"You ought to get some sleep," he told her.

"I know. But I can't." she got to her feet, and they strolled around the clearing together. He watched her with interest. She was certainly a lovely girl. In the past, he had never had much time to spare for women. His studies had always come first.

"How old are you?" he asked after a while.

"Nineteen," she said. "You?"

"Twenty-seven."

"You're an anthropologist?" she asked.

"Yes."

"A good one?"

"Not very," he admitted. "Just run of the mill. I came here hoping to make my fame and fortune by discovering the native life of Loki."

"You still may," she said. "Aren't they supposed to live somewhere in the jungle? Maybe we'll find them while we're travelling east."

Marshall chuckled quietly. He had been so busy with the sheer problems of survival that he had never even stopped to consider that possibility. Of course, he thought! Wouldn't it be wonderful if I stumbled right into an alien village!

They talked for a while longer, mostly about her. She went to school on Thor, the neighboring world; she had stopped at Marleyville to visit her brother, who was in business there, before going on to see her father at New Lisbon. Evidently, Marshall thought, she had led a rather plush and sheltered life up till now. But she was bearing up pretty well under the jungle life, he thought.

When his watch read half past four, he woke up Estelle Garvey. "Your turn," he told her. "Your husband relieves you at six o'clock."

He returned to his clump of grass. Lois settled down across the way from him. He was asleep within minutes.

They were all up at dawn. Garvey, who was very good with his hands, had made use of his time on watch to fashion a pair of fishhooks and some line. They discovered another small brook not too far from their campsite, and some patient angling by Garvey and Marshall provided their breakfast: small herring-like fish which had a sharp, pungent taste when cooked. After breakfast they washed up, the women bathing first, then the men. Personal privacy was being respected as best as possible among them.

They marched until noon, when the heat became almost intolerable and they were forced to stop for a siesta. Lois found a bush with round blue-green fruits the size of apples growing on it, and, after Garvey had boldly tasted one without immediate ill effects, they lunched on those and moved on half an hour later.

The forest creatures showed no fear of them. From time to time small rodents with huge hind legs would hop rabbit-fashion almost defiantly close to them, peering curiously out of gleaming blue eyes. Once a big beast clumsily blundered across their path—an animal the height of a man and about fifteen feet long, which clumped along on four immense legs. It was obviously a vegetarian, and just as obviously it had poor eyesight. It crossed their path only twenty feet in front of Marshall, who was in the lead, and paused briefly to gulp down a hillock of grass before continuing on its myopic way.

Morale remained high in the little band. Marshall estimated that they covered better than fourteen miles during the day, and when they stopped at sundown Garvey shot a long-eared gazelle-like animal for their dinner. Sniffing little hyenas came to investigate the kill, but rapidly scattered when Marshall hurled a rock at them. It was not worth wasting a blaster shot on such vermin.

The next day they moved on again, and that day they ran into their first serious problems in the jungle.

The initial snag came in mid-morning. The party was hacking its way through a particularly tangled stretch of pathless underbrush. Abruptly, a torrential rain descended on them—a warmish rain that fell by the bucketfull, drenching them within instants. There was no time to seek cover, and no cover to be had.

The rain lasted fifteen minutes, though there were moments when Marshall felt it was going to go on forever, cascading in endless sheets. They were soaked to the skin by the time it was over. Their clothing, already shredded and soiled after three days of jungle life, clung to their skins as if pasted there. Gnatlike insects came to hover around the bedeviled Earthmen, stinging and buzzing and flying into ears and eyes and noses and mouths. A glorious rainbow arched across the sky, glowing in the golden-green sunlight, but none of the Earthmen were in any mood to appreciate its beauty. They were wet and sticky and miserable. After a while, their clothes dried somewhat, though the humidity assured that nothing would ever dry completely. By noontime that day, colorful molds were already beginning to form on the soaked clothing. By the time they finished the trip, Marshall thought, their clothes would have rotted completely away.

The prospect of regular drenchings of this sort was not an appealing one. But, in the middle of the afternoon, a new problem presented itself. The stream that they had been following most of the day had widened suddenly into a river—and the river had taken a broad swinging curve out in front of them, where it blocked the eastward passage completely.

Marshall shaded his eyes and looked upriver. "Think we ought to try heading north for a while?" he asked.

Garvey shook his head. "Don't think it's wise to leave course, Marshall. We'd better build a raft."

It took them most of the rest of the day to complete the raft, with Garvey, as the best hand craftsman of the group, directing the work. The raft, when it was finished, was a crude but serviceable affair—several dozen logs lashed solidly together by the tough, sinewy vines that grew everywhere in the jungle. The river that had so unexpectedly blocked their route was almost a mile wide. The Terrans huddled together while Marshall and Garvey poled the rickety raft across.

They were midway across when Kyle, who was holding the blaster, suddenly pointed and shouted: "L—look!"

A snout was rising from the river's murky depths. Turning, Marshall saw the head that followed it—a head about the size of a large basketball, and mostly teeth. The neck came gliding up from the water next, yards of it. Ten, fifteen feet of neck rose above them, and still more lurked beneath the water—along with who knew how many feet of body.

The head was swaying from side to side, looming above the raft and rocking gently as if getting into the rhythm of a spring. Kyle's trembling hands held the blaster. The river creature followed smoothly along the side of the raft, studying the five people aboard, deciding which one would make the juiciest morsel.

"For God's sake, fire!" Marshall called. "Shoot, Kyle, shoot!"

But Kyle did not shoot. With a muttered curse, Marshall sprang forward, nearly upsetting the delicate balance of the raft, and snatched the blaster from the financier's numb fingers. He lifted and fired. The river-serpent's head vanished. The long sleek neck slipped gracefully into the water. A trail of blood eddied upward toward the surface.

Lois gasped and pointed toward the water. It boiled with activity: Creatures were coming from all over to devour the dead monster.

"I'm sorry," Kyle muttered thinly. "I had the gun—I tried to fire it—but I couldn't shoot, I just couldn't. I was too scared. Marshall, dammit, I'm sorry!"

"Forget it," Marshall said. "It's dead and no harm was done." But he made a mental note to the effect that Kyle could not be trusted to act in an emergency. In the jungle, you were either quick or you were dead.

✸

They reached the other side of the river without further mishap, and, abandoning the raft where it had beached itself, they continued inland.

During the next five days, they plodded steadily along. Marshall figured they had covered about a hundred miles—which sounded like a great deal, until he realized it was only one tenth of the total journey.

The five of them were changing, in those five days. Becoming less prissy, less civilized. The barriers of restraint were rapidly breaking down. They ate foods they would never have dreamed of eating normally, ripping and rending almost raw meat to assuage their hunger. They ate less frequently, too, and from day to day they grew leaner, tougher. In the past few years Marshall had let himself get slightly out of shape, but that roll of flesh around his middle had disappeared utterly in only a few days. Muscles that had not worked for many years came into regular play.

The little band did not present a very imposing picture. The men had week-old beards; the women, despite sporadic attempts at self-tidiness, were growing unkempt and very unfeminine, with ragged, stringy hair and no makeup. As for clothing, it was diminishing rapidly, the effects of continual humidity and rain and jungle life. Marshall's shirt had been so encrusted with violet and green molds that he had been forced to discard it. His trousers were frayed and tattered, and ended at the knee. Garvey looked similarly disheveled, while Kyle was even worse. The insubstantial fabrics of the women's dresses had suffered the most. Lois' violet synthofab dress, which had attracted Marshall so much back in Marleyville, was a bedraggled ruin. She shed it completely on the fourth day, making do with her underclothes and some foliage bound around her breasts for the sake of modesty.

But modesty mattered very little in the jungle. It was futile to maintain the old civilized taboos under such conditions. Before the end of the first week, the five of them were bathing unashamedly together, and there was no more niggling concern with modesty or other social graces that were irrelevant in the cruel world of the jungle.

Marshall became an adept hunter. The jungle abounded in strange life-forms of every description: thick furred creatures like little teddy-bears, that soared on bat-wings from tree to tree, forming easy targets in mid-glide and yielding deliciously tender white meat; big-beaked jungle birds of astonishing color, who ranged themselves in groups of a dozen along a tree-limb and obediently waited to be shot; curious amphibious creatures who looked like oildrums with eyes, and whose hind legs tasted like fine chicken; graceful fawn-like creatures that flitted through the forest like tawny ghosts, occasionally coming within range. Making the most of his two hundred blaster charges, Marshall kept the group supplied with meat. Kyle became a surprisingly able fisherman, while the women made themselves responsible for gathering fruits, nuts, and vegetables, and Garvey took care of the mechanical aspects of jungle life, the building of clearings and the fashioning of clubs and sandals and the like.

They forged forward, keeping careful track of the days and careful watch of the skies, in case a rescue ship should pass overhead. None did. But the general mood of the party was one of quiet determination. The conviction now gripped them that they would return to civilization alive. Except for occasional brushes with the larger jungle wildlife, and a few small incidents involving snakes underfoot, there had been no serious problem. The rain, the humidity, the insects—these were inconveniences which could be tolerated. There was no reason to suspect that they would get into difficulties. All they had to do was to keep on plugging ahead.

Until the ninth day. When it suddenly became clear that their eastward march had come to an unexpected halt—perhaps permanently.

It had been a coolish day, by jungle standards, and the group had been moving at a good pace all morning. They stopped at noon and feasted on a pair of the small green amphibious oildrum-creatures, and then moved on. Marshall, his blaster in his hand, led the way, with Lois at his side. The girl wore only sheer pants round her waist, but despite this she did not show the embarrassment she had displayed originally when it had been necessary for her to discard her useless city clothes. Her body was tanned and handsome.

Walking behind Marshall came Nathan Kyle, holding the flare-gun, with the Garveys bringing up the rear. On one of his recent evening watches Garvey had fashioned a bow and arrow outfit for himself, and he now wore the bow slung over his thick barrel chest. His wife carried the survival kit.

They cut their way through some reasonably open territory for about an hour after the lunch halt. Marshall, keeping his compass constantly in hand, maintained the consistent eastward course which he hoped would, in time, bring them to the coastal area where the colony of New Lisbon and the other smaller coast settlements could be found.

The course took them up the side of a small, heavily-wooded rise.

Marshall strode through the thick shrubbery, ignoring as best as he could the droning insects that nipped at his bare legs, and down the other side of the low hill.

He stopped, staring ahead. His eyes ranged toward the next hill in the gently undulating series. Sudden amazement surged through him.

"Good God!" he muttered. "Look at that!"

The others came up to him and paused with him, an anxious, frightened little group. Garvey, squinting out into the distance with his keen, experienced eyes, said finally, "I've never seen anything like it. The beast must be fifty feet high!"

"Are you sure?" Marshall asked.

"At least that much. It's standing in a clump of rhizome trees that grow to about forty feet, never less, and you can see the creature's head bobbing up over the damned trees!"

Marshall was conscious of Lois pressing up against him, her hand gripping his arm in sudden fright. He put his free arm around her to steady her. But he was frightened himself. He had never seen anything quite like the beast that stood squarely in their path, no more than five hundred yards ahead.

The creature was vaguely humanoid in shape—that is, if it had any meaning to describe such a monster as humanoid. It towered above the trees, but through the shrubbery Marshall could see that it stood on two massive legs that seemed almost like treetrunks themselves. The being was covered entirely with thick, metallic-looking scales that glinted blue-green in the sunlight. Its immense head consisted mostly of mouth; fangs more than six inches long were visible. The eyes were like blazing beacons, as big as dishes—but they were not the eyes of a beast. There was unmistakable intelligence in them.

As they watched, one gigantic arm swooped upward through the air. For an instant, eight huge fingers were spread wide. Then they closed tight, imprisoning a bat-like flying reptile the way a man might pounce on a small insect. The trumpeting sound of the frightened pterodactyl echoed for a moment in the forest; then, the mouth yawned, the arm went toward it.

The mouth closed. The monster had devoured an appetizing morsel—a pleasant midday snack. As if to signal its pleasure it rumbled groundshakingly, a fierce bellow of content. Then it turned, and, sending saplings crashing all around, began to stride toward the group of humans huddled at the foot of the hill.

✳

Marshall was the first to react. "Come on," he said harshly. "Maybe it senses us. Let's split up before we all wind up as lunch for that thing."

With a rough shove, he sent Nathan Kyle plunging away into the underbrush. Garvey needed no hint; he and his wife faded off the road into a sheltered spot. Marshall glanced at him, saw him stringing his bow and nocking an arrow into place.

Marshall and Lois crouched down behind a thick shrub and waited. He gripped the blaster tight, holding it in readiness, but even as he opened the safety he paused to think that the blaster was a futile weapon to use against a monster of this size.

Lois whispered, "What *is* that thing? I've never heard of a life-form that size."

"Neither have I. This is just something that's lurked in this unexplored jungle without ever getting seen from the air. And it's just our luck to be the ones to discover it!"

"Does it know where we are?"

Marshall shrugged. "Something that size probably doesn't have very highly developed sense organs. But it may have seen us. And it may be hungry."

"I hope not."

The creature was getting closer. Marshall could feel the ground quivering as each ponderous foot descended to the jungle floor. It was like a distant drumbeat....*boom....boom....boom....boom....*

Abruptly the booming stopped. That meant, Marshall thought, that the monster had to be very close—and perhaps was pausing a few yards away, searching for the small creatures it had seen from the distance. He held his breath and warily looked over his shoulder.

Two legs were planted like treetrunks no more than twenty yards from him. He caught his breath sharply. Lois turned to see what he was looking at; her mouth widened as if she were about to scream, and Marshall instantly slapped his hand over it.

She relaxed. He lifted his hand from her mouth and put a finger to his lips, indicating silence.

They turned round to see the creature.

✳

It did not seem to notice them. Marshall's gaze rose, up the giant legs, past the thick midsection of the body, to the head. Yes, there was no doubt about it—there was intelligence in those eyes. But an alien intelligence. And it was the face of a carnivorous creature that would hardly stop to wonder before devouring them.

It had come to a halt and was peering round, spreading the brush apart with its monstrous paws, hunting for the hidden Earthmen. Marshall prayed that Garvey, on the other side of the creature, would not decide to open fire with his bow. The monster evidently had a poor sense of smell, and the humans were well hidden under the shrubbery. With luck, they might avoid being seen. Perhaps the creature, cheated of its prey, would simply continue on its way through the jungle, allowing them to move along toward New Lisbon without harm.

Long moments passed. The creature, with seemingly cosmic patience, was still standing there, probing the underbrush with its enormous fingers. Marshall kept the blaster cocked and ready in case he should be uncovered. No doubt Garvey was waiting, too, with his wife.

How about Kyle? Marshall remembered the way Kyle had choked up when the sea-serpent had risen from the depths of the river. How was the financier reacting now, with hideous death looming not far overhead?

Marshall found out a moment later.

Kyle began to scream.

"Help! Help me! It's going to find me! Marshall! Garvey! Kill it before it catches me!"

His pitiful wails rang out loudly. Marshall saw the feet of the monster rise and move in the direction of the sound.

"No! No!" Kyle yelled

"Stay here and don't move from the spot," Marshall told Lois. "I've got to protect Kyle. The idiot! The absolute idiot!"

He moved in a half-crouch through the underbrush. Kyle was still yelling in hysterical fear. Marshall kept going until he reached Garvey. The solidly built colonist had his bow drawn tight and was looking around.

"The creature's just over to the left," Garvey informed him. "It heard Kyle squalling and now it's going to have a look."

Marshall craned his neck back. Yes, there was the creature, hovering high above the forest floor.

"Help me! Please don't let it get me!" Kyle was still wailing.

The creature stopped suddenly. It reached into the underbrush; its fingers closed around something. Then it straightened up. Marshall saw something impossibly tiny-looking held in the monster's hand, and he had to force himself to realize that the kicking, squirming creature the monster held was a human being.

"Let's go," Marshall said. "It's caught Kyle. Maybe we can kill it."

※

The monster was staring at Kyle with deep curiosity. The Earthman blubbered and screamed. Gently, the huge creature touched Kyle with an inch-long fingernail. Kyle moaned and prayed for release.

"Should we fire?" Garvey asked.

"Wait a minute. Maybe it'll set him down. It seems fascinated by him."

"It's never seen an Earthman before," Garvey said. "Maybe it'll decide Kyle isn't edible."

"He deserves whatever he gets," Marshall grunted. "But it's our duty as Earthmen to try to save him. Suppose you take a pot-shot at the hand that's holding Kyle. Think you can hit the alien without nailing Kyle?"

"I'll do my best," Garvey said grimly.

He drew the bowstring back and let the arrow fly—straight and true, humming through the air and burying itself deep is the wrist of the hand that grasped Kyle round the middle.

The creature paused in its examination of Kyle. It probed with a forefinger of the other hand at the arrow that was embedded in its flesh. Suddenly, it tossed Kyle to the ground like a doll it had tired of, and advanced toward the place where Marshall and Garvey crouched hidden behind two gigantic palm-fronds.

"Here it comes," Marshall muttered. "We'd better shoot to kill. You go for the eyes with your arrows, and I'll aim for the legs and try to cut the thing down to our size."

The ground was shaking again. Marshall's hand gripped the blaster butt tightly. Suddenly the monster emitted an earsplitting howl of defiance and kicked over the tree that had been sheltering them.

Marshall fired first, aiming his blaster bolt straight into the thick leg in front of him. The energy beam was opened to the widest possible aperture. It played on the leg for a moment but barely seemed to pierce the surface. The creature was virtually armor-plated. Marshall glanced back at Garvey. The colonist had already shot two more arrows—

Marshall saw them sticking out of the creature's face—and he was nocking a third arrow.

The monster stooped over, slapping at the foliage as if irritated by the sudden attack rather than angry. One paw swept inches over Marshall's head. He fired a second bolt into the same place as the first had gone, and saw a break in the scales now. The monster roared in pain and lifted its wounded leg high.

The leg thrashed around, kicking and trampling. Suddenly a sidewise swipe of an open hand caught Marshall and sent him sprawling, half unconscious. He landed near Kyle. The financier, Marshall saw, was not in good shape. Blood was trickling from his mouth and one of his legs was grotesquely twisted. Kyle's face was a pale white with fear and shock. He did not seem to be conscious.

Marshall struggled to his feet. He became aware that the alien's struggles had slackened somewhat. Running back to Garvey's side, he looked up and saw an arrow arch upward and bury itself in the center of one huge yellow eyeball.

"Bullseye!" Garvey yelled.

The scream of pain that resulted seemed to fill the entire jungle. Marshall grinned at the colonist and gripped his blaster again.

He fired—three times. The charges burrowed into the weakened place in the monster's leg, and suddenly the great being slipped to one knee. Unafraid now, the two men dashed out into the open. Garvey's final arrow pierced the remaining eye of the giant. A shrill cry of pain resulted. Marshall raised his blaster, centering the sights on the monster's ruined eye, hoping that his shot would supply the *coup de grace.*

"Yes," a deep, throbbing voice said. "*Kill me. It would be well. I long to die.*"

* * *

Marshall was so stunned he lowered his blaster. Turning to Garvey he said, "Did you hear that?"

"It sounded like—like a voice."

"*I was the one who spoke. I speak directly to your minds. Why do you not kill me?*"

"Great Jehosaphat!" Garvey cried. "The monster's talking!"

"It's a telepath," Marshall said. "It's intelligent and it's able to communicate with us!"

"I ask for death," came the solemn thought.

Marshall stared at the great being. It had slumped down on both its knees now, and it held its hands over its shattered eyes. Even so, its head was more than twenty feet above the ground.

"Who—what are you?" Marshall asked.

"I am nothing now and soon will be even less. Twenty thousand years ago my people ruled this world. Today I am the only one. And soon I too will be gone—killed by tiny creatures I can hardly see."

Marshall heard a rustling sound behind him and glanced over his shoulder to see Lois and Garvey's wife come hesitantly out of hiding, now that the danger seemed to be past.

Marshall felt a twinge of awe. To think of a world ruled by beings such as these—and to think of them all gone except this one, their cities buried under thousands of years of jungle growth, their very bones rotted by the planet's warmth and lost forever. What a sight it must have been, a city of titans such as these!

"Why do you not kill me?" the being asked telepathically.

"What's happening?" Lois asked.

Marshall said, "Garvey hit the creature in the eyes with arrows and I knocked him down by blasting his legs. But he seems to be intelligent. And he's pleading with us to put him out of his misery."

"That thing—intelligent?"

"Once we had sciences and arts and poetry," came the slow, mournful telepathic voice. *"But our civilization withered and died. Children no longer were born, and the old ones died slowly away. Until at last only I was left, eating animals and living the life of a beast in the jungle...."*

"How can you be sure you're the last?" Marshall asked. "Maybe there are other survivors."

"When others lived my mind was attuned to them. But for many years I have known nothing but silence on this world. I did not know beings your size could be intelligent....I beg your pardon if I have injured the companion of yours who I seized in my curiosity. Will you not give me the satisfaction of death at last?"

❋

Marshall felt deep sadness as he watched blood stream down the alien's face—yellow-brown blood. If only they had known, if only the being had not been so fearsome in appearance, if only it had made tele-pathic contact with them sooner—

If. Well, it was too late now.

"Isn't there some way we can help it?" Lois asked.

Marshall shook his head. "We're hundreds of miles from civiliza-tion. We'll be lucky to get back alive ourselves. And I crippled it with my blaster."

"Only thing to do is put it out of its misery," Garvey said flatly.

"Yes. I am in great pain and wish to die."

Marshall lifted the blaster regretfully. Only a few moments before he had been shooting to kill, shooting what he thought was a ferocious and deadly creature. And, he thought, unwittingly he had destroyed the last of an ancient and awe-inspiring race.

Now he had no choice. It was wrong to permit this noble creature to suffer, to be eaten alive by the blood-hungry jungle creatures.

His finger tightened on the blaster.

"I thank you for giving me peace," the alien telepathed. *"My loneli-ness at last will end."*

Marshall fired.

The energy bolt pierced the already broken eye of the monster and seared its way through to the brain. The vast creature toppled forward on its face, kicked convulsively as the message of death passed through its huge and probably tremendously complex nervous system. In a moment it was all over except for a quivering of the outstretched limbs, and that soon stopped.

Marshall stared at the great body face down on the jungle floor. Then he turned away.

"Let's go see how Kyle is," he said. "The alien picked him up and dropped him again when we opened fire. I think he's in bad shape."

The four of them stepped around the corpse of the fallen alien and made their way to the place where Kyle lay. The financier had not moved. Marshall bent over him, pointing to the livid bruises that stood out on Kyle's body.

"Fingerprints," Marshall said. "The big boy had a pretty strong grip."

Kyle's eyes opened and he looked wildly around. "The monster," he said in a thick, barely intelligible voice. "Don't let it touch me! Don't—"

Kyle slumped over, his head rolling loosely to one side. A fresh trickle of blood began to issue from between his lips, but it stopped almost at once. Marshall knelt, putting his ear to Kyle's chest.

After a moment he looked up.

"How is he?" Garvey asked.

Marshall shrugged. "He's dead, I'm afraid. The shock of the whole thing, and the internal hemhorrage caused by the creature's grip on him—"

"And he fell about twenty feet," Garvey pointed out.

Marshall nodded. "We'd better bury him before the local fauna comes around for their meal. And then we'll get back on the path to New Lisbon."

●

They dug a grave at the side of the clearing and lowered Kyle's body in. Garvey bound two sticks together crosswise with a bit of vine, and planted them at the head of the grave. No one even suggested a burial for the dead alien. It would have been totally impossible to move a creature of such bulk at all. Its weight was probably many tons, Marshall estimated.

It was nearly nightfall by the time they were finished interring Kyle, but the party moved along anyway, since no one was anxious to camp for the night close to the scene of the violence. Few words were spoken. The brief and tragic encounter with the huge alien, and Kyle's death, had left them drained of emotion, with little to say to each other.

The next day, they continued to forge onward. Marshall was still obsessed with the thought of the dead alien.

"Imagine," he said to Lois. "An entire planet full of giants like that—can you picture even a city of them? Fantastic!"

"And all gone," Lois said.

"Yes. Every one. Not a fossil remains. If we ever get back to civilization, I hope to be able to organize a search party to bring back the skeleton of that giant. It'll be quite an exhibit at the Galactic Science Museum, if we ever find it."

In the distance, a hyena cackled. A huge shadow crossed the path in front of them—the shadow of an enormous flying reptile winging its solitary way over the jungle. Far away, the rhythmic bellowing of some jungle creature resounded echoingly.

Marshall wondered if they ever would get back. They had covered many miles, sure enough, but they had not yet even reached the halfway point in their journey to New Lisbon. And who knew what dangers still lay ahead for them?

They marched on, through that day and the next, and the one after that. Heat closed in around them like a veil, and the rain was frequent and annoying. But they managed. They killed for meat, and fished when they came to water, and by this time they had all become experts on which vegetables were edible and which were likely to provide a night of indigestion and cramps.

Day blurred into day. Marshall's beard became long and tangled. They looked like four jungle creatures rather than Earthmen.

And then one day shortly after high noon—

"Look!" Garvey yelled shrilly. "Look up there, everyone! Look!"

Marshall could hear the droning sound even before he could raise his eyes. He looked up, feeling the pulse of excitement go through him. There, limned sharply against the bright metallic blueness of the afternoon sky, a twin-engine plane circled the jungle!

For a moment they were all too numb, too stupefied with joy to react. Marshall was the first to break from his stasis.

"The flare-gun—where is it?"

"In the survival kit!" Garvey exclaimed.

Hasty hands ripped open the fabric of the kit that had served them so long. Marshall hurriedly jerked out the flare-gun, inserted a charge with fumbling fingers, lifted the gun, fired.

A blaze of red light blossomed in the sky. Shading his eyes, Marshall saw the plane wheel round to investigate. He inserted another flare and fired it.

"Shirts off, everyone! Signal to them!"

They waved frantically. Minutes passed; then, the hatch of the plane opened and a small dark object dropped through. A parachute bellied open immediately. The plane circled the area and streaked off toward the east.

Through some sort of miracle the parachute did not become snagged in the trees on the way down, and the package came to rest not far from where the four stood. Marshall and the others ran for it. They found a note pinned to the wrapping:

We were just about to give up hope of ever finding any of the crash survivors when we saw the flares go up. Your area is too heavily wooded to allow for a landing, and so we're returning to New Lisbon to get a 'copter. Remain exactly where you are now. We expect to be back in about two hours. In the meantime we're dropping some provisions to tide you over until we return.

"We're going to be rescued!" Lois cried. "They've found us!"

"It's like a miracle!" Garvey's wife exclaimed.

The two hours seemed to take forever. The four squatted over the provisions kit, munching with delight on chocolate and fruit, and smoking their first cigarettes since the day of the crash.

Finally they heard the droning sound of a helicopter's rotors overhead.

There it was—descending vertically, coming to a halt in their clearing. Three men sprang from the helicopter the moment it reached the ground. One wore the uniform of a medic. They sprinted toward the survivors. Marshall became uncomfortably aware of his own uncouth appearance, and saw the women attempting to cover the exposed parts of their anatomy in sudden new-found modesty.

"Well! I'm Captain Collins of the New Lisbon airbase. I certainly didn't expect to be picking up any survivors of that crash!"

"My name's David Marshall," Marshall said. He introduced the others. "You the only survivors?"

Marshall nodded. "A fifth man was thrown from the plane alive, but he died later. We're the only ones who survived. How far are we from New Lisbon?"

"Oh, three hundred fifty miles, I'd say."

Marshall frowned. "Three hundred fifty? That means we covered better than six hundred miles on foot since the crash. But aren't you a little far from home base? How come you searched for us here?"

The New Lisbon man looked uncomfortable, "Well, to tell the truth, it was a kind of a hunch. We got this crazy message—"

"Message?"

"Yes. A few days back. Damn near everyone in the colony heard it. It was a kind of telepathic voice telling us that there were still a few survivors from the crash, and giving an approximate position. So we sent out a few scouts. Say, any one of you folks a telepath?"

"No, not us," Marshall said. "It must have been the alien."

"Alien? There's an alien here?"

"Past tense. He's dead." Marshall smiled oddly. "But he must have decided to do us one last favor before he died. In return for the favor we were doing him. He must have broadcast a telepathic message to New Lisbon."

The New Lisbon man eyed Marshall strangely. "Are you telling me that you found an intelligent alien in the jungle?"

"That's right. And we're going to go back and locate the body, and see if we can preserve it for science. It's the least we can do for him. At least one remnant of his race will be preserved. They won't die away without leaving a trace," Marshall said, as he walked toward the helicopter that would take him back to civilization.

VAMPIRES FROM OUTER SPACE
(1959)

Three of the five stories in Super-Science Fiction's *glorious* SPECIAL
MONSTER ISSUE! *of April, 1959 were my work: the lead novelet,
"Mournful Monster," under the Dan Malcolm pseudonym, a short called "A
Cry for Help" bylined Eric Rodman, and this one, the second lead, which
ran under the name of Richard F. Watson.*

*I wrote it in September, 1958, right after my first visit to San Francisco,
which is why the story is set there. (I lived in New York then, the city of my
birth, and had not the slightest inkling, then, that thirteen years later I was
going to move to the San Francisco area.) The title on the manuscript when
I turned it in was simply "Vampires from Space," but the meaningless
phrase "outer space" was just then establishing itself as a cliché, and
Scottie stuck it right in. It is, I think, the only place the phrase can be found
in all my millions of words of science fiction.*

The first report of what was quickly to become known as the Vampire
Menace reached the central office of the Terran Security Agency half
an hour after the attack had taken place. The date was June 11, 2104.
Agency Subchief Neil Harriman was busy with routine matters when the
courier burst into his office, carrying a message pellet gaudy with the
red-and-yellow wrapping that meant Top Level Emergency.

Harriman reached one big hand out for the message pellet. "Where's it from?"

"San Francisco. It just came in by simultaneous visi-tape. Marked special for your office, with all the emergency labels."

"Okay," Harriman said. He flipped the switch that darkened the office and brought the viewing screen down from its niche in the ceiling. As Harriman unwrapped the message pellet and began to slip it into the viewer, he glanced up at the courier, who was standing by with expectant curiosity. Harriman scowled darkly. No words were necessary. The courier gulped, moistened his lips, and backed out of the office, his curiosity about the emergency message doomed to be unsatisfied.

Alone, Harriman nudged the starter button and the tape started to unwind past the photon-cell eye of the viewer. An image formed in glowing natural colors at the far side of the room.

The voice of the speaker said, "This is Special Agent Michaels reporting from San Francisco, chief. There was a killing out here twenty minutes ago. The local police sent for me because it looked like Agency business."

The screen showed one of San Francisco's steep hills. Some twenty feet from the camera's eye a body lay grotesquely sprawled, face downward, head toward the foot of the hill. Gray fog swirled over the scene. It was nearly noon at Harriman's New York office, but it was still quite early in the morning across the continent in California. Transmission of the message-tape was virtually instantaneous, thanks to progress in communications science.

Harriman watched patiently, wondering why it had been necessary to bring to his attention a routine West Coast murder. The image bounced as the man holding the camera walked toward the corpse

Special Agent Michaels' voice said, "This is just the way he was found, twenty minutes ago."

A hand reached down and turned the cadaver over so its face was visible. An involuntary gasp broke from Harriman's lips. The dead man's face was the color of chalk. Harriman had never seen so pale a face before. The victim's eyes were open, and frozen in them was an image of pain, of shock, of horror beyond human comprehension.

There were two dark little holes an inch apart on the dead man's throat, just over the jugular.

"There isn't a drop of blood in him, chief," Michaels said quietly in commentary. "He's as dry as if he was pumped clean with a force-pump.

We've identified him as Sam Barrett, a salesman in a used car show-room. Unmarried, lived with his aged mother. He worked around the corner on Van Ness Avenue. There were two eye-witnesses at the scene of the crime."

The camera's eye panned to a balding man in his forties who stood at the edge of the sidewalk, nervously twisting his hands together. He looked almost as pale as the ghastly body on the ground.

Go on," prompted Michaels. "This is for the record. Tell us who you are and what you saw."

"My name is Mack Harkins," the balding man said in a thin, hesi-tant voice. "I live over on Austin Street, couple of blocks from here. Work at the Dynacar showroom around the corner. I was walking along and suddenly I looked up ahead and saw a man struggling with—well—some kind of *thing*."

"Describe it," Michaels prodded gently.

"Well—bigger than a man, purple-colored, with big bat-wings. You know, one of those bat-people, what do you call them?"

"Nirotans?"

"Yeah, that's it. One of them Nirotans, bending over the man's throat like he was sucking blood from him. Before I knew what was going on, the bat-thing saw me and bolted away into an alley." Harkins shuddered. "I went to look at the body. No blood at all, just like he is now. Drained."

"You're sure it was a Nirotan you saw?" Michaels asked.

"I ain't sure of anything. But there was this big purple thing with bat-wings wrestling with poor Barrett. If it wasn't one of them Nirotans, I'd like to know what it was, then."

"Thank you, Mr. Harkins. I think the local authorities would like to ask you some questions now." The camera flashed toward the second witness.

The second witness was not human. He was a member of one of the half-dozen different species of alien beings that frequented Earth since the opening of the age of interstellar travel some three decades earlier.

The camera focused on the short, stockily-built being whose only external physical differences from humanity were the two tiny, heat-sensitive antennae that sprouted just above each eye.

"You are from Drosk?" Michaels asked.

The alien nodded. "I am Blen Duworn, attaché to the Drosk Trade Commission office in San Francisco," he said in smooth, faultless English. "I was out for a morning stroll when I came upon the scene this man has just described to you."

"Tell us what you saw."

"I saw a large winged entity vanishing into that alley. I saw a man falling toward the ground, and another man—Mr. Harkins, rushing toward him. That is all."

"And this large winged entity you saw—can you identify it more precisely?"

The alien frowned. "I am quite sure it was a Nirotan," he said after a brief pause.

"Thank you," Michaels said. The screen showed another view of the bloodless corpse. "That's where it stands as of now, chief. I'll keep in touch on further developments as they break. Awaiting your instructions."

The screen went dead.

＊

In his darkened office, Neil Harriman sat quietly with folded hands while a chill of terror rippled quickly through him. He recovered self-control with a considerable effort, and switched on the light.

His mind refused to accept what the message tape had just told him.

Harriman's particular job in the workings of the Terran Security Agency was to deal with crime involving Earthmen and aliens. There was plenty of bad blood between the people of Earth and the strange-looking visitors from space. A planet which had not yet fully reconciled itself even to racial differences in its own one species of intelligent life could not easily adjust to the presence of bizarre life-forms, some of them considerably superior to the best that Earth had.

Up till now, Harriman's job had largely been to protect the aliens from the hostility of Earthmen. The green-skinned Qafliks, for example, had touched off demonstrations in those parts of the world where white skin was still thought to be in some way superior to all other colors of skin. In other places, the peculiar sexual mores of the uninhibited Zadoorans had angered certain puritanical Terrestrials. So Harriman's wing of the Agency had been given the task of protecting Earth's many alien visitors until the people of Earth were mature enough to realize that it was not necessary to hate that which was strange.

But now an entirely new and dangerous aspect had entered the picture. One of the aliens had murdered an Earthman. And, thought Harriman bleakly, it *would* have to be a Nirotan that had committed the crime.

The Nirotans were recent additions to the Terran scene. They had first landed on Earth less than a year previously, and no more than a few thousand were present at this time. They were not pretty. Descended from a primitive bat-like form, they were frightening in appearance— purple-hued creatures seven feet tall, their bodies covered with thick coarse fur, their eyes tiny and set deep in their skull, their faces weird and strange. They had wings, bat-like membranes of skin stretched over vastly elongated finger-bones, while a small pair of well-equipped hands provided them with the manipulative abilities necessary for the development of a civilization.

They were traders, bringing with them curiously fashioned mechanical contrivances that were in great demand on Earth. But they had little contact with Earthmen. The Nirotans seemed to be a with-drawn, self-contained race, and few Earthmen cared for the company of such repellent-looking beings in any event. So little was known about them. Dark rumors had arisen that they were vampire beings, thirsty for human blood. The ordinary people of Earth regarded the Nirotans with fear and loathing for this reason, and gave them a wide berth.

So far as anyone had known, the vampire story was nothing but a terror-inspired myth. Until now.

The murder story, Harriman thought, would have to be hushed up somehow. At least until the investigation had definitely proven the guilt or innocence of the Nirotans. If the world ever learned of the "vampire" attack, there would be an hysterical uprising that might bring about the death of every Nirotan—or every alien of any kind—on Earth. Reprisal from the stars would be swift.

Harriman scowled tightly. This was too big for him to handle on his own. He restored the message tape to its container and picked up his phone.

"Harriman speaking. Let me talk to Director Russell. And fast."

His call went through rush channels, and a moment later the deep, resonant voice of the Director of the Terran Security Agency said, "Hello, Harriman. I was just about to call you anyway. I want to see you in a hurry. And I mean *hurry.*"

✦

Director Russell was a short, rotund man who normally wore an affable expression during even the most grave crisis. But there was nothing cheerful about his plump face now. He nodded curtly to

Harriman as the Subchief entered. Harriman saw two message pellets lying on Russell's desk, both of them wrapped in the red-and yellow emergency trimmings.

Russell said, "I've been reading some of your mail, Harriman. You know that I'm always notified when an emergency message arrives here. You got one about half an hour ago. Then another one showed up for you, and I figured I'd save some time by having a look at it myself. And no sooner did I finish scanning that one when another one showed up." Russell tapped the two message pellets on his desk. "One of these is from Warsaw. The other is from London. They're both about the same thing."

"The Nirotans?"

Russell nodded darkly. "Tell me about your tape."

"A man was murdered in San Francisco this morning. Body found completely drained of blood, with puncture-holes over the jugular. Two witnesses—a Drosk and a man named Harkins. They saw the victim struggling with something that looked like a Nirotan."

The Director's eyebrows rose. "Witnesses? That's more than we have on these other two."

"What are they?"

"Murder reports. One in Poland last night, the other in London about two hours ago. An old man and a girl, both bloodless."

"We'll have to keep this quiet," Harriman said. "If the people find out—"

"They have. There's already been a vampire-hunt in Warsaw. Two Nirotans were flushed by the mob and just barely escaped with their lives. Londoners are talking vampire too. It looks damned bad for the Nirotans, Harriman. Especially with this eye-witness thing in San Francisco. Everyone called the Nirotans vampires all along—and now there's something concrete to pin suspicions to."

"But they've been here for almost a year," Harriman protested. "Why should they suddenly break out in a wave of blood-drinking the same night?"

"Are you defending them?" Russell asked.

"I'm just speculating. We have no definite proof that they're guilty."

"Maybe," Russell said, "they just couldn't hold out any longer with all that nice fresh blood tempting them."

Harriman eyed his chief strangely. He knew Russell did not have much liking for the alien beings on Earth. The Director was, in many respects, an old-fashioned man.

"You aren't pre-judging the Nirotans, are you?" Harriman asked.

"Of course not. But it certainly looks bad for them. I've ordered all Nirotans taken into protective custody until things cool down a little."

"Good idea," Harriman agreed. "If some of them got lynched by the mobs we might find ourselves at war with Nirota tomorrow."

"I'm aware of that," Russell said. "Also, I'm having the three bodies flown here for examination. And I want to get a live Nirotan to examine, too."

"That won't be so easy," Harriman said. "They don't like Earthmen peering at them up close."

"They'd *better* like it," Russell said. "Take a trip over to the Nirotan consulate downtown and talk to the head man."

Harriman nodded. "Right. But I don't think they're going to cooperate."

❂

The news sheets picked up the story with almost supernatural speed. THREE VAMPIRE VICTIMS, screamed the headlines of the afternoon editions. BLOODLESS BODIES FOUND IN FRISCO, LONDON, WARSAW. NIROTANS SUSPECTED.

Harriman made an appointment to see the ranking member of the Nirotan Consulate at half past two that afternoon. Until that time, he busied himself with keeping up on news reports.

Angry mobs were beginning to form. A country-wide pogrom was under way in Poland, the object to hunt down any Nirotans that could be found and destroy them. Ancient superstitious legends had been reawakened in Central Europe. There was talk of silver bullets, of wooden stakes through the heart.

"Dracula-men from the stars," shouted a West Coast newspaper. In Los Angeles, crowds surrounded the Nirotan headquarters, climbing towering palms to hurl bricks at the windows. A major incident was brewing as news of the triple killings swept the world. Fear and hatred were turned against alien beings of all sorts. Harriman sent out a world-wide order instructing authorities everywhere to give sanctuary to aliens of any kind, in case the mob generalized its hate and struck out against all non-humans.

At two that afternoon the first body arrived—from London, flown over by transatlantic rocket. Harriman had a moment to view the corpse before heading downtown to the Nirotan consulate.

The victim was a girl of about seventeen, with plain but pleasant features. The sheet was lifted from her body and Harriman saw its paper-whiteness, and the two dark little holes at her throat. Horror crept down his back. It was a ghastly sight, this bloodless body. The girl's mouth was locked in the configurations of a terrified scream. She looked like a waxen image, not like a creature of flesh and blood.

Harriman's special car was waiting for him outside the Agency building. He rode downtown in deep silence, his mind still gripped by the sight of those chalky young breasts, those dead white thighs. Despite himself he could picture the huge revolting form of the Nirotan huddling around her, its wings half unfolding as the gleaming teeth plunged through the soft flesh of the protesting girl's throat—

Harriman shook his head. He was an officer of the law, he reminded himself. An impartial investigator dedicated to justice. He had to keep from letting his emotions enter into the case. Maybe the Nirotans *were* hideous; maybe they *did* look like the Devil's own nightmares. It made no difference. His job was simply to determine guilt or innocence.

If the Nirotans were guilty, if three of their number had committed the crimes, then there would be grave interstellar repercussions. Probably the Nirotans would be asked to leave Earth permanently.

But if they were innocent—somehow—then it was his job to protect them from the wrath of the mobs, and find the real culprits.

The Nirotan consulate was a sturdy four-story building on Fifth Avenue—an old building, dating back nearly two centuries. Just now it was surrounded by a boiling, screaming mob. Eight armed men in the gray uniforms of the Security Corps held the rioters back.. The door, Harriman saw, was barred. One of the Security men had a cut over his left eye; the result, probably, of a thrown missile.

The crowd melted to one side as Harriman's official Security Corps car came to a halt outside the building. Escorted by three armed Corpsmen, Harriman made his way up the steps of the building. He waited outside the door while a scanner beam examined him. There was the sound of relays groaning as the heavy protective bars were electronically drawn back.

The door opened. A Nirotan stood in the shadows within, looming high above Harriman.

"Enter," the alien said in its strange, hoarse, dry-sounding voice.

Harriman stepped inside and the great door clanged shut behind him, obliterating the raucous screams of the mob outside. Three

Nirotans faced Harriman, the smallest of them better than half a foot taller than he. They conducted him silently through the building to the office of the Nirotan consul.

There was a faintly musty odor about the place. Despite himself, Harriman felt a twinge of revulsion as he was ushered into the presence of Trinnin Nirot, ranking Nirotan diplomat in North America.

The Nirotan was standing in one corner of the office—Nirotans never sat. His small, muscular arms were folded in a surprisingly human posture. The great sleek wings sat huddled on his shoulders. On Earth the atmosphere was too thin, the gravitational pull too strong, to make it possible for the Nirotans to fly: Their home world had a thicker atmosphere and lighter gravity, and there they soared on wings that measured fifteen feet from tip to tip.

Harriman tried to hide the irrational fear he experienced at the sight of the huge bat-like creature. He stared at the face, covered, like the rest of the Nirotan's body, with fine, purplish fur. He could see the dog-like snout, the tiny yellow eyes, the enormous fan-like ears, and, gleaming behind the Nirotan's thin lips, the teeth. Teeth that might, perhaps, be able to drain blood from an Earthman's throat.

Harriman said, "You understand why I am here, of course."

"I understand that there are rioters outside this building, and that my people on this planet must take cover for fear of their lives," said the Nirotan crisply. Like most aliens on Earth, his command of the language was flawless. "More than that I do not understand. I am waiting for an explanation."

Harriman's jaws tightened. He felt awkward standing halfway across the room from the Nirotan; but there was no place to sit down, and the alien did not offer any sort of hospitality. Harriman fidgeted, crossing and uncrossing his arms. After a brief pause he said—quietly, since the Nirotans were extraordinarily sensitive to sound—"Last night and this morning three Earthmen were found dead in widely separated places, their bodies drained of blood. Many people believe that they were killed by members of your race."

The alien's facial expression was unreadable. "Why should they believe this? Why choose us as the killers, and not the Qafliks or the Zadoorans or some other race? There are many alien beings on this planet."

"There are two reasons for suspecting Nirotans," Harriman said. "The first is an ancient superstitious belief in vampires. Bats who drink human blood. The people of Nirotans are closest in physical appearance to the popular image of the vampire."

"And the other reason?"

"The other reason," said Harriman, "is more pertinent. Two eye-witnesses in San Francisco said they saw a Nirotan in the process of attacking one of the victims."

The alien was silent for a long moment. Finally he said, "Tell me, Mr. Harriman: if you could, would you kill and eat me?"

Harriman was stunned. "Would I—kill and *eat* you?" he repeated slowly:

"Yes. Do you feel any inclination to feast on a roasted Nirotan?"

"Why—of course not. The idea's monstrous!"

"Exactly so," the Nirotan said calmly. "Let me assure you that a member of my race would no sooner drink the blood of an Earthman than an Earthman would dine on Nirotan flesh. Pardon me when I say that we find your physical appearance as repugnant as you seem to find ours. The whole concept of this crime is beyond our belief. We are not vampires. We do not feed on animal matter off any sort. The crime we are accused of could not possibly have been committed by a Nirotan."

Harriman silently regarded the alien, staring at the flashing teeth, needle-sharp, at the vicious little claws, at the folded, leathery, infinite-ly terrifying wings. Appearance seemed to belie the calm denial of guilt that Harriman had just heard.

The Earthman said, "It might be possible to determine guilt or innocence quickly. If you would lend us a member of your staff for examination—"

"No," came the curt, immediate response.

"But our physicians might be able to establish beyond doubt the impossibility of any—ah—vampirism. I can assure you that no harm would come—"

"No."

"But—"

"We do not tolerate any handling of our bodies by alien beings," said the Nirotan haughtily. "If you persist in accusing us of this incred-ible crime, we will be forced to withdraw from your planet. But we can-not and will not submit to any sort of examination of the sort you sug-gest, Mr. Harriman."

"Don't you see, though, it might clear your people at once, and—"

"You have heard my reply," the Nirotan said. He rustled his wings in an unfriendly gesture. "We have stated our innocence. I must take your refusal to believe my statement as a deeply wounding insult."

There was crackling silence in the room. This was an alien, Harriman reflected. On Nirota, perhaps, the idea of lying was not known. Or perhaps the Nirotan was a very subtle devil indeed. In any event, the interview was rapidly getting nowhere.

"Very well," Harriman said. "If your refusal is final—"

"It is."

"We'll have to proceed with your investigation as best we can. For your own sake, I must ask you not to let any of your people venture out unprotected. We can't be responsible for the actions of hysterical mobs. And, naturally, we'll do everything in our power to discover the guilty parties. Your cooperation might have made things a little easier all around, of course."

"Good day, Mr. Harriman."

Harriman scowled. "For the sake of good relations between Earth and Nirota, I hope none of your people is responsible for this crime. But you can be sure that when we do find the murderers, they'll be fully punished under the laws of Earth. Good day, Trinnin Nirot."

*

Harriman was shaking with repressed disgust as he made his way down the consulate steps, through the path between the gesticulating rioters, and into his car. The Nirotan stench seemed to cling to him, to hover in a cloud about him. And he knew the Nirotan's hideous face would plague his dreams for weeks to come.

He rode uptown, back to the skyscraper that housed the headquarters of the Terran Security Agency, in a bleak and bitter mood. For the ten years that he had held his job, he had devoted himself to protecting the alien beings on Earth, guarding them from the outcroppings of superstitious hatred that sometimes rose up to threaten them. And now, he could no longer defend the extra-terrestrials. Three vicious crimes had been committed. And Trinnin Nirot's cold refusal to permit investigation made it that much harder to believe in the innocence of the Nirotans. The vampire image was ingrained too deeply.

When he returned to his office, Harriman found a message instructing him to report to Director Russell at once. He found Russell in conference. In the Director's office were four men—George Zachary, Secretary-General of the United Nations; Henri Lamartine, Commissioner of Extraterrestrial Relationships; Dr. David van Dyne, chief medical examiner of the Security Agency; and Paul Hennessey, Commissioner of Justice and Russell's immediate superior.

Director Russell said, "Well, Harriman? Did you see the Nirotans?"

"I saw Trinnin Nirot himself," Harriman said. "And I got nowhere."

"What do you mean, nowhere?"

"Trinnin Nirot categorically denies the possibility that any Nirotan might have committed the crimes. He says that Nirotans are vegetarians, and that the whole idea of their being vampires is beyond belief. But he won't let us have a look at any of his men to confirm it."

"We expected the denial," muttered Commissioner Hennessey. "But where do we go from here?"

"Isn't there any evidence on the bodies?" Harriman asked.

Dr. van Dyne said, "All three bodies are here, and I've examined them. All that can be definitely determined was that two needle-like instruments penetrated the jugular veins of the victims and rapidly withdrew their blood. The withdrawal might have been done with teeth, or it could have been done mechanically. Of course, if we could get hold of a Nirotan and examine his teeth, we could probably find out readily enough whether one of them actually committed the crime or not. If they're really vegetarians, they probably don't have the equipment for doing it."

"Are we trying to decide whether a Nirotan actually did it?" Director Russell asked in some surprise. "I thought that was all settled. There were witnesses, after all, for the San Francisco murder."

Commissioner Lamartine said, "Before we can start to take legal action against the Nirotans, we'll have to rule out all possibility that any other race might have done it—or that the crimes were committed by Earthmen."

Russell blinked. "Earthmen? Are you suggesting—"

The bearded little commissioner shook his head stubbornly. "We're dealing with a proud and stubborn race here, as Mr. Harriman can confirm. We can't simply accuse them of a crime like this without proof."

"Eyewitnesses constitute some beginning of proof," Russell snapped.

Commissioner Hennessy held up a hand to cut short the dispute. "Please, gentlemen. I think Trinnin Nirot's refusal to permit examination of any Nirotans speaks for itself in the matter of guilt or innocence."

"I'm not so sure," Harriman put in. "They seem to have some kind of taboo against letting other species get too close to them."

"But certainly they'd be willing to let the taboo go by the boards for the sake of clearing themselves," Russell objected.

"Not necessarily," said Lamartine. "We're dealing with alien beings, remember. They don't see things the way we do."

"In any event," said Secretary-General Zachary, "we'll have to reach some solution in a hurry. There's rioting going on in every city where Nirotans are located. And the bitterness is starting to spread to take in other aliens, too. If we don't restore order in a hurry, we're going to find all the extraterrestrials pulling out—and turning Earth into a backwater world considered not fit for civilized beings to visit."

Harriman stared at the five grim faces. These men, like himself, were shaken to the core by the notion that the beings from the stars might be blood-drinkers in fact as well as in appearance. And it was hard to believe in the innocence of the Nirotans.

The phone rang. Director Russell reached out with a plump hand and snatched the telephone nervously from its cradle. He listened for a moment, snapped some sort of reply, and slammed the instrument down again.

"Bad news," he said, his face becoming grimmer. "A mob broke into the building where the Nirotans were taking sanctuary in Budapest. Dragged three Nirotans out and killed them. Drove wooden stakes through their hearts."

Harriman felt chilled. Legends weighted with medieval dust were erupting into the neat, ordered world of the twenty-second century. Wooden stakes in Budapest! Ominous mutterings against the winged people—and three bloodless bodies lying in the morgue ten floors below.

"Heaven help us if the Nirotans are innocent," Secretary-General Zachary said tonelessly. "They'll never forgive us for today."

"I'll order triple protection," Russell said. "We don't want a massacre."

Hysteria was the order of the day on Earth in the next six hours. Three murders in themselves were not of any great importance; round the world each day, hundreds of human beings met violent deaths without causing a stir. But it was the manner of the deaths that dug deep into humanity. The killings struck subconscious fears, and brought to the surface the old myths. It was dread of the unknown, dread of the people from the stars, that touched off the rioting round the world. The relative handful of Nirotans waited behind the walls of their shelters, waiting for the mobs to come bursting in.

The United Nations General Assembly, which had become the world government in fact as well as in name during the past seventy-five years, met in an extraordinary session that evening at U.N. headquarters. The purpose of the meeting was simply to vote additional appropriations for the protection of extraterrestrial beings against mob violence—but during the session a delegate from the United States rose in wrath to demand the immediate withdrawal of what he termed the "Nirotan vampires" from Earth.

The resolution was declared out of order, and did not come to a vote. But it represented the sentiments of a great majority of Earth's nine billion people on that evening.

Harriman flew to San Francisco that evening aboard a midnight jet-liner that made the journey in four hours . A waiting taxi took him to the downtown San Francisco offices of the Nirotan Trade Delegation, in the heart of the city on Market Street. The summer fog shrouded everything in gloom.

Special Agent Michaels was waiting for him outside the heavily protected building. The agent's face was set tightly. Fifty or sixty people were parading wearily around the building, despite the lateness of the hour. They no longer seemed violent, but they carried hastily constructed placards which bore slogans like VAMPIRES MUST DIE! and NIROTANS GO HOME!

"Been any trouble with the pickets?" Harriman asked, indicating the mob.

"Not as much as earlier," Michaels said. "There were about five hundred people out here around nine o'clock, but they've all gone home, except the diehards. They were parading the mother of the murdered man around the building and screaming for justice, but they didn't try to do any damage, at least."

Harriman nodded. "Good. Let's go in."

There were fifteen Nirotans standing inside. Michaels assured Harriman that the group included every Nirotan who had been in the San Francisco area in the past three days. If a Nirotan had been the murderer of Sam Barrett, then the murderer was in this room.

Harriman stared at the group. As always, the facial expressions of the aliens defied interpretation. They seemed to be waiting for the disturbance to die down, so they could resume their normal way of life.

Conscious of their dread appearance, of his own insignificance, of the nauseous odor of fifteen Nirotans in one room, Harriman moistened his lips. A mental image came to him unexpectedly—the fifteen bat-like creatures surrounding him, throwing themselves on him with once accord, fastening their fangs in his throat and sucking away his lifeblood. He winced involuntarily at the vividness of the picture.

Then he remembered that he was an officer of the law, and that these beings facing him were simply suspects in a murder case.

He said, "Early yesterday morning a man was killed in this city. I'm sure you all know *how* he was killed. I've come here from New York to talk to you about the murder of Sam Barrett."

None of the aliens spoke. In the solemn silence, Harriman continued. "Two witnesses claim they saw a Nirotan struggling with the murdered man in the street. If the witnesses are telling the truth, one of you in this room committed that crime."

"The witnesses are saying that which is not so," declared an immense Nirotan boomingly. "We have committed no crimes. The offense you charge us with is unthinkable in Nirotan eyes."

"I haven't charged you with anything," Harriman said. "The evidence implies that a Nirotan was responsible. For your sake and the sake of interstellar relations, I hope it isn't so. But my job is to find out who *is* responsible for the killings."

Harriman shook his head. "My first step has to be to establish guilt or innocence in this room. As a beginning, suppose I ask each of you to account for your whereabouts at the time of the murder?"

"We will give no information," rumbled the Nirotan who seemed to be the spokesman.

A stone wall again, Harriman thought gloomily. He said, "Don't you see that by refusing to answer questions or permit us an examination, you naturally make yourselves look suspicious in humanity's eyes?"

"We have no concern with appearances. We did not commit the crime."

"On Earth we need proof of that. Your word isn't enough here."

"We will not submit to interrogation. We demand the right to leave this planet at once, in order to return to Nirota."

Harriman's eyes narrowed. "The Interstellar Trade Agreements prevent any suspected criminals from leaving Earth for their home world.

You'll have to stay here until something definite is settled, one way or the other, on the murder."

"We will answer no questions," came the flat, positive, unshakeable reply.

Anger glimmered in Harriman's eyes. "All right, then. But you'll rot here until we decide to let you go! See how you like that!"

He turned and spun out of the room.

※

He slept fitfully and uneasily on the return journey to New York. It was mid-morning when the jetliner touched down at New York Jet Skyport, and it was noon by the time Harriman returned to his office at the Terran Security Agency. He felt deep frustration. There was no way for the investigation to proceed—not when the only suspects refused to defend themselves. Earth couldn't accuse members of an alien species of murder on the basis of two early-morning eyewitnesses and a lot of circumstantial evidence rising out of old hysterical legends. It was always a risky business when one planet tried people of another world for crime—and in this case, the evidence was simply too thin for a solid indictment.

On the other hand, Earth clamored for a trial. The overwhelming mass of the people, utterly convinced that the Nirotans were vampires, stood ready to enforce justice themselves if the authorities lingered. Already, three Nirotans had died at the hands of the jeering mobs—an incident which would have serious consequences once the hysteria died down.

Director Russell growled a greeting at Harriman as the Agency subchief entered the office. It was obvious from Russell's harried expression and from the overflowing ashtrays that the Director had been up all night, keeping in touch with the crisis as it unfolded and as new complications developed.

"Well?" Russell demanded. "What's the word from San Francisco?"

"The word is nothing, chief," Harriman said tiredly. "The Nirotans clammed up completely. They insist that they're innocent, but beyond that they refuse to say anything. And they're demanding to be allowed to return to their home world now."

"I know. Trinnin Nirot petitioned Secretary-General Zachary late last night to permit all Nirotans on Earth to withdraw."

"What did Zachary say?"

"He didn't—not yet. But he doesn't want to let the Nirotans go until we get to the bottom of this vampire business."

"Any word from anyplace else?"

"Not much that's hopeful," Russell said wearily with a tired shrug. "There are thirty Nirotans under surveillance in London, but they're not talking. And we have twenty cooped up in Warsaw. Zero there too. Right now we're busy protecting a couple of thousand of the bats. But how long can this keep up?"

"Couldn't we seize a Nirotan forcibly and examine him?" Harriman asked.

"I've thought of that. But the high brass says no. If we happen to be wrong, we'll have committed what the Nirotans are perfectly free to consider as an open act of war. And if we're right—if the Nirotans were lying—then we still have the problem of finding out *which* Nirotans did the actual killing."

"Maybe," Harriman said, "we ought to just let the bats clear off Earth, as they want to do. That'll solve all our problems."

"And bring up a million new ones. It would mean that any alien could come down here and commit crimes, and go away untouched if he simply denied his guilt. I wouldn't like to see a precedent like that get set. Uh-uh, Harriman. We have to find the killers, and we have to do it legally. Only I'm damned if I know how we're going to go about doing it."

We have to find the killers, Harriman thought half an hour later, in the solitude of his own office. *And we have to do it legally.* Well, the first part of that was reasonable enough.

But how about the second, Harriman thought?

Legally they were powerless to continue the investigation. The forces of law and order were hopelessly stalled, while fear-crazy rioters demanded Nirotan blood in exchange for Terran.

The main problem, he thought, was whether or not a Nirotan—any Nirotan—had actually committed the atrocities. According to the Nirotans, such crimes were beyond their capacities even to imagine. Yet the heavy weight of popular belief—as well as the damning fact of the two San Francisco witnesses—lent validity to the notion of the Nirotans as blood-sucking vampires.

Medical examination of a Nirotan might settle the thing in one direction or another. If it could be proven that the Nirotans might possibly have committed such a crime, it would be reasonable to assume that they had. But, on the other hand, if the Nirotans had definitely not done it, Harriman would have to begin looking elsewhere for the authors of the atrocities.

If only the Nirotans would cooperate, he thought!

But some alien quirk, some incomprehensible pride of theirs, kept them from lowering themselves to take part in anything so humiliating to them as an official inquest. The Security Agency was stymied—officially. They were at an impasse which could not be surmounted.

How about unofficially, though?

Harriman moistened his lips. He had an idea. It was a gamble, a gamble that would be worth his job and his career if he lost. But it was worth taking, he decided firmly. Someone had to risk it.

Picking up the phone, he ordered his special car to be ready for him outside the building. Then, without leaving word with anyone of his intended destination or purpose, he quietly departed.

There were several dozen Nirotans cooped up at the consulate on Fifth Avenue. Any one of those Nirotans would do, for his purposes. The thing he had to remember was that he was in this on his own. He did not dare risk taking on an accomplice. His plan was too risky to share with another person.

The consulate was guarded by armed Security Corpsmen. And, unless there had been a slackening of public animosity, the building was probably still surrounded by a howling mob.

It was. More than a thousand shouting New Yorkers clustered around the building, pressing close to the steps but not daring to approach for fear of the guns of the Security men. The mob, frustrated, kept up a low animal-like murmur beneath the hysteria of the shouts and curses it hurled forth.

Harriman ordered his driver to park his car several blocks north of the scene of the disturbance. The Agency subchief proceeded cautiously, on foot, making his way between the packed rows of angry demonstrators toward the consulate. He felt a dryness in his throat. He was gambling everything, now.

He needed a Nirotan—dead or alive, preferably alive. And there was only one way for him to get one, he knew.

He made his way up the steps of the consulate. The guards, recognizing him, gave way. Harriman called them together.

"I've got orders to bring a Nirotan out," he whispered. "Just one. They want him down at Headquarters. When I get him out, I want an armed convoy through this crowd—eight of you on each side of me, with drawn guns, in case anyone in the crowd tries to make trouble. All that understood?"

They nodded. Tension pounded in Harriman's chest. He was taking a tremendous risk, putting a Nirotan in front of the crowd in broad daylight. But there was no help for it. If he came at dead of night, when the mob had diminished, he would get no response from within. Nirotans slept the sleep of the dead at night—this much had been definitely established.

Harriman waited in the scanner beam while the Nirotans within examined him. At last, he heard the heavy door begin to clank open. Beady yellow Nirotan eyes stared at him from within.

"Yes? What do you want?"

"To talk," Harriman said. "Something new has come up that you must be told about."

The door widened a little to admit Harriman. But, instead of stepping inside, he extended a hand and seized the wrist of the Nirotan. Harriman tugged. The Nirotan, for all his great height, had the light bones of a flying creature; besides, surprise was on Harriman's side. The astonished Nirotan came tumbling through the half open door before he knew what was happening. A great shout went up from the mob at the sight of the bat-creature. Harriman felt a twinge of fear at the raucous roar of the crowd. The Nirotan was squirming, struggling to break Harriman's grasp. His wings riffled impotently.

"What is the meaning of this?" demanded the bat-creature indignantly.

"Just come with me, and don't struggle, and everything will be all right," Harriman said soothingly. He let the alien catch a glimpse of the tiny needle-blaster he held in the palm of his free hand. "We want to talk to you at headquarters. The crowd won't hurt you if you cooperate with me."

For an uneasy moment Harriman wondered if the alien might not prefer suicide to cooperation. But evidently the Nirotans' pride did not extend that far. Eyes blazing with fury but otherwise meek, the Nirotan allowed himself to be led down the consulate steps by Harriman.

"Keep back!" the Security Corpsmen shouted, gesturing with their weapons, as they formed an enflankment to protect Harriman and his captive. An ugly menacing buzz rose from the crowd; some began to jostle forward, evidently impelled by hotter heads behind them. But they gave way as the little convoy proceeded past.

The trip to the car seemed to take hours. Harriman was limp and sweat-soaked by the time he finally reached the vehicle and thrust the Nirotan in. There had not been a single overt act of violence on the part of the crowd. It was as if the actual sight of a Nirotan walking safely through their very midst had left them too stunned to react.

"This is an outrage," the Nirotan started to say, as the car pulled away. "I will protest this kidnapping and I—"

Smiling in relief, Harriman took from his pocket the anesthetic capsule he had prepared, and crushed it under the Nirotan's snout. The bat-creature slumped instantly into unconsciousness and said no more.

✹

Some fifteen minutes later, a stretcher was borne into the headquarters of the Terran Security Agency. The form on the stretcher was totally swathed in wrappings, and it was impossible to detect what lay beneath. Harriman supervised delivery of the stretcher to the inner office of Security Corps Medical Examiner van Dyne.

Dr. van Dyne looked puzzled and more than a little irritated. "Would you mind telling me what all this mystery is about, Harriman?"

Harriman nodded agreeably. "Is your office absolutely secure-tight?"

"Of course. What do you think—"

"Okay, then. I've brought you someone to examine. He's currently out with a double dose of anesthetrin, and I'll guarantee his complete cooperation for the next couple of hours, at least. Don't ask any questions about where or how I got him, Doc. Just examine him, and get in touch with me the instant you're finished."

Harriman reached forward and yanked the coverings off the figure on the stretcher. Even in sleep, the face of the Nirotan was hideous. Dr. van Dyne's jaw sagged in disbelief.

"My God! A Nirotan! Harriman, how did you—"

"I told you, Doc, don't ask any questions. He's here, that's all, and until the anesthedrin wears off he won't say a word. Look him over. Find out whether or not a Nirotan can be a vampire. Let me know the

312

outcome—and don't breathe a syllable of this to anybody else, *anybody*, or it'll be worth your head and mine. Clear?"

The pudgy medico looked troubled by the obvious irregularity of the situation. But he remained silent for a moment, eyeing the slumbering Nirotan on the stretcher. Finally van Dyne said, "Okay. I've always wanted to have a close look at one of these fellows. And we can get a lot of things settled this way."

Harriman smiled. "Thanks, Doc. Remember, you don't know anything. If there's any blame to be taken, let me be the one to take it. How soon will you have any information to give me?"

"That's hard to say. Suppose you stick around the building for a while. I'll phone you in—oh, say, an hour and a half."

"Right. I'll be waiting."

As Harriman walked toward the door of van Dyne's office, the medical examiner had already begun to select the equipment he planned to use in the examination.

✺

Back in his own office, Harriman dropped down wearily at his desk and ran tensely quivering hands through his hair. In ninety minutes, he would have the answers to some of the questions that were plaguing him about the Nirotans.

He had kidnapped a Nirotan in front of a raging mob. It had been bold, foolhardy—but necessary. Without a close look at one of the bat-creatures, it was impossible to take even the first steps toward solving the vampire mysteries.

Now, he needed information. He rang up the library circuit and requested everything they had on Nirota—immediately.

The tapes started arriving a few minutes later. Harriman sorted through them. The first ones were dry statistics on Terran-Nirotan trade over the past ten months. But at length Harriman came up with something that was more useful to him—a tape about Nirota itself.

The Nirotans are a proud, aloof people, Harriman read. *They do not welcome contact with other races except for the purpose of trade.*

Their historical records stretch back for nearly fifteen thousand Terran years. They have had space travel for ten thousand of those years. The Nirotan Federation extends over some thirteen worlds, all of them settled by Nirotan colonists many centuries previously.

The Nirotans are superb mechanical craftsmen and their wares are prized throughout the galaxy. In general they do not take part in galactic disputes, preferring to remain above politics. However, the Nirotans have been engaged in fierce economic competition with the artisans of Drosk for the past thousand years, and several times during this period the rivalry has become so

Harriman's reading was suddenly interrupted by the strident sound of the telephone. As he answered, his eye fell on the wall-clock, and he discovered with some surprise that he had been immersed in Nirotan history for rather more than an hour. Perhaps, he thought hopefully, van Dyne has completed his examination and was reporting on his findings!

"Harriman speaking."

"van Dyne here, Neil. I've just finished giving our specimen a good checkdown."

"Well?" Harriman demanded eagerly.

In a quiet voice said "If a Nirotan committed those murders, Neil, then I should have been a streetcleaner instead of a medic."

"What do you mean?"

"Item one, the Nirotan's big front incisor teeth are wedge-shaped—triangular. The holes in the victims' throats were round. Item two is that the Nirotan's jaws aren't designed for biting—he'd have to be a contortionist or better, in order to get his teeth onto a human throat. And item three is that metabolically the Nirotans are as vegetarian as can be. Their bodies don't have any way of digesting animal matter, blood or meat. Human blood would be pure poison to them if they tried to swallow any. It would go down their gullet like a shot of acid."

"So they were telling the truth after all," Harriman said quietly. "And all they had to do was let us examine one of them for ten minutes, and we'd be able to issue a full exoneration!"

"They're aliens, Neil," said van Dyne. "They have their own ideas about pride. They just couldn't bring themselves to let an Earthman go poking around their bodies with instruments."

"You haven't done any harm to your patient, have you?"

"Lord, no!" van Dyne said. "I ran a complete external diagnosis on him. When he wakes up he won't even know I've touched him. By the way, what am I supposed to do with him when he wakes up?"

"Does he show any signs of coming out from under the anesthetrin yet?"

"He's beginning to show signs of coming around."

"Give him another jolt and put him back under," Harriman said. "Keep him hidden down at your place for a while, until I can figure out where to go next."

"You have any ideas? Now that we know definitely that the Nirotans didn't pull the vampire stunt, how are we going to find out who did?"

Harriman said, "That's a damned good question. I wish I had an equally good answer for it."

Then his eye fell to the tape of Nirotan history, still open at the place where he had been reading when interrupted by the telephone call.

He read: *However, the Nirotans have been engaged in fierce economic competition with the artisans of Drosk for the past thousand years, and several times during this period the rivalry has become so intense that it has erupted into brief but savage wars between Drosk and Nirota—*

"I've got a hunch," Harriman said. "It's pretty wild, but it's worth a try. Keep that Nirotan out of sight for the rest of the day. I'm going to make another trip to San Francisco."

※

The San Francisco Security Corpsmen knew exactly where to find Blen Duworn, attaché to the Drosk Trade Commission office. For one thing, all non-human beings were kept under informal surveillance during the emergency, for their own protection. For another, Blen Duworn was a material witness in the killing of Sam Barrett, and therefore was watched closely so he could be on hand in case authorities cared to question him again.

Which they did. Early in the day, after his night flight to the West Coast, Neil Harriman was shown into a room with the Drosk and left alone. Blen Duworn was short, about five feet three, but sturdily built, with thick hips and immensely broad shoulders, indicating the higher gravitational pull of his home world. The Drosk was, at least externally, human in every way except for the half-inch stubs above each eye that provided a sixth sense, that of sensitivity to heat-waves. Internally, of course, the Drosk was probably totally alien—but non-terrestrial beings were not in the habit of letting Terrans examine their interiors.

Harriman said affably, "I know you must be tired of it by now, Blen Duworn, but would you mind telling me just what you saw that morning?"

The Drosk's smile was equally affable. "To put it briefly, I saw a Nirotan killing an Earthman. The Nirotan had his fangs to the Earthman's throat and seemed to be drawing blood out of him."

Nodding, Harriman pretended to jot down notes. "You were not the first one on the scene?"

"No. The Earthman named Harkins was there first."

Harriman nodded again. "We of Earth know so little about the Nirotans, of course. We have some of their history, but none of their biology at all. They claim to be vegetarians, you know."

"They're lying. On their native worlds they raise animals simply to drink their blood."

Harriman lifted an eyebrow. "You mean they have a long history of—ah—vampirism?"

"They've been blood-drinkers for thousands of years. Luckily for us, Drosk blood doesn't attract them. Evidently Terran blood does."

"Evidently," Harriman agreed. In the same level, unexcited tone of voice he went on, "Would you mind telling me, now, just how you managed to convince Harkins that he saw a Nirotan draining blood from Barrett—when it was really you he saw?"

The antennae above Blen Duworn's cold eyes quivered. "On my world, Earthman, a statement like that is a mortal insult that can be wiped out only by your death."

"We're not on your world now. We're on Earth. And I say that *you* killed Sam Barrett, not a Nirotan, and that you deluded Harkins into thinking it was a Nirotan he saw."

Duworn laughed contemptuously. "How preposterous! The Nirotans are known for their blood-drinking, while we of Drosk are civilized people. And you can yet accuse me of—"

"The Nirotans are vegetarians. Human blood is poison to them."

"You believe their lies?" Duworn asked bitterly.

Harriman shook his head. "It isn't a matter of belief. We've examined a Nirotan. We *know* they couldn't possibly have committed those murders."

"Examined a Nirotan?" Duworn repeated, amused. "How fantastic! A Nirotan wouldn't let himself be touched by Earthmen!"

"This one had no choice," Harriman said softly. "He was unconscious at the time. We gave him a thorough going-over and found out beyond question that the Nirotans have to be innocent."

"I don't believe it."

"Believe as you wish. But who might be interested in seeing the Nirotans blamed for such crimes? For thousands of years Drosk and Nirota have been rivals in the galaxy, trying to cut each other out of juicy trading spots. Here on Earth we've allowed both of you to come peddle your wares, in direct competition with each other. But Drosk didn't like that, did it? So an enterprising Drosk did some research into Terran folklore, and found out about the vampire legend—about the dreaded giant bats who drink human blood, and who happen to resemble the people of Nirota. And someone cooked up the idea of murdering a few Earthmen by draining out their blood, and letting us draw our own conclusions about who did it—knowing damned well that there would be an immediate public outcry against the Nirotans, and also knowing that the Nirotans were culturally oriented against defending themselves. You figured we'd never find out that the Nirotans couldn't possibly have done it. But you didn't count on the chance that we might violate Nirotan privacy, drag one of them off to a medical laboratory, and see for ourselves."

Blen Duworn's muscular face remained impassive, but his tiny antennae were stiff and agitated. "You forget that there was an Earthman who *saw* the Nirotan drinking blood."

"We know the Nirotans *can't* drink human blood," returned Harriman sharply. "Therefore, Harkins was either lying, bribed, or not responsible for what he was saying. I rather think it was the last, Blen Duworn. That you manipulated his mind in such a way as to have him think he saw a Nirotan. And then that you gilded the lily by coming forth as a witness yourself—never dreaming that we'd be uncivilized enough to look at a Nirotan despite his wishes, and find out the truth."

Blen Duworn's eyes suddenly gleamed strangely, and the antennae above his eyes rose rigidly. "You're very clever, Earthman. You seem to have figured everything out quite neatly. Only—we of Drosk are not blood-drinkers ourselves; medical tests could easily prove that we are just as innocent as the Nirotans are. Why try to fix the blame on us? I've never been positive that I saw a Nirotan that morning; it was dark and foggy. If I was the vampire, how did I do the killing?"

"Drosk is noted for its mechanical skill," Harriman said. "It isn't hard to devise an instrument that can tap the jugular, pump out a few liters of blood, and immediately turn the blood to vapor and discharge it into the atmosphere. I'm sure you could create such a device the size of a signet ring, with Drosk's microminiaturizing techniques. Plunge it into the jugular, draw out the blood, dispose of it—who would be the wiser?"

"The Nirotans are equally clever at such contrivances," retorted the Drosk.

"Yes, they are. But what motive would they have for confirming the popular stereotype of themselves as vampires? No, Blen Duworn, you've exhausted all your arguments. I say that the so-called Vampire Menace was cooked up by Drosk conspirators, with an eye toward driving your Nirotan competition off Earth. And—"

The gleam in Blen Duworn's eyes grew more intense. Harriman tried to avert the alien's gaze, but the Drosk snapped, "Look at me, Earthman! At my eyes! You've been very clever! But you haven't counted on one thing, the Drosk hypnotic power, the power with which I persuaded Harkins that he had seen a Nirotan, the power which I will use now to obtain my freedom—"

Harriman rose, reeling dizzily, as the alien's mind lashed out at his own. It was impossible to look away, impossible to break the alien's hold—

Harriman began to sag. Suddenly the doors opened. Three Security Corpsmen rushed in, seizing Blen Duworn.

Harriman shook his head to clear it, and smiled faintly. "Thanks," he muttered. "If you'd waited another minute he would have had me. I hope you got every word down on tape."

❁

After that, the rest was simple. "Duworn cracked and gave us the name of his conspirators," Harriman reported the next day to Director Russell. "Half a dozen Drosk were in on it. The idea was to make it look as if the Nirotans were going vampire all over Terra."

"And if you hadn't illegally examined that bat-creature," Russell said, "we'd still be going around in circles. You ought to hear the apologies Secretary-General Zachary's been making to the Nirotans."

"Couldn't be helped, chief. Duworn and the others were banking on our lack of knowledge about the Nirotans. And they came close to succeeding. But what kind of an investigation can you conduct if you don't know anything about the suspects, even?"

Russell nodded. "You'll have to take a reprimand, Neil. That's just for the record. But there'll be a promotion coming along right afterward, to take the sting out of it."

"Thanks, chief."

Secretary-General Zachary managed to convey Earth's apologies to the Nirotans for the recent indignities they had suffered, and the bat-beings decided to remain on Earth. Drosk, on the other hand, felt compelled to withdraw; it was decided that the six guilty conspirators would be taken back to their home world for punishment according to Drosk law, and all members of the species departed from Earth at once.

Neil Harriman received his promotion, and once again it was safe for the Nirotans to walk the streets of Earth. But, despite the well-publicized findings that the Nirotans were harmless vegetarians, and despite the confession of the Drosk, few Earthmen passed one of the hulking bat-like beings without a slight shiver of revulsion, and a thought for the ancient legends of the era of superstition, which had so shockingly come alive for a few days during the so-called Vampire Menace of 2104.

THE INSIDIOUS INVADERS
(1959)

Super-Science Stories, *which by now was my only surviving market for action-oriented science fiction (Bill Hamling had closed his magazines and the Ziff-Davis pair, under the new editorship of Cele Goldsmith, had ceased to be a haven for staff-written formula fiction), continued to make with the monsters as circulation went on dipping. The June, 1959 number was the glamorous* SECOND MONSTER ISSUE!, *to which I contributed "The Day the Monsters Broke Loose" and "Beasts of Nightmare Horror," though other hands than mine were responsible for "Creatures of Green Slime" and "Terror of the Undead Corpses." August, 1959 was the gaudy* THIRD MONSTER ISSUE!, *with no less than four pseudonymous Silverberg offerings ("Monsters That Once Were Men," "Planet of the Angry Giants," "The Horror in the Attic," and "Which was the Monster?"). Then Scottie stopped numbering them: the October, 1959 issue, with three more of mine, was labeled simply* WEIRD MONSTER ISSUE! *That one was the last in the sequence: when I turned those three stories in in March of 1959, Scottie sadly notified me that he would need no more science-fiction stories from me after that. Though* Trapped *and* Guilty *were going to continue (for the time being),* Super-Science *had walked the plank.*

I would miss it. It had supported me in grand style for three years, and the income from it would be hard to replace.

"The Insidious Invaders" appeared in that final issue under the pseudonym of Eric Rodman. The attentive reader will detect at once the fine hand of W.W. Scott in the story's title. I called it "The Imitator," not exactly an inspired title either. The story's theme—a predatory absorptive alien—is not

one for which I can claim any particular originality, but it has, at least, been one that I've dealt with in a number of interesting ways over the decades, most notably in my short stories "Passengers" of 1969 and "Amanda and the Alien" of 1983. So "The Insidious Invaders" can be considered an early draft of those two rather more accomplished pieces.

One oddity that jumped to my attention here when I dug the story out for this book involves the names of the characters—Ted Kennedy and his sister and brother-in-law Marge and Dave Spalding. It's not the use of "Ted Kennedy" as a character that I'm referring to, for in 1959 John F. Kennedy himself was only then beginning to make himself conspicuous on the national stage and the existence of his kid brother Teddy was unknown to me. But the protagonist of my novel Invaders from Earth, *written in the autumn of 1957, was named Ted Kennedy too; his wife's name was Marge; and there was also a character named Dave Spalding, unrelated to Marge, in the book. There is no other link between the story and the book. The Ted Kennedy of the story is a spaceman; the one of the novel is a public-relations man, as is the Dave Spalding of the novel. Why I used the same names for these two sets of characters, two and a half years apart, is something I can't explain, nearly fifty years later. Some sort of private joke? Mere coincidence? I have no idea.*

At any rate, with this story I was just about at the end of the phase of my career that had been devoted to writing quick, uncomplicated stories for the low-end science-fiction magazines. All the magazines that published that kind of story had folded, by the middle of 1959, or else had shifted their policies in the direction of the more sophisticated kind of s-f that Astounding *and* Galaxy *were publishing. Since I was committed, by that time, to a life as a full-time writer who depended for his income on high-volume production, I needed to change markets, and I did. My records for the second half of 1959 show that I had begun to write fiction and articles for such slick men's magazines of the era as* Exotic Adventures, Real Men, *and* Man's Life, *and that I had found another new slot for my immense productivity in the suddenly hyperactive genre of soft-core erotic paperbacks, where I began turning out two and even three books a month—*Suburban Wife, Love Thieves, Summertime Affair, *and an almost infinite number of others of that ilk. I was still writing the occasional story for the top-of-the-line s-f magazines, too. Just ahead for me lay an entirely new career as a writer of popular books on archaeological subjects (*Lost Cities and Vanished Civilizations, Empires in the Dust, *etc.) and then, in the mid-1960s, a return to science fiction with the novels (*The Time Hoppers, To*

Open the Sky, Thorns) *that laid the foundation for my present reputation in the field.*

I have no regrets over having written those reams and reams of space-adventure stories back in the 1950s for Amazing, Super-Science, *and their competitors. The more of them I wrote, the greater my technical facility as a writer became, something that would stand me in good stead later on. They provided me, also, with the economic stability that a young married man just out of college had to have. Nor was I wasting creative energy that might better have been devoted to writing more ambitious fiction. You would be wrong if you thought that I had stories of the level of "Sundance" or "Enter a Soldier" or "The Secret Sharer" in me in 1957. I may have been a prodigy, but that prodigious I was not, not in my early twenties. Beyond a doubt, though, I was capable back then of "Cosmic Kill" and "Mournful Monster" and the rest of the works reprinted here. So—with a respectful nod to my hard-working younger self—I call them forth from their long stay in obscurity and bring them together for the first time in this book, as a kind of souvenir of the start of my career.*

After the incident of the disposal unit, there was no longer any room for reasonable doubt: something peculiar had happened to Ted Kennedy while he was away at space. Marge and Dave Spalding, Kennedy's sister and brother-in-law, had been watching him all evening, growing more and more puzzled by certain strangenesses in Kennedy's behavior. But this was the strangest of all.

He had been wandering around the room, examining the new gadgets that now were standard household fare. They were strange to him, after all the years he had been away. He had been standing by the wall disposal unit, which efficiently and instantly converted matter to energy, and he had suddenly, curiously, stuck his hand near the open entryway to the unit, saying, "This house is so full of new gadgets that I hardly know what anything does. This thing over here—"

"Watch out, Ted!" Marge Spalding screamed in alarm. "Don't—"

She was too late. There was the brief crackling noise of the disposal unit functioning. And Kennedy had thrust his arm in up to the elbow!

"Ted!" Marge wailed. "Your arm—!" She closed her eyes and felt hysterics starting.

But Kennedy said in the same calm, strange voice he had been using all evening, "My arm's all right, Marge. What's all the excitement about?"

"But—but that was the wall disposal unit," Marge muttered bewilderedly. "Anything you put in there gets converted to energy."

Kennedy held up an obviously intact arm and smiled, the way one might smile when talking to a child who misunderstands. "Look, Marge. I pulled my arm back in time. See?"

Dave Spalding, who had been watching the scene with growing confusion, said, "But we heard the sound, Ted. When you activate the unit, it crackles like that."

"And I saw you stick your hand in there all the way up to the elbow, Ted!" Marge insisted.

Kennedy chuckled. "You're both imagining things. All I did was toss a piece of candy in to see what would happen. My hand didn't go anywhere near the field."

"But I saw your hand go in, Ted," Marge repeated, getting more stubborn now that the evidence of her own eyes was being contradicted. "And yet—your hand's all right. I don't understand."

"I tell you my hand didn't come anywhere near it, Marge," her brother said forcefully. "Let's not discuss it any more, shall we?"

❖

That was the strangest part of the evening so far, Marge thought. But Ted had been behaving peculiarly ever since he came in.

He had been late, first of all. That was unlike the old Ted. He had been expected about nine, but he was long overdue. Dave Spalding had been pacing the apartment with increasing irritation.

"It's past ten, Marge. When's this spaceman brother of yours getting here? Three in the morning?"

"Oh, Dave, don't start getting upset about it," Marge had said soothingly. "So he's a little late! Don't forget it's five years since he was last on Earth."

"Five years or no five years. His ship landed at half past seven. It doesn't take three hours to get here from the spaceport. I thought you said he was so punctual, Marge."

"He used to be. Oh, I don't know—maybe there was some routine he had to go through, before they would let him leave the spaceport. I understand there's a comprehensive medical examination for all returning spacemen—"

"That's all we need," Spalding snorted. "Some weird disease he picked up on Alpha Centauri Five, or—"

"You know they wouldn't let him near civilians if he had any such diseases."

"Well, all I want to say is that if he doesn't show his face here by eleven, I'm going to go upstairs and go to bed," Spalding grumbled. "Spaceman or no spaceman. I need my sleep."

The doorbell chimed.

Marge cried, "There he is now, Dave! I knew he'd get here any minute! Be nice to him, Dave. He is my brother, after all. And I haven't seen him since '89."

"Okay," Spalding said. "Don't worry about me. I'll be polite."

He walked to the door, hesitated before it a moment, and opened it. A tall young man in spaceman's uniform stood in the hallway, smiling. There was something about the quality of that smile that made Dave Spalding instantly uncomfortable. As if—as if it were not the smile of a human being, but of some alien *thing* wearing the mask of humanity.

"Hello, there," Spalding said with forced geniality. "Come right on in. My name's Dave Spalding."

"Thanks. I appreciate this, Dave." Kennedy stepped in. His voice, when he had spoken, had a curious otherwordly undertone.

Spalding closed the door.

Marge ran toward her brother, throwing her arms around him. "Ted! Oh, Ted!"

"Hello, Sis!" Kennedy replied He thrust her gently away from him. "Stand back—let me look at you." He whistled appreciatively. "Sister's a big girl, now, isn't she?"

"I'm almost 24," Marge said "I married Dave three years ago."

"You haven't changed much in the five years I've been away," Kennedy said. "The same red hair—that dimple—the freckles on your nose—"

"Was there much red tape before you could leave the spaceport?" Spalding broke in brusquely.

"Just the medical exam," Kennedy said. "They gave me a quick look to make sure I wasn't carrying the plague. I was cleared through around quarter past eight."

Spalding gave an unfunny chuckle. "You must have stopped off for a little nip or two before coming here, eh?"

"Nip? No. I came straight here from the spaceport."

"But it only takes half an hour by rocket-tube," Marge said, frowning.

Kennedy shook his head. "No one said anything to me about a rocket-tube. I took the subway."

"The subway!" Spalding laughed. "Oh, really now—the subway, all the way out here! No wonder it took you so long!"

Marge said, "Dave, the rocket-tube line has only been in operation three and a half years. That's why Ted didn't use it. He didn't know it existed!"

"The world changes more than you think in five years. The new-model autos that drive themselves—the three-D video—the robots—those things were still brand new and strange, when I was last on Earth. And now they're commonplace. To everyone except me."

Marge stared keenly at her brother. When he spoke like that, he seemed real. But there was something unconvincing about him, all the same.

What am I thinking? she wondered. *Am I nuts? He's my brother, that's all. He looks and acts a little different because he's been away so long.*

Dave said, "Come on into the living room, Ted. You probably want to rest up. I'll give you a drink—put a little music on—"

"And you can tell us all about your five years in space," Marge said.

Ted smiled. "Good ideas, all of them."

They adjourned to the living room, where Kennedy made himself comfortable in an armchair. Spalding turned the phonograph on. Chamber music welled out into the room. Kennedy nodded his head in time with the music.

"Mozart," he said. "You miss him, out in space."

"Can I dial you a drink?" Spalding asked.

"Scotch, thanks. I take it neat."

"Same old Ted!" Marge said, reassuring herself. "Still likes the same music, still drinks then same kind of drink."

"It's only been five years, you know. I haven't been away forever."

Marge nodded. But, still, the nagging feeling persisted that there was something different about Ted that a mere absence of five years could not account for.

"Can you tell us where you've been?" Spalding asked. "Or is that classified?"

"Well, some of it is," Kennedy said. "But I covered a lot of ground. You ought to see the night sky on Deneb Nine, Marge—five hundred little moons up there, like whirling knives in the darkness. And the 17th planet of the Vega system—two billion miles from its sun, and yet there's that great blazing light in the sky, so bright we had to wear special eye-lenses."

"Join the Space Force and see the galaxy!," Marge exclaimed. "That's what the recruiting commercials say. I guess it's really true."

Kennedy sipped his drink slowly. "It was good of you two to put me up here while I was on ground leave. It's no treat to come back to a world where you have no friends and just one living relative."

"Oh, don't mention it," Spalding said. "Ah—how long did you say you'd be staying?"

"Three weeks, if it's all right with you."

"And then you have to go back to space for another five years?" Marge asked.

"That's right. Survey trip, this time—around the galactic rim."

"How exciting that must be!" Marge exclaimed.

"It's just his job, after all," Spalding said in offhand tones.

"But how much more exciting it must be to be a spaceman, than a—a *newspaperman*," Marge said.

Kennedy turned to his brother-in-law. "Are you a newspaperman, Dave?"

"I work for one of the systemwide wire services."

Kennedy shrugged. "Then you've got a job that keeps humming *all* the time. We spacemen spend three quarters of our time drifting through nowhere, between planets, playing solitaire and watching corny old films and thinking about Earth."

He rose and began to prowl around the room, eyeing the mechanical implements. The Spaldings liked new gadgets, and the room had plenty of them—the automatic drink-mixer, the wall disposal unit, the light-dimmer, and half a dozen more.

"But when the waiting's over," Spalding pursued, "When you finally reach another sun and walk on alien soil—"

"Ah! Then it all becomes worthwhile." He yawned. "But you must excuse me. I've had a busy day aboard ship, and then getting out here on that subway—"

"Of course," Spalding said sympathetically. "Do you want me to show you to your room?"

"I'd appreciate that," Kennedy said.

Marge watched her brother carefully. Half the time he seemed so normal, and the rest—

"Hmm," Kennedy was saying. "This house is so full of new gadgets that I hardly know what anything does. This thing over here—"

That was when he put his hand into the disposal unit and withdrew it unharmed. Despite Kennedy's repeated insistence that his hand had not gone in, Marge was certain that she had seen it enter the field and be consumed. But there it was, whole. She frowned and shook her head.

Kennedy said, "Dave, would you show me to my room? I'm pretty worn out."

Her brother and her husband went upstairs together. Marge Kennedy sank limply into the enveloping depths of the sofa. "But I saw his hand go in," she muttered softly to herself. "I saw it!"

※

When her husband returned from the guest room, fifteen minutes later, Marge was still sitting on the sofa, staring off into nowhere—obscurely worried, and not even fully understanding *why* she was worried.

Spalding said, "Well, he's all moved in upstairs in the guest room. He seems pleased with the layout. Suppose we turn in, now. Past eleven, isn't it?"

Marge shook her head. "Dave, I'm worried."

"About what? That business with the disposal unit." He laughed nervously. "It must have been just our imaginations that—"

"No." Marge locked her hands together. "I saw him clearly put his arm into the field. But when he took it out again the hand was whole. And there are other things that worry me, too."

"Like what?"

She struggled for words, wondering if she were being utterly silly even to start this sort of discussion. After a pause she said, "He's *different*, somehow, Dave."

"Different? Sure. Five years, and—"

"Not just the five years. That's part of it, maybe. But some things about a person just don't change, not even after five years. And he's changed. His voice isn't quite the same any more. There's something— well, weird—about the way he speaks now. And his eyes—that far-away look he has. He never had that before, either. Dave, he's *changed*. I'm afraid of him now!"

Spalding glowered scornfully at his wife. "Afraid of your own brother?"

She felt her face going hot. "I'm afraid that—that he isn't my brother any more."

"*What!*"

Marge fought to keep the hysterical sobs back. "Dave, I don't know what I'm saying, I guess. But I feel strange, with him upstairs. As if—as if something very dangerous has entered our house."

"Don't be idiotic, Marge!"

"I tell you I'm worried."

"What do you want me to do about it?" he burst out impatiently. "Go upstairs and ask him if he's a monster in disguise? Look, Marge, he's your brother and you invited him here."

"I didn't know he'd be—like this."

"And what, am I supposed to do about the way he is? This thing is all in your imagination, anyway. For the umpteenth time, are you going to come to bed, or—"

"Didn't you see him stick his hand into the disposal field?" Marge demanded.

"No, I didn't!" Spalding snapped angrily.

Marge's eyes widened in surprise and anger. "But you said—Dave, you're just making that up! You saw it as clear as I did."

Exasperated, Spalding let out his breath slowly. "Do you want me to go upstairs and ask him to leave? If you think he's dangerous, he can spend his furlough in some hotel."

"No—we can't do that—"

"Then leave me alone. Stop this crazy talk and let's go to bed."

"Would you do one thing for me?" Marge asked.

"What is it?"

"Go upstairs—to *his* room. He probably isn't asleep yet, but maybe he's getting undressed. Try to get a look at him."

"Huh?"

"My brother had a scar on his chest—about five inches long, starting from the left collarbone and running down diagonally. He got it when we were kids. See if—if the man upstairs has that scar too."

"Now, look, Marge," Spalding said irritatedly, "you already admitted that he liked the same drinks and the same music he always did, so why—"

"Will you go upstairs and look? You could tell him you just stopped in before you went to bed, to see if he was comfortable."

"This is ridiculous, Marge. Spying on your own brother to see if he's actually a Thing from Outer Space—it's absurd!"

"I'll feel happier if you go up. Will you?"

Spalding shrugged resignedly. He would get no peace this night until he did, and he knew it. "Oh—all right. If it'll stop you from worrying." He started toward the staircase. "I'll go see if he's still awake. But if his light is out, I'm not going to bother him."

✺

The light, however, was not out. Dave Spalding stood for a long moment in front of the guest room door, peering regretfully at the thin wisp of light streaming underneath the door, and finally knocked. He pushed the door open and said apologetically, "I saw your light was still on, Ted, so I figured I'd stop in and—what the devil—" He stopped and gasped.

Kennedy said in a voice of cold, iron-hard menace, "Why do you enter my room without knocking?"

Spalding backpedaled on numb, watery legs. "Your face— you—it's—"

"My face is different?"

Whispering incredulously, Spalding said, "Why—you look like me, now! My face, that is. Not yours!"

"I'm simply practicing," Kennedy said in the same flat, metallic tone.

"Practicing?"

"Don't go away," Kennedy said quickly, as Spalding continued to back toward the hallway. "Come here, Dave. Right over here to me."

"What *are* you?" Spalding muttered. He felt a trickle of cold sweat run tinglingly down his back.

Kennedy chuckled. "What am I? I'm your brother-in-law, Dave."

"But your face—and your hand, before, in the disposal unit—"

"Yes. You *did* seem surprised. It was an error of mine, putting my hand in there. But I didn't know the consequences, or I'd have kept my hands away from it." He circled around, deftly putting himself between Spalding and the door. Paling, Spalding stood his ground, resisting the temptation to try to fight his way out. Kennedy went on, "I couldn't do things like this before I visited Altair VI, two years ago. Altair VI has a very interesting form of native life. At the moment nobody knows of the existence of this life-form but me. It's a mimic, Dave."

"Mimic?"

"When the spaceman known as Ted Kennedy was exploring Altair VI two years ago," Kennedy continued, "he wandered off alone, away from his ship, to look for lifeforms. There was a big brown stone in his way; he kicked it. But the stone clung to his boot. It wasn't a stone, you see. It was a mimic."

330

Kennedy's words made no sense. Spalding shook his head in confusion. He was close to panic. "I don't know what you're talking about, Ted. Get out of my way and let me out of this room. You—you must be out of your mind to talk this way—"

"Ted Kennedy never knew what happened to him," the other continued serenely, as though there had been no interruption. "Within ten seconds the mimic had absorbed him—swallowed him up, flesh, brain, memories, and all. When the mimic had fed, it realized what a lucky find it had made. A spaceman—who would be going back to Earth some day. The mimic can divide itself infinitely, you see. It left part of itself there, in its old disguise as a stone, waiting for unwary beasts to come along and be absorbed. The rest of itself went back to the spaceship—wearing the disguise of Ted Kennedy."

"Marge *said* you were different—that something had happened to you—"

"I have all of Ted Kennedy's memories. So far as anyone can tell, I *am* Ted Kennedy, down to the last molecule. And my crewmates, who were all absorbed by the mimic and who are all here on Earth, enjoying ground leave, now—"

Spalding shuddered. "No! You mean—there's a whole ship full of you on Earth now—all over—"

"Exactly. Come here, Dave."

"No! Get away from me."

"Come here, Dave!"

Spalding backed away, but Kennedy advanced toward him, his eyes gleaming, his hands reaching out. Spalding felt the cold fingers seize his shoulders with a burning grasp. Felt himself being drawn closer, closer, to the body of the thing that wore the guise of his brother-in-law. Felt the framework of his soul giving way, felt himself being pulled apart, demolished, absorbed—

He fought to free himself. But every move he made only increased the destruction.

"Don't try to resist," Kennedy murmured. "It'll just take a few seconds, Dave."

In a muffled, indistinct voice, Spalding cried, "Marge! Marge, help me!"

"Just a moment more," Kennedy whispered calmly. "Don't waste your breath. She can't hear you, anyway. Just a moment more, then it will be over."

Spalding felt himself growing limp. He had no will of his own remaining. His mind and body were fusing with that of the creature from Altair VI. He was being swept away on the tide.

"Marge...." he whimpered. "Marge...."

The Kennedy-thing laughed exultantly. "There! Finished!"

He released Spalding. Spalding staggered back, then straightened up suddenly.

He smiled at the Kennedy-thing. The union was complete. The entity Dave Spalding had been totally absorbed, and....replaced.

※

Downstairs, Marge waited impatiently. Five minutes had gone by, and Dave had not yet returned. She had thought she heard the sound of a scuffle upstairs. Were Ted and Dave fighting, she wondered? What if—

Oh, no, she thought. Nothing serious could be going on up there. It was all her imagination, her feverishly overwrought imagination. But she wished Dave would hurry up down.

A moment later, she heard footsteps, and Dave appeared.

Marge looked up anxiously. "You were up there a long time. I was getting worried."

Spalding shrugged. "He hadn't gotten undressed yet when I came in. I had to wait until he took his shirt off—so I could see the scar."

Marge frowned faintly. Dave's voice—it sounded a bit hollow, and unnatural. The way—the way Ted's voice had sounded. Prickles of fear crept along her spine. She tried to calm herself.

In a level voice she said, "He had it, didn't he? The scar, I mean?"

"Of course. A big purple slash right across the side of his chest, where he got cut the time he climbed over the picket fence."

"Eh?" Marge was surprised. "He—he told you how he got that scar?"

"What? Oh, yeah, sure," Spalding said. "He told me all about it. How you and he were stealing apples years ago, and how the farmer came to chase you." Spalding laughed. "He jumped over the fence, but he cut himself going over, and you were stuck in the orchard because you couldn't get over the fence."

Marge felt cold chills racing over her skin. Uncertainly she said, "He told you—*that?*"

"Yes."

"Funny," she said. "He never would tell anyone that story. He was always so ashamed that he had left his kid sister behind when he tried to get away. He made me swear I would never tell anyone about it."

"Well," Spalding said, "he told me."

"Five years does change a man, I guess." Marge paused. Wild accusations rose up in her mind. But all this was too fantastic to consider. It made no sense.

She said, "Well, almost midnight, now. You'll be useless in the morning if you don't get some sleep now, Dave. Let's turn in."

"Just a minute, Marge," Spalding said slowly.

Marge began to tremble. Her husband's face was deathly pale, set in a strangely rigid mask. "Why are you looking at me that way?"

"Come here."

"I *am* here. Dave, what's—"

She took an uncertain step toward him. "No. Closer," he said. "Let me hold you in my arms."

Marge laughed hollowly. "Why get so lovey-dovey here in the living room, Dave? Let's go upstairs and—Dave? You look so strange, Dave."

"Let me hold you," he said, his voice flat, toneless, mechanical.

Marge took a step away from him, now, clenching her fists to keep herself from screaming. "Dave—your eyes! You look different! What's wrong with you, anyway? Something happened to you upstairs, I know it! What's going on in this house?"

"Let me hold you, Marge!" Spalding said, more loudly, stepping toward her. His thick, muscular arms snaked out and met behind her back, drawing her to him in a rough, choking hug.

Tendrils of force reached out, searching, probing, absorbing....

"Let go of me!" Marge yelled, writhing in his tight grasp. "You're holding me too tight, Dave! Are you drunk? That's what it is! He has some otherworld liquor upstairs, and he gave you some. Dave, I can't breathe—"

"Just one more moment, Marge," Spalding said softly. "And then you'll be one of us."

She pummeled against his chest with her fists in an impotent attempt at freeing herself. But he held her tight, feeding on her, consuming the substance of Marge Spalding and transforming it.

"Dave, what are you doing to me?" she whimpered. "Dave, I don't understand this. Please let go. I—you're hurting me—"

"Only a moment more before absorption. Then you'll be part of us, Marge, you and me and Ted, and then soon the whole world—"

"Dave! No!"

She screamed, high, shrill, filling the entire room with her voice.

"Quiet, Marge," Spalding said.

She screamed again, louder this time—but the scream came to an abrupt halt before it had reached its peak of volume, and died away.

"That's all there is to it, you see," Spalding said gently, a few moments later, when the transformation was complete. "A few moments while our organism absorbs yours—then the split, and a new Marge Spalding appears."

The creature that had been Marge Spalding nodded. "It's very odd, isn't it? I remember everything I ever did as Marge Spalding, clear and sharp. But I'm not Marge Spalding any more, am I? I'm—something else. Part of you, Dave. And of Ted. And of all the members of the crew of Ted's ship."

"And soon everyone in the world, too. All merged into *us.*"

The form of Ted Kennedy came down the stairs. The spaceman stood at the foot of the stairs, taking in the scene.

"I see it's all over. I waited to come down until you had converted her."

"We'd better sleep now," Spalding said. "Build up our energy. And then, tomorrow, every time one of us gets someone alone—"

"We convert him into *us,*" Marge said.

Kennedy nodded. "Simple. Quick. All this food waiting for us on this planet—billions of human beings we can convert. All ours!"

They gloated quietly, wordlessly for a moment. Then the doorbell chimed.

"At this hour!" the creature that had been Marge Spalding exclaimed.

"Answer it," Kennedy said.

Spalding walked toward the door and opened it. A man in his middle fifties stood there, looking abashed and uncertain about having rung the bell so late at night.

"It's Mr. Adams from next door," Spalding said.

Adams said, in an apologetic voice, "Hello there, Mr. Spalding. I know it's late at night, and I hope I'm not intruding—but I was just coming home from the movies, and as I passed by outside our house I seem to have heard screams, and I think they were coming from in here—"

"That's right," Spalding said calmly. "It was my wife Marge who was screaming."

Adams blinked. "Mrs. Spalding? But you all seem so calm now—I mean, I guess everything's under control—"

"Yes. Everything is under control," Spalding said quietly.

"If that's the case," Adams said, "I guess I'll just be going along on home, then. Sorry to have bothered you. Just that I thought you might be needing help—"

"We appreciate that very much, Mr. Adams. Wouldn't you step in for a moment?"

"Oh, but it's late, and you say everything's under control—"

Spalding smiled. "All the same, if you'd come inside—"

"Yes, do come in," Marge urged. "We'll fix you a little nightcap."

Adams hesitated doubtfully, wavering between his desire to be a good neighbor and his wish to get home and to bed. At length he said, "Well, just for a moment. I've always believed in being neighborly. Guess I'll come in, if you're nice enough to ask me."

"We're glad to have you, Mr. Adams. There—don't stand in the hall. Come on in and close the door. This is my brother-in-law, Ted Kennedy."

"How do you do," Adams said, as Spalding closed the door. The little man looked around, suddenly confused. "Why—you all look so grim—"

Hands reached for him. Mr. Adams uttered half a cry of surprise before Spalding's hand tightened over his mouth. The absorption began....

There was no stopping it. Mr. Adams was absorbed and transformed.

The hunger of the mimic of Altair VI was insatiable. Today, Mr. Adams; tomorrow, the universe....